The City of Tears

BOOK TWO
of The Burning Chambers

Kate Mosse is an award-winning novelist, playwright, essayist and non-fiction writer, the author of eight novels and short-story collections, including the multimillion-selling Languedoc Trilogy, The Burning Chambers Series and number one best-selling Gothic fiction *The Winter Ghosts* and *The Taxidermist's Daughter*. Her books have been translated into thirty-seven languages and published in more than forty countries. The Founder Director of the Women's Prize for Fiction, she is the Founder of the global Woman In History campaign.

KATE MOSSE

The City of Tears

PAN BOOKS

First published 2021 by Mantle

First published in paperback 2021 by Mantle

This edition first published 2022 by Pan Books
an imprint of Pan Macmillan
The Smithson, 6 Briset Street, London EC1M 5NR
EU representative: Macmillan Publishers Ireland Ltd, 1st Floor,
The Liffey Trust Centre, 117–126 Sheriff Street Upper,
Dublin 1, D01 YC43
Associated companies throughout the world
www.panmacmillan.com

ISBN 978-1-5098-0689-8

1 3 5 7 9 8 6 4 2

A CIP catalogue record for this book is available from the British Library.

Typeset by Palimpsest Book Production Ltd, Falkirk, Stirlingshire
Printed and bound by CPI Group (UK) Ltd, Croydon, CR0 4YY

Visit **www.panmacmillan.com** to read more about all our books
and to buy them. You will also find features, author interviews and
news of any author events, and you can sign up for e-newsletters
so that you're always first to hear about our new releases.

As always, for my beloved
Greg & Martha & Felix

And for Peter Clayton
20 June 1964–18 June 2018
Much missed

But He that sits and rules above the clouds
Doth hear and see the prayers of the just,
And will revenge the blood of innocents
That Guise hath slain by treason of his heart,
And brought by murder to their timeless ends.

Christopher Marlowe
The Massacre at Paris (1593)

The mind is its own place, and in itself
Can make a Heav'n of Hell, a Hell of Heav'n.

John Milton
Paradise Lost, Book I (1667)

I have said before
That the past experience revived in the meaning
Is not the experience of one life only
But of many generations – not forgetting
Something that is probably quite ineffable:
The backward look behind the assurance
Of recorded history, the backward half-look
Over the shoulder, towards the primitive terror.

T. S. Eliot
'The Dry Salvages', *Four Quartets* (1941)

CONTENTS

Historical Note

The Wars of Religion in France were a sequence of civil wars which began, after years of grumbling conflict, on 1 March 1562 with the massacre of unarmed Huguenots in Vassy by the Catholic forces of François, Duke of Guise. They ended, after several million had died or been displaced, with the signing of the Edict of Nantes on 13 April 1598 by the formerly Protestant King, Henri IV or Henri of Navarre. The most notorious engagement of the Wars of Religion is the St Bartholomew's Day Massacre in Paris, which began in the early hours of 24 August 1572. But there were many such slaughters the length and breadth of France both before and after it, including in Toulouse in 1562 (the period covered in *The Burning Chambers*) and copycat massacres that occurred in twelve major cities following the Paris massacre in 1572.

The events of spring and summer 1572 leading up to and immediately after the St Bartholomew's Day Massacre – the death of Jeanne d'Albret, the marriage of Marguerite de Valois to Henri of Navarre, the assassination of Admiral de Coligny and the responsibility for ordering the massacre itself – have been heavily interpreted, not to say fictionalised, by generations of librettists, artists, filmmakers, playwrights and novelists, key amongst them Christopher Marlowe, Prosper Mérimée and Jean Plaidy. However, the most enduring creative interpretation of the real historical events is Alexandre Dumas's 1845 novel *La Reine Margot*. In this same spirit I, too, have allowed myself a certain amount of artistic speculation and licence . . .

Henri IV, the first Bourbon monarch of France, converted to Catholicism (for the second time and for good) in July 1593 – in an attempt to unite his fractured kingdom and win over France's fiercely Catholic capital city – reputedly with the words: *'Paris vaut bien une messe'*: Paris is well worth a Mass . . . He was crowned in Chartres in February 1594 and his excommunication was lifted a year later.

The Edict of Nantes, when it came into force in 1598, was perhaps less a genuine reflection of a desire for true religious tolerance than an expression of exhaustion and military stalemate. It brought a grudging peace to a country that had torn itself apart over matters of doctrine, religion, citizenship and sovereignty – and all but bankrupted itself in the process.

Henri IV's grandson, Louis XIV, revoked the Edict of Nantes at Fontainebleau on 22 October 1685, precipitating the forced exodus of those Huguenots still remaining in France. Every country which accepted the refugees was enriched by their presence – indeed, the word 'refugee' comes from *'refugié'*, a French word first used to describe the Huguenots.

The Eighty Years War in the Low Countries was no less complicated. Beginning in 1568, it was a revolt of the Seventeen Provinces – what are today the Netherlands, Belgium and Luxembourg – against the violent occupation of Hapsburg Spain. Under the leadership of the Prince of Orange, Willem the Silent, the invasion forces under the Duke of Alba – working for Philip II of Spain – were eventually expelled from the north and west of the country. On 18 February 1578, the Satisfaction was signed, reconciling Amsterdam and Holland, and on 29 May that same year, Amsterdam – the last major city in Holland remaining Catholic – finally became Calvinist in what was known as the Alteration. What is extraordinary, in the context of the bloody history of the times, is that no one was killed. I have allowed myself many artistic liberties in the imagining of this event, too.

Hollanders, Frisians, Zeelanders, Gelderlanders and others gradually started to think of themselves as Dutch. On 26 July 1581, the Provinces signed the Act of Abjuration, the first step to self-rule for the Netherlands. In 1588, the Republic of the Seven United Provinces was established and in 1609, one year before the assassination of Henri IV in Paris, the Dutch Republic was recognised. All the same, it would be another generation before the Peace of Munster was signed in 1648, marking the end of the Eighty Years War and the beginning of the so-called Golden Age of the seventeenth century.

The story of French Protestantism and the beginning of the Dutch Republic are both part of the larger European story of the Reformation – from Martin Luther hammering his ninety-five Theses to the church door in Wittenberg on 31 October 1517, Henry VIII of England's dissolution of the monasteries, which began in 1536, to the missionary Evangelist Calvin setting up his safe haven in Geneva for French refugees in 1541, and the sanctuary offered to Protestant refugees in Amsterdam and Rotterdam from the late 1560s onwards. Key points at issue were: the right to worship in one's own language; a rejection of the cult of relics and intercession; a more rigorous focus on the words of the Bible itself and a desire to worship simply, based on the rules for living laid down in scripture; a rejection of the excesses and abuses of the Catholic Church that were repugnant to many; and the nature of the host in communion. For most people, though, these matters of doctrine were remote.

There are many excellent histories of the Huguenots and the influence of this small community is extraordinary, a diaspora that took them – as skilled immigrants – to Holland, Germany, England, Ireland, the New World, Canada, Russia, Denmark,

Sweden, Switzerland and South Africa. The origins of the word 'Huguenot' are unclear, though there are indications that initially it might have been a term of abuse and contemporary followers tended to refer to themselves as members of *l'Église Réformée* or the Reformed Church. For the sake of the narrative, however, I have used Protestant, Calvinist and Huguenot within the text.

The City of Tears is the second in a series of novels set against this backdrop of three hundred years of history, travelling from sixteenth-century France and Amsterdam to the Cape of Good Hope in the eighteenth and nineteenth centuries. The characters and their families, unless otherwise specified, are imagined, though inspired by the kind of people who might have lived: ordinary women and men, struggling to live, love and survive against a backdrop of religious war and displacement.

Then, as now.

Kate Mosse
Carcassonne, Amsterdam & Chichester
January 2020

Principal Characters

In Puivert

Marguerite (Minou) Reydon-Joubert, Châtelaine of
 Puivert
Piet Reydon, her husband
Marta, their daughter
Jean-Jacques, their son
Salvadora Boussay, her aunt
Aimeric Joubert, her brother
Alis Joubert, her sister
Bernard Joubert, her father

In Paris & Chartres

Vidal du Plessis (Cardinal Valentin), Personal
 Confessor to Henri, Duke of Guise & later
 Lord Evreux
Louis (Volusien), his illegitimate son
Xavier, his steward & manservant
Pierre Cabanel, a captain in the Catholic militia
Antoine le Maistre, a Huguenot refugee from
 Limoges

Principal Characters

PROLOGUE

The woman is lying beneath a white sheet in a white room, dreaming of colour.

Hier Rust. Here lies.

She is no longer in the graveyard. Is she?

The woman is caught between sleeping and waking, surfacing from a place of shadows to a world of harsh light. She lifts her hand to her head and, though she feels the split skin on her temple, finds there is no blood. Her shoulder aches. She imagines it purple with bruises where his fingers pressed and pinched. Pictures now how the tan leather journal fell from her unwilling hand down onto the red Cape soil. That is the last thing she remembers. That, and the words she carries with her.

This is the day of my death.

The woman opens her eyes. The room is indistinct and unknown, but it is a typical room in a Cape Dutch homestead. White walls, plain but for a piece of embroidery with verses from the Bible on the wall. Bare-board floors, a chest of drawers and a nightstand made of stinkwood. On her journey from Cape Town, through Stellenbosch and Drakenstein and Paarl, she has lodged in many such houses. Settlers' houses, some grand and some small, but each with a nostalgia for Amsterdam and the life left behind.

The woman sits up and swings her legs off the bed. Her head

spins and she waits a moment for the sickness to pass. She feels the wooden floor through her stockinged feet. Her white shirt and her riding skirt are stained with red dust, but someone has removed her boots and placed them at the foot of the bed. Her leather hat is hanging from a hook on the back of the wooden door. On the chest of drawers stands a brass tray with an earthenware jug of wine – strong local wine the colour of cherries – and a piece of white bread and strips of dried beef beneath a cloth.

She does not understand. Is she prisoner or guest?

Unsteady on her feet, the woman moves to the door and finds it locked. Then she hears the whistling of a chattering of starlings outside. She laces her boots, walks to the window. A small square frame with thin metal bars on the inside. To keep her in or to keep others out?

She reaches through the bars and pushes open the glass. The sky at dusk in the Cape is the same as it is in Languedoc. White, with a wash of pink as the sun sets behind the mountains. The woman can see the chapel at the top of the town; another small white building in the Cape Dutch style, with a thatched roof and peak-arched windows either side of the arched wooden entrance. Ever since the new church opened its doors to its Protestant congregation a few years ago, it has served as the school. The sight of it gives her hope, for at least she is still within the boundaries of the town. If he meant to kill her, surely he would have taken her up into the mountains and done it there?

Away from prying eyes.

She can make out the fruit orchards, too, growing Cape damsel and damask plums, sweet saffron pears and apples hanging from the trees; in these weeks she has learnt to identify each variety and the farmers who grow them: the Hugo family and the Haumanns, the de Villiers and descendants of the du Toits.

Now she can hear the rise and fall of girls' voices playing a skipping game. A mixture of Dutch and English, no French, the legacy of years of struggle for control of this stolen land. The Cape is once again a British colony, the main road renamed Victoria Street in honour of the English Queen. Further away, the plangent singing of the men coming home from the fields. Another language, one she does not recognise.

Her feeling of relief is fleeting. Quickly, it gives way to grief at the loss of the journal, the map, the precious Will and Testament which has been in her family for hundreds of years. Though the journal is gone from her possession, she knows every word of it off by heart. She knows every crease of the map, the terms and provisions of the Will. As she waits and waits, and the light fades from the sky, she thinks she hears the voices of her ancestors calling to her across the centuries.

'*Château de Puivert. Saturday, the third day of May, in the year of Grace of Our Lord fifteen hundred and seventy-two.*'

Then her sorrow at the loss of the documents turns into fear. If he has not killed her yet, it can only be because there is something more he wants from her. She regrets her caution now. Remembers reaching to scrape the lichen from the stone. She shivers at the memory of the cold muzzle of the gun and his pitiless voice. His shadow, the smell of sweat and clinker, a glimpse of white in his black hair.

She'd drawn her knife, but had only grazed his hand. It was not enough.

The light is fading from the sky and the air is still, though filled with the whining and the buzzing of insects. The children are taken inside and, in every house, pinpricks of light appear as candles are lit. Though she is tired, the woman keeps vigil at the window. She picks at the bread and drinks only a little of the smooth Cape wine, then pours the rest out of the window. She cannot afford to dull her senses.

She sits on the end of the bed, and waits.

The church bell in its solitary white tower chimes the hour. Nine o'clock, ten o'clock. Outside, darkness has fallen. The mountains have faded into shadow. On Victoria Street and the criss-cross of smaller roads and alleyways, the candles are extinguished one by one. Franschhoek is a town that goes early to bed and rises with the sun.

It is not until past eleven o'clock, when she is fighting sleep and the throbbing in her head has started again, that she hears a sound from inside the house. Instantly, she is on her feet.

Footsteps on the floorboards beyond the door, but quiet. Walking slowly, as if trying not to be heard. She has had hours to decide what to do, but it is instinct that takes over now.

She slips behind the door, holding the empty wine vessel in her hand. Listens to the rattle of a key being pushed into the lock, then the clunk of the catch as it gives and the door is slowly opening inwards. In the dark, she cannot see properly, but she glimpses the flash of white hair and smells the leather of his jacket so, the instant he is within reach, she launches the earthenware jug at the height of his head.

She misjudges. She aims too high and though the man staggers, he does not fall. She throws herself towards the open door, intending to try to get past, but he is faster. He grabs her wrist and pushes her backwards into the room, clamping a hand over her mouth.

'Be quiet, you little fool! You'll get us both killed.'

Immediately, she is still. It is a different voice. And in the moonlight filtering through the window, she can see the back of his hand. No sign of where her knife grazed her assailant's skin. And, seeming to trust her, the man releases her and takes a step away.

'Monsieur, forgive me,' she says. 'I thought you were him.'

'No harm done,' he says, also speaking in French.

Now, in the silver shadows, she can see his face. He is taller than her attacker in the graveyard and his black hair is shorter, though split through by the same twist of white.

'You do look like him.'

'Yes.'

She waits for him to say more, but he does not.

'Why am I here?' she asks.

He holds up his hand. 'We have to go. We have little time.'

The woman shakes her head. 'Not until you tell me who you are.'

'We –' He hesitates. 'I saw what happened in the graveyard. I've had to wait until now. He's my brother.'

She crosses her arms, not knowing whether she should trust this man or not. Waits.

'We do not see eye to eye.'

Again, she expects him to say more, but he glances at the door and is restless to be gone.

'Whose house is this?' she asks.

'It belongs to our mother. She is bedridden, she doesn't know you are here. None of this is her fault.' He briefly touches her hand. 'Please, come with me. I will answer all your questions once we are safely out of Franschhoek.'

'Where is your brother now?'

'Drinking, but he will be back at any moment. We must go. I have horses waiting at the eastern boundary of the town.'

She unfolds her arms. 'And if I don't come with you?'

The man looks directly at her and she sees the determination, the concern too, in his eyes.

'He will kill you.'

The calm statement convinces her better than any entreaty or fierce persuasion could. Better to take her chance with this stranger than to remain here, passive and waiting for what the dawn might bring. She takes her hat from the back of the door.

'Will you tell me your name?' she whispers, as she follows him along the dark corridor and towards a door at the rear of the house.

He puts his finger to his lips.

'Will you at least tell me where we are going?'

He hesitates, then answers. 'To the old stone bridge across the ford. The others are waiting there.'

'I don't understand.'

'Jan Joubertsgat,' he says. 'Where Jan Joubert died.' He turns. 'Isn't that why you are here?'

The woman catches her breath, feeling suddenly exposed. 'You know who I am?'

The man's face creases into a smile. 'Of course,' he says, unhooking the latch and pushing open the door. 'Everyone knows who you are.'

PART ONE

AMSTERDAM & PUIVERT
May & June 1572

CHAPTER ONE

Old Mariken knelt before the altar of the chapel in Begijnhof, as she had each night since receiving the letter, and prayed for guidance.

Written in an elegant hand, on fine paper, sealed with wax and a noble crest; it was her duty to answer. Yet the days had passed and still she had not replied. The words seemed to burn through her clothing, branding her skin with the hiss of calumny. A promise made thirty years ago at a deathbed in a boarding house off Kalverstraat.

'*Heer, leid mij,*' Mariken whispered. 'Lord, guide me.'

The author of the letter was a French cardinal, a powerful man. It would not do to refuse him. The request for information about the boy and his mother seemed harmless, couched in plain and reasonable language. There was no cause for alarm. Yet Mariken could sense a malignancy beneath the official words. She feared if she gave his Eminence what he sought, not only would she be breaking her vow to a dying woman, but she would also be signing the boy's death warrant. Such knowledge as she possessed was powerful and dangerous.

For an instant, Mariken smiled at her foolishness. If the boy still lived, then he was a man of some thirty-five years standing. Yet he was forever fixed in her memory as a child sobbing over the cold body of his mother, clasping a package given to him.

Mariken had entrusted the package to her friend, Sister Agatha, for safekeeping, intending to retrieve it and return it to the boy when the time was right. But in the passage of the years, she had forgotten about it. She never knew what was in the package, though she suspected what it might contain. A common enough story: details of a betrothal, a promise made and broken, an illegitimate birth, another woman ruined.

'*Domine, exaudi orationem meum.*' Lord, hear my prayer.

Mariken's words echoed loud in the empty space, too loud. Her heart stumbled and she turned from the altar, fearful of being discovered alone in the chapel at such an hour of the night. But no one lifted the latch, no one stepped into the nave.

She raised her eyes to the Cross and wondered if anyone else would remember Marta Reydon and her son. She doubted it. Most of her companions of those days were gone. Though many years had passed, she still prayed for Marta's soul. She had been a woman as ill-served in death as she had been ill-used in life.

Mariken had first made Marta's acquaintance in the alleyways around the old parish church of Sint Nicolaas, where the women who sold themselves to the sailors coming off the ships gathered. Mariken and her friend Sister Agatha, a nun from a nearby convent, had done what they could for the poor creatures.

Mariken shook her head. It was so long ago. Her memories had lost their colour. Her fist tightened around the letter concealed beneath her long plain robes. She could delay no longer. It would go ill for her if she failed to furnish the cardinal with the details he wanted – no, the confirmation of what he appeared already to know. For although the Beguines were religious women, not cloistered nuns, they, too, took a vow of obedience and service, and their community also needed protection in these lawless times. Though Amsterdam had not yet joined the Protestant rebels, Mariken feared it was but a matter of time before the city fell. The Calvinists were gathering at the gates. Many of their Catholic sisters and brothers had already been forced from their convents and monasteries and quiet gardens, and had fled. The Mistress of Begijnhof would expect her to do her duty to the Holy Mother Church.

All the same.

When receiving the letter, Mariken had first made inquiries up towards the harbour, where information could be bought in the taverns of Zeedijk and Nieuwendijk for the right price. Then, she had turned to a powerful acquaintance on Warmoesstraat. A wealthy grain merchant, Willem van Raay was a pious man, a discreet man, a keeper of secrets. Mariken had nursed his daughter back to health some years previously, so she trusted him well enough to ask if he might have heard of a Pieter Reydon, or if there was gossip about why so eminent a French cardinal might have his gaze fixed upon Amsterdam. He had taken a letter for Reydon, to pass on if he managed to find him, and promised to investigate.

But two weeks had passed and still she had heard nothing.

Mariken accepted now the only thing was to call upon Willem van Raay in person. It was another burden on her conscience. They were forbidden to go out during the day without permission and, since she could not confide her reasons for wishing to leave the community, she would have to lie. At least by slipping out at night, she tried to persuade herself, she was avoiding that second transgression.

She had purloined the key to the outer gate earlier, though she hadn't absolutely decided to use it: not least, Mariken didn't relish the thought of being out unaccompanied in the dark streets at such an hour. But God would surely watch over her. Once she had spoken to Burgher van Raay, she would have information enough to compose an appropriate letter to the cardinal and her conscience would be clear. The burden would be lifted from her shoulders.

Mariken crossed herself and rose slowly to her weary feet, still feeling the cold imprint of the tiles on her knees. Every single bone seemed to ache with the pain of living.

She rearranged her *falie* over her wisps of grey hair and went out into the night. It was dark in the courtyard, though a few midnight candles were burning in one or two of the wooden houses around the green. The brook babbled its night-time song between the thorn bushes. Mariken glanced up at the Mistress's window, praying she had not woken and found the key gone, and was relieved to see her window was dark.

Fearful and troubled, Mariken fumbled and dropped the key. In all her years in the community she had never disobeyed the rules in such a manner. Her old heart thumping, she finally succeeded in unlocking the gate. She stepped onto Begijnensloot and into the narrow medieval streets beyond the bridge. Mariken was so anxious that she did not observe the shadows shimmer behind her. As she crossed Kalverstraat, head bowed, she did not feel the shifting of the air. So when the blow came, pitching her forward into the Amstel, she had no time to think.

Like many Amsterdammers who lived their lives ringed by canals, Mariken could not swim. As the first mouthful of water filled her lungs, she just had time to think how glad she was that now she could not be forced to betray the trust placed in her. She was aware of a man standing on the quay watching her drown. As her heavy grey robes quickly pulled her under, Mariken prayed that the boy Pieter and his mother would, in time, be reunited in God's grace.

And that the cardinal would never know the truth.

CHAPTER TWO

Two Weeks Later

CHÂTEAU DE PUIVERT, LANGUEDOC
Friday, 6 June

There was barely a whisper of wind.

Minou held her long, pale fingers to her temples and pressed. Her head continued to pound. She could feel the approaching storm in the prickling of her skin and the sheen of sweat at the base of her throat.

Her family would be gathering now to hear her decision. She could delay no longer, yet still she hesitated. Minou glanced around the musicians' gallery. The familiarity of it soothed her spirits. But when she turned back to the window, and saw black storm clouds mustering above the valley, unease caught in her chest.

What should she do?

Minou loosened the high collar at her neck, the brocade stiff between her finger and thumb. It was unlike her to be so indecisive. She presumed it was because so many of her family were here, bringing back dark memories of the last time they had all been together in Puivert.*

'*Les fantômes d'été*,' she murmured. The ghosts of summer.

Blood and sinew and bone. The thrust of the sword and the

---

*The Burning Chambers (2018)

swing of the rope, the roar of the fire as it took hold in the northern woods. Many had been lost between that dawn and dusk.

Ten years had passed. The forest had come back to life. New green shoots had replaced the black, charred trunks, soft dappled light painting new pathways between the trees. A carpet of pink and yellow woodland flowers blossomed in the spring. But if the land no longer bore the scars of the tragedy, Minou still did. She carried the horror of what she had witnessed deep inside her, like a shifting splinter of glass. She never forgot how closely Death had walked beside them. How his breath had scorched her cheek.

It was why she had invited her whole family to a service of remembrance in the chapel to mark the anniversary and to lay the past to rest once and for all. Afterwards, Minou had gone alone into the woods and laid flowers at the overgrown grave of the previous châtelaine of Puivert. There had been other tributes, poesies and scraps of ribbon. A Latin prayer. For although the castle was now a Huguenot enclave, many in the surrounding countryside remained committed to the old Catholic faith. The flourishing Église Saint-Marcel in the village of Puivert below attested to that.

As if mirroring the pattern of her thoughts, the bells of the church began to call the hour. Minou picked up her journal. It was her custom to write in the afternoons, carrying parchment and ink up to the open viewing point at the top of the keep. It was her way of linking the girl she had been to the woman she had become. So, though duty was calling, she decided to allow herself a few moments more of solitude. Writing helped her make sense of the world, a testimony on life as she lived it. Writing, if nothing else, would calm her conflicted thoughts.

Quitting the chamber, Minou climbed the narrow stone staircase to the roof, up steps worn thin by generations. At the narrow landing at the top of the keep, she took her old green travelling cloak from its hook beside the door, lifted the latch and was about to step out onto the roof when a voice rang out below.

'*Maman!*'

Feeling as if she had been caught out, she turned quickly.

'*Je suis ici, petite.*'

Minou heard footsteps, then the inquisitive face of her seven-year-old daughter appeared on the floor below. Marta was never still, in body or mind. Always rushing, always impatient. As usual she was holding her linen cap, stitched with her initials, crumpled in her hand.

'Maman, where are you?'

Minou took her fingers from the latch. 'Up here.'

'Ah.' Marta peered into the gloom and nodded. 'I see you now. Papa says it is time. It is past four o'clock. Everyone is waiting in the solar.'

'Tell Papa I will be there presently.'

She heard Marta draw breath to protest but then, for once, think better of it.

'*Oui, Maman.*'

'In point of fact, Marta, could you also ask Papa to –'

But only the echo of Minou's own voice swam back at her. Her quicksilver daughter had already gone.

PUIVERT WOODS

The assassin crouched in the tangled undergrowth, his finger and thumb stiff in position around the wheel-lock pistol. His gaze was fixed upon the highest point of the castle.

He was ready, had been so since first light. He had made his

15

confession and prayed for deliverance. He had laid his offering at the grave in the woods of the previous châtelaine, a pious and devout Catholic lady murdered by Huguenot vermin. His soul was pure. Shriven.

He was ready to kill.

On this day, he would rid Puivert of the cancer of heresy and be blessed for it. He would purify the land. For ten years, the Protestant harlot, an imposter, had filled the château de Puivert with refugees from the wars. She had given sanctuary to those who should be driven down into the fires of Hell. She'd taken food from the mouths of the true Catholics who belonged here.

No more. Today he would fulfil his vow. Soon, the bells of the castle would ring out for Mass once more.

'Thou shalt not suffer a heretic to live.'

Had not the eminent priest preached those very words from the pulpit in Carcassonne? Had he not fixed him with a gimlet eye, selecting him of all the congregation to fulfil God's command? Had he not given him benediction and provided him with the means?

The assassin's right hand tightened on the pistol, as his left slipped to the heavy purse hanging at his waist next to his rosary. Though his greatest reward for his most Christian service would come in the hereafter, it was only fair he should have some credit on this earth too.

The man rolled his shoulders and flexed his fingers. He could be patient. He was a poacher by trade, well used to tracking and hunting his prey. The blood-stained sack at his feet gave testament to his skill. A rabbit and an entire colony of rats. The kitchen gardens in the upper courtyard of the castle attracted all kinds of scavengers. It would have been a sin not to profit from his presence there.

The assassin shifted position, feeling the taut muscles spasm in his right thigh. He looked up through the canopy of green leaves. The sun was shrouded by dark clouds as he heard the solitary toll of the village bell strike the hour. The Huguenot whore customarily took the air at the top of the keep at this time in the afternoon, so why did she not show herself today?

He listened, alert to the slightest sound, hoping for the creak of the wooden door. He heard nothing save for the rumble of distant thunder in the mountains and foxes on the slopes of the garrigue beyond the boundary of the woods.

It was God's will that the heretic should die. If not today, then tomorrow. France would never be great again until the last Protestant had been driven from her shores. They were the enemy within. Man, woman, child – it mattered not. Dead, imprisoned, exiled – it mattered not. Only that the wound be cauterised.

The assassin sat back to wait for his quarry. At his feet the blood of his catch continued to seep through the hessian of the sack, staining the green woodland grasses red.

CHAPTER THREE

SAINT-ANTONIN, QUERCY

In the burnt-out ruins of the Augustinian monastery, a boy stood in silence in the shadow of the blackened church where so many Catholics had died. In his dreams at night, he could still hear their screams. He could see the woman's bloodied face, her cracked voice telling him to run, to save himself.

The priest's thin fingers pressed down hard on his narrow shoulders, pinching and tensing with each word uttered to the cardinal standing on the broken steps in front of them. The boy did not understand why he'd been ordered to gather his few belongings or to what purpose he had been brought here, only that something of significance was about to take place.

'I should not have been so bold as to trespass upon your time, Cardinal,' the priest stuttered. 'Your Eminence, I beg your pardon.'

The boy felt a ball of spittle strike the back of his neck. It trickled down between his cap and his collar. He did not move. If he could withstand the rod upon his bare back and the kiss of the fire against his naked legs, he could withstand this, too.

'I would not have trespassed, had I not felt it my duty to inform you . . .'

'Such a sense of pious duty is commendable in these dark times,' the cardinal replied.

It was the first time the visitor had spoken and the boy

struggled not to raise his eyes and look at the stranger's face. A voice of distinction, of authority and power.

'Of course, you can rely upon my discretion, Cardinal –'

'Of course.'

'– but the good fortune of your presence in our beleaguered town is the answer to our prayers. A sign from God. That someone of your stature should –'

'Who else knows of this matter?'

'No one,' the priest answered hastily, his fingers spasming so fiercely that the boy knew he was lying.

'Is that so,' the visitor said drily.

'We have learnt to hold our tongues. In this part of France, in this godless town, we are pariahs. Outcasts. A stray word would bring the Huguenot dogs back to our doors. We are so close to Montauban. So many Catholics have been sacrificed.'

The visitor's voice did not soften. 'Provided you hold fast to God's commands, He will protect the righteous.'

'Yes, of course, your Eminence.' The boy heard the pause, the intake of breath. 'All the same, our church in hiding would benefit from your largesse.'

'Ah, so we come to it,' the cardinal murmured.

'Only so we may continue to bring God's word to the faithful who live in fear, you understand.'

Another bead of spit dribbled down the boy's neck. This time he could not prevent himself from shuddering.

'Oh, make no mistake,' the cardinal said coldly. 'I understand.'

For a moment there was silence. The boy forced himself to keep his eyes fixed firmly on the ground: a square of dry earth, a scattering of white pebbles, blades of trampled grass. The visitor moved and he caught a glimpse of the red hem of his robes: fine cloth, dark stitched shoes without a speck of dust on the toes.

'You need have no fear that there will be any further calls upon your charity after this,' the priest added, attempting to drive home his advantage.

The visitor exhaled. 'I have no fear of that.'

'No, my lord?'

'You are a man of true faith, are you not? A man of your word.'

'I am known in Saint-Antonin for a most pious man.'

The boy heard the vanity in the priest's voice and wondered at it. Did he not realise he was being mocked, not flattered? He was a vicious and crafty man, but a fool all the same. Then he felt the jab of the priest's hands in the small of his back.

'The boy is strong, healthy. From noble stock.'

'What proof do you have?'

'This.' The boy felt the cap pulled from his head. 'And his mother's confession.'

Now he felt the full force of the visitor's gaze upon him.

'Look at me, boy. There's no need to be afraid.'

He raised his head and looked into the face of the stranger for the first time. Tall, with pale skin and dark brows, his cardinal's red robes were all but concealed by a hooded, black cloak. He had never seen him before.

And yet. There was something.

'I am not afraid, sire,' he lied.

'How old are you?'

'He has seen nine summers,' the priest replied.

'Let him speak for himself. He has a tongue in his head.'

To the boy's astonishment, the visitor removed one of his leather gloves and reached out to touch the white streak in his hair, the cause of so much of his ill treatment. A devil's mark, a sign of pestilence. Countless men of the cloth had tried to rid him of it by plucking out the hairs. Always, they grew back whiter than before. The visitor rubbed his thumb and forefinger together, then replaced his glove and nodded.

'It is not chalk. There is no intent to deceive.'

The visitor gave no indication he had heard, only reached beneath his robes and produced a small hessian bag. The priest's eyes widened with greed.

'No more will be spoken of this.'

'Of course, your Eminence. The boy's mother died at his birth. He has been raised in the love and affection of our Holy Mother Church. We let him go with great reluctance.'

The visitor ignored his words.

'Would you come with me, boy? Would you serve me?'

The boy thought of the priest's flaccid white flesh and his shrivelled member hanging between his thin legs, the quiet weeping of the other boys who failed to understand that showing weakness only encouraged a greater cruelty.

'Yes, sire.'

The faintest of smiles flickered across the visitor's face.

'Very well. If you are to serve me, I should know your name.'

'Volusien is the name my mother gave me.'

'But he goes by Louis,' interrupted the priest. 'His guardian thought it more suitable for a child of his unfortunate situation.'

The visitor narrowed his eyes. 'Unfortunate?'

The boy saw the priest flush an ugly red, and he wondered at it, but now the visitor was holding out the bag. The priest stretched out a rapacious hand but, at the last moment – too quickly for Louis to be sure if it was accident or by design – the prize was let fall. The coins rattled loose to the ground.

'Come, boy.'

He hesitated, caught between excitement and fear. 'Am I to accompany you now, sire?'

'You are,' the cardinal said, turning and walking away.

Louis stood fixed by the sight of his tormentor on his knees harvesting his blood money, and realised he felt nothing. What reserves of pity or compassion Louis had once possessed had been beaten out of him in the orphanage. He did not even feel disgust.

He ran to catch up. Was he to be an equerry or a page? He had dreamt of such things, though never with expectation. He had never known his mother – only that there was some shame about his circumstances and that his guardians resented the care of him.

As they turned the corner of the ruined church, two men stepped out of the shadows. Kerchiefs were tied across their faces and their blades were unsheathed. Louis instantly raised his fists, ready to defend his new master, but instead felt the weight of the visitor's hand on his head like a blessing.

The cardinal nodded.

The men walked away and out of sight. Moments later, a sound somewhere between a squeal and a grunt split the still air, then silence. The visitor paused, as if to be sure, then continued forward to where a carriage-and-pair stood waiting.

'Come, boy.'

'My lord.'

Though Louis had never before left Saint-Antonin and had never received any formal schooling, he was sharp witted. He watched and he listened. So at this extraordinary moment, on this extraordinary day, he recognised the thistle crest and colours of the Duke of Guise.

His head was spinning, wondering if the misery he knew was about to be replaced by something worse. He had no choice but to go. All the same, as he climbed up into the carriage, he found the courage to ask one more question.

'How should I address you? I would not offend through ignorance.'

The cardinal gave a cold smile. 'We will see, Volusien known as Louis,' he replied. 'We shall see.'

CHAPTER FOUR

CHÂTEAU DE PUIVERT, LANGUEDOC

As Minou hurried down the narrow steps from the keep, she heard the first rumble of thunder. She could not believe how the time had flown. She'd intended only to write for a few minutes, but nigh on an hour had passed.

The afternoon shadows had lengthened and the oppressive early heat of the day had been replaced by a silent chill. The air sparked with a sense of threat and menace. Minou shook her head, impatient. There was no prophecy in the sky. A summer storm in the Pyrenees was far from unusual at this time of year. Though the villagers were inclined to see each and every one as a portent of some catastrophe or judgement, she believed it was Nature, not the designs of God, that shaped the world.

Minou paused at the foot of the steps and glanced back at the coat of arms carved above the main door to the tower with the letters b and p – for Bruyère and Puivert. For ten years, she had been Marguerite de Bruyère, Châtelaine of the castle of Puivert, its lands and its living. The Bruyère family had built the fortified square tower in the thirteenth century and, when coming into her unexpected inheritance, Minou had taken the name as her birthright. But although she'd come to love this green valley set in the foothills of the mighty Pyrenees – and was proud of the refuge it had become for all those of the Reformed faith fleeing persecution – the title meant nothing to her. She considered herself a custodian of Puivert, nothing more.

Her married name – Reydon – was a gift bestowed upon her by her husband, Piet, courtesy of the French father he had never known. His affection lay with his Dutch mother, Marta, lying some thirty years dead in a graveyard in Amsterdam. Their daughter was named for her.

The truth was she was still – and ever would be – Minou Joubert. Those two words painted the truest portrait of the woman she was.

In the woods beyond the castle walls, the assassin jolted awake, his pistol still in his hand.

Had he missed his quarry?

He threw his gaze up to the keep. There was no one there. No glimpse of the green cloak. The door to the roof was still firmly shut. He rubbed his face with a grimy hand, then stiffened at another sound, this time in the undergrowth behind him. He put the pistol down and, slowly, moved his hand to the hunting knife at his waist.

He narrowed his gaze. The rabbit, sensing danger, raised its ears and turned tail. Too slow, too late. The blade flew through the air, striking the animal in its soft, white belly. The assassin went to claim his prey, pulling his weapon free with a gush of guts and fur.

Taking the creature by the scruff of its neck, dripping a trail of blood on the ground, he added it to his sack. Whether or not the Protestant harlot showed her face this afternoon, he'd had a good day's work all in all.

The assassin wiped the knife on the sleeve of his jerkin, took a mouthful of ale from his flask. He checked that his box of gunpowder and shot were still dry, then settled back to wait.

The afternoon was not yet over. There were many hours more of light. It was close to the longest day of the year.

Composing herself, Minou looked across the courtyard to the main family dwelling as the door opened and her husband strode out.

'Minou, at last! It's almost five o'clock.'

She rushed forward and held out her hands. 'I am sorry.'

Piet frowned. 'We have been waiting on your arrival in the solar.'

'I know.' She kissed him on the cheek. 'I was writing and lost track of the hour. Will you forgive me?'

His expression softened. 'As if, after all this time, I still do not know what happens when the words claim you!'

'Truly I am sorry.'

A match for one another in height, they walked slowly together back towards the house. Minou could see the spider's web of lines around her husband's eyes and how his shoulders hunched, and wondered what was troubling him. She knew the music of Piet's heart as well as she knew her own. But in the past few weeks – no, longer – she had felt a drift of distance between them. He had taken several unplanned journeys to Carcassonne and, even when at home, he had held his innermost thoughts close.

'How goes it with you, my love?' she asked lightly.

'All is well,' he said, but his attention was clearly elsewhere.

Since the Battle of Jarnac some three years past – an engagement that had cost Piet the use of his fighting arm – her husband had been obliged to lay down his sword and find other ways of serving the cause. He had organised secure networks of messengers to carry confidential orders, arranged safe passage for their refugee brothers and sisters from Catholic-held cities in France to Huguenot enclaves, and raised significant monies to keep the rebel Calvinist forces in the Dutch Provinces in boot leather.

Piet had followed reports of the Protestant rebellion there with great attention. When word of the success of the Watergeuzen, the Sea Beggars, vanquishing the Spanish forces in the north reached Puivert, Minou remembered how it had grieved him that he had not been alongside them on the battle-field, especially now as Amsterdam was teetering on the brink between the old faith and the new.

She glanced at him. Minou thought he'd accepted his situation, but perhaps she was mistaken. It was why her decision about Paris was so important. It would be a chance for Piet not only to be reacquainted with many of his former comrades but also to be at the heart of things once more. God willing, the adventure would give back to her husband something of what he had lost.

'Are you resolved, Minou?' he said, as they reached the threshold.

'I am,' she lied.

A rumble of thunder rolled over the distant hills.

'You are sure? We could wait another day if—'

Minou squeezed his arm, touched by the hope in his voice. 'You have done nothing but wait, my love. The anniversary has come and gone, everyone is here assembled, June advances.' There was another rumble of dry thunder, then a cuckoo calling. 'There. No truer herald of the arrival of summer than that. There will be rain before nightfall.'

She heard him take a deep breath. 'Minou, before we go in, there is something I must tell you . . . something I have wanted to say for some time.'

Minou felt her heart lurch. 'You can tell me anything, you know that.'

'Some weeks past, I learnt—'

'Maman!' their daughter shouted, leaning dangerously out from the casement overlooking the courtyard. 'Hurry! We are all quite fatigued with waiting!'

'Marta!' Minou waved her hand. 'It is not at all safe to hang out of the window like that, go back inside.'

'Then come quickly.'

'We will be there presently.'

Minou turned back to Piet. 'Really, Marta is too bold. Quite fearless.' She rested her hand on his cheek, feeling the stubble of his trimmed red beard, flecked with grey now, rough beneath her fingers. 'What was it you wanted to tell me, *mon coeur*?'

Piet smiled. 'No matter. It can wait. We are summoned!'

Minou laughed. 'Mademoiselle Marta can be patient a moment longer.'

'Not for all the violets in Toulouse would I try her patience further. We should go in.'

In the months and endless years to come, when Minou looked back, she saw this first quiet misunderstanding as the tipping point: that briefest of beats in time when – had Marta not called out – a different story might have been told.

But as Minou stood with her Piet in the upper courtyard of the château de Puivert on that day in June, she could not possibly have imagined how all the grief and pain she had suffered in the past would be as nothing compared to the loss and despair to come.

CHAPTER FIVE

The main family living room, the solar, occupied the entire length of the first floor of the castle. A generous and comfortable chamber, benefiting from the best of the afternoon light, it was one of the first alterations they had made when taking possession of the castle. Minou had demolished several internal walls and reconfigured the stairwells and corridors so that no memory of the old chamber – or the abuses that had taken place within it – remained.

Three tall double-casement windows with latticed lights, each framed by brocade curtains, looked south over the upper courtyard. Above the door, a heavy single curtain hung on a brass pole. In summer it was held back by a thick rope tie, and kept drawn in winter to keep out the icy winds sweeping down from the mountains. There was a limestone fireplace with two wooden settles positioned at right angles on either side of the hearth with several upholstered footstools and high-back chairs set about. At the far end, a large dining table of walnut with two long benches filled the space, with an answering dresser and chest where the table linen and crockery were stored.

What gave the chamber its particular character were the wall hangings. Filling the space from floor to ceiling were two tapestries, commissioned by Minou from a Huguenot weaver in Carcassonne: one was a representation of Puivert; another was an artist's impression of Begijnhof, the religious community in Amsterdam nestled between Singel and Kalverstraat. A third, much smaller, was a family portrait completed last winter.

As Minou stood with Piet on the threshold, she enjoyed a rare moment of seeing her loved ones unobserved: her father Bernard, his old eyes clouded and unseeing now but his wisdom undimmed; her sister Alis with her dark Midi complexion and her wild black curls tamed into a long plait, her solid and sturdy frame speaking of strength more than grace; next, her brother Aimeric, also stocky and strong and, though twenty-three years to Alis's seventeen, so alike her that they might be taken for twins. He stood in conversation with their Aunt Salvadora, her double-chins swaddled in her black widow's hood. Finally, Marta and two-year-old Jean-Jacques, listening to their grandfather recite a story of chevaliers and the Carcassonne court in medieval times that Minou remembered from her own childhood days.

Where their daughter favoured Minou in her appearance – not least in having the same mismatched eyes, one blue and the other brown – their son had Piet's colouring: russet hair, green eyes and a freckled skin that owed more to his Dutch mother than his French ancestors.

Then the creak of a loose floorboard gave their presence away.

'*Enfin*,' cried Marta, throwing herself down from the window seat. 'We are all quite worn out with waiting.'

'You must learn to be patient, *petite*,' Minou said fondly.

'Aunt Salvadora says that in the royal rooms in the Louvre Palace, the most noble ladies wear skirts this wide.' Marta spread her arms. 'Too big to get through a doorway without turning sideways. Is that so? Because how would—'

'That is not at all what I said,' Salvadora objected. 'I was explaining how the fashions of the court are intended to demonstrate the elegance and grandeur of the crown. Our noble king – and his sister and brothers – represent the best of France and, thus, must pay heed to the impression they give. In portraiture, as in their daily lives.'

Minou saw Aimeric and Alis exchange a look. They had no regard for the Valois court. Aunt Boussay was another matter. Despite her affection for her nieces and nephew – and theirs for her – Salvadora held true to the old faith in which she had been raised. Despite the rumours about King Charles, his tantrums and ill health – not to speak of the common knowledge that it was Catherine de' Medici, the Queen Mother, who truly ruled at court – Madame Boussay would hear no word of censure against the royal family. Her admiration remained steadfast.

'The ladies and gentlemen of the Paris court wear elegant attire for official occasions, but dress with less grandeur for the everyday, like us.' Minou gestured to the delicate family tapestry on the wall. 'Papa does not wear his blue doublet with the silver slits except on special occasions, does he?'

Marta, considering herself wise at seven years old, mused: 'Nor I my jewelled hood. It is for best only.'

'Exactly so.' Minou stroked her daughter's cheek. 'It is the same even in the Louvre Palace.'

The child nodded. 'It is wise for even queens and princesses to have everyday clothes, for how else would they be able to play?'

Everyone laughed, even Salvadora, and Minou felt a surge of gratitude for the love and companionship they all shared. She glanced back at the tapestry. She and Piet were sitting clothed in gold thread and adorned in silver and jewelled beads: on cushions in front of them sat Marta in her bleached-white cap beside two-year-old Jean-Jacques in velvet breeches with his wooden rattle. The colours were vibrant and the stitching full of life, of movement. Though no bigger than a lady's shawl, it was Minou's favourite. Of all of the tapestries, it spoke most to who they were.

Were they to risk all this for Paris?

Minou pulled herself up at such a thought coming unbidden into her mind. Certainly, the journey would be long. Certainly, the steady pattern of their lives, which had been hard won, would be disrupted. But whatever discomforts they might endure, seeing Paris with their own eyes would surely be worth it? To stand before the mighty towers of the Cathédrale de Notre-Dame and witness history as it was made was not an honour to be missed.

Minou was conscious of Piet's eyes fixed upon her. No man could have worked harder to promote a message of tolerance, nor to attempt to bring those of differing faiths to common ground. Her husband believed not only that a permanent peace was possible, but also that the majority of women and men of France – Catholic or Huguenot – wanted it. He cited their own family as proof of it. While Bernard, like Salvadora, remained within the old faith, they had brought their children up in the light of the Reformed Church. If their family could manage to accommodate and respect one another's differences over a decade of civil war, why not other families also?

'Minou,' Piet said lightly, 'will you speak?'

Then he smiled and, even after ten years of companionship, her heart sang. She felt her indecision leave her. Whatever doubts she had, she owed it to her husband to be by his side in Paris.

CHAPTER SIX

'My thanks for your patience,' she said, looking around the chamber. 'And I ask your forgiveness for my poor time-keeping.'

At the sound of her voice, everyone fell silent. Bernard turned in his chair. Aunt Salvadora folded her fan and placed it in her lap. Alis stopped pacing and stood beside Aimeric. Even little Jean-Jacques felt the gravity of the moment and stopped kicking his fat little feet as Marta sprang up onto the bench beside the nurse and whispered at her brother to be still.

'I am grateful, too, that no one –' Minou glanced at her daughter – '*almost* no one has attempted to rush me to make my decision.'

'But you say we should always speak the truth,' Marta protested.

'Hush,' said Piet, putting his hand on her shoulder. 'Let Maman speak.'

'It is an honour that our family has been invited to attend the royal wedding. For some –' she looked at Aimeric – 'to be present on this auspicious day is a matter of duty. For others, it is a matter of reconciliation.' She looked to her husband, and he smiled his encouragement.

'Catherine de' Medici and Jeanne de Navarre. Two queens, two mothers, adversaries for many years. Through this marriage contract, they signal their intent to put aside their differences in order to rebuild a land fit not only for their children, but also for their children's children. If Marguerite de Valois – Margot – can take the Protestant Henri of Bourbon for her lawful husband, then surely all Catholics can learn to live in peace with their Huguenot neighbours.'

'Well said,' said Bernard. 'Is not that so, Salvadora?'

'Indeed, it is.'

Minou looked at each of her family in turn. 'You all know how hard I have found it to arbitrate between what I consider is in the best interests of our family, and what are our responsibilities to our friends and comrades. But, after much reflection, I consider it will be an honour to stand witness, after these long years of war, to this agreement brokered between former enemies.' Her gaze came to rest on Piet. 'That being so, I propose we should all accept the invitation and travel with you to Paris for the wedding.'

For a moment, as everyone in the chamber took a moment to absorb what she had said, the air seemed to shimmer and pulse. Then, Marta clapped her hands and the world came rushing back.

'I am glad,' Piet said, his eyes sparkling as he took Minou's hand. 'So very glad.'

Aimeric laughed. 'Brother, did you not know what your wife intended?'

Piet flushed. 'I was confident in your sister's decision!'

'As was I, though I admit as much on my own selfish account as for any nobler purpose. I am summoned to rejoin Admiral de Coligny's entourage. He has stayed away from Paris of late – hence my liberty to return to Languedoc for these weeks – but now the King calls for him and he cannot refuse. Knowing you all are somewhere within the city walls will make the discharging of my official duties all the more pleasant.'

Minou smiled. 'And it will be a joy to have the benefit of your companionship there, brother.' She waved her hand, taking in the room. 'Of course, there is no obligation for anyone else to come, though all are welcome.'

Bernard shook his head. 'I am too old for such a journey, *Filha*. I shall return to Carcassonne and look forward to hearing all about it when you return.'

'We will lack your company, but I quite understand. What of you, dear Aunt?'

Salvadora flicked open her fan, sending a single black feather dropping to the ground. 'How you think I would deprive myself of such a spectacle, I cannot imagine! It will be the wedding of the age. Though the Queen of Navarre might be misguided in her faith, her son is a prince of the royal blood and was indeed born a Catholic –'

'Though a convert to the Reformed Religion as soon as he could speak,' Alis said under her breath.

'He is a prince of the royal blood,' Aunt Boussay repeated firmly. Her expression softened. 'And to see Paris at last. Notre-Dame and the Sainte-Chapelle, where the holiest of the relics of the Passion are to be seen: the Crown of Thorns, a piece of the true Cross—'

'Of old wood, more like . . .'

Minou muttered a warning. 'Alis . . .'

'Whenever my official duties permit me to do so, I shall be honoured to show you the sights, dear Aunt,' Aimeric said quickly, frowning at his little sister.

Marta picked up the stray black feather and tickled Jean-Jacques under his chin, then slipped it into the folds of her skirt.

'I, too, have given the matter due consideration,' she said in her solemn voice. 'I shall accompany you and Papa to Paris, not least of all to keep an eye on this little devil.'

'Really!' protested Salvadora. 'Minou, you should not allow her to speak like—'

'But he is!' Marta insisted.

Salvadora pursed her lips. 'Well, it is impolite to say so.'

'All brothers are devils, Marta,' Alis grinned, pointing at Aimeric, 'which is why I, too, feel obliged to come to Paris. To keep an eye on him!'

Aimeric clamped his hand to his chest. 'You wound me!'

'Is that true, Maman?' Marta demanded.

'What is true, is that your Aunt Alis and Uncle Aimeric have spent a lifetime teasing one another! Pay them no heed.'

'Come, sit with me, Marta,' Alis said, leading her to the table. 'We can talk of vexatious brothers and how to tame them!'

Piet turned to Aimeric. 'Is it still your intention to leave tomorrow?'

'Yes. I will travel via Chalabre to bid farewell to my wife, then ride on to join my comrades in Saint-Antonin. All being well, I should be in Paris by the end of June.'

'Might you be able to secure suitable lodgings for us?'

'For how long?'

'Given the wedding itself is on the eighteenth day, I think we should aim to arrive during the first week of August – when, God willing, the city should not yet be too crowded – and depart after the celebrations are completed, a day or two past the Feast Day of St Bartholomew. That will allow us some three weeks in Paris.' He looked to Minou. 'That should be sufficient, do not you think?'

Minou smiled. 'Quite sufficient.'

Salvadora brandished her fan at Aimeric. 'I would be close to the Louvre Palace, nephew. On the grand rue Saint-Martin or the rue Vieille du Temple. Not in some insalubrious district.'

'The university quarter on the left bank might be better,' Bernard said mildly. 'The air is cleaner there.'

Salvadora tutted. '*Appropriate* lodgings I said, Bernard. I do not wish to be among tradesmen, or poets or—'

'Protestants?' called Alis.

Aimeric's lips twitched. 'I give you my word, revered Aunt, that I will keep you safe from the contaminating evils of poetry and the printing presses of the Sorbonne.'

His aunt narrowed her eyes. 'You know perfectly well what I mean.'

'I do,' he answered fondly. 'I shall secure lodgings appropriate to everyone's needs. Have no fear.'

'That is settled,' Piet said, his voice alive with the promise of the adventure. 'I propose we should leave around the longest day, some two weeks hence, and take our time to travel.'

'Do you have a route in mind?' Aimeric asked.

Piet glanced, almost shyly, at Minou and all at once, she understood. Though he had been waiting on her decision, he had already been planning for her and the family to go with him. Was that what he had been on the point of confessing earlier?

Her responsibilities acquitted, Minou took a cup of wine from the dresser and raised it in a toast to her husband.

Piet smiled with relief at her blessing. 'Indeed yes,' he said, turning back to his brother-in-law. 'I have some thoughts.'

In the forest beyond the castle walls, a blackbird called to its mate. A fox made its stealthy way along a woodland path, a buck and doe broke cover to forage for food in the glades. In the mountains, eagles wheeled and soared, riding the currents of the stormy air.

Still the assassin watched. He had no hope now of fulfilling his mission before night fell. He wondered what had happened to change the usual pattern of things, for he had no doubt the intelligence he had been given was good. Every afternoon, the heretic went to the top of the tower. Why not today?

He heard the changing of the watch at dusk. He saw the lamps in the towers lit, one by one. An owl came out to hunt. Finally, as the light faded from the sky, the assassin took shelter in the deeper recesses of the wood. He laid down the pistol, covered his box of gunpowder tightly to keep it dry, then reached in his pocket for the meagre rations he had left, and settled back against the trunk of a beech tree to pass the night.

'If not today, then tomorrow,' he said, zeal burning in his eyes. 'The Lord's will be done.'

Little by little, the day sank down behind the hills.

Aunt Boussay returned to her needlepoint. Alis took Marta to see the kittens in the kitchen gardens. Jean-Jacques slithered from his nurse's lap and stumbled back to his grandfather begging for the end of the story.

Minou sat on the bench in the long windows, listening to the tempest. It gave her pleasure to watch Piet, as excited as any boy planning his first hunt, leaning over the table with his leather jerkin untied and his sleeves rolled up. Aware of her observance, he turned. He gestured to the chaos of papers and maps on the table.

'Would you like to see what—'

Minou held up her hand. 'Two heads are better than three. I am content to leave the planning to you and Aimeric.'

'You are sure of that, my lady of the mists?'

Minou smiled. 'Quite sure, my lord. Indeed, I am grateful not to have to think on it.'

When the bells of Saint-Marcel struck the ninth hour, the nurse took the children to their beds and the servants brought wine and victuals for supper. As the bells were tolling ten, Bernard retired, followed shortly afterwards by Salvadora. The candles danced and guttered. Alis stayed a little longer, offering suggestions and commentary, then took herself to her chamber. At the approach of midnight, with no sign that Piet or Aimeric had exhausted their discussions, Minou also withdrew.

Finally, the storm broke with wild winds and rain lashing against the glass. She was bone tired, but when she got to her chamber, she found she could not settle. The voices in her head were too clamorous.

At two o'clock, she rose and opened the casement to freshen the air in the room. She heard the indistinct voices of her husband and brother, now standing in the courtyard below, then returned to her tangled bedsheets, wondering what kept them from their beds.

Finally, the tempest blew itself out. All the same, it was still not until a pale dawn came creeping across the sill, that Minou surrendered to the inky arms of sleep.

CHAPTER SEVEN

Vidal du Plessis – known now as his Eminence, Cardinal Valentin – looked down from the window to the small courtyard below, which was bathed in morning light. The boy was playing with other children.

The more Vidal watched, the more he observed how Louis held himself apart. Vidal approved of such caution. To be part of the group without drawing attention, all the better to watch and listen, showed good judgement. Yes, he approved.

They had ridden north all the previous day and through the night, covering some fifty leagues distance from Saint-Antonin to reach the outskirts of Limoges by morning. But although Vidal had taken refreshment and bathed his temples, he remained fatigued, short tempered. The relentless rattling of the carriage wheels continued to reverberate in his skull. Every bone in his body ached. His head ached.

He turned away from the casement and cast his eye around the well-appointed chamber. Limoges fell within one of the principalities controlled by Jeanne d'Albret, the Huguenot Queen of Navarre, and was currently under the control of Huguenot forces. However, a handful of noble estates had been left in Catholic hands, not out of compassion or mercy, but because the Queen admired the enamel boxes and trinkets produced in Limoges itself. Papist or not, she did not want those businesses destroyed.

Vidal considered the situation absurd and resented being confined in this enclave surrounded on all sides by heretics. Only a few weeks more, he told himself, then he could return to his purpose. Come the feast day of the Nativity of Our Lady in September, he would be free to return to his private estate outside Chartres, purchased with the promise of his inheritance from his wealthy uncle, Philippe du Plessis, and fulfil the next stage of his life's plan. Having had no son of his own, Vidal was his sole heir.

At least, Vidal had thought it so. He shook his head, unwilling to entertain such troublesome thoughts, then wished he had not. His temples started to pound.

Vidal was a star in the firmament of the Catholic Church. Having risen to prominence quickly during the wars, and with little opposition, he had long ago shaken the dust from his southern heels and aligned himself to the North. He was a personal confessor to the Duke of Guise himself and, for ten years, had profited from the misery of civil war. He was now wealthy, he was powerful. But at this particular moment, for his private ambition to be realised, he needed the current cessation in hostilities to hold. Until Michaelmas at least, when the last of his arrangements would be in place. Then the country could go to the Devil, for all Vidal cared.

Yet, for all his influence, Vidal felt matters slipping out of his control. The situation in Amsterdam – though he had taken steps to contain it – gave him cause for concern. He had money enough for the time being, but a claim against his uncle's estate would ruin him. His plans were costly. And his current sojourn in Languedoc had served to confirm that the feverish atmosphere in Paris was repeated the length and breadth of the country. France was a tinder box of resentments, disagreements and grudges.

Everything depended upon the royal wedding going ahead. Though the marriage contract had been agreed between the Queen Mother and the Queen of Navarre in April – and an August date set for the ceremony – the Louvre Palace was still waiting for dispensation from his holiness the Pope. That was just one obstacle. There were others, not least the Duke of Guise's continuing love affair with the bride-to-be.

Vidal wiped his face with his kerchief, the furrows on his brow evidence of ten years' service to the Guise family. He neither knew nor cared if there was genuine affection between Marguerite of Valois and Guise. However, he was certain that when – if – Guise did show his hand, it would not be love sickness which moved him to action but rather an implacable hatred of his rival, Henri of Navarre. That the Huguenot was about to be married into the Catholic royal family, so uniting the Bourbon and Valois dynasties, was a savage blow to Guise's own ambitions. Vidal had no doubt his master would do anything he could to destabilise the alliance.

His fingers began to tap on the back of his chair, accelerating as his vision took hold. No, he could not waver now. And though God had long since stopped listening, Vidal raised his eyes towards Heaven.

'Your Eminence.'

Vidal turned. His steward, Xavier, stood in the doorway. The man was as pale as milk, despite the southern sun, and his eyes were a sickly yellow. Yet he was robust and never faltered.

'What is it?' he said sharply, replacing his red biretta on his head.

'Forgive me for intruding upon your repose, sire, but word has come from Paris.'

'Oh?'

Vidal held out his hand for the letter. Xavier crossed the room in two strides, gave the missive into his master's hands, then stepped respectfully back.

Vidal broke the familiar wax seal, already a little cracked from the journey, and scanned the words. He frowned, read them again a second time to be certain there was no mistake, then held the parchment to the candle and watched it flame.

'Eminence?'

He tossed the blackened remains into the cold grate. 'We are summoned to return immediately to Paris. It seems the Queen of Navarre is unwell. A fever.'

'Was she previously in ill health?'

'I believe she was,' Vidal replied carefully.

'Then it is to be hoped that her Majesty recovers, although...'

Vidal narrowed his gaze. He had a network of spies working the length and breadth of the country – and beyond – of whom Xavier was one of the most reliable. He did not enquire how the man acquired his information, nor from whom, but his intelligence was rarely at fault. The ends always justified the means in the service of Christ.

Vidal waved his hand. 'Although?'

'I would not wish to talk out of turn, my lord.'

'I will not censure you if your words are not to my liking. Speak.'

The steward hesitated. 'Though I am sure it is a common fever . . .'

'Do not try my patience, Xavier.'

'The messenger who brought the letter confided that, but three days previously, Catherine de' Medici had made a gift of gloves to her royal guest.'

Vidal's eyebrows shot up. 'Perfumed gloves?'

'Fashioned by her own glove maker,' Xavier elaborated, 'they are said to have been delivered by the Queen Mother herself to the Hôtel de Bourbon, where the Queen of Navarre is currently residing.'

Vidal considered. There wasn't a woman or man in Paris who had not heard of René the Florentine, perfumier to Catherine de' Medici, or that, in addition to his legitimate business, the Italian was also the purveyor of poisons. His shop was never empty.

'This is common talk in the streets?'

'The messenger said it is spoken abroad in both Catholic and Protestant quarters.'

Vidal's fingers drummed harder. This did not suit his purposes at all. If there was rumour of a plot against the Queen of Navarre – even if there was no evidence, but the populace believed it – then relations between the Louvre Palace and the Hôtel de Bourbon would become strained and the marriage might not go ahead.

'Bring the messenger to me. I would question him myself.'

Xavier raised his hands in apology. 'I did not think to detain him. He has already gone.'

'Gone? Gone where?'

'I know not. I am sorry, sire.'

Vidal frowned. 'No matter. We have our instructions. We cannot let such gossip distract us from our purpose. It is not for Man to question the ways of God, Xavier, for His wisdom and mercy are beyond our comprehension. The soul of the Queen of Navarre is in His hands.'

'Yes, your Eminence.'

'Prepare the horses. I will give my apologies to our host for our premature departure. We leave immediately.'

Xavier's eyes snapped up. 'We are not to wait for news from Puivert?'

Vidal understood his concern. The intention had been to remain in Limoges until receiving word his orders had been successfully carried out.

'The Duke of Guise would have me back in Paris without delay – indeed, he commands it so. I shall be forced to assume the matter has been resolved satisfactorily.' He paused. 'However, leave instructions that, should any communication be received, word should instantly be sent after us. I would know for certain.'

'Very good, sire.'

'On which point, is there word from Amsterdam?'

Xavier met his eye. 'The situation was as you thought, Eminence. However, the matter is concluded.'

'Discreetly?'

'There is no possibility of any connection being made to you, sire. And there was no evidence – if indeed it ever existed – found in the nun's quarters. Nothing.'

Vidal exhaled in relief. 'Good. You have done well, Xavier. I will see you are rewarded for it.'

'It is my honour to serve, sire.'

A shout in the courtyard below drew Vidal back to the window. The child's game had shifted from play to battle. Louis had his right fist clenched but it was the other boy – a son of one of the prefects of Limoges – who sported a bloody nose.

Despite the fact that he would be obliged to issue some form of reprimand, Vidal was not displeased. Louis had a fighting spirit, a sharp sense of self-preservation and an apparent lack of conscience. Whether he claimed Louis as his own, or continued the fiction that he was the child of a distant cousin taken into his service out of Christian charity, Vidal believed he would prove himself useful.

'And what of the boy?' Xavier asked.

Vidal looked down into the courtyard again. His son seemed to sense he was watching, for he glanced up and without a hint of shame in his face. The briefest of smiles crossed Vidal's lips. He shut the casement.

'The boy comes with us to Paris.'

CHAPTER EIGHT

CHÂTEAU DE PUIVERT, LANGUEDOC

Evidence of the storm was everywhere, broken branches and twigs strewn on the wet ground. The heavy smell of damp straw and the bright day assailed them as Minou left the family's private quarters.

As the rising sun painted its pattern upon the grass, the solemn group walked from the upper courtyard and through the castle grounds towards the gatehouse to bid farewell to Aimeric. Marta skipped ahead while Minou and Alis walked at a steadier pace, with little Jean-Jacques jumping between them.

The *basse cour* courtyard was given over to the working life of the castle – the stables and blacksmith, the kennels for the hunting dogs, the stores of provisions to support the household, the salting house. Each Saturday, the lower courtyard served as the weekly market for Puivert. Tradesmen and artisans had begun to come up from the village as soon as the gates were opened to set up their stalls. Farm women with willow panniers and wide-brimmed hats bearing the first fruits of summer; the cooper and his boy rolling rattling barrels of ale over the drawbridge and into their position in the shadow of the western walls; a poulter with a brood of hens gathered within a make-shift wooden pen. The fires of the forge were already burning, the farrier with his rasp in hand. Even a travelling bookseller appeared with his chap books and pamphlets. Minou had never seen him before and made a mental note to look over his stock.

Women bobbed their heads as they walked by, men touched their caps. Minou smiled and raised her hand in greeting to those she knew. It had taken her some time to learn to accept and to acknowledge these signs of fealty. Nothing in her modest upbringing in Carcassonne, or her childhood spent in her father's bookshop in the Bastide, had prepared her for such status or position.

Minou had come into her unexpected title from her birth mother, Marguerite, for whom she was named. That Bernard and Florence were not her blood parents was a secret that had been kept from her until she was nineteen. So, although Minou felt a gratitude for the woman who had died giving birth to her – and in whose image she was fashioned, tall and pale, with straight brown hair and mismatched eyes – she considered Florence, some fifteen years buried, her true mother. It was love, not blood, that mattered. It was from Florence that she had learnt her life lessons, not least to respect and pay heed to antiquity: 'Without knowing of the mistakes of the past,' she used to say, 'how can we learn not to repeat them? History is our teacher.'

Minou had held the advice close to her heart and so, without intending it, had modelled herself on the great medieval hero of Languedoc, Viscount Trencavel.* She ran her estates in Puivert – their estates – in the same spirit of toleration and was proud that in this, one of the southernmost points of the Midi, Huguenots and Catholics lived side by side as Christian neighbours, not enemies.

When Piet had been away in the early years of the wars, Minou had governed Puivert alone. She had become reliant on her own counsel and instincts, adjudging who was the injured

*Labyrinth (2005)

party in a broken engagement or a dowry unpaid; listening to charges of adultery and ill faith and stolen inheritance; protecting the innocent against unwarranted charges and administering justice to the guilty.

'*Merci infiniment, madame*,' said Marta prettily.

Minou looked round to see her daughter accepting a handful of ripe, red cherries from an old woman, dressed head-to-toe in black, in the custom of the mountains. Marta's pale blue dress, with its delicate cream beads, dazzled in comparison.

'*Mercé a vos, madomaisèla*,' the woman responded in the old language.

Minou had learnt how to fulfil her duties by trial and by error, so it amused her how Marta took it all in her stride. She was very much the treasured daughter of the castle. Minou glanced at her son and wondered if he would be the same. She doubted it. Jean-Jacques was a steady, good-natured child, constant in his emotions, not quicksilver curious like his sister. Jean-Jacques would inspire loyalty. Marta would inspire devotion.

The assassin jolted awake and slapped his cheeks to sharpen his senses.

Yes, there it was. Close at hand, voices and the sounds of horses, the gust and whinny of their breath, their hooves tramping on damp ground. The noise was coming from some-where around the main entrance to the castle. Was it her? Was the false châtelaine leaving the castle? His spirits lurched at the thought he might have missed his chance, but then he remembered. He'd heard that her heretic brother was to ride north today. He looked up at the tower and saw there was no one there. The door to the roof remained shut.

The assassin rolled his shoulders and stretched his legs to

loosen the night from his bones, then undid his hose and pissed against a beech tree.

He took a swig of ale from the bottle, chilled from the dew, and chewed on a mouthful of bread. Then he sat back in position again, with the wheel-lock pistol balanced across his knees. It was beautiful. Perhaps they would let him keep it when the deed was done.

'*Domine, exaudi orationem meum.*' Lord, hear my prayer.

His blood stirred at the thought of the killing to come.

Piet and Bernard were waiting at the gatehouse with Aimeric.

Minou watched as father and son embraced one another. She was touched to see her brother was wearing Piet's old dagger at his waist. A talisman for good fortune? At that moment, Piet dropped his hand on Aimeric's shoulder and leant in. Minou wondered they still had anything left to say to one another, having talked all night.

'Why do you whisper?' demanded Marta. 'Maman says it is rude to whisper.'

The two men stepped apart. Piet stroked his daughter's long brown hair. 'There are some things that are not for young ears.'

'What kind of things?'

'Things,' Aimeric repeated, his black eyes sparkling.

'I don't think that is fair. Maman says—'

'No more, *petite*,' Minou said, drawing Marta to her. 'Stand with me.'

She thought Aimeric looked fine in his black doublet and hose. His wild hair was tamed beneath a felt cap and his beard trimmed to a perfect point. The country landowner was gone, he was now every bit the soldier once more.

'I wish with all my heart he would not go,' Alis whispered.

'Are there not others who stand as high in the admiral's esteem? What need Monsieur de Coligny of our brother?'

'It is his duty,' Minou replied. 'He has pledged his service.'

'Paris is so distant.'

'No further than his previous postings, Alis, and hasn't he always come back to us?'

'But what if —'

Minou squeezed her sister's hand fondly. 'Give him your blessing. Let him leave with proud words in his heart.'

Alis hesitated, then stepped forward, her green dress vivid beside her brother's black clothing. Her face was drawn but, from the set of her jaw, Minou knew she would not cloud his departure with her melancholy.

'Though the very air in Paris pulses with papistry, fire-and-brimstone preachers on every street corner, Brother, I dare say there is much to amuse and engage, too.'

Aimeric smiled. 'I will shut my ears to any and all corruption.'

'You will cut a fine figure, I have no doubt. But stay out of trouble, do you hear? Be guided by caution as much as by courage —'

'Because brothers are little devils,' Marta added.

Alis smiled gratefully. 'Exactly so. Because brothers, little and less so, are devils.'

Taking everyone by surprise, Alis threw her arms around Aimeric, hugged him, then strode away back across the courtyard towards the house without another word.

'What's the matter with Aunt Alis?' Marta said. 'Where's she going?'

'She is sad,' Piet replied. 'What say you and I go and amuse her? You can challenge her to a game of Queen's Chess.'

'Chess is boring. I don't—'

'In which case you can help me with mapping our route.'

Instantly, Marta brightened. 'Can I use *Gran'père*'s box compass?'

'*If* you ask his permission to do so,' Minou said, 'and *if* he says you may, then yes.'

'Can I borrow it, *Gran'père* Bernard?'

Bernard steadied his stick. 'Let us go and find it. Give me your arm, Marta, and we shall walk together.'

'I'll go with her to make sure she doesn't wreak some new havoc.' Piet grinned, hoisting Jean-Jacques up onto his shoulders. 'We shall be in the solar, my love, when you are ready to join us.'

Minou watched them go, three generations – her father, her husband and her son, with her quicksilver daughter leading the way across the courtyard. Then she turned back to Aimeric and held out her hand.

'I shall lack your company.'

'And I yours. These weeks here at Puivert have been quite like old times. The Joubert family together again.'

'It has been a pleasure to have you with us for so long. I hope your wife will forgive us for keeping you.' Minou hesitated. 'Did you and Piet resolve matters between you last evening? You were talking late into the night.'

Aimeric nodded. 'There is much to attend to. Despite the terms of the peace, some territories are less safe than others. Piet is right to take such care in the planning.'

'That is all?' Minou asked lightly. 'Nothing more than that?'

'What more should there be?'

'He does not seem distracted to you?'

Aimeric frowned. 'Piet has matters on his mind, of course, but nothing out of the ordinary. A great deal is riding on this wedding going ahead without mishap.'

'It's just . . .' Minou stopped, not sure what she was trying to say. 'Piet did not give you any other reason for his distraction. He did not confide in you?'

Aimeric shook his head. 'No. That is to say, he did ask that I should seek news from Amsterdam when I arrived in Paris. He's followed the uprising there against the Spanish occupation closely and would hear first-hand reports of how things are going.'

The sound of clinker and bridle as Aimeric's groom arrived with his piebald palfrey brought their conversation to a close. Beyond the gates, his travelling companions were now waiting: three fellow soldiers armed and already mounted. Plain livery, nothing to mark them out. They would don the insignia of Admiral de Coligny once reunited with their comrades in Saint-Antonin.

She saw Aimeric's eyes glint with purpose and, though she wished to question him further, she knew her brother's thoughts were already on the road ahead.

'God speed,' she said brightly.

'Take good care of my niece and nephew.'

'I will.' She squeezed his hands. 'Until we are together again in Paris.'

'Until Paris.'

The groom cupped his hands and Aimeric leapt up into the saddle. He snapped his reins and the horse leapt forward.

'*Hie!*'

As he crossed the drawbridge, Aimeric turned and raised his hand in a last farewell. Then he pressed his knees into the horse's flank and broke into a gallop, his men following at his heels.

CHAPTER NINE

PUIVERT WOODS

Two horses, a grey stallion and a bay mare, crested the brow of the hill.

Manes and tails flying, the thunder of their hooves reverberated through the damp earth as they galloped across the plains of the river valley, before turning up towards the woods.

The sun was high in the sky and the hills were alive with colour – yellow-tipped broom and purple cypress, pink and white meadow flowers. On the ground, a carpet of silver-coated leaves. Twigs and dead branches, brought down in last night's storm, snapped under the iron shoes. The tones of the riders' apparel were needlepoint bright. Minou's old green cloak and red skirts, Piet's forget-me-not blue doublet and hose. Feathers in each cap.

After the emotion of Aimeric's leave-taking, Minou suggested they should excuse themselves from the normal business of the castle and blow the cobwebs away. At ten o'clock, she and Piet had set out to ride north along the river valley. The plan was to meet Salvadora, Bernard and the children in their favourite bower in the woods to dine, before returning home to Puivert in the mid-afternoon.

As she drove her horse faster, Minou did not believe there was any freedom on God's earth that could compare to the joy of riding through the forest in summer beneath the cloudless blue of the Midi sky, when the going was firm but not too hard, when the sun was bright but not fierce.

'The prize is mine,' she cried. Taking her husband by surprise, she gripped her reins and flexed her whip.

'*Par force!*'

The bay leapt forward, neck stretched, the white blaze on her nose a perfect diamond. Minou pulled quickly away, flying up the last of the track to the outskirts of the woods, some three hundred acres of forest that lay to the north of the château de Puivert.

At the brow of the hill, Minou slowed to a lazy trot, then into a walk. She loosened the reins, let her hands rest on the pommel of her saddle and followed the track that led to the glade where they were to rendezvous.

'*Brava*,' she said, patting her mare's steaming coat.

Dappled light filtered through the canopy of leaves, transforming the mossy ground beneath them into a patchwork of shifting shapes. A sweet breeze rustled the underside of the leaves, turning the green to white, to silver, back to a shimmering green.

Minou pulled up as her destination came into view. Ahead, in the heart of the glade, the servants were setting the midday table beneath a line of beech trees. The corners of the white linen cloth were being lifted lightly, then let drop, by each gentle gust of wind. A handcart, used to transport the victuals, wine and crockery, stood close by. A little further away, the large trap, its wooden arms pointing to Heaven, tilted back on two large wheels. The sturdy bay carthorse, tethered to an alder tree, was grazing nearby.

Her father was established with Marta at a small, folding table a few paces from the makeshift kitchen. Minou marvelled again at how, of all the family, Bernard was able always to still her daughter's restless spirits. With him, Marta was never bored.

The nurse was sitting with Jean-Jacques on a blanket in the

shade and Minou was pleased to see Salvadora had joined the party. She considered eating *en plein air* a ridiculous affectation. But Minou was disappointed not to see Alis. She knew her sister's need to mourn the loss of Aimeric, her boon companion, in private. At the same time, it would not do to let her brood.

CHÂTEAU DE PUIVERT

Alis stared blindly through the window of the chapel.

She had come to the keep, away from watching eyes, and wept herself dry. Usually so steadfast, this time she felt quite hollow with misery.

Alis rested her head against the glass. Neither the azure sky nor the red-specked orchards in the valley lifted her spirits. They only reminded her of how three days previously, she and Aimeric had gone walking arm in arm through the apple trees, talking until the sun went down.

It was foolish to be so affected by her brother's departure. She should consider it a blessing that he had been able to spend any time at Puivert with them at all, especially without his wife in tow. There had been times, during the worst of the fighting, when they had not heard tell of him for months.

But what if, this time, he never came back?

As Alis turned back to the altar, something about the quality of light caught at her memory. Without warning, she was suddenly assaulted by the image of her seven-year-old self, being held captive in the castle here by the priest with the white streak in his hair. A child, lost and alone.

Image after image flashed unbidden into her mind, lightning sharp: being dragged into the woods where the pyre was burning, a rope tethered around her neck; of Minou tied to the stake in the flames; of Aunt Salvadora lying bleeding upon the ground; of the previous châtelaine turning the knife upon herself and her unborn child. So much blood.

'No!'

She would not walk in the shadow of the past. She had survived. It had left her strong and self-sufficient. It was only that, today, the person she loved most had gone. Solitude did not suit her, Minou always said so. It made her a prisoner of her own anxious thoughts.

Time would do its work. Each day, the ache of Aimeric's absence would lessen. June would pass, then July. In a matter of weeks, they would be together in Paris. For now, company was what she needed, the guileless chatter of her niece, even her aunt's endless discussions of the latest fashions of the court.

Alis exhaled. She would heed Minou's advice. When she heard the bell ring for two o'clock, she would go to the top of the tower to watch out for her family coming home from the woods. She would have a clear view from up there. She would spend the afternoon in their company and brood no more on Aimeric.

August would come soon enough.

PUIVERT WOODS

At the rumble of hooves behind her, Minou turned.

'My lord, what kept you?'

'The victory is yours.' Piet smiled, leaning across to kiss her as he drew level.

'You concede, sire?'

'I concede,' Piet said, kissing her gloved hand, then the inside of her wrist, then her lips.

Struggling to hold his restless stallion, he dismounted, then reached to assist Minou as she unhooked her leg from the pommel and slid from her saddle.

'*Vas-y*,' Piet said, summoning the groom to hold the horses.

Minou threaded her arm through his, rejoicing in the dappled sunlight and the heady scent of the pine trees. On a branch, a mistle thrush with its boldly speckled breast sang for the arrival of summer.

'What were you and Aimeric whispering about?' she asked.

Piet laughed. 'I told him that if he did not find us adequate lodgings in Paris – and I was obliged therefore to endure Salvadora making complaint for the duration of our sojourn – I would be forced to take my dagger back and turn it upon myself!'

'That is indeed a fate none of us wish for! Though, in point of fact, I did not mean this morning at the gatehouse, but rather last evening. You were talking until dawn.'

Piet drew his arm away.

'What do you mean by that?' he asked sharply.

Minou stared at him. 'Mean by it? Why, nothing more than I said. I could not sleep, so I got up and opened the window. I heard you talking in the courtyard.'

'You were eavesdropping?'

'Eavesdropping! Piet, how can you say such a thing?'

'Listening to a private conversation, what else would you call it?'

She was bewildered by the cold expression on his face.

'It was humid after the rain, the chamber was airless . . .' She touched his arm. 'Why have you taken offence when none was intended? Do you doubt the wisdom of us accompanying you to Paris?'

'No! I would not leave you here without my protection.'

'Protection! Whatever do you mean?' Minou held his gaze,

trying to read the story in his eyes. 'Husband, whatever it is that occupies your thoughts, please tell me.'

Piet sighed. 'I am only concerned that the mere presence of so many Huguenots in Paris will be seen as provocation to many, regardless of the wishes of the King or the Queen Mother.'

'Is it this you were going to say to me yesterday?'

Piet didn't meet her eye. 'Of course.'

'We are safe here,' she said.

'Safe!' he exploded. 'Nowhere is safe! There are spies everywhere.'

Minou looked at him in astonishment. 'Piet, please tell me what is wrong. There is something more, I know you well.'

For a moment, he held her gaze. She could see the indecision in his face, then his eyes slipped away and a tiny piece of her heart broke.

'Forgive me, Minou,' he said, his voice suddenly weary. 'I am tired. Pay no heed to my ill-humour. You are not at fault.'

Without giving her the chance to say more, he mounted his horse and galloped away through the woods, leaving Minou at a loss to know what had actually taken place between them.

CHAPTER TEN

For a moment or two, Minou just stood watching the empty space and wondered what secret her husband was keeping that he thought too troubling to share with her. Then she realised Bernard, Salvadora and the servants were all looking in her direction.

Minou forced a smile upon her face, as if the quarrel had not happened, and walked forward into the green glade to join them.

'*Maman!*' Marta cried. 'See what I have drawn.'

The small folding table was now covered with paper, pens and ink, a hinged ruler and colouring chalks.

'Show me, *petite*,' she said, as brightly as she could manage.

'It's a map!' Marta said, pointing at a drawing. '*Gran'père* let me use his compass to put things in their rightful place.'

'That was kind of him.'

'We are here.' The little girl pointed at a rough outline of the castle. 'And this is the route we shall travel, though I need to show it to Papa to make sure it will serve.' Marta peered around her. 'Where has he gone?'

'Papa has urgent matters of business to attend to. You can show him later.'

Marta pouted. 'I wanted to—'

'Go and play with your brother,' Minou said firmly, gesturing to where Jean-Jacques was balancing on a fallen tree trunk with his nurse's assistance. 'And this,' she added, removing the box compass from her daughter's hand, 'can stay here. It is not yours. Unless *Gran'père* said you might keep it with you?'

'He did not,' said Bernard mildly, though he was smiling.

'I was going to keep it safe.'

'I warrant it will be safe enough here,' Minou said, putting the treasure back on the table. Marta had the grace to blush.

Minou watched her daughter skip to join the others.

'*Filha*,' Bernard said, patting the bench. 'Sit with me.'

'Marta is a magpie,' she said. 'She should not take things that do not belong to her.'

'She is curious. She will learn,' he replied. 'Is her drawing serviceable?'

'In point of fact, it is excellent. She has a good hand and a fine eye for detail, though perhaps her perspective is not quite what it might be. Puivert is rather larger than it warrants. She has fashioned it the same size as Paris!'

Bernard smiled. 'Puivert is the centre of Marta's world. If she spent all her days in Carcassonne, I have no doubt La Cité and Paris would be the twin pillars on which France is founded.'

Minou laughed. 'That is true.'

'Your mother drew you a map of Carcassonne when you were about the age Marta is now. Red chalk for La Cité, green for the Bastide, blue for the river in between, our bookshop in the rue du Marché and our house in the rue du Trésau both coloured in yellow. Do you remember?'

'Of course. I have it still.'

Bernard's old face brightened. 'I had thought it lost these many years.'

'I keep it inside my journal for safekeeping.'

'Ah, your journal! Florence would be astonished to know her rough sketch has done such good service.'

A gentle silence fell between them. Minou sensed Bernard

was waiting for her to speak and, though she did not wish to be disloyal to her husband in any way, she was in need of her father's wisdom.

'You heard our quarrel?' she asked, and was grateful when he did not feign ignorance.

'I did.'

She sighed. 'One moment we were at ease in one another's company, then the next . . . I don't understand it.'

'If you will forgive me for giving voice to what you know, *Filha*, but since his injury, Piet has struggled to find a role he can play with honour, with purpose. For the most part, he has succeeded.'

'Do you think I do not know that!'

'Perhaps watching Aimeric depart with his companions this morning was an unwelcome reminder of what he has lost?'

Minou felt her eyes prick with unexpected tears. 'Perhaps. It is just I overheard him talking with Aimeric in the courtyard last evening. I feel sure there is something he is holding back from me.'

Bernard raised his eyebrows. 'Overheard . . .'

Minou flushed. 'I should have withdrawn. I did, as soon as I realised. But what distresses me, Father, is when I asked – without any guile – what had been the substance of their conversation, Piet behaved as if there was some terrible secret. I even entertained the thought he might have a mistress in Toulouse.'

Bernard roared with laughter. 'Daughter, you can dismiss that from your mind. I have never known a man so constant in his affection for his wife as Piet.'

Minou blushed. 'I know. I felt guilty for even allowing such a disloyal thought to enter my head. But there is something. He has been so withdrawn of late. And yesterday, before we came into the solar to join you all, he said there was something he needed to tell me. His demeanour was sombre and measured. Then Marta interrupted, and the moment was lost.'

Bernard sighed. 'The key to a long and happy marriage is not to avoid discord, nor to be scared of it or deny it. Rather, it is about trying to find ways of turning differences – especially those that seem insurmountable – into a source of strength. Speak to him again.'

'I have tried, but he refuses to hear.'

Bernard considered. 'If not infidelity – which we both agree it is not – then go through the possible reasons for his pre-occupation and strike those from your mind: financial matters, concern for the children, the prospect of further fighting, this year's harvest, the journey to Paris. Then ask yourself what else could it be?'

Minou thought, then a trickle of dread ran down her spine. It was suddenly so obvious.

'Vidal . . .' she breathed.

Vidal, Piet's dearest friend from his student days in Toulouse. They had been as close as brothers once. Vidal had first betrayed him and then – in league with the previous châtelaine of Puivert – had attempted to kill him, hunting them down from Carcassonne, to Toulouse and finally to Puivert.

So many dead for the sake of a fragment of old cloth, a holy relic.

Piet never spoke of Vidal – and Minou never asked him for fear of putting an unborn idea into his head – but often she wondered if his dreams were tenanted by the man he once had loved. And if, in those dishonest hours between dusk and dawn when the night terrors came, the memory of Vidal's piercing black eyes and white streak of hair still haunted him, as much as they haunted her.

Minou caught her breath. Could it be? The events that had brought them so violently into conflict with one another were in the past. Vidal had acquired what he wanted. A decade had passed without evidence of his continuing malice or interest in them. Why would Vidal bother with them now?

But what if that was not true?

'Vidal,' Minou said again, hating how even speaking his name polluted the soft, afternoon air.

'Has there been word of him?' Bernard asked sharply.

'Not that I know of. However, Vidal is certain to be present at the royal wedding. He is high in the Duke of Guise's esteem. Perhaps it is the thought of seeing him again which disturbs Piet's peace of mind.'

'You will not know, *Filha*, unless you ask him. For the sake of the love between you, encourage him to open his heart to you.'

'And if he will not?'

Bernard laid his liver-marked hand over hers. 'You will resolve matters between you, of that I have no doubt. Piet loves you, and you him.' He pulled himself to his feet, signalling the conversation was over. 'Now is it not yet time to eat?'

Minou put the stick into her father's hand and, side by side, they walked towards the dining table. A wooden bowl of cherries, a platter of *fromage de chèvre* with mountain honey, baskets of *pan de blat*, earthenware bowls brim full with ale. All that remained was for the salted ham to be unwrapped from the damp muslin cloth.

'Go, Minou. We will manage here without you.'

'I should stay. The children—'

'– are content.'

She looked over. Jean-Jacques was curled sleeping against the nurse, who was singing a gentle lullaby in the old language

Minou remembered from her own childhood. Marta was trailing after Salvadora, who was rearranging crockery on the table, and criticising the state of the linen.

'Go,' Bernard repeated. 'Resolve matters with your husband.'

Minou hugged him, feeling how sharp his ribs were through his doublet. 'Thank you. What would I do without your good counsel?'

'What are fathers for, if not to advise their daughters?'

They walked a few steps further, then Minou stopped. 'Do you still miss her, Father? Even after all these years?'

'Every day, *Filha*. I miss your mother every single day.'

CHAPTER ELEVEN

Piet gave the stallion his head.

He wanted to shout, to clear the poison from his blood and the bile in his stomach. He bent low in the saddle, riding faster and harder, as if he could outrun his malevolent thoughts.

He was limed in a trap of his own making, each untruth twisting and winding around the next, until he could not breathe. Minou was his love, his affectionate companion and helpmate. They completed one another. So how to explain the reluctance to confide in her? A situation that made him, if not a liar exactly, certainly a man who concealed? His silence was building a wall between them, he knew it. Yet on each occasion when he steeled himself to speak, fear took his tongue.

It was his duty to look after his family, to keep them safe.

Piet felt shame working its way up from his chest and into his throat until he could barely breathe. He kept telling himself he remained silent for Minou's own good, as he had each day since receiving the letter from Amsterdam. He told himself there was no sense sharing the dread that held him, helpless, in its grip until he had proved the letter was genuine. That the threat was genuine. Minou was inclined to worry, so why burden her unless he had to?

Even now, he remembered the initial shock of reading the single name at the foot of the paper: Mariken. Her compassionate face was linked forever in his mind with his mother's blue lips in that cold and derelict room on Kalverstraat. He remembered the lap of the canals and waterways as if it was yesterday, the smell of peat and of herring, as Mariken led him later through narrow Amsterdam streets to safety.

Piet had spent the past weeks attempting to prove the veracity of Mariken's letter. He had sent word to his comrades in the Low Countries, rebels in Brielle and Utrecht, with no success. He could only hope that once Aimeric reached Paris, and made contact with Dutch communities there, he might know more.

Once he knew for certain, he vowed to himself, he would tell Minou. But for now, he owed her an apology. The last thing he wanted was to hurt her. He looked around, and realised how far north he had ridden.

'*Hie*,' he said, turning back towards home. '*Vas-y*.'

The bell in the village below struck two o'clock. The assassin waited. Then, above the whispering of the wind, he caught the sound of the door and then a flash of green.

She was early today.

'*Sancte Michael Archangele, defende nos in proelio*,' he prayed, sending words up to the archangel for whom he was named. 'Defend us in battle.'

This single act of assassination would be as much an act of war as any siege or infantry charge. He was a soldier in the army of Christ.

The assassin quickly crossed himself, then stepped out of the cover of the undergrowth. He had assessed the range and angle to the parapet, where it was the châtelaine's custom to sit, and calculated the optimum position. If she remained by the door, he would not have a clear shot. He needed her to come closer to the edge.

'Come on, come on,' he urged his victim. 'A few steps more.'

He steadied his breathing and fixed his gaze on his quarry.

The powder, ball and shot were in place. His grip tightened upon the trigger. He set his eye along the muzzle.

He watched as the false châtelaine walked to the far side of the roof to look out over the lands to the north. He kept his arm steady. Finally, the heretic whore turned towards her accustomed spot on the crenellated parapet. The angle wasn't quite right, she was standing further away than usual, but he had her in his sights all the same.

At last.

Tilting his arm by some forty-five degrees to keep steady the priming powder in the pan, he squeezed his finger and thumb, and fired. In one seemingly simultaneous moment, he heard the clicking of the wheel, the tension of the mainspring, the sharp white-hot sparks of the fool's gold as the pyrite hissed and spat and the bullet left the gun.

The sound reverberated around the woods, abrupt and harsh, as the bullet was discharged towards the keep. A white-backed woodpecker flew up into the sky in a startle of wings.

The assassin watched the whore sway, then saw the blossoming of red on green as she fell. He exhaled, then relaxed his shoulders. He could not be sure she was mortally wounded, but it was a palpable hit. Thanks be to God, his shot had found its target.

Slowly he let his arm drop. He took a deep breath, surprised to find his palms were damp. Then time rushed back. There was not a moment to lose. He had to put as many leagues between Puivert and himself before the alarm was raised.

The assassin stepped back into the cover of the woods, restless now to be gone. He gathered his meagre belongings, dismantled the pistol and placed it in his leather satchel, and kicked over the flattened leaves and bracken where he'd slept. He picked up the sack, stiff with dried blood, then dropped it back to the ground. It was a good haul, but the stench of decay was seeping through the hessian and, though the skins would keep for a while yet, the meat was already turning putrid.

He turned and headed for the track through the woods that would take him first to Chalabre, then north some ten leagues to the Catholic safe house in Carcassonne, where he would receive his reward.

As he ran low through the army of beech trees and silver birch, the assassin wondered again if the cardinal might allow him to keep the pistol. It was costly, but had he not fully earnt it in God's service?

'Steady,' Minou murmured to her mare. The report of a gun, close at hand in the still afternoon, had startled the animal. She had nearly been thrown. 'Steady now, steady.'

Minou had listened out for a second shot, but none had come. She hadn't given permission for a hunt – and she did not think Piet would have done so without telling her – and, besides, the poachers of the Pyrenees still preferred a knife or bow and arrow to any kind of firearm. It was odd.

As soon as she had quietened her horse, Minou continued gently on towards the castle, still rehearsing what she was going to say to Piet. She hated there to be discord between them. Her anger at being unfairly criticised had given way to a desire for conciliation. Her father was right. If they could talk their troubles away, all would be well.

It wasn't long before the outline of the keep came into view, then the long, low curtain of grey wall between the towers of the château de Puivert.

Nothing was stirring. The low arched gate that led into the kitchen gardens was closed, though she could hear the usual household sounds beyond the walls.

She patrolled the length of the northern walls, her watchful gaze switching between the château and the woods. Looking for something out of place, evidence of a gun being fired. She turned and this time, when she drew level with the outside of the Tour Bossue, she spied something in the undergrowth. Minou dismounted. The bay would not come near, so she tethered the animal then walked forward alone.

A dirty hessian sack was lying beneath the trees. Minou untied the neck and recoiled from the stench of the rotting flesh. She tipped the contents out on the ground. Several rats and two rabbits, one with its belly sliced open. Why would a poacher leave behind his spoils, meagre as they were?

Minou crouched down and ran her fingers over the leaves, noting how the grass was flattened in places. A single crust of bread, bone hard. Someone had sat here long enough to leave his mark.

As she stood, she heard banging. Steady, rhythmic, repetitive, the music of wood against stone? Minou raised her head and saw how the door that led onto the roof of the keep was ajar, swinging backwards and forwards in the wind.

Her first reaction was impatience. The top of the tower was so exposed to the elements – the harsh breath of the Tramontana, the driving rain, the snows in winter – that the door was always supposed to be kept secured. Then she wondered. Since no one else but her ever went up there, why was it now unlatched?

Leaving her horse, Minou hurried through the arched gate into the kitchen gardens, then, with a mounting sense of unease, she ran to the keep and up the stairs, her cloak flowing behind her.

On the roof, the wind cracked and blustered. Minou paused in the doorway, then her blood turned cold.

'No . . .'

She was unwilling to trust the evidence of her eyes, but there was no doubt. Someone was lying collapsed on the ground, her arms stretched wide. A green hood, a green dress stained red by the blood pooling beneath her.

'Alis!' she cried, running to her sister. 'Alis!'

Minou rolled her onto her side, trying to find the source of the bleeding. There was a deep gash on Alis's temple, but the worst of the blood was flowing from a bullet wound in her back.

Using her kerchief as a tourniquet, Minou tried to stop the flow. Fresh blood instantly stained the white linen cloth red. She unpinned Alis's hood, folding the material to make a pillow beneath her sister's head, then ran to the edge of the keep and looked down into the main courtyard below. She needed help urgently, but where was everyone?

In the furthest corner by the gatehouse, she saw an old man with a cart of hay moving slowly across the courtyard.

'Help me!' she shouted. 'Bring help!' She waved her arms, but she couldn't tell if he had heard her or seen her. Minou ran back to Alis, knowing she couldn't leave her for fear her condition would deteriorate. She pressed harder, desperately trying to stem the flow from the wound in her back as best she could.

The white kerchief continued to turn red.

'*Il n'y a personne?*' she shouted again, twisting her head towards the pass door. 'Will somebody help me?'

As Piet approached the castle, he practised what he was going to say to Minou. Words of apology and of love, he for her and she for him.

But when he came within hailing distance, and saw Minou's mare tethered outside the side gate in the wall, his words vanished. Why would she have left her horse here rather than take it to the stables? Then he saw the corpses of the butchered animals on the ground and his heart started to drum.

Piet leapt down from his stallion, secured the horse beside Minou's bay mare, and ran through the gate into the castle as if the Devil himself was at his back.

Time dragged its heels, marked only by the uneven pattern of Alis's ragged breathing. Her pallor was worsening. Minou tapped her cheek, trying to rouse her, but her sister's eyes remained closed. The moment she took her hand away blood pumped out. If she left her, Alis would die. No doubt of it.

'Help is coming,' she said, pressing her green cloak against the wound. 'It won't be long.'

At last, Minou heard footsteps on the stairs and suddenly Piet was in the doorway, with two servants behind him.

'Minou!' he cried.

She saw how, in an instant, Piet took in the sight of her cloak soaked with blood, then Alis lying lifeless on the ground.

He rushed towards her. 'What happened, are you hurt?'

'No, not me.'

Minou heard him catch his breath. 'I feared . . .' he whispered, crouching beside her. 'When I saw you, I thought—'

'Alis has been shot,' she said. 'I heard the sound some while ago.'

Piet recoiled. 'What! Did you see anyone as you came through the woods?'

Minou shook her head. 'No, but he left behind a sack of ripe carrion.'

'I saw that.'

'Someone has been keeping watch, I think.'

'How bad is it?'

Minou half lifted the kerchief and another gush of blood

spurted out. 'The ball is still in there. We should get it out. It's the best chance of preventing an infection from taking hold.'

Piet nodded. 'Hold her hand.'

Taking his hunting knife from his belt, he wiped the tip on Minou's cloak, then pressed the sharp point into the wound. Alis stirred, but did not wake.

'I almost have it,' he said, twisting the blade as gently as he could. This time the shot came out in a slick of fresh blood. Minou instantly plugged the deeper wound with the sodden kerchief.

Piet sat back on his haunches, his face grey with relief. 'I thought it was you, Minou,' he said again. 'I thought I'd lost you.'

Minou placed her bloody hand across his. 'I know.'

For a heartbeat, she held his eyes. Then she summoned the servants.

'Mademoiselle Joubert is badly injured. Have hot water, cloths and vinegar taken to my bedchamber. Honey too. It's good for purifying the blood. It might stop a fever from taking hold. And you – Marcel – ride down to the village and tell the physician we are in urgent need of his services. Make haste.'

The servants bowed, then ran.

'I fear moving her will agitate the bleeding, but we have no choice. If you carry her, Piet, I'll keep my hand pressed against the wound.'

He nodded. 'On my count. One, two and three.'

Between them, they managed to lift her from the ground. Alis didn't even murmur. She lay lifeless in Piet's arms.

'Hurry,' Minou said desperately, feeling another slick of blood between her fingers.

Together, they staggered towards the door and clumsily down the stairs, a red trail on the stone steps betraying their route.

CHAPTER TWELVE

'Why does the physician not come?' Bernard asked again.

With each moment that passed, Alis's breathing became shallower, more laboured. The colour was draining fast from her cheeks. Bernard squeezed his younger daughter's hand while Minou continued to apply fresh bandages to the wound. Press and replace, press and replace. Eventually, the flow of blood lessened.

'She grows colder,' Bernard murmured.

'Help is on its way. Piet will bring the doctor.' Minou had lost count of how many times she had said the words. 'They won't be long now.'

All the same, it was not for some time until, finally, she heard Piet's voice in the hallway below their bedchamber. The step of boots upon the stair, the scent of the world outside, then a stooped grey man was ushered into the chamber.

'This is Monsieur Gabignaud,' said Piet. Minou and Bernard both jolted at the familiar name, unheard for so many years. 'He has been away in the wars these past years.'

She rose to meet him. 'Monsieur, you are well met.'

'At your service, my lady. Monsieur Joubert.'

Bernard inclined his head. 'Monsieur Gabignaud. Your aunt did us a great service once, my late wife and I.'

'She would have been honoured to be remembered.'

The physician's skin was pock-marked and he was clutching a wooden box of instruments tightly in his hands, as if he feared to be robbed, but Minou saw his eyes were keen with intelligence.

'Your patient is here, monsieur,' she said swiftly. 'Did my husband explain what had happened?'

'Only that Mademoiselle Joubert had been shot.'

'We ourselves know no more than that. We took out the ball and purified the wound with vinegar.'

'It is what I would have done, my lady.'

'I will go to Salvadora and let her know how things are,' Piet said quietly. 'Will you be all right?'

Minou lightly touched his fingers. 'Yes, but come back when you can.'

With her hand upon her father's shoulder – to comfort him or to comfort herself, she wasn't sure – Minou watched Gabignaud make a preliminary examination. Her fear that he might be a butcher-surgeon who had learnt his trade on the battlefield vanished as he gently studied the wound, a single jagged hole at the base of Alis's spine where the bullet had penetrated the flesh. From his questions, she discerned he was also a compassionate man.

'Will my daughter live, Gabignaud?' Bernard said, his voice loud in the silence of the chamber.

'I will do everything I can, monsieur. There is no sign of fever – though it is early – and no discharge either. You were right to take the shot out, Madame Joubert.'

'I'm glad you think so.'

'But this gash on her head . . .'

'We think she did that when she fell,' Minou replied. 'Is it serious?'

Gabignaud raised his hands. 'It is harder to treat what we cannot see than what we can,' he said cautiously, 'but I am hopeful.'

As he cleaned the wounds and applied fresh strips of cloth, Minou acted as her father's eyes. In a low, steady voice, she described every action the physician was taking to save his child.

For the rest of that long afternoon, Gabignaud laboured to save Alis's life.

Minou cindered hawthorn and rosemary and wild thyme in the fireplace to purify the air. Servants went to and fro, bringing copper pans of hot water up from the kitchens. Bernard sat white and silent, his old face lined with grief and fear for his youngest child. The maids tore fresh strips of cotton and laid them on the nightstand, while others carried away the old, bloodied bandages to be burnt in the yard.

In the solar, Salvadora sewed the same patch of cloth over and again, pricking her fingers and leaving marks of blood on the yellow fabric. She prayed and, from time to time, drank a little wine to ease her fears. The nurse occupied the children with card games and stories. Piet came and went, leaving Minou each time with the gentle touch of his hand or an affectionate kiss upon her cheek.

The sun sank lower in the sky, yet still Alis did not stir.

'You should go and rest,' Minou said to her father, seeing how his head was drooping onto his chest.

Bernard sighed. 'Ah, *Filha*. I have spent so very many nights like this – sitting by your bedside, or by Aimeric's or Alis's, waiting for a fever to break or a nausea to pass. Though I serve no purpose now, I like to think she knows I am here.'

'Of course, she does,' Minou said fiercely. 'And yours will be the first face she sees when she wakes.'

'God willing, yes.'

'Might I at least bring you something to drink or eat?'

'You are a good daughter, but do not concern yourself with me. I will do well enough here.'

Minou's heart broke at the desperation in his voice. She leant forward and placed a kiss on his forehead, then returned to her own vigil at her sister's side.

'Please wake up', Minou whispered in Alis's ear. 'Please.'

As the evening shadows began to fall, casting long ribbons of golden light across the floor of the chamber, Minou spied a thick trail of blood oozing down the side of the bed.

'Monsieur Gabignaud . . .' she said quietly, but Bernard heard her all the same.

'What is it?'

Gabignaud lifted back the cover and Minou caught her breath. The top sheet was clean, but the undersheet glistened with fresh blood the colour of rubies.

'Pass me a bowl, if you will.'

'What is happening?' Bernard said. 'Tell me.'

'I think Mademoiselle Joubert's body is attempting to cleanse itself,' the physician replied in a taut voice, examining the wound.

'Is that not a good sign?' Minou asked.

'It may be,' Gabignaud replied carefully. 'But if it is God's will to take her to Him, then . . .'

The sound of Bernard's stick striking the ground made Minou jump.

'No! This is not God's will, it cannot be!'

For a moment the words seemed to hang in the air between them.

'Father, Monsieur Gabignaud is doing all he can. You know that.'

Bernard waved her away. 'This is not God's doing. If a man did this, a man might repair this. Gabignaud, I beg you. Save my child.'

Minou took her father's hand.

'Save my daughter, Gabignaud,' he whispered, as the fight went out of him.

'Come and sit over here,' Minou said, steering him towards a chair at the open window. The air will do you good.'

'I am not leaving the chamber.'

'Of course not. But let us give the good doctor room enough to make his ministrations.'

'Is she in pain, do you think?' Minou asked when she returned to Gabignaud's side.

'I cannot be certain, my lady, but I think not.'

'And why does she still not wake?'

He shook his head. 'It may be that, by remaining in this half-state, Mademoiselle Joubert is protecting herself. Her breathing has eased, her pulse is steady. There is a little fever, but that might even be a good sign. A sign her body is resisting. See how she catches at the bedclothes with her hands? There is life in her for the fight.'

As Saturday slipped over into Sunday morning, Alis's fever broke.

Minou was dozing at her sister's bedside, as Gabignaud was checking his patient's pulse for any indication of a change in her humours, when Alis opened her eyes.

'Minou?' she murmured into the darkened room.

At first, Minou didn't hear.

'Minou,' Alis said again, a little louder. 'Where am I?'

'Doctor! She's awake!'

'What happened? Why am I here?'

'Alis, you're awake!'

Gabignaud smiled. 'Mademoiselle Joubert, how goes it with you?'

Alis stared at him. 'Who are you?'

Minou's voice broke with relief. 'This is Monsieur Gabignaud, Alis. He saved your life.'

She felt Alis squeeze her fingers, then she closed her eyes again. 'It is a pleasure to make your acquaintance, Monsieur Gabignaud.'

Minou took a moment to compose herself before going over to where Bernard was asleep in his chair.

'Father,' she said, putting her hand softly on his shoulder. 'Alis has woken. It's too soon to know, but for now that's all that matters. She's awake.'

There was a stillness, a silence. Minou felt a fist tighten around her heart.

'Father?' she whispered, putting her hand on his shoulder. Bernard didn't stir. Minou put her hand to his cheek, and realised it was cold.

In the dark hours before dawn, Minou sat at her escritoire, hollow with grief. With her quill in hand, and a blank sheet of paper before her, she attempted to compose a letter to Aimeric.

As light thickened, bringing shape back to the valleys and hills of Puivert, she continued to wrestle with words that would not come, words that were too cruel, too definite, when so much was unclear. Her duty as a sister kept her there, finally writing what needed to be written. Only the barest of facts. That, on the seventh day of June, his cherished sister Alis had been shot by an unknown hand. And that, in the early hours of the eighth day of June, their beloved father's old heart had finally stopped beating.

As the first rays of the sun lit the chamber, Minou signed, blotted and sealed the letter, then rang the bell. The servant came to carry it away, words to break another heart.

PART TWO

AMSTERDAM & PARIS
June, July & August 1572

CHAPTER THIRTEEN

BEGIJNHOF, AMSTERDAM
Monday, 9 June 1572

The bells of Sint Nicolaas church and the Nieuwe Kerk were ringing out over the canals and waterways. In Plaats, buyers and sellers haggled over the price of herring and peat, of slabs of butter on wooden boards and rich, yellow cheese. The shop-keepers piled their wooden shelves high with produce. Women and men rested their legs on stone benches beneath the colon-nades of the old medieval Stadhuis, the town hall.

It was a bright day in Amsterdam. The sun was shining and the streets were busy. Though times were hard, with blockades and hunger stalking the countryside beyond the walls, within there was an atmosphere of summer and plenty. Amsterdam was a city built on trade and finance.

Cornelia van Raay stood in the shadow outside the gate waiting to be admitted into Begijnhof. Of medium build and stature, her heavy brows and forthright gaze made it seem as if she was frowning even when perfectly content. Today, however, she was anxious. Her father had sent her to deliver a message to one of the inhabitants, Mariken Hassels. Cornelia wished he had not. She disliked the stifled atmosphere within Begijnhof, the religious women scuttling around with their eyes to the ground, too scared to speak or laugh or raise their faces to the sun. But she was an obedient daughter and her father, usually a man of little visible emotion, had seemed much perturbed.

Cornelia folded her hands and tried to be patient.

Around her, she heard the familiar melody of Amsterdam. The pull of rope and winch as goods were transported into warehouses in Oudezijds Voorbugwal and Warmoesstraat, where her father's lucrative business was situated. The air humming with the roll of the cooper's barrels down rickety wooden pathways lashed together on the quays of Nieuwe Zijde. The swell of shallow-bottomed barges and lighters sailing from Damrak to the harbour, where stevedores loaded and unloaded provisions ferried from the sailing ships anchored beyond the floating palisade in the IJ. A forest of masts, a floating woodland riding at anchor outside the city walls.

When Cornelia was a child – and before his civic responsibilities as a burgher took up so much of his time – her father used to carry her up to the harbour to inspect his fleet of ships, which transported grain across to the Baltic states and south down into France. She loved to watch the sailors and bargemen of every colour, yelling to one another in unfamiliar tongues as they unloaded their cargo: the pale features of Zeelanders; the brooding eyes of carpenters from Denmark; the pale servants of rich timber merchants from Poland; the lucrative herring fleet; the messenger service carrying letters from Amsterdam to Antwerp and back six times a day. Sometimes, they would return home to their handsome house past In 't Aepjen, the boarding house on Zeedijk, where it was claimed foreign sailors could pay for their lodgings with monkeys instead of coins.

Things were hard for many. The wars had destroyed countless thriving businesses, though her father had weathered the storm better than most. She saw the hollow eyes of refugees who came stumbling into the city seeking shelter. She saw the boarded-up warehouses when a merchant went out of business, how their name was painted out and another man's took its place. Cornelia knew they were lucky.

She knocked again on the gate, but the metal grille remained closed. Had the Sisters forgotten she was here? She understood their caution. In these times of resistance and rebellion, where most other towns in Holland had fallen to the Calvinist rebels, Amsterdam remained a Catholic city, surrounded by Protestants. Soldiers with matchlock muskets patrolled the streets at night. The five city gates were closed when darkness fell and manned day and night to prevent refugees from the wars – or those too ill or diseased – from entering. Special guards held the entrances to the harbour and the IJ at night with floating beams and chains.

Even so, both within the walls – and outside the gates, at the hedge sermons held in the countryside that drew hundreds of worshippers – skirmishes between the Calvinists and the city's militia were increasing, as were attacks on Catholic priests and nuns. Cornelia knew the destruction of statues and icons was commonplace enough for any visitor to Begijnhof to be thoroughly investigated before they were admitted.

Finally, the grille slid back and a narrow face, framed by the distinctive grey headscarf worn by the Beguines, appeared.

'The Mistress will see you now.'

'*Dankuwel.*'

The rasp of a bolt and the turn of a heavy key. Cornelia slipped through the gate, which was locked quickly behind her.

She followed the Beguine through the pretty gardens, spiked with rose trees and thorn bushes and streams, past the small brick church with its high thin tower to the largest of the wooden houses surrounding the green. In silence, they climbed the plain wooden staircase. A knock upon the door, a peremptory instruction to enter, and she was ushered into a large, light room.

'Good afternoon.'

Cornelia bowed her head. 'It is gracious of you to receive me, Mistress.'

'Your father is a true friend to our community. He is in good health?'

'He is. He is recently returned from France, where he contributed to the building of a new church in Paris.'

The Mistress nodded, as if no more needed to be said of his piety. 'You are enquiring after one of our community, Mariken Hassels?'

'I am.'

'Why?'

The abrupt question took Cornelia by surprise. 'I – because . . .'

'Why do you wish to see Mariken?' the Mistress pressed.

'My father –' She began again. 'That is to say, Mariken did my father – did me – great service once. She nursed me back to health when our physician had given up hope.'

'I am aware of that,' the Mistress said, her black eyes dark in her heavy face. 'That was some ten years ago. So although I do not question the gratitude you owe Mariken, my question is why you wish to speak with her now?'

Cornelia felt her chest tighten. Her father, though by nature a mild-mannered man, had been quite explicit on the point.

'My father impressed upon me it was a private message,' she replied, 'for Mariken's ears only. I would not disobey him.'

Cornelia raised her eyes and, for a heartbeat, they held one another's gaze. A battle of wills. Because of Willem van Raay's financial largesse to Begijnhof and the stature of their family in Amsterdam, Cornelia was gambling that the Mistress would not push her further.

'Of course, my father wished for me to obtain your permission to speak with Mariken, as a matter of courtesy. But forgive me, he was most clear I should pass on the message in person, and to her alone.'

Cornelia watched irritation flicker across the Mistress's face, then anger that although her authority was being challenged, financial considerations dictated she could do nothing about it.

'There is a complication,' she finally admitted. 'The fact of the matter is that Mariken is no longer with the community.'

'How can that be!' Cornelia exclaimed, then she remembered herself. 'Forgive me, I did not mean to be disrespectful.'

The Mistress held up her hand. 'It was a shock to us, too. Mariken had been with us for all of her adult life, some fifty years. That being so, for reasons I do not claim to understand, she chose to leave our community some weeks ago. She gave no prior indication of it, she left no letter, she did not ask permission or seek guidance.'

'You are sure she left voluntarily?'

'You forget yourself.' The retort was sharp.

Cornelia apologised again. 'But is it likely she would simply go?'

'Likely or not, that is what has happened. If you might inform Burgher van Raay of that.'

Looking back, Cornelia couldn't say what first drew her attention: the shifting of the air, the way the Mistress's eyes darted to the right-hand corner of the room, the tenor of her voice. Just a little louder than necessary, just a little clearer than before. Cornelia realised with a jolt that their conversation was being overheard.

By force of will, she kept her gaze fixed on the older woman's face.

'My father will be most distressed to hear this news. I will explain you did everything you could to help.'

'Just so.' The Mistress inclined her head, then added, as if it was of no consequence at all, 'Might I now ask you what was the message?'

Cornelia smiled. 'Only that there was nothing to report,' she lied.

Her expression did not change, but Cornelia sensed a loosening of her shoulders, the slightest exhalation of trapped breath.

'I don't know what he means by that,' Cornelia said, 'but since Mariken is no longer here, I imagine this will be the end of the matter.' She stood up. 'Thank you for granting me an audience.'

Now there was no mistaking the older woman's relief.

'It was my duty. As I said previously, your father has been a loyal and generous friend to our community.'

'And will continue to be so.' Cornelia bowed her head. 'I will not take up any more of your time.'

The Mistress reached out for a small bell sitting on the table beside her chair. Again, in that instance, Cornelia saw her eyes slip once more to the corner of the room. This time, she spied a pair of dark eyes looking back at them from behind the screen.

'May God go with you, child.'

Cornelia crossed herself, then stepped back.

She had hoped to speak to other women of the community, in case Mariken might have confided in anyone in the days before her departure, but there was no opportunity. The same Beguine who had shown her into the compound returned, leading her back through the gardens past the wooden houses and the old church. Before she knew it, Cornelia was standing again on the little bridge looking back at Begijnhof. An island community ringed by water, divided by water, in the heart of the teeming city. A sanctuary or a prison?

As Cornelia retraced her steps towards Warmoesstraat, she

replayed in her mind the message she was supposed to have passed to Mariken: that the boy Pieter Reydon had lived to adulthood and now prospered in Languedoc. A Huguenot convert, he was married with two children, a daughter and a son, and his family estate in Puivert – inherited through his wife, Marguerite Joubert – was some leagues south of Carcassonne.

That he had no idea of his birthright.

Cornelia suspected that, far from being the end of the matter, it was only the beginning and, despite the heat of the Amsterdam day, she shivered.

CHAPTER FOURTEEN

Three Weeks Later

Château de Puivert, Languedoc
Sunday, 29 June

Beneath the light of a full moon, the marshal of the stables at the château de Puivert was making the final preparations for the family's journey to Paris.

The horses were shod and rested, the bridles and harnesses ribboned and repaired. Every stirrup and buckle had been cleaned and cleaned again. The leather saddles and saddlebags glistened with beeswax and the scent of ash. The carriages for the family and open traps for the household servants and luggage gleamed, with every wooden spoke and axle checked and tested.

At eight o'clock, a service would be held in the chapel to bless their forthcoming endeavours, and then their adventure would begin.

So far as the eye could see, there were signs of a glorious, abundant summer: fields of filigree flax swaying in the wind, the blue flowers peeking out from the thin, green stalks and silver-grey olive groves; in the orchard, blood-red cherries and the first of the new crop of apples, russet and gold.

But for Minou, the beauty of the world and the rhythms of her own heart were at odds with one another. Their departure could not come soon enough. For ten years their sanctuary, her father's death and the unexplained assault on Alis had stolen her peace at Puivert. Too often she found herself reliving every moment of that long day, brooding on what might have happened differently. She discerned in Piet the same restlessness to be gone. Memories that hitherto had been rendered harmless by time, secrets of the past dulled by the passing of the years, were suddenly sharp and vivid once more. Not knowing whether Aimeric had yet received her letter also gnawed away at her. As did her grief at having to bury their father without either her brother or her sister at her side.

From the outside at least, Minou and Piet's intimacy seemed restored. They were united in their shared grief for Bernard and their concern at leaving Alis behind. But beneath the surface, the reserve between them remained. Their conversation was gentle and mostly practical, neither wishing to upset the status quo. Minou's hope was that Paris, a place with no shared memories, would give them the space to find their way back to one another.

She had spent most of her remaining days with Alis. Though still confined to bed, her sister was showing signs of a fuller recovery than the doctor had first diagnosed. Some significant measure of feeling had returned to her legs and her spirits were lighter.

'While I'm gone, you must follow Dr Gabignaud's instructions to the letter,' Minou repeated. 'He is confident there is no permanent damage.'

'You truly think I'll walk again?'

'In time, I do. I believe it and so should you.'

Alis's dark eyes glistened with frustration. 'I hate being waited on. Not to be able to go outside or to ride, it's torment.'

'You have to be patient.'

Alis sighed. 'Can you do one last thing for me?'

'Anything.'

'Take Salvadora with you to Paris! She is threatening to stay here, to nurse me, and, truly, I could not bear it.'

'Alis!'

'I swear on my life, Minou, that if I have to endure one more day of her talking about the unsurpassable beauty of Marguerite de Valois and the glories of the royal family, I shall throw myself out of the window and be done with it!'

At first, the going was easy.

The weather was kind. The colours of summer painted Languedoc brilliant with pinks and yellows and violets. For the first hundred leagues, the sun was warm, yet lacking the fierce heat and dust of the Midi that would come with August. Cloudbursts of rain at night kept the ground soft for the horses and, each morning, ushered in air mild and fresh with promise.

Wherever possible, Piet had plotted their route through Huguenot-held territories or across lands that had avoided the worst excesses of civil unrest. They stayed in the houses of friends and colleagues of the Reformed faith when they could. On the rare occasions when they found themselves without an introduction, wayside lodging houses mostly proved adequate for a night or two.

Chalabre, Toulouse, Saint-Antonin and on. During those early days of July, their slow passage was pleasurable. Since no one but Piet had travelled beyond the boundaries of Languedoc before, there was much to amuse and engage: Jean-Jacques, soothed by the steady rolling of the carriage wheels, sat plump on his nurse's lap pointing at birds, at weasels and stoats; Marta asked endless questions – about why the buildings were brick not stone, why the roofs were made of timber not tile, why those toiling in the fields wore different clothes, why and why and why.

'Hush now,' Minou admonished, when Piet's patience began to wear thin. 'Let Papa be.'

Dust and dirt, Minou felt the passage of France beneath the wheels of their cart, beneath the hooves of their horses, as they journeyed from south to north. The colours of the Midi gave way to the overcast skies at the heart of the country, the *sabots* of the mountains replaced by the leather shoes in the valleys of the Massif Central.

In a blaze of purple lavender and pink dogbane, the Joubert family crossed into Berry. The old language of Occitan vanished, replaced by the sharper tones of the *langue l'Oil*. The skies were overcast and the people working in the fields looked grey.

'Papa, tell me the story of how you and Maman met,' Marta pleaded.

They were in a boarding house south of Limoges. It was a stormy evening in mid-July and torrential rain had confined them to their quarters. They had taken a modest but clean room of white-washed walls and plain wooden furniture, large enough to sleep the whole family, but the taphouse below was noisy. Salvadora had insisted on her own room – which could not be too close to the kitchens or the stables, not on the ground floor where the men were drinking, and not in the attic where there were bound to be fleas. It had taken all of Minou's patience not to lose her temper.

'You have heard it a thousand times,' Piet protested.

Marta tilted her head. 'But I like to hear it.'

'Papa is tired, *petite*,' Minou admonished. 'And you should be in bed.'

'I'm not at all tired.'

'I don't mind,' Piet said. He got up from the window ledge,

sat down on the end of their pallet bed and pulled his daughter onto his lap. 'The very first time I set eyes upon your mother—'

'— in La Cité.'

'— in La Cité, no more than a step from *Gran'père* Bernard's house, where the wild roses grow around the door—'

Marta's face momentarily clouded. 'I miss *Gran'père*.'

'I know, *petite*,' Minou said, sitting in the rocking chair. 'As do we all.'

Piet went through the familiar tale, grown threadbare with the retelling, while Minou watched the expressions on their faces: her husband, imbuing the tale with peril and valour, her daughter jumping in whenever he tried to miss a step or change the order of the narrative. She could not help but wonder if Piet still felt the same love for her now? He was courteous and considerate, but Minou felt the distance between them was growing, not diminishing.

Marta pulled on her father's sleeve. 'And then?'

'Careful,' Minou said. 'Do not leave a mark on Papa's robe.'

'My hands are clean. Nurse made me wash them a hundred times.'

Minou raised her eyebrows. 'A hundred?'

'At least. Papa, carry on!'

Piet held up his hands in surrender. 'It was a cold and dark night in Carcassonne, a long, long time ago. The bells for Vespers had been rung and it was the hour for the lighting of the lamps. It was then that this most beautiful lady appeared before me—'

'Like an angel sent from God.'

'No, not an angel,' Piet said firmly. 'A real lady, flesh and blood.' He reached over and took Minou's hand. 'This lady.'

Marta clapped her hands in delight, as she always did. Piet placed his hand over his heart, as he always did.

'Quietly, *petite*,' Minou hushed. 'Jean-Jacques is already sleeping. And you, *mon coeur*, you are just as bad.'

Piet put his finger to his lips and Marta giggled. 'It was a *coup de foudre* – a lightning strike,' he said in a loud whisper.

'You fell hopelessly in love.'

'Hopelessly.' He pretended to swoon. 'And though we had not been introduced, I made so bold as to speak to this beautiful lady.'

'And though we had not been introduced,' Minou said, taking up the story, 'I was minded to listen.'

'But Papa could not tarry.'

'Indeed, I could not, for I was in Carcassonne on important business.' Minou pretended not to see a shadow flicker across his face. 'I was bound to take my leave,' he continued. 'So not knowing the name of this beautiful lady, I christened her my—'

'Lady of the mists,' Marta said triumphantly. 'That is to say, you, Maman.'

'Me.' She reached forward and took her daughter's hand. 'And then we were married and lived happily for the rest of our days.'

'No,' Marta protested, 'you have left out all the in-between.'

'That's enough,' Minou said firmly. 'It's time for you to go to bed. We have an early start tomorrow if we are to make up the time and arrive in Limoges as planned.'

Marta was tired now, so she didn't argue. She put her arms around her father's neck. Piet stood up, carried her across the chamber and laid her gently in her bed.

'*Bonne nuit*, little one.'

'Good night, Papa,' Marta replied, her voice heavy with sleep. 'Good night, lady of the mists.'

CHAPTER FIFTEEN

LIMOGES, LIMOUSIN

The following day, they made good going and arrived in Limoges as the bells were striking noon.

Their host, Antoine le Maistre, had once served in the Prince of Condé's army. Like Piet, he had been injured at Jarnac and had then retired to his country estate in the Huguenot-held heartlands of the Limousin. As a welcome gift, his sweet-faced wife presented Minou with a beautiful blue-and-gold *champlevé* enamel box and went to great trouble to arrange an afternoon banquet with the children, giving Piet some hours alone with his old friend.

'We will not be long,' Piet said.

Minou smiled. 'Take as long as you wish. Madame le Maistre and I will pass a few pleasant hours. To be in a house, to eat at a table and sleep tonight in a clean bed, I am more than content.' She gestured to the far end of the chamber. 'And Marta has already taken charge.'

Piet followed her gaze to where their daughter was marshalling the four le Maistre children – two of whom were older than her – into costumes to perform an entertainment.

'They are to do a masque,' Minou said wryly.

Piet raised his eyebrows. 'Lord . . .'

'Of the royal wedding! Needless to say, Marta is Marguerite de Valois.'

'Of course. And which of the boys is to be her beau?'

Minou smiled. 'She is asking Monsieur le Maistre's two older sons questions to decide between them.'

Piet laughed. 'Don't allow her to be too bold, mind. I would like to be invited to stay here again on our way back to Carcassonne in September!'

'Don't worry. Go. Enjoy the companionship of your friend. We will see one another again at dinner.'

'This is our local *vin paille*,' le Maistre said, handing Piet a goblet of rich yellow wine. 'Many of the vineyards were destroyed during the wars but now, our vignerons are starting again to produce wines to grace any table.'

'My thanks.' Piet took an appreciative sip, then looked around the room. 'You have a beautiful home, le Maistre. Do you enjoy life away from the battlefield?'

His host laughed. 'I was never like you, Reydon. I fought out of necessity and duty, because there was no choice. Us or them, no man could stand aside while his comrades fell.' He paused. 'But every night in the field, in my orisons I asked God to spare me in order that I could come back to this. The life of a country landowner suits me. I am happy sitting by my hearth with my good wife and children, attending church on Sunday and serving on the Consistory, helping to keep our city safe and pious and respectful of God's commands. I hope never to have to pick up my sword again.'

Piet laughed, though he shook his head. 'I am happy that the Lord was listening to you, my friend.'

'How goes it with you?'

'Well.' Piet hesitated. 'I envy you your contentment. My wife is the finest of women, our lands are beautiful, my children . . . We have been able to do a great deal of good for our cause.

But, I confess, I miss the thrill of the battlefield. I would that I could still serve.' He raised his dead hand. 'You remember Jarnac?'

Le Maistre nodded. 'You were injured, of course I remember – though not before saving the lives of four of our men.'

'I've trained myself to hold my dagger in my left hand. Were it not for the fact that I can no longer grip the hilt of a sword, I would be fighting alongside our Protestant brothers in the Dutch provinces against the Spanish occupation.'

'Does your wife know you feel thus?'

Piet smiled. 'Yes. Minou does everything within her power to help me see the goodness in our lives.'

'She's a wise woman.' Le Maistre studied him over the rim of his goblet. 'Though you wish, from time to time, she would not worry so . . .'

Piet grinned. 'But listen to me, so full of complaint. Tell me, le Maistre, are the rumours I am hearing about the death of the Queen of Navarre true?'

The two old friends took their drinks to the settle, and sat.

'It is hard to divide truth from falsehood these days,' le Maistre said, 'and the news takes a while to reach us here. But what appears to be beyond doubt is that the Queen passed away on the ninth day of June in the Hôtel de Bourbon in Paris. The common gossip holds that she was poisoned by the Queen Mother, Catherine de' Medici.'

Piet's eyebrows shot up. 'Is there cause for such an allegation?'

'The long enmity between the two ladies and the fact that, some five days before her death, she received a gift of a pair of white leather gloves from the Queen Mother.'

'Said to be infused with poison?'

Le Maistre shrugged. 'That's what is spoken, in both Protestant and Catholic quarters.'

'But to what purpose? The Queen of Navarre brokered the marriage deal between her son and Catherine's daughter herself.'

'I only report what I've heard,' le Maistre said.

Piet thought for a moment. 'And what of the bride-to-be? The stories of her notorious affair with the Duke of Guise have reached even as far as Languedoc. Will she consent to marry Navarre? He is a king, it's true, but of a southern kingdom and a Huguenot to boot?'

Le Maistre gave a wry smile. 'I think it unlikely Marguerite de Valois will have much choice in the matter.'

'So the Pope has given his dispensation for the union to go ahead?'

'That I do not know.' Le Maistre refilled their goblets. 'Take good care of your family in Paris, Reydon. By the sounds of things, the city is even more divided than usual.'

'Is that why you have chosen to remain in Limoges?'

Le Maistre shook his head. 'I have everything I need here, Reydon. I have no need for my face to be seen in the crowd by our leaders, noble as they are. This simple life is enough for me.'

Minou and Piet took their leave from Limoges in the middle of the last week of July.

The confinement in one another's company, night and day, started to take their toll. Everyone was quick to temper. Marta in particular became more restless and inclined to quarrel. Jean-Jacques was plagued with colic, so when the nurse's back was turned attending to the stricken little boy, Marta took to wandering off on her own. Salvadora complained about everything, from the hardness of the beds to the paucity of their diet to the dismal weather. And Piet, frustrated by the petty irritations of their travelling life, took to riding ahead of the carriage to arrange their lodgings for their night, and rejoining them only when dusk was falling.

Minou started to wish they had remained in Puivert.

The further north they travelled – from areas mostly sympathetic to the Huguenot cause into Catholic-held territories – the rumblings of discontent grew louder. Taxes had been raised to pay for the royal wedding, even higher than during the wars, and after three years of poor harvests, people were suffering. Catholics blamed the Huguenots, the Protestants blamed the papists; the legacy of the past ten years of civil war was now evident in every town in which they stopped.

July tipped over into August.

Some ten leagues north of Orléans, the taphouses were buzzing with stories of how the bridegroom-to-be, Henri of Navarre, had arrived in Paris with nine hundred Huguenot armed noblemen at his side. To honour his royal mother, or to avenge her death, no one knew. To honour the terms of the marriage contract or to challenge it, the gossip was divided.

As they crossed into the Catholic heartlands around Paris, whispers that a Huguenot army was intending to march upon the royal city to prevent the wedding filled the taverns. One thousand men, ten thousand, and, as le Maistre had warned, it was impossible to separate true report from false.

On their last night on the road, in airless lodgings some ten leagues south of their destination, Piet stayed awake. Minou watched him from the bed, his right arm resting on his leg drawn up on the bench in the window, barely moving, looking down across the plains to the city walls of Paris below. Only the occasional sigh and the way his green eyes flickered in his drawn face revealed how deeply his thoughts held him.

Minou slipped from beneath the sheets and sat silently beside him in the casement, her head resting on his shoulder. She could sense the anxiety moving in him now the journey's end was in sight. Minou felt a fluttering of anticipation. As she waited for the dawn, she remembered how she had felt when glimpsing Toulouse for the first time. A gentle spring day, with Aimeric reluctant and homesick, in a carriage taking them to a new, unknown life. She had been a girl then, innocent and hopeful, dreaming of a boy.

Dreaming of this boy.

Minou squeezed Piet's arm. Despite everything and all that had happened, they were together still and she loved him.

'I am still your lady of the mists,' she whispered, though he seemed not to hear. 'You have my heart.'

CHAPTER SIXTEEN

Two Weeks Later

RUE DES BARRES, PARIS
Sunday, 17 August

The maid stood shuffling from foot to foot in the doorway.

'A gentleman is here to see you,' she said, pulling at her apron.

Minou looked up from her journal. 'What manner of gentleman?'

'One of them, my lady.' She sniffed. 'Begging your pardon, my lady, that's to say a soldier . . .'

Minou sighed. 'Go and ask his name and his business.'

The servants in their rented lodgings made few attempts to hide their dislike of the Protestants in Paris, seeming to forget their guests were Huguenots, too. All the same, Minou liked the house. Though the quartier Saint-Gervais was in the heart of Catholic Paris, rather than in the university quarter where the majority of Huguenots were lodging, it suited them well. It was a four-storeyed corner building, with an entrance hall favoured by a small square window overlooking the street, and a steep wooden staircase winding up the centre of the house like a spine. The main family living room on the first floor had generous windows facing north and west and was full of light. On the second floor, there was a good library and, above that on the third floor, comfortable sleeping quarters large enough to accommodate everyone. The entire top floor of the house was given over to the nursery, with a single window in the eaves that looked out over the apse and transepts of the Église Saint-Gervais.

The stables were set some distance from the house, so the air was clean, and a small internal courtyard, next to the kitchens and servants' quarters, provided welcome shade in the hot afternoons. A discreet latched wooden gate gave into an alleyway. From there, it was only a few steps to the Place Saint-Gervais, where, at midday, they could hear the cries of the men who came to repay and settle debts beneath the elm tree that stood in front of the imposing Gothic church. Marta had taken to mimicking them in her games and was trying to teach Jean-Jacques to do the same.

'*Attendez-moi, sols l'olme, attendez-moi.*'

In the late afternoon, Minou watched the nuns flock into the church from their *maison à colombages*, like black birds, to Vespers, then back to their half-timbered dwelling after their orisons. Most convenient, the house was a mere fifteen minutes' walk from the house in rue de Béthisy where Admiral de Coligny was lodging with his entourage, Aimeric amongst them.

White friars and black were everywhere, the Cistercians and Franciscans, the Jesuits, the Augustinians. The air was heavy with papistry and incense, yet Minou did not find it oppressive. Towers and spires split the skyline, some thirty-nine different parishes each dedicated to its own saint. On the rue Saint-Jacques stood the medieval tower and Église Saint-Jacques-de-la-Boucherie, the starting point on the journey to Santiago de Compostela, the travellers wearing scallop shells pinned to their clothes to mark them for pilgrims.

Most days since their arrival in Paris, Minou had set out to explore, accompanied sometimes by Salvadora and the children, sometimes alone: walking round the marshy swamplands of the Marais and the fortress prison of the Bastille; admiring the flying buttresses and splendour of Église Saint-Eustach, growing more magnificent each day as the stonemasons worked; visiting the market place at les Halles and the flower sellers down at the river. Too often, Minou thought of things she would like to tell her father, in the joy of the moment forgetting he was gone. Then, the same dull ache of grief would come over her and she would mourn his passing as if it had only just happened. She lacked her sister's company too. Though Alis despised anything that smacked of idolatry, Minou thought she would have loved Paris all the same.

Minou knew she walked and walked, in part, to combat the loneliness she felt at the lack of Piet's company. He was rarely at home. A few days past, when rearranging her possessions in her wooden casket, her fingers had touched the loop of dried twine. She had fashioned it herself the day before Piet asked her to be his wife, so they could travel as husband and wife. She'd smiled at the memory: May 1562 with the sun rising over the Pyrenees, their faces flushed with sleep, an overnight hideaway on their flight from Toulouse. Piet had been a blushing boy, promising to buy her a true ring to mark their betrothal as soon as he could.

They had been so full of hope then.

Minou had held the delicate memento in her hand a moment, then slipped it onto her ring finger, though she did not think Piet had noticed. And since her hope that they would find their way back to one another's affections more easily in unfamiliar surroundings had not been realised, she continued to map Paris with her feet, the twine betrothal ring sitting next to her silver wedding band.

Minou soon learnt that the footprint of the old medieval

town sat in sharp contrast to the white marble of the Italianate palaces and new manor houses of the great Catholic families with their turrets and grey slate roofs. The rue Vieille du Temple was where the privileged households of the Catholic nobility, chief amongst them the Duke of Guise, were situated, the finest manor houses and Gothic palaces, the seat of government and commerce. Orchards hidden behind high walls.

But for her, nowhere showed the marriage of the old capital of Gaul and the beating heart of the emerging France more than the Louvre Palace itself. The transformation of the Louvre from fort to palace had begun in the reign of King François I. Though only the bare bones of the medieval fortress remained – its defensive moats and walls overlooking the Seine – everywhere Minou went, she heard talk of the glories of the new palace: how courtiers could walk from the workaday military corridors through chamber after chamber into the inner sanctum of the royal family; of high ceilings and tapestries; of the paintings and sculptures of an Italian artist, Leonardo da Vinci, who had designed the new west wing and the Salle des Caryatides; how the Queen Mother was having a new palace built next to the Louvre, on the site of the Tuileries, once an old tile factory.

The mighty Seine, the pulsating artery of the city, was a teaming waterway as busy as any coastal port. Piet said it reminded him of Amsterdam, the wharves and piers endlessly working, constantly peopled. And between the banks, like a jewel in a blue belt of the river, lay the Île de la Cité, joined to the left and right quartiers by four bridges. It was there, in the glorious cathedral of Notre-Dame, that the royal wedding would take place.

The maid reappeared on the threshold, waiting impatiently for permission to speak.

'Well, did he give his name?' Minou asked.

The girl sniffed. 'No, my lady, but he says he is your brother.'

Minou leapt up from her desk. 'Don't leave him standing in the hallway any longer. Show him up.'

Her heart lifted. She was finally to see Aimeric. In the weeks they'd been in Paris, though he had sent his best wishes, he had not been to visit. Minou quickly tidied away her journal and writing implements, then turned to greet him.

'Aimeric!' she cried, welcoming him with her arms outstretched. 'It has been too long.'

They hugged until she thought the breath had been squeezed out of her, then she stepped back and looked at him.

'Upon my word, you have grown.'

Aimeric laughed. 'You always say so when we have been parted a while, and it is never true! You will always be just that little bit taller than me, Minou. It's perfectly humiliating.'

'Nonsense, it shows your courtesy and your good sense, for this is a fine height to be!' She linked her arm through his. 'Aimeric, I am so glad to see you. How are you? How have you been so busy that you could not call upon us before now? What are your—'

'Sister, let me at least sit down before you assail me with questions!'

Minou grinned. 'Forgive me.'

Aimeric settled himself in an upholstered chair and removed his hat and cape. Minou poured him a goblet of wine.

'I am sorry I haven't visited before now – waiting upon the admiral fills my every waking hour. Receiving visitors on his behalf, listening for signs of trouble, guarding him in the streets, eavesdropping on every proclamation read in market squares and sermons thundered from the pulpit on the Lord's Day. Paris is full of fire-and-brimstone preachers.'

Minou laughed. 'You are a spy, now, not a soldier!'

'Quite! De Coligny is convinced that there are forces that would disrupt the wedding. I fear he is right, on both sides of the religious divide, to be fair. There are many of our number who do not think it appropriate that Navarre should marry into the Valois family. On their side, the idea of a Protestant standing so close to the throne fills them with horror.' He took a long sip of his wine. 'But enough of affairs of state, such as they are. I want to hear all your news. Does Paris please you?'

Minou smiled. 'Much to my surprise, it does. I find myself charmed by this very Catholic city of cathedral churches, abbeys and monasteries.'

Aimeric nodded. 'I understand. I feel her charms too. What of the children and Salvadora? Do they also find Paris to their liking? I wager Alis is in her element, for all she would try to resist. Is she here at present? I have much missed her.'

Minou's heart plummeted. 'You did not receive my letter,' she said heavily.

'What letter?' he said, putting his goblet back on the table. 'Minou, what's happened?'

She took a deep breath. 'I fear I have terrible news.'

Aimeric put his hands on his knees and listened as she told him about the events of the seventh and the eighth of June: the assault on Alis and the death of their father. When she had finished, he remained very still.

'Our father is gone,' he said in a hollow voice.

Minou nodded. 'Yes. He felt no pain, he just slipped away.'

'You are sure of that?'

'He looked as if he was sleeping. Peaceful. At rest at last.'

Aimeric dropped his head and, though there was no sound, Minou saw his shoulders were shaking as he sobbed.

'I would you had known of it before now,' she said. 'All these weeks, I prayed the letter had found you.'

'It does not seem possible,' Aimeric said, his voice breaking. 'All this time, whenever I saw something remarkable or perturbing, even, I imagined myself telling Father about it. Saving things up when I would be able to see him again in Puivert or Carcassonne. To learn now that, all this time, he had gone.'

He quickly raised his eyes to her face, then dropped them again as if not wanting to see the truth written there.

'I do that too.' Minou put her hand to her brother's chest. 'But you carry him here, Aimeric. As do I. He'll always be with us.'

He clasped her hand hard, like a drowning man grasps the person who would save him. For a few moments they sat without speaking, Minou respecting the shock of his grief, which had come so unexpectedly.

'Forgive me,' Aimeric said eventually. 'I am poor company. I had come so full of news and stories to share with you, but now I cannot think.'

'There will be time enough in the days ahead.'

Aimeric wiped his cheeks with the back of his hand. 'But what of Alis? Does the doctor think she will recover? Will she walk again?'

'In time, yes. I had a letter from her yesterday.' Minou paused. 'Salvadora had threatened to stay behind in Puivert and tend to her, so her good progress is a relief.'

She was pleased this comment raised a ghost of a smile.

'That would not find favour with Alis.' Then his eyes filled with tears once more. 'My poor, dear sister. I will write to her and hope that this communication, at least, does not go astray.'

'She will be so happy to receive a letter from you.'

Aimeric ran his hands through his wild black hair, then leant back in his chair. Minou thought how young he looked, the traces of the boy he had been suddenly so obvious in the pain darkening his eyes.

'Will you stay a while? Dine with us, perhaps? The children would be delighted to see you.'

Aimeric sighed. 'I wish I could, Minou, but there is too much to do ahead of tomorrow. In any case . . .' He spread his hands. 'I don't think I would make good company. I need time to make sense of this ill news. I must pray for them.'

'I understand. Your grief is fresh, you need time to make sense of what's happened. For us, it is something we have learnt to live with these past two months.'

'It's as if there is a band around my ribs. I can't breathe.'

'It will pass,' Minou said gently. 'Though our father is never far from my mind – and a hundred times a day – the sharp pain of those first days has given way to a quieter sadness.'

Aimeric clasped his hands together. 'He is in God's hands now. Alis too. He is watching over her, I am sure of it.'

Minou smiled, glad at least that Aimeric could find some comfort in his faith. Though she had never admitted it, she felt only a hollow anger and a disbelief that such things could happen. It weighed heavily on her heart that their father had died unshriven and unblessed, for she knew Bernard would have wanted to go to his Maker with his sins forgiven.

Aimeric stood up.

'Will you come again to visit once the wedding has taken place?' Minou asked, slipping her arm through his. 'Salvadora will be sorry not to have seen you. Piet too.'

'I will, I have missed you all greatly. Though, of course, I have seen Piet a number of times.'

Minou felt her heart grow tight in her chest. 'You have? When?'

'He did not tell you?'

'No, he neglected to mention it.' Minou paused. 'I would not be disloyal, but in truth Piet is rarely at home. He spends much of his time visiting colleagues in the Dutch quarter and former acquaintances from the wars. I try not to begrudge him, though I lack his company.'

Aimeric pulled at his doublet, clearly uncomfortable. 'It is good for him to be reunited with past comrades he fought alongside.'

'Of course.' Minou hesitated. 'Aimeric, when you took your leave from Puivert, I asked you whether there was some particular matter that had kept you and Piet talking into the early hours on the eve of your departure. You said there was not. Is that still your answer?'

Now it was Aimeric who hesitated. 'I would not betray a confidence,' he said awkwardly.

'There is something, Brother, that troubles him. I know my husband well. His face is an open book.' She paused. 'According to the maid, a woman came to the house earlier, asking for him. Now I wonder if this might be connected to the same matter? If it affects me, or the children, I have a right to know.'

Aimeric's face folded with indecision, then he exhaled a long sigh of surrender. 'I admit there was something Piet asked me to look into on his behalf. It concerns his mother and his child-hood in Amsterdam, but I can say no more than that. You must ask him.'

Minou pulled her arm away. 'I knew I wasn't imagining it!'

'If he is keeping the matter from you, Minou, there will be a reason. He will confide in you in his own time. You have to be patient.'

CHAPTER SEVENTEEN

'Hey! You, girl. *Guenon de hus.*'

Since arriving in Paris from Amsterdam on her father's orders, Cornelia van Raay had been subjected to many abuses and calumnies when she ventured out alone: *putain*, whore, Dutch bawd, doxy, Huguenot sow. '*Guenon de hus*' was a term she had not heard before, though the tone of the man's voice made its meaning crystal clear.

As the August heat intensified and travellers continued to arrive footsore from all corners of France for the wedding, the insults had become more frequent. There were not enough beds. The taverns were full, the boarding houses were full. Tempers were frayed.

Cornelia hated Paris, but until she had delivered her father's message to Pieter Reydon, she could not return home. With the help of loose-tongued Dutch servants from the embassy and in taverns where the Netherlander rebels gathered, she had identified the house where the Reydon family were lodging. It only remained to pass the letter into his hands. She was hopeful that today would be the day. If she succeeded, then she could quit the city by nightfall and be gone before the wedding took place.

Cornelia lowered her head, her face concealed beneath her plain hood and cloak, and kept walking up and down the rue des Barres, waiting for Pieter Reydon to return. She had approached the corner house at first light, but the maid informed her he had already gone out. Her plan had been to wait and accost him as he returned, but her presence in the street was starting to attract attention. An hour ago, a Huguenot soldier, in his distinctive black, had come and gone. Then a few moments ago, another man – a merchant or businessman, by the looks of things – had been admitted.

'*Putain.*'

She pretended not to hear.

'Are you a false Christian? A Huguenot.' Her accuser seemed to spit out the word. 'Is that why you are not at Mass? Is that why you pay me no heed?'

Another man laughed, a third called out another insult. Cornelia turned away. Why did these rich Parisian boys, the sons of courtiers, of noblemen she supposed, have so little to occupy their time? The Protestant nobility, French as well as Dutch, wore their modest black attire proudly, a challenge to the profligacy of the garish peacock silks and jewelled caps of the court.

'Hey!' He clicked his fingers. 'Hey, Huguenot sow. I'm talking to you.'

A bellow of laughter and the rattle of a purse. 'A Catholic man not good enough for you?'

Alarm sparked in her chest. Cornelia fixed her mind on the rhythm of her feet on the dry ground, willing herself not to turn around. If she looked into their eyes, she would be lost. The only thing was to pretend nothing was happening. Holding her basket tighter, she continued along the *impasse*, praying either that her tormentor would lose interest in his sport or – she knew it unchristian even to think it – fix upon another victim. She walked faster, heading for a busier street and the safety of the crowd. She could return to the Reydon house later.

'Whore!'

Something struck her on the back of the neck. A pebble? A coin. Cornelia flinched, but did not miss her step.

'Or do you not come so cheap? *Une fille de l'escadron*, is that it?'

Another coin struck her shoulder blade. Then suddenly she felt his presence behind her and then – a shock, though she was half expecting it – the clamp of a hand upon her arm.

'Monsieur!'

'Oh, a foreigner,' he said, pushing her into the alleyway that ran alongside the Reydon house. The stink of stale wine on his breath and yesterday's perfume on his clothes repulsed her. His two companions stepped behind, trapping her between them. She glanced up – taking in the trimmed beard, the wide white ruff, the feathered velvet cap despite the muggy heat, the tempered steel at his waist. A pock-marked nose too large for his face. She felt the pinch of his fingers on her chin.

'I only wanted to talk to you, but now you have offended me.' His grip tightened. 'Do you foreign whores not know Parisian manners?'

Cornelia knew it was wisest to do nothing to provoke him.

'My lord, by your leave, let me go,' she said in French. 'My husband is waiting.'

'My husband is waiting,' one of his lackeys jeered, mimicking her Dutch accent. 'You are not one of the Queen Mother's courtesans?'

Cornelia felt the press of something hard against her back, something intimate, and she recoiled in disgust. A guffaw of sour breath, then a hand clawed at her private places.

'Leave me be!'

Cornelia tried to step to one side, but her attacker blocked her path. She twisted her head, trying to slip his grip, but he only pinched her the harder.

'Look at you! Pretending to virtue when, under this pious exterior, you're all the same. Your colour is high.' He dragged at the clasp of her cloak until it came loose. 'Oh, what do we have here? These are rather fine clothes beneath this drab modest exterior.' He placed his hand on her breast.

'Monsieur, no!'

'We know what Protestant girls get up to behind closed doors when you believe yourselves unseen by Christian eyes.'

'I am a truer Catholic than you!' The words were out of her mouth before she could stop them.

The man's eyes narrowed. 'What did you say?'

His hand moved so fast, Cornelia did not see it coming: the strike of skin on skin, her cheek burning, but the shock numbed any pain. He ripped off her bonnet, taking a fistful of her dark brown hair and pushed her back against the wall.

'How dare you address me in such a manner? Maybe, despite your drab clothing, the Queen Mother does have you for one of her own. A little Dutch *fille de l'escadron*.'

'Monsieur, please.'

His question was lost in a second blow, harder this time. Cornelia tasted blood in her mouth, the shift of a tooth come loose. When her attacker's arm drew back for a third time, finally she found her voice to scream.

Above them, a casement window opened and an elegant woman of middle years looked down.

'What disturbance is this?'

Her assailant gestured his companions back into the shadows of the alleyway. Then, clamping his hand over Cornelia's mouth, he stepped out into view.

'Madame, I beg your pardon for disturbing you.'

Cornelia struggled to get free, so she could cry out again, but she was limed like a bird in a trap.

'My companions are in their cups. It is high spirits, nothing more.'

'This is the fabled Parisian courtesy of which we have heard so much?'

'As I say, madame, high spirits.'

'I suggest you take your high spirits elsewhere, monsieur!' the woman commanded. But then, to Cornelia's despair, she withdrew and closed the window.

Far from quelling his mischief, the intervention had heated his blood. Cornelia felt his arousal as he pushed the entire weight of his body against her.

'Foreigner you may be, and you are plain, but your skin is unpocked,' he hissed, his spiteful blue eyes inflamed with the thrill of the hunt. 'And since you have humiliated me in such a manner, I am due some recompense.'

In a practised motion, he thrust his hand between her legs. Cornelia wrestled, trying to push him off, but his perverted desire made him stronger still and she could not get free. She kicked at his shins, but made no impression. She kept fighting, but the sotten voices of his companions were in his ear, urging him on.

'My turn next.'

Cornelia could not believe such villainy was happening in the middle of the afternoon in the most populous city in France. It was not possible. In Amsterdam, she had spent her life protected from such lewd behaviour, though she knew the tiny streets behind Zeedijk and Sint Nicolaas church drew such men.

'Messieurs, did Madame Reydon not say to take your high spirits elsewhere?'

Behind them now in the rue des Barres stood the man Cornelia had observed going into the Reydons' lodgings. Wearing a bright doublet and hose, holding a sheaf of papers in his hand, his expression was one of contempt.

Cornelia sighed with relief. For a moment, no one spoke, then her attacker released her. His companions shrank into the shadows.

He gave a half-bow. 'Forgive me for disturbing you. We will take our leave. Your servant.'

He clicked his fingers and his followers scuttled after him towards the river, quickly losing themselves in the crowds on the rue de la Mortellerie. Cornelia let her shoulders drop with relief.

'Monsieur, my thanks. If you had not—'

The man pointed. 'You and your kind disgust me. Coming to a Christian city, plying your vile trade in broad daylight. Polluting Paris. Go back to where you came from.'

Cornelia stepped back as if she'd been struck, then realised that because of her dishevelled clothing, her loose hair and the coins scattered on the ground, she was being taken for the very thing the men were trying to make of her. A whore.

'Monsieur, you mistake me.'

'We don't want foreigners here.' He gave a half-glance up at the house. 'None of you.'

Cornelia straightened her cloak and hood, picked up the basket, and walked out of the alleyway into the humid, grey afternoon with what dignity she could muster.

Fury kept her going all the way back to the river, determined in some way to be avenged on the men who'd treated her so badly. Little by little, her anger abated. Though she had failed to deliver her message to Pieter Reydon, she had at least learnt something: that Madame Reydon had accompanied her husband to Paris, and that she was an honourable woman.

CHAPTER EIGHTEEN

The landlord came back into the chamber, still holding his papers.

'You sent them away?'

'The gentlemen were sorry to have disturbed you.'

Minou raised her eyebrows. 'Gentlemen, I think not! Did you know them, monsieur?'

He shook his head. 'The girl was a foreigner.'

'That makes no difference,' she said sharply.

He shrugged. 'One good turn deserves another, Madame Reydon. To return to our negotiations . . .'

'I shall not yield, monsieur. Terms were agreed prior to our arrival. My brother, who is in the service of Admiral de Coligny, was acting on our account.'

'If you are not able to pay this little more, Madame Joubert, there are many others who will,' the landlord replied. 'Paris is full. There are no beds to be found.'

'It is not a matter of whether or not we can afford it, but a matter of you honouring our contract. Terms were accepted and confirmed. If you now consider the fee you set too low, I am sorry for it. But we agreed a fair price for the month.'

'As I say,' he repeated in his oily voice, 'one good turn deserves another.'

Minou held his gaze, then she sighed. 'I will pay an additional livre each week. Will that satisfy you?'

The landlord bowed. 'It has been a pleasure doing business with you, Madame Reydon. By your leave.'

'Good day.'

When he had gone, Minou looked back over the alleyway. She was appalled that the royal city contained such men. It was not just their manner, but their lack of shame. Then again, she supposed that, given the court was so decadent, it should be no surprise that such wild and licentious behaviour dripped down like poison into every corner of Paris. She hoped the girl had got away unmolested.

Minou picked up her summer gloves from the oak chest. She had been looking forward to today's visit to the Sainte-Chapelle, an outing originally planned to please her aunt. She refused to allow the machinations of their landlord or brazen street behaviour to cast a shadow over the day.

She smiled. It was odd that her spirits should be lifted at the thought of standing in a place of worship dedicated to the faith against which she had turned her face. But elegance and grace of architecture or music knew no boundaries. Minou thought of her younger self – her Catholic self – hurriedly sewing the Shroud of Antioch into the lining of her old green cloak, marvelling at the history of the relic in her hands. Then her face clouded when she remembered Vidal. She assumed the Shroud was still in his possession.

'Maman, what is a *fille de l'escadron*?'

She spun round. 'Marta! I did not know you were here.'

Her daughter joined her at the window. 'Does not the Queen Mother have a daughter of her own?'

'She does,' Minou replied carefully.

'Then why did that man say she would have her for one of her own?'

Minou sighed. 'It doesn't matter. The men have gone now.'

'What's a courtesan?'

'Marta, that's enough,' she said firmly. 'It does not concern us.'

Marta pushed out her bottom lip, preparing to sulk, then thought better of it. 'As you wish.'

Minou narrowed her eyes. 'You are not to pursue this matter, do you heed me?'

The child was a picture of innocence. '*Oui, Maman.*'

'Marta, I mean it. You must not bother Great-aunt Boussay with your questions – nor indeed anyone else – otherwise you will not accompany us to the Sainte-Chapelle.'

Marta gave a fleeting curtsey, then skipped from the chamber.

'Marta, I am not in jest!' Minou called after her without any hope of receiving an answer. She did not wish her daughter to be less curious, but sometimes she wished she was less sharp of hearing.

The wedding was tomorrow, followed by three days of feasting. After that, they were free to depart Paris. Though she had not seen Aimeric until today, and she had hopes that would change once the ceremony was over, Minou couldn't deny it would be a relief to deliver Salvadora back to her house in Toulouse, then to be able to return home to Alis and her own bed. Minou had received a letter from her sister two days past, full of how she could now walk a few steps with the help of a stick. The postscript from Monsieur Gabignaud, the physician, had been more measured and cautious about his patient's recovery. Minou was keen to see for herself.

She smiled, thinking of the beauty of Languedoc in the dog days of summer. The woods would be alive with colour: copper and burnished gold and the claret-red of the vines, the orchards plump with apples and pears. There, the air would be clear and the sunflowers would be singing their last yellow song on the plains.

Life would go on. Though her grief for her father would be

sharper in Puivert, their lives would return to normal. Paris would be no more than a memory.

Salvadora Boussay sat on the high-backed wooden settle in the entrance hall, waiting patiently for her niece. Her hands fidgeted in her lap. She was as excited as a girl making her first holy communion.

In the dark days of her marriage, imagining herself in the streets of the holiest city in France had given her courage to withstand the beatings and her husband's disdain. But now, today at last, she was to go to the Sainte-Chapelle, a place she had dreamed of seeing her entire life, a place of devotion where—

'Great-aunt Salvadora, may I ask you a question?'

Salvadora looked up to see Marta racing down the last flight of stairs, launching herself over the last two steps to land in front of her on the floor on all fours like a cat.

Her hand flew to her chest. 'Really! Where are your manners?'

Marta scrambled up and gave an insolent curtsey. 'Sorry. I want to ask you a question. What is a *fille de l'escadron*?'

Salvadora's cheeks flamed. 'Where on earth did you hear such terrible – not in this house, I warrant.'

'Spoken here but some few minutes past.'

'I cannot believe that.'

Marta had the grace to blush. 'Perhaps not *in* the house, I admit. I heard a gentleman. Below in the street. Maman reprimanded him and sent that weasel of a landlord to speak to him. Is a *fille de l'escadron* the same as a courtesan?'

'Good lord,' Salvadora said, scandalised that the seven-year-old girl knew such a word, 'that is quite enough!'

'But if no one will tell me, how shall I learn? It is important for girls to learn. Aunt Alis always says so.' Marta tapped her head. 'I won't tell anyone you told me. I'll keep the information here with my other secrets.'

'You are a precocious child.'

Marta tilted her head. 'And I am fair, too. Everyone says so.'

'It was not a compliment,' Salvadora said, flapping her fan. 'You are too boastful.'

'Maman always says we should not lie,' Marta countered. 'So will you tell me what a *fille de l'escadron* is?'

'I most certainly will not. And I shall speak to your mother about your behaviour, make no mistake.'

Marta frowned, then quit the hall as quickly as she had taken possession of it.

The air settled once more.

Salvadora was shocked by the entire conversation. She continued to wave her fan so vigorously that three more feathers came loose. Such ill behaviour. She didn't know what girls were coming to these days.

'But what does it mean, nurse?' Marta pestered.

Having abandoned her great-aunt in the hall, Marta had run all the way up to the nursery at the top of the house. She was now precariously perched in the open window swinging her legs back and forth against the wall.

'Stop that fussing, mademoiselle; you'll leave marks on the wall.' The harried nurse was bouncing Jean-Jacques up and down in her arms, trying to calm him. His belly was swollen with colic.

'I won't tell anyone you told me.'

'I haven't time for your questions, can't you see your brother is upset?'

'He's always upset. If you just answer, I will go and leave you in peace. Cross my heart and hope to die.'

'Don't say such things.'

The little boy gave another wail of pain.

'Pretty please,' Marta coaxed in her sweetest voice.

The nurse huffed. 'The Queen Mother is rumoured – I don't know if this is true, mind – to have some . . . ladies who . . . in return for favours – trinkets, jewellery and what have you – persuade gentlemen to tell them secrets.'

'So *escadron* means "friends", does it?'

'Hush, little man,' the nurse cooed. 'That's better, *mon brave*.'

'Nurse! What does *escadron* mean?'

'A group.'

'A group of girls?' Marta frowned, trying to put the pieces together. 'Is courtesan a saucy word?'

Finally, she had the nurse's full attention. 'Mademoiselle Marta!'

Realising she had gone too far, Marta kissed her little brother on his hot, flushed cheek.

'Thank you, nurse!' she said, and skipped from the room.

CHAPTER NINETEEN

Minou and Salvadora stood arguing, in their outdoor clothes, face to face in the hall, the air hot with angry words.

'I cannot believe you would be so unwise as to answer such a question,' Minou said furiously. 'Marta is far too young to understand.'

Salvadora snapped her fan shut. 'If you give me leave to speak, Niece.'

'I know she is persistent, but there are ways of deflecting—'

'Do you truly think,' Salvadora interrupted, 'that I would tell Marta, who is a wilful child and liable always to speak out of turn, that *filles de l'escadron* are courtesans who seduce men for secrets?'

Behind them, the front door opened and Piet entered.

'What on earth is happening? The whole street can hear you quarrelling.'

Salvadora puffed out her plump cheeks. 'Your wife has so low an opinion of me as to think I would explain the workings of the Queen Mother's cadre of painted mistresses to your seven-year-old daughter!'

'What!' Piet looked at them in astonishment. 'I don't understand. Where on earth did Marta even hear such a thing in the first place?'

Minou looked at him. 'She overheard an altercation in the street. When I would not explain what the men meant, against my express orders Marta went to Salvadora. Who did.'

'I most certainly did not!'

Minou threw her hands in the air. 'If not you, Aunt, then who? I came upon Marta marching up and down the corridor pretending to be . . .'

Minou noticed Piet stifle a laugh and she glared at him.

Salvadora bridled. 'If you will forgive me, Niece, if you kept a firmer hand over the child, then she would not have been in a position – running unsupervised around the house at all times – to hear such vulgar words spoken in the first place.'

'Are you suggesting I do not know how to care for my own child?'

'I don't think that was what Salvadora meant,' Piet intervened.

Minou now turned on him. 'You take her part over mine?'

'Salvadora, might you excuse us?'

The older woman hesitated and then, with a final disapproving glance at Minou, withdrew.

Minou folded her arms, her eyes sharp with grievance.

Piet loosened the ruff at his neck, then walked to the sideboard, poured two goblets of wine from the decanter, and handed one to Minou.

'We cannot be at one another's throats like that.'

'The quarrel was not of my making. When I remonstrated with Marta, it was evident someone had told her. When I pressed her, she said she had come upon Aunt Boussay in the hall—'

'Which you took to mean that Salvadora answered her question?'

'Well, who else could it be? You were not at home – again – and Aimeric had left. There's no one else.'

'My love,' Piet said mildly, 'our resourceful daughter will have gone to the nursery and badgered the nurse. Or to the kitchen; she is a favourite there. Any one of the maids would have had great delight in enlightening her.'

Minou frowned. 'Marta would not lie to my face.'

'She would not tell a direct lie, no. But, by your own account, what she actually said was that she "came upon" Salvadora. She did not say your esteemed aunt had answered her question.'

Minou took the goblet. 'Oh.'

Piet touched his goblet to hers. 'Oh indeed. Our daughter, wonderful as she is, is a precocious child to whom spinning tales comes as naturally as breathing. You know that. It is not like you to be gulled so easily.'

Minou leant back against the sideboard. 'I must apologise to Salvadora. Not only for what I said, but for the fact of it delaying our visit to the Sainte-Chapelle.'

'You were intending to go today?'

'It is what we'd planned.' She gestured to her cloak, hat and gloves. 'Hence this, despite the heat.'

'I did wonder.'

'The landlord came to put his case for increasing our rent.'

'What did you say?'

'I refused, then the altercation in the street happened. He was kind enough to go down and manage the matter, so after that I felt obliged to agree to another livre.'

'That's all right, I think.'

Piet opened the little latticed window. Hot August air slunk over the sill, bringing with it the stink of the river and the over-crowded streets.

'When Marta told you what she'd learnt about the *escadron*, how did you respond?'

'I told her that the young women of the court who behaved in such a manner to gather secrets were silly and unadmired. Dull creatures.'

Piet grinned. 'And what did Marta reply to that?'

Minou felt the shadow of an answering smile on her lips too. 'That she despised those who could not keep a secret and how she would never break her word nor exchange gossip for trinkets. Oh, and then she added that she presumed those who betrayed their secrets were boys because it was common knowledge that boys were unable to hold their tongues!'

Now Piet laughed out loud. 'It reminds me of the back-and-forth quarrels Aimeric and Alis used to have when they were little. Alis also believed boys were beneath contempt.'

'With one or two notable exceptions, I do not think her opinion has much changed.' Minou took a sip of her wine. 'I meant to tell you, I received a letter from her a few days ago saying all was well at Puivert and that she was walking almost unaided.'

'This is wonderful news.'

'Yes, though Monsieur Gabignaud was more circumspect. Alis would not want us to worry.'

'We'll be home soon and will see for ourselves. And as for Alis's low opinion of men, she will feel differently when she falls in love.'

'She still says she will never marry. She says there is nothing a husband could give her that she does not already have on her own account.'

'Not even children?'

Minou smiled. 'Her reply was that she had no need of a child of her own when she had the delights of Marta's companionship.'

'Delights!'

'Also, that she feared that a child would undo her.'

'Whatever does she mean?'

Minou thought for a moment. 'From the instant you hold your first child in your arms, your heart is no longer your own. One becomes weakened in resolve, fearful of the evil in the world.'

'Do you feel that?' Piet asked, surprised.

'Sometimes.'

'But surely the joys of a child outweigh by far the assault on one's emotions?'

Minou curled her hand against his cheek. 'It is easy for you to say. You are a man. But for a woman? My lack of judgement today – if I can call it that – was, in part, driven by concern for Marta. That need to protect her from the worst of the world. It will be the same for Jean-Jacques. Worrying over them governs my waking hours more than anything I might feel on my own account.' Minou gestured in the direction of the new Tuileries Palace. 'Even the Queen Mother, though she has borne ten children and buried six, is quite undone by the love she holds for her youngest son. This despite his *mignons* and their peculiarities.'

Piet took her hand. 'Why are you really so out of sorts, Minou? At the thought of the wedding tomorrow? Or because we are here in Paris at all?'

'No, not that. Against my expectations, I have found my heart stolen by Paris. It's more . . . I don't know. I would that tomorrow was over and done with, the celebrations concluded, and we were on our way home.' She took a deep breath. 'And you, my love, you are so rarely here. I lack your company.'

Piet's face clouded. 'I am enjoying the companionship of those from whom I have long been separated. You would not deny me that.'

'Not in the slightest.'

Minou paused. The last time she had tried to persuade Piet to confide in her, it had led to a quarrel. But, after what Aimeric had said, she did not feel she could today keep her peace.

'Aimeric came to visit.'

'That's wonderful,' Piet said genuinely. 'I know how much you miss him.'

'He said he had seen you on one or two occasions. That you had asked him to make certain inquiries on your behalf. He assumed I knew.'

Piet's expression darkened. 'He had no business to tell you.'

'You cannot blame Aimeric, he was in an impossible situation. He only confided in me when I told him how a woman came to the house earlier in search of you.'

'What manner of a woman?' he asked quickly.

'I don't know. I didn't see her.'

'Was she in her later years? Did she give her name?'

Minou held his gaze. 'Piet, do you know who she is?'

Piet flushed, then hesitated. 'I may do. Was she a nun?'

'A nun!'

'Someone in religious orders, at least.'

'As I say, I did not see her, though I tend to think if she had been so the maid would have said.' She took a breath. 'Aimeric counselled me to be patient, but I have waited for weeks for you to confide in me. It has put a wall between us, you on the one side and I on the other.'

'Minou.'

She kept talking. 'All I would say is this. If the reason you hold your peace is because you are trying to protect me from something, or trying to shield me from distress, I beg you – as always – to reconsider. There should be nothing you cannot share with me.'

Piet stood a moment, swirling the wine in his cup. 'Might Salvadora be kept waiting a moment longer?'

Minou's heart skipped a beat. 'She will understand.'

He gave a sharp nod of his head. 'Very well, you have the right to know.'

Now the moment had come, Minou was suddenly anxious about what Piet might tell her. Then, she felt the slightest shifting of the light. It was better to know and face the truth head on than always to be wondering. Imagination had a habit of painting the world darker than it truly was, wasn't that what the philosophers said? And what her own pernicious thoughts in those dark hours between midnight and dawn taught her?

'Let us repair to our chamber,' Piet said. 'I would not be overheard.'

CHAPTER TWENTY

Marta stormed down the stairs, still in a fury about the scolding she had received from her mother.

'If I was not so dismissed, I would have no need to ask the servants,' she complained. 'It's not fair. Aunt Alis would have answered me.'

The portrait upon the wall kept his silence.

Marta stopped at the small window on the half-landing, her heart full of injustice, just in time to see their carriage pull away at the end of the rue des Barres. Marta's hands balled into fists. She had not thought for an instant her mother would make good on her threat to go to the Sainte-Chapelle and leave her behind.

She had been going to ask if they might detour via the street where all the glove makers had their shops. All being well, she had even intended to suggest they might return from the Île de la Cité via the other side of the river. She'd overheard the scullery maids talking about how the *mignons* of the Queen Mother's youngest son – men who were half-girl and half-boy – paraded along the Boulevard Saint-Germain carrying lapdogs, even monkeys, in little waistcoats and hats.

Now she was to be denied all of these astonishing sights.

Marta pressed her face against the glass. In the bright world beyond the confines of the house, she could see people walking in rich and lavish clothes. 'All for show,' Maman would say, 'speaking nothing of a man's true worth.' But what harm was there in colourful things? If a person was favoured by wealth or fortune, Marta did not understand why they should not be allowed to display it.

And here she was, stuck inside, with the prospect of another dull day, closeted within the four walls of the house. And Jean-Jacques constantly shrieking and the nurse fussing over his every move.

Marta sighed. She was so neglected. Even when everyone was at home, time hung heavy on her hands. There was nothing to do. Papa was mostly absent, doing whatever it was he did. Uncle Aimeric spent his days in the company of Admiral de Coligny and never came to visit, Maman was always distracted and Great-aunt Boussay was, well, herself. If only Aunt Alis had come with them. She was amusing. Alis would have taken Marta on a new trip every day, had she wished it.

Then she had a thought. Marta raised her head from the window, feeling a flutter of excitement in her stomach. She would be told off again, if she was caught, but since the nurse would be occupied with Jean-Jacques and everyone else had gone to the Sainte-Chapelle, who was there to catch her?

She walked as quietly as she could, up the stairs to the family sleeping quarters on the third floor, then along the corridor towards her parents' chamber. She knocked, just in case, though she had no expectation there would be anyone in there at this time of day. She knocked again, a little louder, to be certain. Then, she pushed open the door and stepped inside.

Every corner of the chamber shimmered with the presence of her mother: her scent, her shoes and clothes. Her hairbrush and glass on the dresser, heirlooms of the Carcassonnais grandmother Marta had never met, the blue-and-gold enamel box given as a gift in Limoges, her green travelling cloak hanging on the wardrobe door.

Of her father's presence, there was less evidence. Just a faint smell of the sandalwood oil he used upon his hair and his riding gloves, lying one on top of the other on the nightstand beside the canopy bed.

Marta closed the door and went straight to her mother's wooden casket, which contained her most precious possessions. Feeling the thrill of transgression, every sense heightened by the promise of wrongdoing, Marta opened the box. She had no plan beyond discovering what sort of trinkets her mother had brought with her from Puivert. It was curiosity, not avarice, that tempted her to look.

Marta dismissed the plain old Bible her mother kept always with her, as well as her journal, tied with a leather cord and filled with scraps of paper and parchment, the shabby map of Carcassonne drawn in chalk. Her fingers rummaged around in the casket, prying and shifting. She found a ring – tourmaline, her mother's birthstone, set in silver. It was pretty enough, and the pink and speckled shards within it glistered in the morning light, but too big to fit her finger. Several lace cuffs were neatly folded, nothing exceptional. Then her fingers touched some beads. They rattled against the side of the casket as she drew them out.

It was a wooden rosary with a plain silver cross. Marta was bewildered. Prayer beads were for Catholics. *Gran'père* Bernard and Great-aunt Boussay followed the old ways, but Maman was a Huguenot, like Papa.

Without warning, the door opened and a servant walked in with a tray of drinks. In a fluster, Marta slammed shut the casket lid and thrust the chaplet into her pocket.

'Mademoiselle Marta!'

'I was waiting upon my mother,' she stammered, guilt loosening her tongue. 'I thought to find her here.'

The maid's eyes narrowed. 'My lady is downstairs with your father.'

Marta was horrified. 'But Maman went to the Sainte-Chapelle. I saw the carriage pull away . . .'

'Madame Boussay went alone.' The servant's eyes swept around the room, as if looking for something out of place, then returned to Marta. 'Will you wait for her, mademoiselle?'

'No!' Marta gave her prettiest smile. 'I had something to tell her, but it can wait.'

She walked out of the room with as much dignity as she could muster, the purloined beads heavy in her pocket. As soon as she was out of sight, she started to run, hoping the servant would hold her tongue. Marta had been denied her promised visit to the Sainte-Chapelle. She would die if she was forbidden to go to the wedding, too.

CHAPTER TWENTY-ONE

LA SAINTE-CHAPELLE, ÎLE DE LA CITÉ

Salvadora Boussay stood in the crowd, breathless with awe, in the upper chapel of the Sainte-Chapelle, and thanked the good fortune that had brought her to stand here in God's presence.

She had memorised every detail and learnt all there was to know about the provenance of the building, but the glory of it surpassed even her expectations. The Sainte-Chapelle had been completed in the year 1248. A labour of grace, commissioned by the greatest of the medieval Christian kings, Saint Louis, to house the treasures of Christ's Passion brought back from the Holy Land via Constantinople – pieces of the True Cross, the Holy Lance that pierced Christ's side when he was crucified, a vial containing drops of Christ's blood and the Crown of Thorns, the biggest prize of all. The King himself had, barefoot and penitent, accompanied the precious relics on the last stage of their journey into Paris.

Diamonds of multi-coloured light, from the flamboyant rose window in the western wall and the stained-glass windows in the vaulted apse, flooded the chamber. Each of them, soaring to some ten times the height of a man, illustrated a scene from the Bible. From Genesis to the Apocalypse, the images changing by the hours of the day with the passage of the sun across the Parisian sky.

Statues of the twelve apostles stood on pillars beneath the exquisite rib-vaulted ceiling. Salvadora looked, and found the particular niches set into the wall intended in the past for the royal families of France and, there beyond, was the Oratory, added some two hundred years after the foundation stone had been laid, allowing later kings and queens to observe Mass privately through a grille in the wall.

But more beautiful than all this was the *grande châsse*, the guilded reliquary box, enshrined atop the tribune at the east end, and built to house the royal relic collection: a casket of gold, enamel, rock crystal, pearl, ruby and sapphires. A symbol of Christ's suffering, of his willingness to lay down his life so that mankind could live for ever. Salvadora felt quite giddy with the miracle of God's love made manifest.

Then, she blinked.

Perhaps it was the heat tricking her senses, or the trial of standing looking up for so long, but she could have sworn she saw movement at the top of the Gothic tribune, behind the screen. Or perhaps the sheer wonder of being present in this holiest of places was more than she could bear.

Salvadora felt a wave of nausea. She flapped her fan, but it did not help. She felt quite faint, both cold and hot at the same time. She stumbled back from the reliquary and turned away, looking desperately for somewhere to sit until the dizziness passed.

High above the chamber, Louis edged his way round the narrow platform until he was in a perfect position, then he crouched on the ledge and peered through the gaps in the screen at the preparations below.

The morning service was over. All that remained were the smell of polish and beeswax and incense grown cold. Motes of dust floated in the air. There was the unmistakable air of abandonment after a celebration was over. Everything seemed a little less bright, a little less special.

In the milling mass of faces and ecclesiastical robes, Vidal – Cardinal Valentin – stood out. Louis took off his cap to cool himself. Though Xavier took spiteful pleasure in blackening Louis's hair each morning with coal tar to disguise the white strip that matched Vidal's, when he thought himself unobserved, Louis saw in his father's eyes a desire to acknowledge him as his son. Though nothing had yet been spoken out loud, the physical similarities and mannerisms were evident to all. Louis knew the steward dripped poison in his ear about Louis's behaviour and that a whipping awaited him if he ever went out with his head uncovered. Xavier had punished him once – with great ferocity – and if he was discovered hiding in the reliquary itself, he would be beaten again even more savagely.

Then again, he did not intend to be caught.

Louis put his cap back on and looked down. Some days previously, he had watched preparations for the feast day of the Crown of Thorns in this cavernous upper chapel. He'd observed the churchmen checking and double checking, the servants running to and fro. The hot morning had been filled with a sense of purpose. With this most Catholic of celebrations, there was no need to compromise or adapt to the requirements of the time. Louis believed no more in this superstition than in any other – it was ridiculous to believe that such an object might have been worn by Christ upon the Cross and survived its journey across continents and centuries – but he understood that the symbolic value of the Crown of Thorns outweighed common sense. The mass of people, the superstitious and the slow-witted, believed such relics could transform their lives. What interested Louis was why his father had given the arrangements such attention and why Xavier, usually such a permanent malignant presence within their lodgings, had spent the days both before and after the ceremony here in the Sainte-Chapelle.

In the event, the ceremony on 11 August had passed without note, yet Louis was certain that it was not an end to the matter. The wedding was tomorrow and he had a suspicion that while all other eyes would be on Notre-Dame, his father's attention would be set here.

Louis had a stillness and a patience that belied his years. He could stay here, hidden in his cramped eyrie, for as long as it took. All day and all night, if need be. Years of staying in the shadows, especially during the treacherous darkness of the boys' bedchamber at night when the priests came, had taught Louis to take up no space in the world.

Once he knew what Xavier's purpose was, it would be another morsel of information with which to bargain. Everything had a value. Everything could be used for advantage or harm.

Louis finally located Xavier in the throng below. On Vidal's business, or his own? He watched the steward take a purse from his pocket. A hireling's filthy hand shot out, quicksilver fast, to seize it. Xavier did not let go. For a moment, the two men stood there, as if swearing an oath upon a Bible, then, finally, the steward released the coin. The ruffian slipped it beneath his cloak, bowed and left through the small wooden door in the far corner of the soaring chapel.

The steward glanced around, as if to satisfy himself no one had witnessed the transaction, then he slunk back to stand close to Vidal.

The adoring congregation had formed a crowd around his father after Mass was over. Louis watched person after person kiss his ring and ask for his blessing. A rich old woman, in a black hood, seemed suddenly to stumble in front of him, and had to be helped away.

Stupid, superstitious fools.

Louis knew how piety masked depravity, how those who

shouted loudest about God's work were often those with the blackest hearts.

The disturbance over – the fat widow had gone – Louis leant back against the side of the narrow tribune platform. He did not care what, if anything, Xavier was planning, only that the steward stood in the way of his own advancement. But he had to play his hand carefully. Vidal relied upon Xavier and seemed to have no suspicions of his loyalty.

Time would tell. Louis would say nothing yet, but he would continue to watch and gather evidence. Xavier would betray himself eventually. Men like him always did.

CHAPTER TWENTY-TWO

RUE DES BARRES

Minou sat patiently in an oak armchair in their bedchamber, sipping her wine and watching Piet pace to and fro. She knew he was trying to find the courage to begin.

'Just talk, *mon coeur*. The story will tell itself.'

Piet looked over at her, his face desperate with indecision. Minou patted the tapestried seat of the companion armchair. 'As soon as you start, the words will come. I promise you.'

Piet hesitated a moment longer, then refilled his goblet.

'Very well,' he said, and it seemed to Minou that in that instant the air in the chamber grew sharper, expectant.

Piet took a deep breath. 'At the end of May last, I received a letter. It purported to come from Mariken Hassels, a woman from the Beguine community, who had known me in my childhood in Amsterdam.'

Minou's mind flew to the tapestry gracing the walls of the solar in the château de Puivert.

'Begijnhof,' she said.

He nodded. 'It was Mariken who saved me. She found me, when my mother was dying, and looked after me until she could find a family to take me in. I spoke French passing well, so they brought me to Languedoc and all remnants of my Dutch past were lost.'

Minou realised she was holding her breath, her heart weeping at the thought of Piet, a bereaved child, left orphaned and alone.

'Seeing Mariken's name at the foot of the page after all these years, it brought back such dark memories, Minou. Memories I'd not thought had the power still to harm me.'

'I understand.' She paused. 'What did the letter say?'

Piet took another breath. 'That this last spring, a French cardinal had been asking questions about me. Asking if any documents pertaining to my birthright had been left in her possession.'

'What! Why now, after so long?'

'She did not say, only that she was delaying answering the cardinal until she knew if I lived. She wanted to warn me, I suppose.'

Minou frowned. 'How did she find you?'

'She wrote a letter and gave it into the hands of a Dutch merchant she trusted, in the hope that he might be able to get it to me.'

'It's extraordinary that it did,' Minou said.

'I found it rather alarming.'

'That your name is well-enough known in Amsterdam?'

'Yes. Though I have made no secret of my support of the Calvinist rebels, it concerns me I was easily found.'

Minou stared at him. 'Do you know what the documents might be? Did Mariken say?'

'No. I suspect she feared the letter might be intercepted. I imagine it is something to do with my father's identity.'

'He was a French merchant, isn't that what your mother told you?'

'The story changed,' Piet said, blushing at the memory of it. 'Sometimes he was a merchant, sometimes he was a nobleman, even a prince! I learnt not to ask when I realised my questions made her sad.' He paused. 'Looking back, I realise she might not . . .'

'Even have known who he was.'

Piet nodded. 'Yes, God forgive me. For so long, I tried to blot out everything about the day my mother died: the sound of her ragged breathing, each gasp more painful than the last; feeling her skin growing colder beneath my hand; the damp of the room and the rotting smell of fish bones in Kalverstraat below . . .'

'You must have been so frightened.'

'I was weak with terror. Even now, the horror of being left alone in the dark as the light faded –' he pressed his hand to his stomach – 'I can still feel it here. Then Mariken came, and she took care of me. Found me somewhere to live, people who would be kind to me. I held my mother's face close to my heart, but I tried to forget everything else about Amsterdam. It was too distressing. So you can imagine, receiving the letter from Mariken was like an old wound being violently ripped open.'

Minou nodded. 'On the day your mother died, can you recall her giving you anything? Documents, letters, a package of some kind? Or giving something into Mariken's safekeeping?'

'I have racked my brain over and again these past months, but I can't remember. Only the loss and knowing the world I'd known was ended. I loved her deeply, Minou.'

'I know,' she said gently.

'I was barely older than Marta is now.' His eyes blazed. 'If such a thing ever happened to her or Jean-Jacques, I don't—'

Minou took his hand. 'If anything happened to us – which, God willing, it will not – our children will never be left alone as you were, *mon coeur*. They are loved, they have aunts and uncles who care about them.'

For a moment, they sat in silence. His distraction over the summer was explained, the waste of the weeks of distance between them, but what was unclear to her was why Piet had not told her before. There was no shame to the story, nothing that reflected badly upon him.

'Do you still have Mariken's letter?'

Piet crossed the chamber, opened their travelling chest and passed it to her.

'Here.'

Minou read it, alert for hidden information between the lines, then looked into her husband's face.

'I don't understand why you didn't tell me about this when you first received it?'

'I wanted to. Several times, I tried to. Then, with what happened to Alis – and Bernard's death – I couldn't risk causing you further distress. If it was a hoax, then why disturb your peace of mind? I had no way of knowing if the letter was genuine.'

Minou's thoughts flew back to that day in early June: Aimeric's departure at sunrise, she and Piet riding out so happily in one another's company through the woods at midday, their bitter argument spoiling the afternoon, sitting with her beloved father at the trestle table in the glade and seeking his counsel. A snapshot of colours and images, each as vivid and present in her mind as if it were only yesterday.

Then suddenly, Minou realised. She looked down again at the paper.

'Is it because you saw Vidal's hand in this that you did not confide in me?' she said, trying to keep the censure from her voice. From the way his face flushed, she knew her words had hit home. 'Piet, how could you have so little faith in me?'

'I understand how much it frustrates you when I think on him,' he said, not meeting her eye.

Minou swallowed her impatience. 'I regret how Vidal has any dominion over your thoughts or spirits when there is no justification – you allow him a power over you he should not have.' She tapped the letter. 'But this is something. Is there any reason to think Vidal is the French cardinal to whom Mariken refers in her letter? Does he have any connection to Amsterdam in general, or Begijnhof?'

'Not that I know,' Piet admitted.

Minou sighed. 'And this is why you asked Aimeric to make inquiries at the Dutch embassy?'

'Yes. They, of course, know of Begijnhof, but no one seems to know Mariken in particular.' A ghost of a smile slipped across his lips. 'Pieter, that's how she addresses me, did you see? I'd forgotten my mother called me that.'

Minou handed the letter back. 'That makes it more likely it is genuine, does it not?'

'I suppose it does.' Piet sighed. 'But if not Vidal, then who? I cannot think of any other French cardinal – anyone, indeed – who would be seeking information about me.'

Minou marvelled at her husband's innocence. 'Piet, you are a prominent and outspoken supporter of the rebels. As you just admitted, your role in supporting Calvinist forces in the Dutch Provinces is no secret. The fact that the letter reached you at all is evidence of that. All this of itself is quite enough to bring you to the attention of Catholic factions in Amsterdam. So, though we cannot rule out Vidal being the author of the letter Mariken received, there are other explanations.'

Minou steeled herself to ask the question she had been dreading.

'Since we have been in Paris, have you sought him out?'

'Vidal?' Piet flushed. 'No, but I saw him once by chance. He's not lodging with the rest of the Duke of Guise's party but, rather, is close by in the rue d'Orléans.'

Minou touched his hand. 'How did it affect you?'

He hesitated. 'I had imagined that moment so many times, Minou, wondering how I might feel – angry, regretful for what was lost, furious for what he did to our family, vengeful, scared even. But though I felt a jolt beneath my ribs, as if I'd been punched, in truth it affected me less than I had expected.'

Minou nodded, though she did not quite believe him. 'Did he see you?'

'No, I stepped out of sight.'

'How did he seem?'

'Older, of course, but the trappings of power hang well upon him. As for his face and his manner – the same Vidal. He has with him a small entourage, including a page said to be recently come into his service. As they passed, I saw him. That is to say, the boy.' Piet paused. 'He is about nine or ten years of age, I would say.'

Minou stared. 'Why does this boy interest you?'

'There was something about him, Minou. The cast of his head, his expression, the way he held himself. To my eye, he bore more than a passing resemblance to Vidal.'

Minou's eyebrows shot up. 'His son?'

'I don't know. It's possible, is it not? We know he was responsible for fathering one child, a child who might have been accepted as the rightful heir of Puivert had things gone differently, so why not another?'*

'That's possible.'

'If the page is his son, and Vidal has taken him into his service, that might indicate some remorse for his past actions.'

Minou didn't answer. Her heart sank as she realised that, even now and after all the misery and spite Vidal had inflicted upon their family, her husband still wanted to believe the dearest

---

*The Burning Chambers (2018)

friend of his youth, whom he had loved and trusted, had not entirely disappeared. They had been as close as brothers once.

'Of course, Vidal took a vow of celibacy,' Piet continued, almost eager, 'but we know such things happen. Don't you think it might indicate a softening of his heart?'

'It is possible,' Minou answered carefully. 'Some men find that the hardness of their youth, their intransigence, fades at the birth of a child.'

'Perhaps, having erred himself, Vidal will be better inclined to forgive the transgressions of others. Perhaps he is making amends for the past.'

Although Minou wanted Piet to worry less, her guts twisted at the hope in his voice. And despite the heat of the day, she shivered, suddenly feeling as if Vidal was in the chamber with them. No longer a ghost from their past, but a very palpable threat.

'And, I confess it occurred to me that he might also have been behind the assault on Alis.'

Minou's eyes widened. 'Why ever would Vidal want to hurt Alis?'

'Not Alis, you. She was wearing a green dress that day, Minou. It would have been easy to mistake it for your green cloak. In the heat of the moment, I did the same. And no one but you ever went up to the roof.'

'Why didn't you say when it happened?'

Piet ran his fingers through his hair. 'There was no time to share my suspicions with you. Bernard was dead, Alis's life hung in the balance, and somehow the moment was lost.' He looked at her. 'Did it never cross your mind Vidal might have ordered the shooting?'

Minou frowned. 'My thoughts were focused solely on Alis surviving.'

'At the time, yes, but afterwards? We both know it cannot have been an accident,' Piet insisted. 'It's against the laws of nature for a shot to go astray that high.'

'I agree that it was a deliberate act. I also agree that I was most likely the intended victim. From a distance, the colour of Alis's dress and my cloak might look the same. But Vidal has let us alone for ten years. If he had wished to harm us, he would have done so before now. Why assume anything has changed?' She gestured to the letter. 'Just the coincidence of this and the assault on Alis? You are linking those two things when there is no evidence.' She hesitated. 'Besides, if the attack was Vidal's doing, then surely the bullet would have been intended for you, *mon coeur*, not me.'

Piet leant forward in his chair. 'If not Vidal, then who?'

'Who wrote the letter to Mariken or ordered the attack?'

'Either, both, I don't know,' he cried, his voice brittle with frustration. Then his shoulders slumped. 'Perhaps you are right, Minou. Perhaps I am seeing connections where none exist.'

Minou kissed his cheek. 'Ah, have you not learnt after nearly ten years of marriage, that I am usually right? As for this letter from Mariken, with Aimeric's assistance we will learn what there is to know about the matter. What happened is in the past, try to put Vidal from your mind. He is just a man like any other. Do not give your thoughts to him nor let him steal the sleep from your nights.'

To her surprise, her husband smiled and, for the first time in many weeks, she saw desire flicker in his eyes.

'Why, my lady of the mists? Do you have another suggestion for how to keep sleep at bay?'

Minou blushed. 'I might . . .' She stepped out of his reach. 'But now, I must go and find Salvadora. She's been waiting nigh on an hour for us to depart for the Sainte-Chapelle. There are limits to even her patience.'

Piet groaned. 'What of tonight?'

She grinned. 'We shall see, my love. We shall see.'

CHAPTER TWENTY-THREE

La Sainte-Chapelle, Île de la Cité

Salvadora Boussay sat back in the carriage, her heart racing. Her chemise was slick against her back and her palms sweated within her gloves. She agitated the confined air with her fan, but there was no respite.

She had not seen the man for ten years, but there was no doubt it was him. Here in Paris. A cardinal now, his robes proclaimed it. Even standing in the crowd of worshippers, she had sensed his malevolence and cold ambition.

Salvadora was a proud woman. She had lived her entire life believing that ladies should not draw attention to themselves. Yet today she had first quarrelled with her niece and then, in the Sainte-Chapelle of all places, she had made a fool of herself. Crying out unguarded, almost falling over at the sight of him, allowing strangers' hands to touch her. She felt humiliated, an emotion she thought she had left behind her. Years of brutal treatment at the hands of her husband – where every transgression, however minor, might bring down his fist, a stick, a belt upon her back – had conditioned Salvadora to feel always ashamed.

The carriage lurched around a corner and Salvadora threw out her hand to stop herself from sliding from the seat. Her thoughts continued to taunt her. For all the talk around the fireside of how they lived side by side in different faiths, Salvadora still prayed each night that her family would return to the true Church. In particular, she prayed for Aimeric's salvation for, although she was fond of her nieces, he was her favourite. The son she'd never had. She had carried a child once, but a particularly unrestrained beating had denied her not only that joy, but also the possibility ever after.

The wheels rattled, shaking her bones over the cobbles.

Had Aimeric not been born a Catholic? Baptised a Catholic? And had not his own father – God rest his soul – remained faithful to God unto death? It was only Aimeric's childhood admiration for Piet that had led him to the doors of the Huguenot Temple. And because Minou was an obedient wife, respecting her husband's judgement and guidance, she'd had no choice but to follow, taking Alis too.

She wished Bernard was still here. He would know what to do. Her brother-in-law had possessed the rare ability of being able to give good counsel with a fair and dispassionate eye. He never judged, merely offered practical advice that always soothed.

Salvadora's thoughts twisted back upon themselves. What were a few years upon this earth compared to the life to come? What if her family had shut themselves out of God's love for eternity? Wasn't it her Christian duty to bring them back to the one true Church?

So, although she had been looking forward to admiring the beauty of the Sainte-Chapelle today, she had gone as much in pilgrimage. To pray in the place where prayer and miracles were seamed in the very fabric of the building.

But instead of finding peace, she had seen him. The words of supplication had died on her lips because Vidal had been there too.

Salvadora closed her eyes to pray. 'Blessed lady, filled with compassion for those who invoke thee, and with love for those who suffer, heavily laden with the weight of my troubles, I cast myself at thy feet and humbly beg of thee to take the present affair which I recommend to thee under thy special protection . . .'

The carriage came to an abrupt halt, rocking as the coachman jumped down and opened the door. Salvadora lifted the gauze curtain, a scant protection against the dust of Paris, and saw that they were back in the rue des Barres.

She sat a moment longer, distressed that prayer had not calmed her spirits. As she walked back into the corner house, the bells of Saint-Gervais ringing for Vespers behind her, she could still feel the murderous black eyes of the cardinal on her back.

CHAPTER TWENTY-FOUR

HÔTEL DE BOURBON

In the Hôtel de Bourbon, Aimeric heard the bells of Saint-Germain-l'Auxerrois ring for Vespers. His eyes were wet with grief for his father and his sister.

A magnificent building, covering a plot of land once occupied by some three hundred dwellings overlooking the river to the south, the embellishments and ornaments of the Bourbon Palace made it one of the most admired townhouses in Paris. The *grande salle* was larger than even the most sumptuous room within the Louvre Palace and so was to host the masque commissioned by the Queen Mother for the wedding celebrations.

However, his thoughts now were only of his wise and honourable father. Some two months cold in the ground without Aimeric even knowing. He could not bear it. It seemed impossible that he would never see Bernard's gentle face again, that he would never sit beside the fire in his little house in the rue du Trésau in Carcassonne and listen to his stories of the past.

Aimeric looked out of the first-floor window to the street below. For two days, the people had been gathering to secure their place ahead of tomorrow's wedding, lining the route along which the royal party would process from the Louvre Palace to Notre-Dame cathedral, where the nuptials would take place. He wondered what his father would have thought of the spectacle? His eyes brimmed with tears again. Now he would never know.

With the crowds had come the entertainers, the cutpurses, doxies and tricksters. The smell of rôtisserie and pâtisserie from the street sellers seeped through the cracks in the open windows. From time to time, Aimeric caught the cheers for the burst of a flame-thrower's fire or a roar for tumblers executing their tricks. He wished he could take innocent pleasure in the delights of Paris. But, each nightfall, he could only see how the tension and belligerence slunk back into the crowded streets.

His thoughts returned to his sister. That Alis had suffered so violent an assault on her person, that she had nearly died and he had not known it, distressed him more than he could say. He felt as if he had failed her and was failing her still. She was his boon companion, the greatest friend he had ever had.

But behind the shock and grief, his thoughts had been turning. Though his time with Minou had been over too quickly, he couldn't help but wonder why Piet had not mentioned the events in Puivert nor made any reference to Vidal. His thoughts had been focused on Amsterdam, he understood that, but all the same. Though Minou had not said as much, the instant she had told him of the circumstances of the attack on Alis, Aimeric had suspected Vidal might be behind it. He was a malignant and vengeful man, he pursued his enemies and acted solely in his own self-interest.

Aimeric shut his eyes. His faith would give him the strength to hold firm. There would be time enough to grieve and pay his respects to his father when he returned to Languedoc in the autumn, to spend time with his beloved Alis.

But for now, his heart and his sword belonged to de Coligny. Aimeric rubbed his eyes and took a deep breath. This was not the time to mourn. That would come later, in the privacy of his own quarters. He had to force his thoughts back to the present.

Admiral de Coligny was in private consultation with Henri

of Navarre, in an attempt to encourage the young king to take a greater interest in affairs of state: topics would range from discussions about the role of the Huguenot armies in the Dutch Provinces and the patchy implementation of the current peace agreement, to the arrangements for his own wedding. Though charming and beloved by his men, Henri was as bawdy as any rank-and-file soldier. Pleasure and drinking amused him more than prayer or politics, and he was easily distracted by a pretty face. High born or a village girl in a summer orchard, he made no distinction. He loved easily and completely, until another caught his eye. How Navarre would fare with the Valois Princess Marguerite, Margot – who was a match for him in wit and influence – Aimeric could not imagine. By reputation, both were independent, manipulative, amoral and used to getting their own way.

Though de Coligny was back in favour with the King, Aimeric also knew his influence sat uneasily with the Queen Mother, who saw her own influence slipping with her sickly son.

The admiral wanted to believe a lasting peace was possible. The Queen Mother was a pragmatist, prepared to compromise if it suited her aims. The King was under her thumb and had no views of his own. The main obstacle to peace was the Catholic Duke of Guise. He hated de Coligny, blaming him for his father's death at Orléans, and had vowed to avenge him. It was common knowledge that Guise was in discussions with Spain, seeking to promote a Catholic alliance to stand against the emerging Protestant nations.

Aimeric sighed, trying to convince himself this wedding was good for the kingdom, good for their cause. Given that both Navarre and the King had a true affection for de Coligny, surely the union could not but deliver a greater freedom to the Huguenots.

'A lasting peace,' he said out loud, as if to imprint the words on the air.

Although he had made his usual observances at first light, and prayed again for the soul of his father, Aimeric bowed his head for a third time. With the steadfast faith of a man who believed God watched over the righteous, he prayed that tomorrow would pass without incident and that all those he loved might be delivered safely into the arms of another day.

CHAPTER TWENTY-FIVE

Marguerite de Valois stood in front of the looking glass in her shift, her bare arms and shoulders touched by the afternoon sun shining through the window. She turned to her left and then to her right, admiring herself from all angles, then back to face centre again.

Margot stretched her arms above her head. Her skin was perfect and white, as unblemished as any of the Italian sculptor da Vinci's statues in the Salle des Caryatides. She had brushed her hair one hundred times until it gleamed as warmly as polished mahogany. Her eyes were clear and well set, and she needed little dye to enhance her black lashes. Her brows were two perfect arches. Margot smiled. Her lips were as naturally red and plump as if painted with cochineal. Tomorrow, of course, what nature had bestowed upon her would be improved by her ladies-in-waiting.

She would be the most beautiful bride Paris had ever seen, of that she had no doubt. She could hear the crowds gathering in the streets already. Today she was a princess, tomorrow she would be a queen. As her marriage vows were pronounced, she would also accede to the throne of Navarre. She spoke several languages prettily, she had studied grammar and the classics, she was a poet and accomplished dancer, and known for her great skill on horseback, too. It was not for nothing that she was known as the 'pearl of the Valois'.

Margot's expression darkened. Navarre was nineteen, a few

months younger than she. She had been favourably impressed when she had first met her husband-to-be at the time of their betrothal. He had turned out to be witty and more accomplished than she'd been led to expect and, against her will, he had charmed her. When Navarre had arrived in Paris in June, dressed all in black and accompanied by some nine hundred Huguenot noblemen, Margot had to admit he had cut a fine figure. But his breath stank of garlic. He wore his hair unfashionably long *en brosse*, swept back from his forehead, and he had rough manners and a provincial accent that grated on the ear. Besides, her heart was not free to give. He did not compare to her first love, Henri of Guise.

Margot placed her hand on her breast, remembering the touch of his fingers on her skin. Remembering the scent of his golden hair and the muscles on his back. They had enjoyed one another's company for many months until, finally, they had been betrayed and caught. The Queen Mother had spies everywhere. Guise had been exiled from the court and she had been beaten black and blue by her mother and locked in her quarters for a month.

Two years had passed. But days ago Margot had watched from the windows of the Louvre Palace as the Duke of Guise rode back into Paris accompanied by a cavalcade of some hundred men. If Guise's intention had been to show her feeble brother the King and her ruthless mother who had the heart of the people, it had worked.

The pain of knowing that Guise was so close at hand, yet forbidden to her, was driving her mad. Each night, even though she knew a guard was set, Margot prayed that he might yet find a way into her chamber. Each day, she prayed that word would arrive from the Pope refusing dispensation for the wedding between a Catholic and a Protestant to go ahead, though she had little hope of that now. This morning, she had overheard her ladies-in-waiting gossiping that her mother had ordered any missives from Rome to be held outside France until sunset tomorrow. Although the Cardinal of Bourbon was Catholic, and could be excommunicated for performing the ceremony without special dispensation, he was also Navarre's uncle. Margot suspected Bourbon would fear the wrath of her mother, close at hand in Paris, more than the censure of the Pope some days' ride away in Rome.

She was trapped.

Margot looked away from the mirror. Her beauty no longer pleased her. Nothing could please her except for Guise's company. There were still twelve hours to go. Time enough for him to come and claim her.

'What are you doing?'

Margot's stomach lurched at the sound of the dreaded voice. All her confidence and elegance fell away from the instant she was in her mother's presence and she became a bullied, uncherished child again. She turned, trying to control herself, but her hands wouldn't stop shaking.

'I am honoured, my lady.'

Catherine de' Medici stood, monstrous, in the doorway. She had gone into mourning at the death of her husband some thirteen years previously and wore nothing but black, save for her talisman bracelet with coloured stones. Margot tried not to look at her sharp, protruding eyes and heavy jowls, her white-powdered face and carmined lips, which failed to disguise a cruel mouth.

'I asked you a question. What are you doing?'

'Nothing.'

Her mother advanced into the chamber. Margot couldn't help flinching.

Catherine gave a cold smile. 'It is right to be anxious before your wedding day. It shows appropriate modesty, even though all of Paris knows you have the morals of a street whore.' She held out a goblet. 'I have brought you something to calm your nerves.'

Margot looked in horror at the red liquid swirling in the cup. Was it possible her mother had never intended the wedding to go ahead? It was common gossip in the court that her mother had poisoned the Queen of Navarre. What if she intended to harm her too? To destroy her good health or her spirit? She could not bear to drink it.

'Take it,' Catherine ordered. 'You offend me by your dis-obedience.'

'I am not thirsty.'

Her mother's eyes narrowed. 'I know what is best for you.' Catherine laughed. 'Do you think I have anything but your best interests at heart?' She held out the goblet. 'Take it.'

Margot knew she had no choice but to do what she was told. She was powerless to resist. Then she felt the pinch of her mother's fingers on her chin.

'I am certain you do not need reminding of this, Marguerite, but you will not do a single thing to bring shame upon the Valois name. I am the wife of a king, the mother of kings and, thanks to my great hard work on your account, I have ensured that you, too, will be a queen.' The pressure increased. 'Nothing at all that could bring disgrace on our family. The eyes of Paris will be on you. If you do anything to jeopardise what I have done for you, your life will not be worth living. Do you under-stand?'

Margot's throat was dry.

'Do you?'

'*Oui, Maman.*'

Catherine released her. 'I will reassure the King and your noble brothers that you will obey them.'

Shaking from fear and rage, Margot managed to curtsey.

She watched in silence as her mother lumbered from the chamber, then a red mist descended. She was so ill-used by her family, so powerless to live the life she wanted, her desires so disregarded. With a roar, Margot threw the goblet with all the force she could muster across the room. The wine went flying as the mirror shattered into a myriad pieces, sending tiny fragments of blood-red glass scattering across the floor of her beautiful prison.

CHAPTER TWENTY-SIX

Rue des Barres
Monday, 18 August

'Wake up!' Marta shouted, rushing into their chamber, bringing the noise of the Matins bells in with her. 'I have been ready since first light. Look at me.' She twirled around, holding her skirts wide.

Minou pulled the bed curtains back and sat up.

Piet, sitting by the window in his chemise and hose, held his finger to his lips. 'You are too loud and too early, Mademoiselle Marta! There were only six chimes. We will not leave for some hours.'

'My lady, my lord, forgive me.' The nurse appeared, flustered, in the doorway. 'Mademoiselle Marta, I expressly bid you to remain in your chambers until I came for you.'

Minou smiled. 'It's all right, nurse, she can stay for a while.'

'Are we to receive the entire household in our bedchamber before the sun has barely risen?' Piet grinned.

'There does appear to be a certain anticipation affecting the usual pattern of things.'

Minou patted the bed beside her and Marta climbed up.

'I was lonely in my chamber, Maman.'

Minou laughed. 'Lonely! I cannot think that possible in a city so full of people.'

'There was no one to play with,' her daughter said, spreading her blue skirts around her. 'I look fine in this dress, do I not?'

'As pretty as a princess,' Piet said. 'As indeed will you, my lady of the mists, when the hour calls for it.' He placed a kiss on Minou's forehead, then rose and put on his robe. 'I shall be the proudest man in Paris.'

'What will the real princess be wearing?' Marta said, her voice bright with excitement. 'Aunt Salvadora says that—'

Minou lifted her daughter down from the bed. 'You may have been ready since first light, *petite*, but I am not. And nor, indeed, is your father.'

Marta tilted her head to one side. 'I can help him dress.'

'Lord save us, a man must have some privacy!'

'Return to your chamber and wait patiently,' Minou said. 'Nurse will make sure you have everything you might need. It will be a long day and we will be standing in the heat for some time.'

'But I have—'

She put on her sternest voice. 'Marta, go.'

The little girl stamped her foot. 'How long do I have to be patient?'

Minou hid a smile. 'Once the bells have rung for the mid-morning prayers, we shall leave. It is not far to the Île de la Cité, but it will be slow going.'

'Why?'

'Because the streets will be very crowded.'

'That is many hours hence,' Marta whined. 'Could we not go earlier—'

Piet put his hand on his daughter's shoulder and propelled her to the door, where he handed her into the care of a servant.

'By your leave, Marta, we shall see you and Jean-Jacques a little later. Go straight to the nursery. Do not give the nurse any further trouble.'

* * *

The instant their daughter was out of earshot, they burst out laughing.

'I'm sure all parents think likewise, but she really is an extraordinary child,' Piet said. 'She is so confident.'

'And a magpie,' Minou added. 'Gathering every titbit of information. Yesterday I overheard her talking to Salvadora about learning Latin, someone having told her that, in addition to Spanish, French and Italian, Margot is versed in Latin and Greek.'

Piet laughed. 'She even tried to persuade me that she should be allowed to accompany us to the evening revels that will follow the marriage. The Queen Mother has arranged an exceptional entertainment – a specially written masque, as well as Italian dancing and the finest musicians in Europe. I told her we had turned down the invitation. She thought that was foolish to miss such an occasion!'

'She would! For my part, I'm so relieved you don't want to go. I suspect it will be one of those evenings better in the retelling of it than the living of it.'

Piet traced his finger along the line of her face. 'I would far rather keep to our own company and make our own entertainments.'

'How very circumspect you are this morning, my lord.'

'At your service, *madomaisèla*.'

'*Madomaisèla!* After all these years and two children, I thank you for such gallantry.'

'You seem not a day older than when I first set eyes on you.'

Minou's heart sang. Since Piet had told her about Mariken's letter and his fears about Vidal, the distance between them had vanished like a summer mist. They were their old selves, companions-in-arms, sweethearts again, lovers.

She kissed him on the tip of his nose. 'Now that, *mon coeur*, is only because you will not admit to needing spectacles. The story of the past ten years, I fear, is writ clearly upon both our faces. It's just that you cannot see it.'

Piet grinned. Then, taking her by surprise, he kicked the door shut with his heel, strode back across the chamber, swept her up in his arms and carried her to the bed.

'How now, my lord! There is no time for—'

He threw himself down beside her. 'There is time enough, my lady of the mists, to honour our happy marriage before we stand witness to one where the participants are far less suited. Indeed, it is our duty.'

CHAPTER TWENTY-SEVEN

THE CATHEDRAL OF NOTRE-DAME, ÎLE DE LA CITÉ

The high square towers of Notre-Dame stood magnificent against a cloudless blue sky. The arched windows flanking the west rose window, with its ancient stained glass, were dazzling in the morning sunlight. Today even the gargoyles seemed to pulse with a more benign air.

The parvis in front of the cathedral was alive with colour: a crowd dressed in jewels and feathers, velvet and ermine; faces pink and glistening in the fierce August heat. At the mighty west door, the snap of white of the clerical robes and the golden glint of cross and thurible stood in sharp relief.

Banks of raked seating for the most honoured guests and dignitaries had been constructed on both sides lining the approach to the west door – Catholics on one side, Huguenots on the other, like a crowd at a joust. Below them was the seating for lesser churchmen and property owners, noblemen like Piet and his family whose loyalty to the Crown or to Navarre, or to the prosperity of Paris, had earnt them a place.

Behind the stands, as far as the eye could see, hundreds of thousands of ordinary citizens stood to witness history in the making. Row upon row, street upon street, lining the banks on both sides of the Seine, their voices filling the air like the sound of thunder in the mountains. Unseen, but always heard.

At the entrance to Notre-Dame stood the Catholic Cardinal of Bourbon beside his Huguenot nephew, Henri of Navarre.

The bridegroom was dressed in pale yellow satin embroidered with pearls and precious stones. Navarre still wore his hair *en brosse*, in the style of Béarn, and his manner and demeanour spoke more of the battlefield and the hunt than the corridors of court, but he looked no less a king for all that. Minou tried, but failed, to find Admiral de Coligny or Aimeric in the procession, though many of the senior Huguenots were still in their customary black.

Minou scanned the platforms opposite, until she found the exquisitely decorated section draped in the red and white, the blue and yellow fleur-de-lys livery of the Guise family. In the centre of the group was the Duke of Guise himself. Even Minou was bound to admit that there was something in his bearing that drew all eyes. He, more than Navarre, seemed to take possession of the day.

Minou steeled herself, then narrowed the focus of her gaze until she found Vidal. And though she had been seeking him, her chest contracted at the mere sight of him as if she was held in the torture of an iron maiden. Her legs seemed to have turned to water and her hands shook, as if she held the memory of every violence inflicted by Vidal in her bones. She reached out, clutching at the wooden railing to steady herself, and tried to master the dread that crawled over every inch of her skin: images of Alis lying bleeding on the roof of the keep, Minou's cloak sodden with blood; the rotting corpses of vermin in the woods below where the assassin had waited.

She shook her head, as if to rid her mind of such terrible images.

Vidal had lost. She was alive, Alis grew stronger each day. Piet was restored to his old self. Vidal had not defeated them and she would not allow fear of him to undo her now. Minou forced herself to breathe in and out, until the rhythm of her heart returned to normal.

Finally, she took her hands from the wooden struts and stood straight. But when she glanced at Salvadora and Piet, she realised neither had noticed anything amiss. No time at all had passed.

'Here,' Piet said to Marta, pulling aside the awning so she could climb up on the struts. 'Can you see better now?'

The little girl climbed up. 'Yes, better.'

'Yes, what?'

'Yes, *thank you*, Papa,' she said, pulling a face. 'Where is Marguerite de Valois? Why is she not here, when the King of Navarre is waiting?'

Piet pointed towards the Louvre Palace. 'The princess will come from that direction in a grand procession. Do you see how they have built a special walkway so she may come directly without having to descend to street level?'

'Floating on golden air.'

Salvadora, her face scarlet in the heat, nodded her approval. 'Marguerite de Valois will be accompanied by her brother King Charles, and the Queen Mother, as well as her younger brothers the Duke of Anjou and the Duke of Alençon, and their attendants.'

'And three ladies-in-waiting to carry her train,' Marta said. 'I heard the maids talking of it.'

'You should not listen to kitchen gossip,' Salvadora sniffed, 'though you are, in point of fact, correct.'

Marta shot her great-aunt a resentful look.

'Careful,' Piet said, as Marta leant further out for a better view.

'Did you see Vidal?' Minou whispered in her husband's ear, surprised that her voice sounded so normal. 'In the party of the Duke of Guise's stand opposite?'

Piet put his arm around her waist. 'I did, but I have taken

your words to heart. Better now, in the distant crowd, than to find ourselves in the same place during these next few days. As you said, he cannot hurt us. It's all in the past.'

Minou nodded, though from the colour of his face, she did not believe he was as sanguine as he claimed.

'Look!' Marta shouted. 'They are coming.'

In a wave of colour, as the ceremonial trumpets were lifted, the parvis was suddenly filled with music. The crowd shifted: anticipation turned to an excitement that stirred the senses and banished the everyday. Despite her jangled emotions, the collision of her past and their present, Minou felt her spirits lift as the first sharp, cracked notes of the trumpets pierced the air.

'The bride looks most fine,' Salvadora said with approval. 'A true princess of the royal blood.'

Marta sighed. 'She will be a queen soon, because she is marrying a king.'

Salvadora nodded. 'Indeed, she will.'

Marguerite of Valois, accompanied by her oldest brother, was dressed in a blue velvet gown embroidered with fleurs-de-lis and a cape of spotted ermine. On her head, she wore a crown and, on her shoulders, a wide, blue, jewel-encrusted mantle with a train of some four ells carried by three princesses. She blazed with diamonds that caught the sun as she walked slowly along the golden walkway towards her bridegroom.

The King looked pale and breathless in the heat. Anxious too, as if fearful of the crowds and the Queen Mother's displeasure, casting nervous glances as he stumbled forward. Though dressed finely, he was eclipsed by his younger brother, the Duke of Anjou. Anjou's darker features were complimented perfectly by a pale jewelled cap set around with heavy pearls. Minou had heard the rumours about Anjou's unnatural tastes and dismissed them as spite. Now she reconsidered. His *mignons*, their hair curled like his, looked as out of place in the royal party as a troupe of wandering players making an appearance at High Mass.

'Isn't she beautiful,' sighed Marta. 'Blue is my favourite colour, too.'

The trumpets fell silent and the crowd stilled as the royal party arrived at the west door of the cathedral and were received by the Cardinal of Bourbon.

They were too far away to hear the words of welcome, too far away to see the expression on the faces of those clustered around Navarre and Marguerite. But no one could miss the desperate glance the princess threw at the Duke of Guise, as if willing him to put an end to the charade; nor the moment of silence when Margot refused to give the response and speak her vows; nor how the feeble King, at a sign from the Queen Mother, seemed to push down his sister's head before the nuptial benediction was quickly spoken.

The trumpets were raised again, the crowds roared. It was done.

'They are married,' Piet said with relief.

'But did she freely assent?' Minou whispered.

He raised his eyebrows. 'Enough to satisfy the cardinal, it seems.'

Now the new Queen of Navarre accompanied the Valois party along the platform into the cathedral itself, leaving her new husband outside with his Huguenot attendants.

'It is most irregular,' Salvadora complained, waving her fan.

'Why does her husband not go with her?' Marta asked.

'The royal party will now hear Mass to celebrate the marriage,' Piet explained. 'Navarre does not attend Mass, so —'

'Because he is one of us, not a Catholic like them?'

'Exactly so. You do not accompany Aunt Salvadora to Mass, do you?'

Marta pulled a face. 'No, but I should not care to be left alone outside on my wedding day.'

'Navarre will not be alone for long. There are three days of feasting and revels to come.'

'Will they come out again soon?'

'Quite soon.'

'Could we not go into the cathedral to watch?'

Minou laughed. 'Not today, *petite*.'

'When?'

'I'll take you another day,' Piet promised. 'We wouldn't be allowed in now and, besides, you'd not be able to see a thing for all the people.'

'Then can we go home?' Marta whined. 'It's too hot and I'm thirsty too.'

'For once, I am in agreement with Marta,' said Salvadora, stirring the air with her fan. 'I do not care for so much sun. It is bad for the complexion.'

Minou was still wondering if the marriage had really taken place in the sight of God. The bride and groom had barely looked at one another. And as she glanced around the *parvis*, she knew she was not alone in her uncertainty. She forced herself not to look back to the Duke of Guise's stand. She was still shaken at how the sight of Vidal had undone her so utterly and was worried for Piet.

She felt a tug on her sleeve.

'Maman! I am bored with standing, can we go home?'

Minou laid her hand on her daughter's shoulder. 'I think that is an excellent idea.'

* * *

Cornelia van Raay watched the Reydon family walk down the wooden steps from their seating. Instantly, she tried to follow. Her new plan was to put the letter into Pieter Reydon's hand in the street.

'*S'il vous plaît*,' she repeated, attempting to push her way through. The crowd seemed only to grow more impenetrable. '*Mesdames, s'il vous plaît. Messieurs.*'

But now the main spectacle was over, all of Paris had the same idea – heading for banqueting halls or taverns, or home to palaces and convents. Cornelia could not make her way through the mass of people.

She tried to keep Pieter Reydon in her sights – his wife tall and stately beside him – but it was hopeless. Though she pressed and pushed, tried to slip between shoulders and backs, she found herself hemmed in.

In the end, Cornelia gave in to the embrace of the crowd. Her plan would not work. She would have to present herself in their lodgings later, even though the after-effects of the assault upon her in the rue des Barres made her reluctant to return. Her father had urged discretion, but what else could she do?

'Follow them!' Vidal shouted, pushing back through the stand towards Xavier.

The steward snapped to attention. 'Eminence?'

'There,' he pointed. 'Piet Reydon. Don't let him out of your sights.' Vidal couldn't believe the evidence of his own eyes. Not only Reydon, but his wife, too. The false châtelaine, who had stolen his unborn child's birthright. Xavier had reported the assassin had hit his mark. Evidently, the man had lied. 'Find out where they are lodging and report back. Make haste!'

'Sire.' Xavier bowed, and slipped away.

Since Vidal's aim in ordering Minou's killing had been, in

part, to keep Reydon in Puivert and away from wagging tongues – at least until he had received confirmation from Amsterdam that the lay sister had left no papers or documents behind – the realisation that the whole family had been under his nose all along in Paris enraged him.

He put his hands to his temples. His headache was worse again.

Louis watched the exchange between Vidal and Xavier with cold interest. Standing with the other household servants, he hadn't seen what had so disturbed Vidal, but he realised his father had been shocked to the quick.

Louis waited until Xavier was out of sight, then slipped forward and climbed the steps until he was standing at Vidal's side.

'My lord?'

What is it?' Vidal snapped.

'Should I accompany Monsieur Xavier in case he has need of assistance? He might be grateful to have a messenger to carry word back to you?' Louis felt his father's sharp eyes turn on him, and, involuntarily, he stepped back. 'I did not mean to speak out of turn.'

He readied himself for a blow, but instead felt the weight of Vidal's hand on his shoulder.

'That's a good idea. Give Xavier whatever help he needs, although—'

Louis looked up. 'Yes, my lord?'

'Be careful,' he said with unaccustomed kindness. 'The streets will be dangerous tonight.'

CHAPTER TWENTY-EIGHT

Three days of feasting had followed the marriage. From dawn to dusk all the bells of Paris peeled in honour of the new Queen and King of Navarre. Ringing for peace and for the union of the most ancient, two most noble, families of France, now joined in union.

Now the celebrations were over. The streets were littered with debris and detritus. Huddles of women and men gathered around braziers in the streets to hear the latest news. Gossip started to spread as to whether the Princess Margot truly had assented. Speculation was rife, too, as to whether the royal marriage had yet been consummated. The appropriate witnesses had been in attendance in the bedchamber, as tradition required, but no one knew for certain.

In the makeshift camps and medieval alleyways, tempers were running high. Irritations broke out over every inch of ground, knives were quickly drawn and insults thrown like stones. Bruised faces, bruised honour. Everywhere, the stench of men and women in confined quarters pervaded the air. In the grand houses and boulevards, wives argued with husbands and servants complained about the endless demands of foreign guests. Neighbours, who once had passed the time of day in the streets, were short-tempered and ill-humoured in the stifling August heat. And in the Louvre Palace, the Guise residence and the

Bourbon Palace, the three factions were as divided as they had ever been. Liquor and spectacle had painted over their differences for a while, but now, like smouldering ashes about to burst into flame again, old grievances resurfaced. Guise was always there, stirring up trouble. Each day, if the King called for de Coligny to advise him, the Queen Mother – united with the Duke of Guise on this one point that Huguenot influence should be limited – flooded the chambers with spies, unwilling to let them be alone.

Only Minou and Piet held themselves apart. Delighting in one another's company, as if they were newly married, they had no need of banquets or masques.

Rue d'Orléans

'And?' Vidal demanded.

Louis watched Xavier bow his head.

'Reydon has not left the rue des Barres since the wedding, Eminence.'

'He has attended none of the celebrations?'

'No, my lord.'

'Visitors?'

'None to speak of.'

Though Louis knew Xavier would punish him, he touched his father's sleeve all the same.

'What is it, boy?'

'My lord, the lady's brother has several times gone to the house. He is in the service of Admiral de Coligny.'

'Is this so?' Vidal demanded.

Xavier threw a sideways look at Louis. 'Forgive me, yes. I forgot. I did observe him entering the lodgings on one occasion.'

Louis cleared his throat. 'Also, there was a woman watching the house this morning.'

Vidal turned on his steward. 'Why did you not tell me this?'

'The boy is mistaken.'

'Are you mistaken, Louis? Speak.'

'No, my lord. A woman of some twenty years, of neither high birth nor low,' Louis replied, ignoring the warning in Xavier's eyes. 'From her clothing, I would say she is a foreigner. She arrived at first light.'

'She does not approach the house?'

Louis set a look of regret on his face. 'Monsieur Xavier ordered me to return with him, so I can't answer for the past hour . . .'

'Then "Monsieur" Xavier will return to the rue des Barres and find out who she is.' Vidal waved his arm. 'Get out of my sight.'

With a villainous final look at Louis, the steward withdrew. Louis knew he would pay for it later with a whipping, but he didn't care.

For the second time, he felt his father's hand on his shoulder.

'Are you hungry, boy?'

Louis pretended to consider. 'Only if it pleases you, my lord.'

'You will dine with me tonight. For now, go to the kitchens and tell them to give you whatever you want. Then return to the rue des Barres. Report back to me what Xavier is doing.'

'Yes, my lord.'

Louis knew better than to show it, but inside his spirits were soaring.

RUE DES BARRES

'She's gone,' Piet said, standing at the casement with his hand on the glass.

Minou looked up from her book. 'Who's gone, *mon coeur*?'

'There was a woman earlier, standing by the back door into the sacristy of the church. She seemed to be watching the house.'

Minou put her book on the oak chest beside her chair and joined him at the window.

'Are you sure?'

'It seemed that way.' Piet frowned. 'Do you think it's the same woman who came looking for me the day before the wedding?'

'She could be.' Minou looked towards Saint-Gervais. 'Did you recognise her?'

He shrugged. 'I've reached the point where everyone looks familiar. We have been in Paris too long.'

'Maman,' cried Marta, running in. 'Please, please, please can we go out today.'

'I'm sorry, *petite*, but Jean-Jacques is still unwell. I don't want to leave him until the fever breaks.'

The little girl spun round. 'Papa, will you take me? You promised we would visit Notre-Dame and that was three days ago. Though, in point of fact, I think I would rather go to the pilgrim church.'

'Saint-Jacques-de-la-Boucherie?'

'Yes. There were so many shells dropped on the ground, I wanted one. They fall from their robes, I think.'

Piet ruffled her hair. 'I promise I will take you, but not today. I am waiting for your uncle to arrive. You'll have to entertain yourself this morning.'

Marta crossed her arms in a sulk. 'There's nothing to do. And Jean-Jacques never stops crying.'

'You should be sympathetic not impatient,' Minou reprimanded her. 'He is so little.'

'He's a nuisance.'

'Marta, that's unkind.'

The child's face brightened with a new idea. 'What if I ask Great-aunt Boussay to take me to the Sainte-Chapelle? If she agrees, may I go?'

Piet put his hands on her shoulders. 'Since you were not taken to the Sainte-Chapelle because you were disobedient – and you offended Aunt Salvadora with your saucy questions – she is hardly likely to take you now, is she?'

'I wish Aunt Alis was here, she would take me.' The little girl stamped her foot. 'I shall die of boredom, and then you'll be sorry.'

Marta flounced from the room.

'Only three days more, then we'll be on our way.' Minou sighed. Since the wedding – since catching sight of Vidal – her peace of mind had been destroyed. Even now, the tips of her toes and fingers tingled with the memory of it. She glanced at her husband. 'Are you really waiting for Aimeric?'

Piet grinned. 'But of course! It's wrong to lie, isn't that what you counsel Marta?'

She laughed. 'For all the good that does.' Her face grew serious again. 'Does his coming mean he has word from Amsterdam?'

'I hope so. This waiting for news is setting my nerves on edge.' Piet turned back to the window. 'I wonder what the woman wanted?'

Minou put her arm around his waist. 'If she comes back, I will go down and speak to her. Try not to worry.'

Cornelia wiped her mouth with the back of her hand. Then, bracing her forearm on the edge of the water trough, she tried to stand up.

She'd hoped the nausea that had confined her to her quarters on the river these past three days had passed. But the sheer effort of walking from the mooring to this quartier seemed to have brought it back worse than ever. She had been on the point of approaching the Reydon lodgings this morning when the first attack took her. She had only just made it into the dank alleyway, to this private spot behind an animals' drinking trough, before she was sick.

Now she felt hollow and light-headed. With her kerchief, she dabbed sweat from her temples and the base of her throat. How could she present herself to Pieter Reydon in this condition?

Cornelia took a few deep breaths and waited for the shivering to stop. The alleyway was secluded, as she'd learnt to her peril some days previously, but an unexpected advantage was that she could overhear snippets of conversation when the servants came out into the courtyard garden. So she'd learnt that Pieter Reydon was at home today; that the Huguenot soldier with the untamed black hair – whom even the Catholic maids of the household admired – was Madame Reydon's brother; that the girl was seven years old and considered saucy; and that the two-year-old little boy was often afflicted by ailments of the digestion.

As if in sympathy, Cornelia's stomach twisted again. Not a morsel of food had passed her lips for days, so how could the sickness still have such a hold? This must be the fault of the under-cooked pork she had bought on the day of the wedding from a street vendor. She prayed it was bad meat, for the alternative didn't bear thinking about. She'd heard the sailors and bargemen whispering about an outbreak of camp sickness upstream of the Île de Louviers.

'Rotten meat, that's all,' she just had time to think before another spasm twisted her stomach, and she doubled over again.

* * *

In the nursery, Marta watched the soft puff of the nurse's sweaty upper lip as she breathed in and out, until she was certain she was fast asleep. Her red, rough hands lay still in her lap, her cheeks were flushed and her cap had slipped, revealing strands of thin, grey hair.

Avoiding the noisiest floorboards, Marta tiptoed across the chamber and peeked into her brother's cradle. His arms were thrown wide above his head and his fat little legs spread like the points of a star. She touched his forehead and felt his skin was cool. He would not wake for hours.

Picking up her shoes and cap, Marta pinched the latch between her thumb and forefinger to quieten the door, then carefully made her way all the way down the stairs, especially quietly past the first-floor chamber – where she could hear the murmur of her parents' voices behind the closed door – then, avoiding the kitchens too, she tiptoed out into the courtyard.

A delicious shiver went down her spine. She would be in more trouble than ever if she was caught but, since she had no intention of being caught, she felt only excitement.

Marta put on her shoes and her cap, then opened the gate and slipped out into the alleyway.

The sun was cresting the top of the building, flooding the narrow street with light. The many dull hours spent staring out of the window, memorising each and every journey in the carriage, had imprinted the shape of the street upon her memory, so Marta felt perfectly at ease.

Each of her senses seemed to be vibrating like strings on a lute as she stepped past a woman slumped by the water trough; jumped over a black-and-tan mongrel chewing a bone; avoided a puddle of ale steaming in the heat. With the thrill of transgression, she turned left into the rue des Barres and headed quickly towards the river.

Marta worried she might be challenged, but although people looked surprised to see a girl unaccompanied, they merely smiled or raised their hats. Her confidence grew. At the junction with the rue de la Mortellerie, she stopped. She closed her eyes and went through the route they'd taken to the wedding: from here down to the river, then west along the bank and over the bridge to the Île de la Cité. It wouldn't take long. She could see the Sainte-Chapelle and be back within the hour. No one would ever know she had gone.

CHAPTER TWENTY-NINE

'Monsieur Joubert,' the servant announced.

Minou stood up. 'Aimeric!'

Piet clapped him on the back. 'You are most welcome.'

'Nephew!' Salvadora's plump face was wreathed in smiles.

Aimeric kissed his aunt and his sister in turn, shook Piet's hand, then unfastened his corse and dagger, put them on the chest with a clatter, and sank into a chair.

'There's no respite from this heat, even this early in the day.'

Piet handed him a gage of ale. 'I hope you're looking after my dagger well?' he said, gesturing to the knife he'd loaned Aimeric in Puivert.

'I am, though I'm also delighted to say that I've had no cause to use it.'

'What news?' Minou asked.

Aimeric took a long gasp of ale. 'Admiral de Coligny is yet again summoned to the King's chamber this morning. The King loves him like a father and wishes to please him. It is so regular an occurrence, the Queen Mother is quite perturbed. For his part, all the admiral wants is to be allowed to return to his estates in Châtillon and his wife – she is expecting another child – but the King will not release him.'

'And what of Navarre?' asked Piet.

Aimeric shrugged. 'He's nowhere to be seen. His interests are limited to carousing, hunting and wenching. He cares not for politics, so absents himself from matters of court. All I pray is that he gives attention enough to his wife, so that she does not rush back into Guise's arms. Now the marriage has taken place, and the royal family has accepted the Huguenot Navarre into their ranks, the King believes Guise's power is much reduced.'

Minou heard the doubt in his voice. 'But it is not?'

Aimeric shook his head. 'Alas, no. There is mounting evidence the terms of the peace are not being observed, particularly in Paris. There have been incidents – a Huguenot killed on the left bank, rumours circulating in les Halles that the Protestant army mustered outside the walls is preparing to storm Paris, allegations of Catholic women being accosted on their way to Mass. The usual kind of rumour and counter-rumour.'

'You think these are falsehoods concocted by Guise?'

'It is hard to separate truth from untruth,' Aimeric conceded, 'but there is no doubt Guise wants unrest. He thrives on it. Though he is careful never to speak out of turn, I do not trust him. He gives one message in public from his own mouth, but yet whips up his supporters in anti-Huguenot sentiments in private.'

'To what purpose?'

'Guise is a man who enjoys exercising power, regardless of the costs to others or the consequences. He despises the King, he thinks him weak, is jealous of Navarre and, as you know, has vowed to be revenged on de Coligny for his father's assassination in Orléans. The sooner he leaves Paris, the better.' Aimeric drained his goblet and put it down on the table. 'But forgive me, I cast a shadow over our company with my complaints.'

'Is that not what families are for?' Salvadora answered drily. 'To listen when all others have lost interest!'

Aimeric laughed. 'You are more than kind, dear Aunt.' He turned to Piet. 'But the reason I came is that I have news from Amsterdam for you. It's not much, but you'll want to hear it.'

Salvadora looked from Piet to her nephew, then she gathered up her embroidery and slowly stood up.

'Minou, we should withdraw. The gentlemen need to talk.'

Minou felt her colour rise. It was ridiculous that, after all these years, Salvadora still would not accept that she and Piet ran their affairs together.

'That is thoughtful,' Piet said quickly, 'but I would like Minou to stay.'

Salvadora pursed her lips. 'If you wish it so,' she said, her voice sharp with disapproval. She starred at Minou. 'Will we lunch at two o'clock as usual?'

'Yes, Aunt.'

'In which case, I shall see you at table.' Her face softened as she turned. 'Nephew, it has been a pleasure to see you, though too fleeting as usual. I hope you will come again soon.'

Aimeric escorted her to the door, then came back into the room whistling.

'She is displeased with you, Sister!'

'Salvadora hasn't forgiven me for failing to accompany her to the Sainte-Chapelle as I'd promised.'

'Well, for your sake, I hope it blows over soon. It will be a long journey back to Puivert if not . . .'

Piet closed the door. 'What do you have to tell me?'

Aimeric threw a glance at Minou.

'I have told Minou everything, as I should have done before – and, indeed, as you urged me to do. She has forgiven me for my tardiness.'

'And other faults,' she said, squeezing Piet's arm.

Aimeric smiled. 'I am glad. When we talked before, Minou, you said that a woman had come to the house asking for Piet?'

'Yes, that's right. The day before the wedding.'

'I believe I know who she is. A woman called Cornelia van Raay.

She's the only child of a wealthy Catholic Dutch grain merchant, Willem van Raay, who lives in Amsterdam, but has many business interests here in Paris. He is well regarded. From what I can gather, van Raay sent his daughter to Paris to find you, Piet.'

'Why would he think to seek me here rather than in Puivert?'

Aimeric raised his hands. 'Since every Huguenot nobleman and landowner was invited to the wedding, it was a reasonable assumption you would be in Paris in August too. I also discovered that van Raay is a major benefactor of Begijnhof. In Mariken Hassels's letter to you, did she not write she had asked a friend for assistance? I assume it was van Raay.'

'Is that all?' Piet said, unable to keep the disappointment from his voice. 'I'd hoped for more.'

'I said it was not much.'

For a moment, they were silent.

'Earlier today, I noticed someone in the street watching the house. It might be the same woman as was previously here – the maid's description was so vague as to be useless.' Piet frowned. 'Though she was dressed plainly, and without any attendants; could she have been Cornelia van Raay?'

'But if it was her,' Minou mused, 'and her purpose is to speak with you, then why has she not presented herself? It doesn't make sense.'

Piet shrugged. 'I don't know.'

Minou turned to Aimeric. 'Do you know where Mademoiselle van Raay is lodging? We could seek her out rather than wait for her to return.'

'Rumour has it she is staying on one of her father's barges.'

'Where on the river is it moored?'

'That I don't know, but I can find out.'

Piet nodded. 'If it is van Raay's daughter, and she has information to share, that would be most welcome. The uncertainty has been preying on my mind for too long. I would have the matter resolved, for all of our sakes.'

Aimeric looked at him. 'And if the French cardinal does turn out to be Vidal?'

Piet frowned. 'We will cross that bridge if, and when, we come to it.'

Remembering the wave of pure terror that had swept through her at the sight of Vidal in the wedding stands, Minou marvelled at the steadiness in her husband's voice. She had not told him, for fear of making the incident seem more significant than it was. But since then, Minou felt Vidal was living beneath her skin. Every nerve seemed raw with dread. She had barely slept last night for thinking he was but a few streets away.

'I am grateful for all you have done, Aimeric.' Piet held up the jug of ale. 'Will you take another gage before you go?'

'I can think of nothing I'd like more, but I have been away from Admiral de Coligny for too long as it is. I need to see him safely back to our quarters.' Aimeric stood up. 'Might I dine with you tomorrow instead? I would see my nephew and niece before you return to Puivert.'

Minou smiled. 'I would be most grateful, not least because Marta has declared herself bored with our company at the dinner table and has been demanding guests to amuse her!'

Aimeric grinned, looking for a moment like the boy he'd once been.

'Marta is so like Alis at the same age. She was always bored, always complaining about having nothing to do. Give my apologies to dear Salvadora for taking my leave without saying goodbye to her. I will make it up to her tomorrow evening.' Aimeric buckled his corse and dagger. 'As soon as I find out where the van Raay barge is moored, I will send word. In the meantime, if Mademoiselle van Raay returns – if it is indeed her – will you get word to me?'

'Of course.' Piet clasped his hand. 'Again, my heartfelt thanks.'

'*À demain*,' Minou said. 'We will dine at six.'

CHAPTER THIRTY

RUE DE BÉTHISY

Marta rubbed her eyes. Though she had been trying to pretend otherwise for some time, the plain truth was she was lost.

The streets looked different on foot. So many landmarks she thought she recognised were unfamiliar when she drew near. This time she had been so sure. But as she looked up at the unfamiliar spire, having been drawn by the bells, she wished there were not so many churches in Paris.

Her eyes filled again with tears. What would Aunt Alis say? She was always brave. Marta frowned. Her aunt would tell her to keep going and that things would come right in the end. But clouds had covered the sun so she no longer knew which way to go. If she could get to the river, that would be a start.

Marta blinked away her misery and tramped on, telling herself all would be well. It was still an adventure, but she was tired. Her fingers slipped into her pocket, looking for a coin. With a jolt, she felt the wooden beads she had taken from her mother's jewellery box. She had meant to put them back, but with the wedding and her brother's endless crying it had slipped her mind.

She turned the corner and suddenly, with the wonderful sensation of the ground becoming firm beneath her feet once more, Marta knew where she was. This was the rue de Béthisy, where her uncle was lodging. Maman had pointed out the house, half concealed behind high stone walls, when they'd first arrived in Paris.

The rest of the street was made up of half-timbered houses, white plaster between the diagonal struts on all the upper floors – Papa had explained it was to stop fire from taking hold of the wood – with overhanging first-floor chambers, like eyebrows scowling down upon the narrow street.

Marta smiled, her spirits instantly restored at this evidence of her own resourcefulness. She was on the point of stepping forward when she heard the noise of boots behind her. She looked behind her to see a cohort of men in black livery marching towards her. As they drew closer, Marta saw the soldiers were surrounding a man of noble bearing, late in years, in austere black doublet and hose, a stiff starched ruff at his neck, and a white beard trimmed to a point. With a jolt, she recognised Admiral de Coligny, who seemed unperturbed by all the attention. Rather, he was studying a document in his hands. Then, to her dismay, Marta saw her Uncle Aimeric approach him. She would be in great trouble if her Uncle spied her here unaccompanied. Lightning quick, she jumped back into the shadow of the nearest building.

Everything seemed to happen at once.

The admiral stopped suddenly. As he turned, to show the document to Aimeric, a shot rang out. The deafening report echoed in the narrow street, bouncing off the walls of the houses.

Shocked, Marta looked up in time to see a puff of powder in a first-floor window opposite and the flash of silver of a muzzle being withdrawn.

Then, a woman screamed and the street exploded in chaos – shouted orders, soldiers pushing through the crowd. The admiral was now clutching his elbow as blood pumped through his fingers. Marta saw her uncle hurry de Coligny into the safety of their lodgings; at the same time the soldiers stormed the house opposite, kicking in the door and sending splinters of wood flying. Moments later, they shouted from the first-floor window that the assassin had fled.

The woman was still screaming. Marta put her hands over her ears, too terrified to move. Her view was mostly blocked by the soldiers, but she caught an occasional glimpse of the silver tip of a sword or the pale shaft of a pike on the dry ground. There was a pool of blood on the cobblestones where the admiral had been hit.

Marta realised her cheek was wet. She couldn't find her kerchief, so she took off her cap and wiped her face. There were smears of red on the pristine white linen. Her stitched initials – M R J – were hidden beneath vivid smudges of blood.

Disgusted, she flung the cap away from her. She couldn't bear to touch it now.

CHAPTER THIRTY-ONE

Rue des Barres

The clock chimed the quarter-hour. Minou, Piet and Salvadora were sitting at the lunch table with full serving dishes and empty plates in front of them.

'Forgive me for speaking plainly, Niece, I do not see why we should all be inconvenienced by the child.'

Minou glanced at the door. 'I understand your vexation, Aunt, but—'

Salvadora kept talking. 'If Marta is thoughtless enough not to come to dine when called, then so be it. To miss a meal might teach her better manners.'

'Salvadora, please.' Minou was not sure she could cope with much more ill temper. She was frustrated too, but she was also worn to a thread by her aunt's endless complaints. 'The nurse should have brought her down at two o'clock as usual. I don't know why she has not.'

'I'll fetch her,' Piet offered, dropping his napkin onto the table.

'No, I'll go,' Minou said, seeing a chance of escape. She pushed back her chair. 'I would like to check on our little warrior in any case. It is miserable for Jean-Jacques to be so afflicted. You both, please start. I'll bring Marta down with me in a while.'

Ignoring Piet's look of desperation at being left alone with Salvadora, Minou went up to the nursery. It wasn't just the oppressive afternoon heat that made each step such a labour, but the nagging sense that they had overstayed their time in Paris. Everything seemed a little tawdry now, worn out. It was as if the curtains had been drawn back at the end of a masque to reveal a stage made only of paper and paste. The stink of the streets, the sour waft of the river, the rancid stench of the abattoirs and slaughterhouses now the wind had changed direction, seemed to seep through the walls.

'*Petite*, it's time to eat,' Minou called out as she pushed open the nursery door.

The chamber was empty: a tousled blanket in Jean-Jacques' cot, an earthenware cup by the nurse's chair, Marta's chalks scattered on the table beside a half-finished drawing of the princess in her wedding gown, evidence of the morning's activities, but abandoned now. Motes of dust floated in the hot and silent air.

Minou retraced her steps, peering into each room as she passed until finally, a lank streak of a maid in the kitchen said she'd been sent to draw water for the little boy to bathe some half-hour past. So she went through into the courtyard, expecting to see both children there.

Beneath the plane tree, Jean-Jacques was laughing and splashing in an oval wooden tub. The nurse, her sleeves folded back and smiling, was tipping water over his head.

'My lady.'

'He seems much improved.' Minou chucked him under the chin. Jean-Jacques giggled. 'How now, *mon brave*!'

'He is ordinarily such a happy soul, it broke my heart to hear him cry so, my lady.'

Minou bent down and scooped a cascade of water over her son's naked, round belly. He squealed with delight.

'And where is Marta?'

'I thought Mademoiselle Marta was with you in the dining room, my lady.' The nurse lifted Jean-Jacques out of the water and placed him on a drying cloth on her lap. 'There, that's right, little soldier. All better now.'

'No. I have not seen her since first thing this morning.'

The nurse frowned. 'She said she was going downstairs to ask you and the master if she might be taken on an expedition.'

'She did, but since we were expecting Monsieur Joubert to call, I bid her return to the nursery.'

'She didn't come back up to me, my lady.'

Minou felt a shiver of unease. 'When did you last have sight of her?'

The nurse started to look flustered. 'I was tending to this little one, waiting for the gripe to pass. Mademoiselle Marta was drawing. He was awake all the night, the poor scrap, he wouldn't settle. When, finally, the attack passed, he slept and I might have closed my eyes for a moment.'

'You fell asleep.'

'Upon my word, it was only for a moment. She'll be hiding somewhere. She won't have gone far. Begging your pardon, madame, but you know how she is.'

'Tend to Jean-Jacques,' Minou said, concern making her sharp. 'I will find her. As you say, there are plenty of places to hide.'

But after half an hour's searching, there was still no sign of Marta.

'Would she have left the house?' Piet suggested.

Minou shook her head. 'She knows not to go anywhere alone.'

'The child is disobedient.'

'Salvadora, please,' Piet said. 'My love, if she had taken it upon herself to explore, where might she have gone?'

Minou raised her hands. 'She was enamoured of the numbers

upon the doors of the houses on the Pont Notre-Dame,' she replied, struggling to think. 'And she wanted to go back to Saint-Jacques-de-la-Boucherie before we left Paris to collect the shells the pilgrims drop.'

Salvadora shut her fan with a snap. 'The child will have gone to the Sainte-Chapelle. She was most put out by having been left behind.'

'Of course.' Minou's heart eased just a little. 'You're right, we should start there. Will you stay here, Aunt, in case she comes back in the meantime?'

'I have no doubt the wilful girl will stroll in here, as bold as brass, without any mind for the trouble she has caused.' Salvadora paused, then added: 'Do not worry, Niece.'

Some few minutes later, Minou and Piet were outside in the rue des Barres.

'We should separate,' she said.

'I don't like the idea of you—'

'I'll come to no harm at this time of day,' Minou said firmly. 'We'll cover more ground, and more quickly. You start with the Sainte-Chapelle. If you have no luck there, head to Saint-Jacques or the Boulevard Saint-Germain on the left bank. Marta is entranced with the Duke of Anjou's *mignons* and their perfumed pet animals.'

'I still think it would be wiser—'

Minou wasn't listening. 'On second thoughts, Piet, go first to Notre-Dame. It is closest and you did promise to take her. It might be uppermost in her mind.'

Piet made to protest again, then stopped. 'Where will you go?'

'To seek Aimeric's help. He knows the city better than do we; he has men at his disposal. His position in de Coligny's high regard confers upon him the authority to ask questions.'

Piet nodded. 'It is some half an hour after two. Whatever we discover, shall we meet back here at the five o'clock bells?'

'I hope to be back well before then,' Minou said, injecting a confidence into her voice she did not feel. 'And how I shall scold her!'

Piet found a smile, but Minou knew he was as worried as she was.

'Until five o'clock,' Piet said, then he kissed her hand and took his leave.

Minou watched until he was out of sight, trying to stop her worst imaginings from taking hold. Then she turned in the direction of the rue du Béthisy.

As she made her way through the crowded boulevards towards Aimeric's lodgings, the scale of the task overwhelmed her: the sheer impossibility of finding one seven-year-old girl in a city of hundreds of thousands of people. Minou stopped in every shop they had ever visited, at the carts and stalls of street sellers along the way, asking if anyone had seen a little girl with long brown hair and a blue dress, but no one had.

With each step she took on the dry Parisian streets she felt her breath was being squeezed from her. The further west Minou went, the more she sensed a growing tension in the air, a sharpness, as if the whole city might erupt into conflict at any moment.

As she passed the Pont aux Meuniers, the water singing beneath the wooden wheels of the mills, Minou came to a halt. With an awful and heart-pounding clarity, she suddenly saw herself years from now, looking back on this day as a sequence of missteps and errors, each leading to the next wrong turn until it was too late. Inevitable, irreversible. A tragedy written in blood.

Minou held her hand to her chest and felt how fast her heart was racing. Then, the shout of a stevedore down on the river caught her attention, and the present rushed back.

She shook her head. She could not allow her own thoughts to make a prisoner of her. She was not a silly girl, easily startled, seeking out the words of necromancers or astrologers to make a decision. This was not the time to give in to self-pity or premonition. Her task was to find her daughter and bring her home.

CHAPTER THIRTY-TWO

RUE DE BÉTHISY

Marta didn't know what to do. She had been hiding forever and, worse, she urgently needed to answer a call of nature. She wasn't sure she could hold on much longer.

She'd thought to slip away as soon as things were quiet. But there were now soldiers everywhere and both ends of the street had been barricaded and cordoned off. No one was allowed to pass.

Marta squeezed her legs together, and tried to think of nice things: her little chestnut pony with the white blaze in Puivert, the rose-water biscuits Maman bought for them at the market in Carcassonne, her beautiful embroidered hood that so well matched her eyes, her mother's blue-and-gold enamelled box from Limoges, which glinted in the light.

'What are you doing?'

Marta spun round at the sound of the voice. 'You shouldn't creep up on people,' she snapped, cross to have been caught out.

'Are you lost?' the boy asked.

She stared at him. He was perhaps a little older than her, but he behaved as if he had every right to be here.

'No, why? Are you?'

'We live in the rue d'Orléans,' he replied, a smile touching his lips. 'I came out to see what all the noise was. Would you like to see?'

Marta tossed her head. 'I would not dream of going with you, my parents would not approve.'

The boy looked around with exaggerated interest. 'I don't see your parents.'

For a moment, Marta faltered. 'With the commotion, we became separated.'

'The King's personal guard are on their way. They will arrest anyone who doesn't belong here.' He leant closer. 'You see, the admiral is not expected to live.'

Marta's eyes grew wide. 'Is that true?'

'Wouldn't you like to know!'

'My uncle is of his household.'

The boy pulled back. 'I took you for one of us.'

'I am as French as you,' she said, suddenly ashamed of her southern accent.

'No.' He pointed to the chaplet in her hand. 'One of us.'

'Oh.' Marta blushed. She hadn't even realised she was holding her mother's rosary beads.

'We have many servants. There is food and drink. You can eat, then rest while you wait for your parents to come.'

Marta looked at the mass of people thronging the street. She didn't think she could hold on any longer and she was hungry. She shouldn't go with strangers, but this boy seemed pleasant and well bred. As he said, she could rest a while in his house, regain her strength, then go home as soon as the streets were clear again.

'We haven't even been introduced!'

'If that is all that concerns you, it's easy enough to remedy.' He took off his hat and bowed. 'Louis, at your service.'

'Marta,' she said, giving a curtsey in reply. 'Why is your hair white down the middle? It's strange.'

'Why are your eyes different colours? That's stranger.'

Marta raised her chin. 'I was born like this.'

'So was I.' Louis held out his hand. 'Come. It's not far.'

In his bedchamber, Admiral de Coligny sat propped up on pillows, while his attendants continued to fuss.

His left elbow was shattered and one of the fingers of his right hand had been taken clean off by the force of the bullet, but the Lord had been watching over him. If he had not thought to show the document to Aimeric at that moment and turned, the shot would have hit his heart.

God had spared him.

Everything seemed to be happening in slow motion. He could hear the stomp of endless boots going up and down the stairs, the shouted orders in the courtyard below his window, the cries in the rue de Béthisy beyond as his men questioned and sought witnesses to what had happened. He knew it barely mattered now.

The house where the assassin had lain in wait was owned by the Duke of Guise. The gate leading out from it to Saint-Germain-l'Auxerrois had been left open, where a horse was waiting. This was no opportunist attack. He knew it and his men knew it. The question was what might happen next.

De Coligny closed his eyes and saw the face of his young wife, picturing her in the orchards of their estate in Châtillon, and prayed he would live to see their child come into the world. He thought of his older daughter and sons, his grandchildren.

'My lord,' said a familiar voice in his ear. 'Forgive me for disturbing you.'

'What is it, Joubert?'

He was so tired and bruised from the hours of poking and prodding. How much time had passed? An hour? Several? The broken bones in his arm were throbbing and he feared his right hand was already swollen with fever.

'My lord, his Majesty the King has sent his personal physician to tend to you.'

'I have no need of more attention. I need only to rest.'

'Forgive me, sire, but his Majesty and the Queen Mother have accompanied him in person.'

De Coligny opened his eyes. 'In that case, I will be honoured to receive them.' He spoke wearily. 'Bid them forgive my being unable to rise.'

As Joubert went to withdraw, he grasped the young man's arm.

'Tell your men – and make sure the message is clearly heard beyond the walls of this house – that there is to be no retaliation. Leave it in God's hands. No tit-for-tat reprisals, do you understand? Guise wants an excuse to move against us. Make sure we do not give it to him.'

RUE D'ORLÉANS

Marta stood at the virginals set upon a table and picked at a tune.

'Are you a servant?' she asked, tilting her head. The surface was polished so brightly she could see her face reflected in it.

The boy had led her through a sequence of the most beautiful rooms Marta had ever seen, golden gilt mirrors above white marble fireplaces, and silver candlesticks and porcelain on each mantel. Long pale-blue silk curtains, the colour of forget-me-knots, framed the tall windows.

In this chamber, the music room, a vivid wall hanging covered the entire wall – a breakfast scene before a summer's hunt – depicting a table laden with victuals and ale, a goshawk, cinnamon brown, hooded on the wrist, alaunt hounds in the care of the *valets de limiers*, a horn raised and weapons clean, a bay and a grey horse ready for a medieval sire and his lady.

Marta struck a last note, then turned back to Louis.

'Well, are you a servant or not?'

He crossed his arms. 'What do you think?'

She considered. 'You seem to have the run of the house – and it is a very fine house – so I think you cannot be. At the same time, the maids pay no heed to you.'

His eyes narrowed. 'What do you mean?'

'They do not bow when you pass, which they would if you were important. In fact, they do not pay any attention to you at all.'

He scowled. 'Do you always speak so plainly?'

'Maman says it is wrong to lie.'

'Even if speaking the truth would lead to a whipping?'

'No one would ever beat me!' Marta replied scornfully. 'I am beloved.'

'If that's true, why were you wandering the streets on your own? That speaks of neglect, not love.'

Marta took a step towards him. 'Take that back.'

'Why should I?'

She raised her hands. 'Take it back.'

He raised his in answer. 'I won't!'

'Boys are foolish. You're a fool.'

For a moment, they stood facing one another, fists ready, eyes blazing. Then Marta couldn't help herself, and she giggled. 'You look so cross.'

Louis grabbed her wrist and twisted. 'Don't mock me.'

Marta tried to shake herself free. His grip tightened, then, as quickly as his temper had come, he released her. The storm was over.

'How old are you?' he asked.

'Nearly eight,' she said proudly. 'The same as you, I'll wager.'

'Guess again.'

'Perhaps nine summers,' Marta suggested, rubbing her wrist. She could see the angry red mark of his fingers on her skin and wondered how she would explain it away. 'I must take my leave. My parents, who *dote* upon me, will worry.'

He laughed. 'Do you know the way back to your devoted family?'

'Why do you not think I belong in Paris?'

'I can hear the mountains in your voice!'

Marta raised her chin. 'Your accent is no better!'

Suddenly, the sound of talking outside in the corridor interrupted them. Louis put his finger to his lips and steered her towards a pass door at the far end of the chamber.

'You're pinching again,' she said, shaking her arm free.

'Do you want me to show you the way or not?' he hissed.

Marta didn't want to be indebted to this strange boy, whose mood changed like quicksilver, but she did need help to find her way home. The adventure had lost its bloom.

'All right,' she replied.

'Where are you lodging?'

'In the rue des Barres. It's in the quartier Saint-Gervais.'

'I know. What's your father's name?'

Marta stared. 'Why do you want to know?'

'Because I have an idea. If I go to your father and tell him where you are, he could fetch you home in a carriage.'

'Oh.'

'You do have a carriage, I suppose.'

'Of course,' she answered indignantly. 'But is it not better if I come with you?'

He shrugged. 'I was only thinking to save your shoes – there's a pretty room, all blue, where you could wait – but it's no odds to me either way. I don't care.'

Marta hesitated. She didn't want to be left on her own, even in such a beautiful house, but the thought of not having to walk any more was pleasing. Her plan had been to slip back into their lodgings without anyone noticing, but she'd been gone too long for that. Since Papa would not be able to scold her in front of strangers, this way might be best.

'My feet are sore,' she admitted.

'Tell me something – for proof – so your father knows to trust me.'

'I'll give you this.' She touched her head. 'Oh, I forgot. I dropped it in the street.'

'What are you talking about?'

'My cap. It was my favourite, with my initials – M R J – stitched in red thread. I was going to give it to you to show to my father.'

'All right. Well, tell me where your family comes from?'

'Languedoc. We have a castle, with a separate keep, and lots of land and woods with good hunting,' she boasted. 'Though I confess our house is not so fine as this, we have our own coat of arms above the door – a lion rampant with a forked and knotted tail and a capital B and P – for Bruyère and Puivert.'

Louis stopped so suddenly that Marta bumped into him.

'Watch what you're doing,' she complained.

'What do the letters embroidered on your cap stand for?' he asked casually, as if the answer was of no matter.

'M for Marta, of course, R for Reydon and J for Joubert. That was my mother's name before she was married.'

CHAPTER THIRTY-THREE

RUE DES BARRES

Minou was still in her outdoor clothes, the dust of Paris thick on her boots and cloak.

Having been turned back by an armed guard at the Grand Rue Saint-Honoré, she had tried to approach the rue de Béthisy from the north. But every road in that quartier appeared to be blocked. There were rumours that someone had been shot – wounded or killed, no one was certain – and there were certainly hundreds of armed men on the streets.

With a wild despair, her stomach twisted with fear for her daughter, Minou had tried to slip through the cloisters of Saint-Eustache but, if anything, more soldiers were guarding the northern perimeter. She had been forced to give up her hope of speaking to Aimeric. She would have to be patient until he came for dinner this evening. God willing, by then it would not be necessary. For all she knew, Piet had found Marta already.

Instead, Minou had visited all the places she knew Marta liked, not caring if she was walking in Piet's footsteps or not: the flower market and the Pont du Change, Notre-Dame and over to the boulevard Saint-Germain. The Sainte-Chapelle had been closed. No one anywhere admitted to having seen a little girl in a blue dress and white cap.

In the end, she had been forced to return home, praying all the while she would find Piet and Marta waiting for her. But when she had stepped into the house, and seen Salvadora's face grey with worry, Minou had thrown herself into a chair and sobbed. She was so exhausted she could barely think. The brandy Salvadora had pressed upon her was burning in her throat, she didn't even have the strength to swallow.

Below, there was a knock on the front door.

'Is it them?' Salvadora said, rising in her chair.

Minou leapt to her feet and ran from the chamber.

Cornelia van Raay tidied her hair beneath her hood and looked up at the Reydon house, waiting for someone to come.

It was past five o'clock. She could not believe how the day had gone. Wave after wave of nausea had stolen the hours. Now, finally, it was over.

Cornelia raised her hand to knock a second time just as the door was opened. Startled by the sight of Pieter Reydon's wife standing there, she involuntarily stepped back.

'Mevrouw Reydon!' she cried in Dutch. She gathered her wits. 'Madame Reydon, forgive me for calling on you unannounced, but I would speak to your husband on a matter of urgency. Is he at home?'

Madame Reydon was staring as if she wasn't there, then her expression changed. Cornelia thought she looked drawn and pale, nothing like the lady she'd watched at Notre-Dame on the day of the wedding.

'It's you,' she said. 'There was some trouble in the street. Some days past.'

Cornelia's face clouded. 'Some persons – I will not call them gentlemen – thought to molest me. You were kind enough to send someone down to help me, for which my thanks.'

'Their mothers should be ashamed of them.' Madame Reydon paused. 'Is your name van Raay?'

Cornelia's eyes widened. 'How could you possibly know that? I have been careful.'

Minou gave a fleeting smile. 'You have been seen here three times, mademoiselle. People talk.'

Cornelia hesitated, then nodded. 'My father sent me from Amsterdam to find your husband.' She peered into the hallway beyond. 'Is he at home?'

'No, though I am expecting him. Our daughter is . . . He has gone to look for our daughter, who seems to have left the house . . . or been taken.' She broke off, her voice cracking.

'She wasn't taken,' Cornelia said.

Madame Joubert grabbed her arm. 'How do you know?' she asked desperately.

'I saw her. At least, I think it was her. A young girl came out of the gate into the alleyway. Of your features, madame, with brown hair. She was wearing a linen cap and a blue embroidered dress. She was on her own.'

'When was this?' Minou gasped.

'Between the nine o'clock bells and the ten.'

'And she was alone, you say?'

'Yes, madame.'

'And her demeanour?'

'Happy, smiling,' Cornelia replied without hesitation. 'As if she was going on an adventure.'

The ghost of a smile briefly lit Madame Reydon's lips. 'Marta is fearless, though with little wisdom, it seems.' Her shoulders slumped. 'Will you come in and wait, Mademoiselle van Raay, until my husband and daughter return?'

'Cornelia . . .' Cornelia said, holding out her hand.

But then, without warning, she was overtaken with another bout of nausea. Cornelia felt as if her insides were being turned inside out.

'It's not a contagion,' she managed to say, seeing the look of alarm on Madame Reydon's face. 'Under-cooked meat from a street seller, I—'

Her last words were lost in a grimace of pain. The last thing Cornelia remembered was feeling a strong arm go round her waist and being helped over the threshold into the house.

CHAPTER THIRTY-FOUR

Rue d'Orléans

Having left Marta in the blue room, Louis ran pell-mell through the corridors of the house to his father's private chambers.

For once, fortune had been on his side. On his father's orders, he had returned to the rue des Barres, just in time to see a little girl steal through a gate at the side of the house he and Xavier had been set to watch. From conversations he had overheard, Louis knew there was a seven-year-old daughter in the household, though he'd never seen her. So he'd followed her winding trail through Paris and into rue de Béthisy; when de Coligny was shot, he had watched her hide and, in the end, decided to approach her. Now he knew for certain, luck had delivered him Reydon's daughter. His father would be pleased.

Louis ran around the corner, skating on the tiles, then came to an abrupt halt. The door to Vidal's chambers at the far end of the corridor was closed. He started to tiptoe, moving closer until he could hear the sound of raised voices within.

He pressed his ear to the wood, and recognised the distinctive voice of the Duke of Guise.

'I am in no need of your counsel, Cardinal Valentin, nor indeed your permission.'

'Sire—'

'And I am giving you the right to decide upon your own course of action, for which you should be thanking me.'

'Of course, my lord, I am conscious of your kindness.'

'In return, what I need is your absolution.'

Louis pressed his ear harder to the door.

'My noble lord, if I may speak. This situation . . . I think you should wait. There is no indication that they will seek retribution. De Coligny lives. I do not think you should act rashly—'

'You forget yourself.' The duke spoke coldly. 'Each time my noble father, may he rest in peace, rode into battle, you gave him God's blessing. He died with his sins absolved. Would you have me go to my Maker unshriven?'

'My lord, no. But scripture says what is permissible in God's holy war will be adjudged differently . . .'

'This, too, is war! Because we are not on the battlefield, do you not class this as God's sacred work? For too long, the Huguenots have polluted our country with their pernicious heresies and lies. They are a canker, infecting the court, infecting our country, the enemy of the people. And now, do you not see, they will use this attack upon the traitor de Coligny as an excuse to act against us? His brother-in-law is already camped outside the gates of Paris with some four thousand men. As for de Coligny himself, he will not be satisfied until he has corrupted the King into their number.'

Louis strained to hear. 'My lord, I do not believe the King would turn away from the true Church.'

'De Coligny has his ear. You are aware they are in the rue de Béthisy now, as we speak – the King and his sow of a mother – to beg the admiral's forgiveness.'

'Is there reason, my lord Guise,' his father was saying, 'to think the attack on Admiral de Coligny is anything more than the work of a lunatic?'

The words hung heavy in the air between them.

'He has been named,' Guise said eventually.

'Who has been named?'

'My lord Maurevert.'

'It was he who fired the gun?' Vidal asked. 'And from a house that you own, my lord?'

This time, Guise did not answer. Louis could picture his father's black eyes fixed upon the powerful man he served. 'Does the King approve your actions, sire?' Vidal continued steadily.

Louis held his breath.

'If the King orders the admiral killed, and those belligerents who follow him, it would be treason not to obey.'

Louis pressed his ear even closer against the door.

'His majesty loves de Coligny like a father.'

'Whereas I have lived these ten years deprived of my own,' the duke shouted. 'My father was taken from me at Orléans, if not by the admiral's actual hand, certainly upon his orders. Should a son not avenge his father? De Coligny is a heretic and a traitor. A murderer.'

'My lord, whilst I admire and applaud your loyalty and duty as a son, I still advise caution.'

'Make no mistake, you cannot stop what is to come. No one can. Things are too advanced. This pretence that the Huguenots wish nothing more than to worship peacefully, this lie is destroying France. Destroying our values. They mask their true intentions beneath a sickening piety, whereas the truth is that all de Coligny and Navarre want is power. They will not be content until they have driven every last Catholic from our shores and made France a Protestant state. I will not stand by and let that happen. Do you understand? I am a prince of the royal blood, a descendant of Charlemagne. This is *my* birthright, not that of any Valois half-blood descendant of that Italian sow.'

In the corridor outside, Louis listened to the silence. When his father spoke again, this time it was in a different tone of voice. Detached and without emotion, practical.

'When will whatever is to happen take place, my lord?'

'We rendezvous at the Tuileries Palace after the sun has set tomorrow. The King must give the order. The entire leadership: the dukes of Anjou and Alençon will rally their men, the Swiss guard will be mobilised, the city militia too. Each will tie a white cloth around his arm to mark him as a loyal Catholic. We expect all true Frenchmen and women, loyal to the Crown, to do their duty.'

Another silence, this of such duration and intensity that Louis wondered if they had left the chamber by another door. Then he realised they were praying. Despite himself, Louis shivered. His father had made his choice.

'Hereupon, I absolve you from your sins. *In nomine Patris et Filii et Spiritus Sancti*. Amen.'

'Amen,' the duke responded.

Louis had only just time enough to throw himself back against the wall before the door flew open and Guise marched out, striding away down the corridor, a look of triumph on his face.

A moment later, his father appeared on the threshold. 'Ah, Louis. I fear we cannot dine together this evening after all. Tell Xavier to prepare the horses.'

'My lord, I have news. I came upon the daughter of the man you wanted observed in the rue de Béthisy and have brought her here. I gave her something to make her sleep and left her in the blue chamber.'

Louis's voice tailed off, aware that his father was not listening.

'Fetch your belongings, then go to the rear of the house and wait. We leave Paris immediately.'

He felt a sudden, sickening doubt. Surely he wasn't going to be taken back to the horrors of Saint-Antonin, not after all his good work in his father's service these past months? Had he not proved himself a worthy son?

Louis forced himself to speak. 'Where are we going?'

'Into the Orléanais.'

'To Chartres?' he said without thinking. It was the only city other than Orléans itself that he knew.

Finally, Vidal turned his black eyes on him. 'Do not make me regret taking you with us, boy. Go!'

RUE DES BARRES

The last of the evening sun made its golden progress across the floorboards as Minou and Salvadora sat waiting for news. It was nigh on eight o'clock, three hours after they had arranged to meet, yet still Piet had not returned.

'How long is the Dutch girl going to be here?' Salvadora asked.

Minou looked up. Locked in her mounting distress for what might have happened to Marta – she had been missing for almost ten, perhaps even eleven, hours now – she'd all but forgotten that Cornelia was still sleeping upstairs.

'Mademoiselle van Raay is unwell,' Minou said again. 'You would not have me turn her out on the street, Salvadora? She comes from a good Catholic family in Amsterdam.'

'What does she want?'

'To speak with Piet.'

Salvadora pinned her with a look. 'About what?'

'About – his childhood.'

'His childhood! What does his childhood matter now? What's past is past. Sometimes it's better to let things be.'

'It's not as simple as that,' Minou said, walking to the casement again. Why had Piet not returned? She opened the window and leant out, as if she could conjure the sight into being of her husband with their daughter in his arms.

'Shall I light the lamps, my lady?'

'What?' Minou turned at the sound of the maid's voice. 'Oh, yes.'

'I have brought more wine, madame.' The servant glanced at the tray of untouched food on the sideboard. 'Would you like something different to eat?'

'I'm not hungry. Salvadora?'

'I couldn't.'

They waited in silence while the girl lit the lamps, then left the room.

'Will you at least take a little wine, Salvadora? It will calm your nerves. You need to keep your strength up. We both do.'

'Maybe a little, then. Medicinal.'

Relieved to have something to do, Minou fussed with the tray and the jug, pouring them each a measure.

'Did you not say that Aimeric was to dine with us this evening?'

Minou put her hand to her head. 'Yes. I had forgotten with all . . .'

'That is good then, is it not?' Salvadora said, accepting the wine. 'Since he has not come, nor sent word, that surely that suggests they are looking for Marta together.'

For a moment, Minou's heart lightened.

When the bells struck ten o'clock, Salvadora began to weep.

'I never thought . . . when I think of how I reprimanded Marta so often – how I . . .' Her words tailed away in a sob.

'Piet will bring her home,' Minou said gently. 'He will find her. I'm sure you're right that Aimeric is with him. Marta is quick witted and courageous. All the qualities that sometimes frustrate us, will stand her in good stead now.'

Unless she's been taken, a spiteful voice in Minou's head whispered. *Unless she's fallen into the river and drowned.*

Unless, unless . . .

RUE DE BÉTHISY

Friday night tiptoed towards Saturday morning.

Piet heard the bells strike midnight. He was still concealed in the rue de Béthisy, where he had been for some hours. All of Paris now knew of the failed assassination attempt on Admiral de Coligny, so although Piet had managed to slip past the guard into the street itself, de Coligny's lodgings were heavily guarded by both Navarre's soldiers and the King's own guard, so there was no chance of speaking with Aimeric. Piet was prepared to wait until his brother-in-law came out, which, God willing, perhaps he would. It was not much, but it was something. He could not possibly have spent the evening in their lodgings. He had briefly returned to the rue des Barres and ascertained from a servant that, though his wife had returned, she had not brought their daughter with her. With a lack of courage that shamed him, Piet had slipped away again and come here in search of Aimeric. He'd known he couldn't face Minou without some news, some hope, however small.

Piet rolled his neck, trying to ignore the cold lump in the pit of his stomach. His confidence that they would find Marta had worn thinner with each hour that passed. Even if Aimeric could spare some of his men to conduct a search, what chance was there that they would find her now in a city of hundreds of thousands of people?

She might no longer be in Paris at all.

Piet closed his eyes, trying to outrun his own thoughts. He had walked Paris again today, from east to west, south to north, returning to every single place they had visited. He was exhausted. His entire body ached, but doing something – even this endless waiting for sight of Aimeric – was better than giving up hope.

CHAPTER THIRTY-FIVE

ORLÉANAIS
Saturday, 23 August

Just after one o'clock in the morning, many hours after quitting Paris, Vidal's entourage arrived at an estate on the outskirts of a small town. The carriages passed between grey stone gates, continued up a long straight drive, the hooves of the horses loud in the stillness of the night, then pulled up in front of a long, low manor house of grey stone and shallow-sloped, tiled roof.

Louis felt a punch on his shoulder and he was instantly awake, ready to defend himself, remembering the stained mustiness of the monks' robes, the stale communion wine on their breath. The trail of blood when it was over.

'We've arrived.'

Louis had never thought to be thankful to hear Xavier's voice. He was not in Saint-Antonin at the mercy of the priests. He had been saved from that hell.

'Yes, monsieur,' he said, relief making him polite.

Xavier narrowed his eyes suspiciously. 'Take this,' he said, thrusting an ornate wooden casket into his arms with more force than necessary. 'Don't drop it, or you'll feel worse than my boot on your arse.'

Louis struggled down from the back of the carriage. In the distance, the solitary bell of a village church tolled.

'Where are we?' he asked.

Xavier spat on the dry ground. 'Never you mind.'

Louis hid his impatience. 'Is this where we are to stay?'

Xavier pinched his ear. 'No more questions.'

'I was only going to ask what day it was.'

As Louis had predicted, Xavier couldn't resist mocking. 'Are you an idiot! We've only been travelling for a day. And to think his Eminence holds you in regard.'

'Chartres,' he muttered, suddenly remembering the look on his father's face when he'd said the name of the city. Louis had a fleeting pang of guilt, remembering the girl, but he smothered it. Someone would find her soon enough, no harm done.

Xavier grabbed his arm. 'Who told you we were going to Chartres?'

'No one! I guessed.'

'You'd better keep your mouth shut.'

The coach rocked as Vidal stepped out of the carriage, and walked past them both without a word into the long and narrow house. Xavier bowed.

In the darkness, Louis smiled. Not only was Xavier unaware it was his father who'd confirmed where they were headed, but now he'd learnt there was some secrecy surrounding their destination.

RUE D'ORLÉANS

'It wasn't my fault!' Marta cried, jolting awake.

For a moment, she couldn't remember where she was. Such strange dreams she'd had. She blinked and her eyes adjusted to the dark: the blue walls, the cushions on the settle, the curtains at the long windows, and she remembered.

The boy – Louis – had brought her in here to rest. He'd

promised to be back soon with her father. Had she slept? She must have slept, for her neck was stiff and her stomach felt funny and her head was all woolly. She swung her legs from the settle and tried to walk, but her feet were as heavy as stones.

'Louis . . .' she said into the empty room, as if he might be hiding.

She wondered if her uncle would be sad if the admiral died. Then she thought of baby Jean-Jacques and, annoying as he was, she felt the tears well in her eyes.

Louis had told her to stay in the blue room until he came back with her father, but that must have been hours ago because the sky outside was now black. Had he forgotten about her?

Marta kicked her heels against the wooden frame of the settle, unsure of what to do. Louis was a boy and was as stupid as all other boys, but he was amusing.

'Come back,' she whispered. Her voice seemed very small and insignificant in the dark, echoing chamber. Tears spilled from her eyes and started to roll down her cheeks. This was a situation of her own making, her own fault. Marta wished she was in her own bed listening to the ugly snoring of their nurse, even Jean-Jacques' snuffling night-time sounds. She would never be impatient with him again. She would never be disobedient again.

Marta shuffled to the end of the settle, paddled her hands around in the dark until she found the table with the tray Louis had brought. She picked up the jug with both hands and poured. The sweet ale was warm now with a film on the surface and tasted sour, but it slaked her thirst. Marta drank it all, then she curled her legs up under her again, put her head on her arms, and waited. Louis would return as soon as he could. She trusted him.

A pleasant drowsiness came over her. Quickly, she drifted back into a heavy and dreamless stupor.

'Maman,' she murmured, as sleep dragged her back under.

ORLÉANAIS

At sunrise, Louis was woken and ordered to fetch the box they had brought with them from Paris.

Xavier watched him like a hawk, as he marched him through the house, which made Louis wonder even more about what he was holding in his arms.

'In here,' the steward grunted, shoving Louis into a well-appointed chamber at the rear of the building.

'Where shall I—?'

'Where do you think, idiot? There, on the table. Careful! Keep it level.'

In the gloom of the narrow room, lit only by the early morning, Louis staggered past the cold hearth towards the long refectory table in the middle of the room, and slid the box onto it.

'Now get out.'

'Where should I go?'

'The stables, the kennels, the privy, I don't care. Just do not be here when his Eminence arrives. He wishes privacy.'

Suddenly desperate to know what was in the casket, Louis looked around the room until he saw what he needed. Edging sideways, he kicked a piece of wood that had fallen from the grate as hard as he could. As he'd hoped, Xavier spun round in the direction of the noise, fearing a mouse or something worse. In that fleeting second, Louis quickly opened the box, looked inside, and closed it again.

He smiled. Now, the visits to the Sainte-Chapelle made sense. The question was why?

'Still here, vermin?' Xavier growled, his eyes darting around for a pair of red eyes.

'I'm leaving. Shall I bring you something to drink or to eat?'

Xavier jabbed him in the chest with his finger. 'You might have deceived his Eminence with your willingness to please, but not me, boy. Get out of my sight or I'll take a strap to you. I won't tell you again.'

CHAPTER THIRTY-SIX

RUE DES BARRES

As dawn came creeping over the window sill, Minou heard a sound in the hall below. Instantly, she was on her feet.

'Marta?'

Her shoulders and neck were stiff with a night spent dozing in the chair. She had persuaded Salvadora to retire to her bed at about three o'clock in the morning, then returned to the chamber. She must have fallen asleep.

Minou heard a creak on the stairs, then Piet appeared in the doorway, his clothes creased and dirty with the streets of Paris. A moment of hope was followed instantly by a sickening disappointment when she saw he was alone.

'You didn't find her,' she said in a voice heavy with despair.

'No.'

Minou handed him her white kerchief to wipe his face. 'Here.'

'You?'

'No,' she replied, and watched the last hope drain from his face.

'I searched everywhere, Minou. Every single place we have visited in the past three weeks and then every single place Marta has ever mentioned – the Sainte-Chapelle, Notre-Dame, Saint-Jacques-de-la-Boucherie, the Pont du Change – but nothing.' His shoulders were slumped with defeat. 'No one could remember seeing a little girl in a blue dress, not a soul.'

Minou sank back into the chair, clutching the armrest as if to anchor herself.

'Where have you been, Piet? I have been so worried.'

'I did briefly return at five o'clock, but when the servant told me you had returned alone, I went straight out again to keep on looking.'

Minou shook her head. 'After all we have said about trusting one another, you didn't think to tell me?'

'I didn't want to disappoint you,' he replied quietly. 'I'm sorry.'

Piet put his hand on her shoulder, an apology or an act of reassurance, Minou wasn't sure. She covered it with hers. She was too weary to quarrel.

'Where did you spend the night?'

'In the rue de Béthisy.'

Minou felt a glimmer of hope. 'Did you see Aimeric? I tried earlier, but I couldn't get anywhere close. All the streets around about were blocked.'

Piet poured himself some wine and sat down. 'There was an attempt on de Coligny's life yesterday when he was coming back from the Louvre Palace.'

Minou sat up. 'What! Does he live?'

'His injuries are serious, but he's expected to survive. The assassin took aim from a property said to be owned by the Duke of Guise – which may or may not be significant. Anyone might have got access. There is a heavy guard around de Coligny's lodgings now. Even the King himself came to pledge his support and to vow he would spare nothing to hunt down the assassin.'

'How did you get past the guards?'

Piet rubbed his fingers together. 'A coin in the right pocket.'

'But did you talk to Aimeric?'

'No. I waited all night, in case he came out of the lodgings, but nothing. In the end, I persuaded a soldier – one of Navarre's men – to deliver a message to him about Marta.'

Minou sighed. 'So we have no way of knowing if he received it, and is looking for her or not?'

Piet shook his head. 'As soon as it is day, and the watch has changed, I'll go back to the rue de Béthisy and try again to make contact with Aimeric.' He let his hands drop. 'I'm sorry, Minou. I did what I could.'

But not enough, she couldn't help herself thinking. It wasn't enough. Their daughter was still missing.

'Something else happened while you were gone,' she said. 'Cornelia van Raay is here.'

Piet put his goblet down on the table, slopping wine over the rim. 'When did she arrive?'

'Late in the afternoon. She saw Marta leave the house, somewhere between nine o'clock and ten yesterday morning. There is some comfort in the fact that we know she went of her own accord.' She caught her breath. 'She was not taken.'

From the expression on Piet's face, Minou realised he had also feared the same.

'That is something, at least.'

'Cornelia said she looked happy and excited.'

'What else did Mademoiselle van Raay say?'

'Very little. She had indeed called before and she is in Paris on her father's orders to seek you out. But before we could talk further, she was struck down with another bout of the food poisoning that had confined her to her quarters for the previous three days. I put her to bed upstairs.'

'Thank you, Minou.'

'You can talk to her yourself as soon as she wakes. Before we go back out into Paris to keep looking for Marta.' Minou looked over to the window. The rising sun was giving shape back to the skyline of Paris. 'We will find her,' she said. 'And as soon as we do, I want to leave for Puivert. I can't bear to remain here a moment longer than we have to.'

CHAPTER THIRTY-SEVEN

EVREUX ESTATE
ORLÉANAIS

The old Roman road ran west out of Chartres, cutting a swathe through the flat countryside.

Louis sat very still. The sun was rising behind them as the team and coach slowed. The chain clattered and the wheels creaked as they turned. Then, with a crack of the whip, they were off again – the drop of hooves on the dry ground, the rattle of bridle and bit, hot white breath in the warm morning air. The carriage started to rock from side to side as they picked up pace on a long straight approach which led into the heart of a vast country estate.

Louis stared at Xavier, his head nodding on his chest, then across to his father. His eyes were closed and he held his biretta upon his lap, but he doubted his father was asleep. Since leaving Paris, Louis had not seen him let down his guard even once, not even in the privacy of his own coach.

'What is it?'

His father's voice, loud in the quiet, confined space, made him jump.

'Nothing,' he said quickly. He hadn't realised he'd been staring.

His father glanced at him, then folded his bare hands over his hat and returned to his thoughts.

'Very well, then.'

Louis lifted the curtain with one finger and looked out of the carriage window. Woodland formed a green belt around the perimeter, but they had cleared the trees already and were cantering through open fields. A man with an ox cart stopped and raised his hat as they passed. A little further, Louis spied a scrawny boy driving a gaggle of geese with a stick. For a moment, he felt the familiar sudden lurch in his stomach – as if falling from a high tower and watching the ground rushing up to meet him – when he thought of the life he might have had if he'd been left in the orphanage at the mercy of the monks. Or he could have ended up like that boy, herding animals in a dirty farmyard in the damp of an early morning, living a life of drudgery and tedium. He was determined never to take his good fortune for granted.

The driveway was relatively flat and the swaying of the carriage was soothing. Though he didn't intend to, Louis found his own eyes closing too. In his liminal state, neither wholly awake nor yet asleep, the pretty face of the little girl in the blue dress stole into his mind. He sat up, startled.

'Boy, speak if you have something to say.'

Louis glanced at Xavier, then to his father.

'I was just wondering where we are, my lord?'

A rare smile broke across his father's solemn face. 'Home, Louis. This is to be our home now.'

CHAPTER THIRTY-EIGHT

RUE DES BARRES
PARIS

'Good morning, Mademoiselle van Raay.'

Their visitor hesitated on the threshold of the living chamber. Cornelia looked pale, and her eyes were bleary under her heavy brows, but Minou was relieved she seemed improved.

'Madame Reydon. You have already been more than kind. Again, please accept my apologies for my indisposition yesterday. I had thought myself recovered.'

'It was no trouble. Please, do join us.'

Cornelia took a step into the room. 'I don't want to intrude.'

'You are not. We've been waiting for you to wake.' Minou gestured across the chamber. 'This is my husband, Piet Reydon.'

Cornelia held out her hand. '*Enchantée*. It is Piet not Pieter?'

'The pleasure is mine, Mademoiselle van Raay.' He smiled. 'And only my mother and Mariken ever called me Pieter.'

'It might not be my place to ask, but is there word of your little girl?'

Minou felt another wave of anguish. 'Not yet. We are about to renew our search, but my husband would—'

'— would be grateful to hear what you have to say before I leave.'

Minou watched Cornelia take stock, then choose the hardest and most upright chair. She was a plain young woman, with honest and broad features, but she showed a clear sense of her own worth. Minou liked her for it.

'You know already, I think, that my father sent me to find you, Monsieur Reydon.'

Piet nodded.

'You know too, then, that Mariken Hassels asked him for help in the spring, having received a letter that greatly troubled her.'

'Do you – or did she – know the author of the letter?' he said, glancing at Minou.

'I regret not. Only that he was a cardinal in France. Mariken told my father she had written to you. Did she not say?'

'No. She gave no name.'

Cornelia frowned. 'My father did what Mariken asked of him, then sent me to report his findings to her: namely, that you had survived your infancy, that you lived now in Languedoc with your family, that you were a Huguenot and known to be a supporter of the rebels in Amsterdam.' For a moment, amusement lit her eyes, transforming her features. 'That was uncomfortable for him.'

'You are Catholic?'

'My father is a good and pious Christian, Madame Reydon. He is also a businessman and war is bad for trade.' Her lightness faded. 'I went on the ninth of June to Begijnhof. This is where things become muddled. The Mistress of the community told me – unwillingly, I might say – that Mariken had, without permission or any prior indication of her intentions, left the community. The Beguines are not nuns. They are, in theory, free to come and go, but not without permission from the Mistress.'

'Are you saying Mariken has disappeared?' Piet said.

'It seems so.'

'When?'

'The Mistress would not, or could not, tell me.'

'And there's been no word from Mariken since June?'

'No, madame. There have been many assaults on convents and monasteries in Amsterdam, as the Calvinists gain the upper hand in the countryside. My father thought it possible Mariken might have sought sanctuary elsewhere, though he has not been able to find her.'

Piet shook his head. 'Surely she would have told your father if she was going to another order?'

'I believe she would, yes.'

'Where do you think she is?'

'I think she has either gone into hiding to avoid the attentions of this cardinal or—'

'Something has happened to her.'

Cornelia nodded. 'When I had my audience with the Mistress of Begijnhof, I am certain someone was listening to our conversation.'

'Who?' Piet said quickly.

Cornelia raised her hands. 'I don't know.'

Piet frowned. 'In her letter to me, Mariken divulged that the cardinal was requesting information about my childhood. Did she confide anything more to your father?'

'She told him only that there were documents – pertaining to your parentage – that your mother had entrusted to her. Mariken gave them to a friend for safekeeping, intending to retrieve them and hand them to you when the time was right.' Cornelia shrugged. 'Again, whether she did so, or if the papers are lost now, that also I do not know. I'm sorry.'

Piet sat back. 'So that's it. We're at a dead end. Mariken is missing, so there is no way of learning where the documents are or why they matter. After all this time, we can go no further.'

'I would not believe that, Monsieur Reydon. My father

continues his inquiries in Amsterdam. But I would say this. He is a pragmatic man, not prone to strong emotions. He believes that whatever is at stake, whatever the information about your parentage might or might not be, it matters to someone a great deal. You have a dangerous enemy. My father bid me warn you that you should take great care.'

'You think Mariken is dead,' Minou said, more a statement than a question.

'Sadly, I do. Killed either by, or on the orders of, the author of the letter. The cardinal.'

Their conversation was suddenly disrupted by the sound of footsteps on the stairs. Everyone spun round as the servant entered the chamber.

'Is there news?'

'I'm sorry, my lady, no. Monsieur Reydon asked me to let him know when we were ready. There are some twenty men gathered below.'

Minou looked at Piet. 'What men are these?'

'It is possible Aimeric received my message,' he said, 'but even if he did, I thought it wouldn't do any harm to gather our servants, and any who might be spared from neighbouring houses, to help us look for Marta.'

And though yet again Piet had failed to tell her what he was doing, tears pricked at Minou's eyes at the thought that she had doubted his resolve.

Piet lightly touched her hand. 'Will you come with us?'

Minou hesitated, then shook her head. 'I want to be here when you return. But might I impose upon you to stay with me, Cornelia? I would be grateful for the company.'

'It would be an honour, Madame Reydon.'

Minou turned back to her husband. 'Bring her home, Piet. Bring Marta home to me.'

CHAPTER THIRTY-NINE

Though it was only ten o'clock, the August sun was already fierce as Piet and the volunteers mustered in the rue des Barres.

'Thank you all – and your masters for releasing you – for your assistance in this matter. You have been told our seven-year-old daughter is missing.' Piet suddenly stopped, fear catching in his throat. 'I am confident that, together, we can find her. You all either know Marta by sight, or have been given a description. When last seen, she was wearing a blue dress and a white cap with her initials embroidered in red upon it.'

Piet looked around the group. Several heads nodded.

'I do not underestimate the difficulty of our task. Each of you has a quartier to search. Ask whatever questions you see fit, go to the places that only you, as Parisians, might know. When you have done what you can, return here and report to my wife. Each man will be given a sol for his trouble and a gage of ale. *Bonne chance*, and may God go with you.'

The sun rose higher in the endless blue sky. The hours passed. The afternoon began to paint long shadows on the buildings. One by one, each of the men returned footsore and disappointed to the rue des Barres, where Minou, Cornelia and Salvadora were waiting.

Only Piet kept going, trying to escape his treacherous thoughts. Tracing and retracing his steps of the previous day, asking the same shopkeepers and tavern owners the same question, yet hoping for a different answer. He was exhausted. His entire body ached, but he could not bring himself to give up.

When night fell, Piet returned to the rue de Béthisy. Twice before during the day he had been turned away at the end of the street. Piet knew it was foolhardy and dangerous even to try to gain admittance to de Coligny's lodgings, but he had to speak to Aimeric. Whatever happened, he had to be able to tell Minou he had done everything he could. He could not face her otherwise.

He was in luck. The guard took his bribe.

'My thanks, friend,' Piet said, handing over another sol. 'All quiet tonight?'

'For now,' the sentry said. He tried the coin with his teeth, then waved him through. 'But I wouldn't tarry, if I were you.'

'I am in your debt.'

Piet slipped under the cordon and into the street. Keeping low and in the shadow of the overhang of the houses, he quietly made his way past the half-timbered buildings towards Admiral de Coligny's lodgings. He noticed some of the houses now had white crosses marked on their doors, the paint still wet.

As he moved closer, hoping for a clearer view, Piet's foot kicked something lying on the ground. He bent down and picked it up. A piece of old cloth rag, stained with blood, lying trampled in the dust.

Then he realised what it was and the world stopped turning.

CHAPTER FORTY

RUE D'ORLÉANS
Sunday, 24 August, Feast Day of St Bartholomew

When Marta woke up again, she was surprised to find it still dark. She felt as if she had been asleep for a long time, yet it still seemed to be night.

She sat up. Her head hurt and her left foot had gone numb from where she'd been lying on it. She pressed her fists to her stomach, to stop it rumbling with hunger. She desperately needed to use the privy.

On legs that didn't feel they belonged to her, Marta stood up and walked gingerly to the window. She stared, then unlatched the casement, not quite trusting her eyes. White crosses had been daubed on the doors of most of the houses in the street below. She frowned, then giggled at the thought of how furious Great-aunt Salvadora would be if someone spoilt their door like that. So far as Marta could see, only three houses in the whole street had been spared.

Marta tapped her toe impatiently, folding and then unfolding her arms, at a loss what to do. Louis should have been back from the rue des Barres by now; he had been gone for hours and hours.

She turned back to the room. Was she not a guest in this house? It was discourteous that she had been left so long alone. She would find a servant and ask for them to bring her something to eat while she waited.

Marta walked to the door and turned the handle. Nothing happened. She tried again, using both hands, but her fingers kept slipping and the door would not open. After a few more attempts, Marta thought to poke her little finger into the keyhole, and felt cold metal.

She was locked in.

In a fury, Marta rattled the handle, then started to shout and bang the door. But despite her noise, the corridor beyond the chamber remained completely silent.

A shiver went down her spine. Someone must have heard her, so why did no one come? Marta took a step back from the door. Was it Louis who had locked her in? She felt a surge of anger. If he had, he had made a mistake thinking he could trick her.

'Boys are fools,' she muttered, as she looked around for what she wanted. 'Ah!'

Taking a sheet of music from the virginal, testing it between her fingers to make sure it was stiff enough, Marta ran back to the door. Lying flat on the floor, she threaded it through the gap until it was set directly beneath the keyhole on the far side. Then she took a pin from her hair, rotated it in the lock carefully, back and forwards, until the key dropped with a clang on the other side. Her heart racing, she put her eye to the lock and saw, to her relief, it had landed on the manuscript paper. Now all she had to do was pull it beneath the door into the room, and she'd be free. Lying on her stomach, Marta carefully slid the music sheet back under the door into the room, bringing the key with it.

'There.' Marta jumped up. 'Boys are stupid.'

In triumph, she slotted the key into the lock, opened the door, and emerged. She couldn't wait to tell Aunt Alis all about how clever she had been when they got home to Puivert.

The corridor was empty. Marta walked on her tiptoes, nervous of being caught, but the further she went without being challenged, the bolder she became.

As she walked through chamber after empty chamber, her pride gave way to unease. She could hear nothing. Marta didn't understand. No voices, no footsteps, no sounds at all. Everyone had gone. She was quite alone inside this beautiful house.

On the ground floor, Marta turned a corner and came upon a long passageway with plain walls. There were no wall hangings nor portraits, nothing but a door at the far end.

Slowly, she turned the handle.

RUE DE BÉTHISY

Piet looked in disbelief at his daughter's linen cap in his hands. Why was it here? A thousand questions were clamouring in his head, each more terrifying than the last.

Marta had been here, surely. But where was she now? Piet ran his fingers over the three red embroidered letters – M R J. The stitching was stiff and stained with dried blood. The horror of it caught in his throat.

Was his daughter dead?

Over the rooftops of Paris, the tocsin bell began to ring the alarum. Piet's head jerked up. It was a call to arms. Then behind him, the sound of horses' hooves. Piet threw himself back into the shadows only just in time as a battalion of armed men thundered into view at the far end of the rue de Béthisy, each of them wearing a white armband. In a flash of crowding images, he recognised the colours of the Duke of Guise, the livery of the Swiss Guard, and the insignia of the King's brothers, the dukes of Anjou and Alençon.

He watched with mounting dread as the group came to a halt outside Admiral de Coligny's lodgings. Rather than challenge them, the musketeers at the gate laid down their arms. Piet felt his guts twist in his belly. Whoever had ordered the first attack on the admiral, there was no doubt this second action was authorised by the Louvre Palace itself.

The guards stood aside and allowed the soldiers to enter. There was a moment of stillness, then a cry went up and the King's men swarmed into the compound with their weapons drawn.

'Kill the traitor!'

A bloodlust seemed to come over the swarm of men. Not only within the walls of the compound, but in the street itself. Soldiers with white armbands began breaking down any door not painted with a cross and, suddenly, Piet realised: the white crosses marked the Catholic houses from Huguenot, the white armbands identified attackers from their victims. When, in the distance, he heard the first echo of cannon and gunshot, his blood seemed to turn to ice in his veins. This was bigger than anything he had imagined. Not a single act of murder against de Coligny. They intended to kill them all.

Piet risked a last glance at the lodgings, then forced himself to turn. He had no choice. He had to get back to the rue des Barres as quickly as possible before the killing spread further afield. He could do nothing to help Aimeric now – he was but one man against many.

His duty was to his wife and family. He could only pray that he was not already too late to save them. His heart aching for his lost daughter, he pushed Marta's cap into his pocket. His fingers touched cloth. Piet pulled out the kerchief Minou had given him earlier. Though grey with the grime of Paris, it was white enough to pass. It might protect him.

Quickly, Piet tied it around his arm. He ran through the labyrinthine alleyways of Paris, the memory of his younger life as a soldier and a spy pounding in his muscles. He had no idea that every step was taking him further away from his last chance to save his daughter.

RUE D'ORLÉANS

Marta stood paralysed with fear. This room frightened her, though it was filled with beautiful furniture and exquisite wall hangings. There was a huge desk, with all the drawers standing open as if someone had left in a hurry, and a huge painting of Christ bleeding on the Cross above a small altar, a single prie-dieu set in front of it.

She wanted to leave. But now the bells were ringing. Not the usual bells, but a terrible clamouring. Harsh. Marta had heard an alarum only once before, when their castle at Puivert had been under attack from Catholic soldiers. It hadn't lasted long, and she had been very little, but Marta had never forgotten how the tocsin had made every part of her body shake.

Marta forced herself to walk to the window and put her hands to the glass. The world was orange, not black like it should be at night. She realised there were flames leaping up into the sky. Paris was burning.

CHAPTER FORTY-ONE

RUE DE BÉTHISY

'My lord,' Aimeric said urgently, 'we must leave. There is no time to waste. Do you not hear the tocsin?'

'I do,' de Coligny replied. 'They are the bells of Saint-Germain-l'Auxerrois, the parish church of the Louvre Palace, if I am not mistaken.'

'But the King posted his own men to guard you,' Aimeric said in disbelief. 'And Navarre's soldiers too.'

'Did you think they would not try again to kill me?'

Aimeric shook his head. 'But the King himself came to ask your forgiveness.'

De Coligny gave a wise smile. 'Whatever his noble majesty believed two nights ago, Joubert, it no longer stands. As for his men, they obey him only for so long as the Queen Mother wills it.'

In the courtyard below, Aimeric could hear the crash of sword clashing against sword, then howls of pain, as the Huguenots tried to defend the house.

'I must help them. We are outnumbered.'

De Coligny took his arm. 'No. Fetch the minister. I would pray.'

'My lord, we should flee.'

'Joubert, it is too late. All we can do now is pray for God to deliver us from this evil.'

Desperately trying to close his ears to the sounds of slaughter below, Aimeric summoned the terrified pastor and guarded the door while the minister stumbled through the prayers.

'Amen,' de Coligny murmured.

Aimeric helped him up from his knees.

'Now I am ready to die in God's grace. Pastor, you may go if you wish.' De Coligny looked around the chamber at his personal guard. 'As may you all. I thank you all for your honest service, but they have come for me. Save yourselves and go in the light of God's love.'

'I will not leave you, my lord,' Aimeric said, as the pastor pushed past in his haste to be gone. 'I took an oath.'

'Joubert, you must,' de Coligny said urgently. 'I need you to take this.' He reached into his private chest and pulled out a manuscript. 'This is a history of our turbulent times, the battles we fought – those we won and those where God was not with us – the peace we struggled to find, the war for faith and for land. I entrust this manuscript to you. I would that my words should live on long after I have been laid in the ground.'

'My lord, if I leave, you will be unprotected.'

The admiral met his gaze. 'If my death spares many others, you included, Joubert, then so be it. It is God's will.'

'I cannot let that happen.'

'This is the last order I will give you. I fear that tonight is about more than just ridding the world of one old servant of God. Find a Catholic house and take shelter there. Avoid our allies, keep away from our safe houses. Do you understand, Aimeric?'

The admiral's unaccustomed use of his given name brought him up quickly. His duty was to obey.

'I do.' Steeling himself, he took the manuscript and bowed. 'My lord, it has been an honour to serve you.'

'God speed, Aimeric. Until we meet again, and we will. Have no fear, for God is with you.'

Aimeric bowed again, then he unlatched the window and climbed out onto the roof at the rear of the building. Behind him, the door splintered as de Coligny's murderers stormed the chamber.

Clutching the precious manuscript beneath his chemise, Aimeric clambered across the rooftops until he could go no further.

He removed his black doublet and soldier's hat, and hid them in a chimney. It would not help much. His face was known for one of de Coligny's men. He knew if he was caught, they would kill him and the papers would be lost. Gauging the distance between the houses ahead, Aimeric decided he could jump it. Provided the soldiers did not look up, he could make for the Catholic heartlands surrounding the Louvre Palace and find somewhere to hide until the worst was over. After that, he had no idea. Only that he had this last duty to fulfil for Admiral de Coligny.

He thought of the games he and Alis had played in childhood, scrambling on the battlements of the walls of Carcassonne, vaulting from parapet to parapet in La Cité. Then he raised his eyes to God, prayed to be delivered safely to the other side, and leapt.

CHAPTER FORTY-TWO

RUE D'ORLÉANS

'In here,' the young Huguenot pastor whispered, leading what remained of his congregation through elegant gardens to an empty stable block. He could not imagine how such a grand house came to be deserted, but there was nowhere else to hide. He barricaded the door with a wooden plank, and gestured that the ladies should conceal themselves at the back of the stalls while those men who could bear arms, should find any weapon they could – a pitchfork, a shovel, a length of wood. Anything would do.

He knew it would not be long before they were found. The flimsy doors of the stables would not hold out against an onslaught of swords and boot leather.

The pastor pushed his hands beneath his robes so his companions couldn't see how they shook with terror: four men – one badly injured – and two women. His courage faltered again at the memory of the servants lying slaughtered in the rue de Béthisy, next door to where they had gathered to worship. A simple service in a private house, permitted under the terms of the peace. They should have been safe.

The pastor swallowed hard. His bowels had turned to water, but he was determined not to surrender. His body was strong, from a childhood working the land before God called him. He would fight to protect his flock.

'Merciful Lord, protect us from Thy enemies,' he said, picking up a pitchfork and gesturing to the men to do the same. 'Confound Thy foes . . .'

The pastor couldn't be sure if it was in his head or the street outside, but he could hear the sound of hooves getting closer, the battle cry of men driven by hatred, and he knew there would be no deliverance, no mercy.

'*Mes amis*,' he said, spreading his arms. 'Let us pray.'

Their pursuers were in the gardens now, the white armbands tied around their sleeves vivid in the filtered moonlight. The younger woman – she was no more than a girl – began to cry.

'Join with me,' he whispered. '*Que Dieu Se lève, et que Ses ennemis soient dispersés; et que fuient devant Sa face ceux qui Le haïssent.*'

Under the force of the soldiers' boots, the horizontal beam of the stable door started to bow, then fractured in two.

'Let God arise,' the pastor repeated, lifting his voice higher still. 'Let His enemies be scattered. May His foes flee before Him.'

He turned to face their attackers. There were fewer than he'd thought and, for an instant, he wondered if they might hold them off.

The ringleader, his face blazing with contempt, stepped forward.

'We have done nothing wrong.'

'Yet you fled.' The captain's voice was swollen with contempt and power.

'In our shoes, would not you have done the same?' For a moment, the pastor held his tormentor's gaze and allowed himself to hope.

'We are all God's creatures.'

One of the other soldiers laughed. 'Shall I kill him, Cabanel?'

'No, he's mine.'

A moment of stillness was broken by the rasp of a sword drawn from its sheath and a flash of steel as the blade slid in. The pastor's eyes widened in surprise. He looked down, saw the hilt protruding from his belly and felt warm blood soaking his black robes. Then, the suck of the blade being pulled free in a slither of flesh and guts. Only then did the pain hit him and he staggered back.

'Do what you will with them,' Cabanel said, gesturing to the women. 'Then kill them. All of them.'

'No!' the pastor cried, as he fell down onto his knees. He had to protect them. Their souls were in his hands.

But these were hunters in need of sport. Their blood heated, they were prowling and jibing, tormenting their victims with the tips of their swords.

'Heretic vermin.'

The older woman screamed as her hood was dragged from her head exposing wisps of white hair beneath. The girl tried to run, but was struck by a blow to the side of her head and went sprawling to the ground. Blood bloomed on the pale, dry straw. One man tried to intervene, but the soldier struck him too and he fell, insensible, beside the girl.

The pastor tried to crawl towards the girl, but his body was failing him now.

'In God's name, let her be. Only the Lord can save you,' he continued, though his head was spinning. 'You are steeped in sin. Repent. Atone for these ill deeds.'

His eyes were flickering shut.

'Let my cry come unto Thee, O Lord,' he said, but the words moved silently on his lips and dissolved like mist.

The man they called Cabanel crouched beside him, put the tip of his dagger into the corner of his eye.

'You are a traitor to the Crown,' he said. 'An enemy to France.'

The pastor felt the blade press into his eyeball, and he shrieked in a final agony.

'Huguenot scum, all of you. Tonight has been a long time coming.'

'*Mon capitaine*,' one of the soldiers cried and everyone cheered. 'To Cabanel!'

As the pastor's lifeblood drained away, he had a last glimpse of the deserted gardens as the stable door swung back and forth on its hinges. He suddenly thought he saw a child in the house, standing at a window with her mouth wide in horror. Or perhaps she was an angel come to carry him into the light.

Concealed on the other side of the gardens, Aimeric bowed his head and prayed for the souls of his sisters and brothers.

He was a soldier. To have watched the slaughter and done nothing surely was a sin, but what choice had he? If he was to keep safe the manuscript that Admiral de Coligny had entrusted to him, he had to remain hidden. It could not fall into the hands of men such as these. The truth must be heard. De Coligny's words would ring down the ages.

Aimeric tracked the progress of the soldiers across the gardens. He had lost his bearings several times in the dark and the chaos of his flight across the rooftops, but he thought he might be in the rue d'Orléans. He had observed this building only from behind its high walls, another of the fine houses owned by the Guise family. It seemed oddly dark.

A movement in a downstairs window drew his gaze. Small hands against the pane. A child? Aimeric narrowed his gaze and tried to see more clearly, but there wasn't enough light. Then, he heard the sound of breaking glass and he realised, with dismay, the soldiers were storming the house.

His conscience burdened by what he had already witnessed, Aimeric knew this time he had a choice. If there was a child, alone and abandoned inside, he had to act.

CHAPTER FORTY-THREE

Numb with horror, Marta took her hands from the window and stepped back. She thought her heart might stop.

There was so much blood. She looked down at her hands, as if expecting to see it there, too.

Then she heard the noise of glass shattering and knew the soldiers were in the house. They had killed those people, two women as well as the men, and now they were coming to kill her, too.

Marta knew she should hide, but her legs wouldn't work. She was pinned to the spot, rigid like the blackbird she had once found frozen to the icy ground one winter's morning in Puivert. In any case, what good would that do? Those people had been hiding in the stables and the soldiers had killed them all the same.

Marta felt a warm trickle down her legs. She looked down and saw a golden puddle around her shoes. Great-aunt Salvadora would scold her for that, but now she wouldn't mind, because that would mean she was safe at home with her family and everything was as it was supposed to be.

Then she heard the sound of boots in the corridor and, finally, Marta found the courage to run. She threw herself into the gap beneath the huge oak desk, pulled her knees up to her chin, and tried to make herself as small as possible. She was shaking with fear, but she had to be brave.

The door was flung back on its hinges, smashing into the wall, and the soldiers staggered into the room. Some of them were clutching flagons of ale, others torches, but they were all shouting and cheering one another as if they were at a celebration. Marta shrank further back into the shadows.

But the next moment, she felt a rough hand clamp around her ankle, and she was dragged out of her hiding place.

'What do we have here, then?' the drunk soldier leered, looming over her in his blood-splattered doublet. 'You waiting for us, little girl?'

She opened her mouth to scream, but nothing came out.

'Leave her be!'

At first, Marta thought she was imagining it. How could her Uncle Aimeric be here too? But then she saw her father's dagger in his hand, and she knew he had come to rescue her.

'She's only a child,' he shouted. 'Don't harm her.'

Aimeric turned. As she saw his eyes widen with astonishment, Marta realised that he hadn't known it was her at all. Then her uncle held out his hand. She scrambled to her feet, and tried to run to him.

Everything seemed to happen at once.

The soldier who'd found her flung out his arm and served her a violent blow, sending her flying backwards. Marta's head cracked into the hard corner point of the oak desk, and she fell dizzy to the floor.

Her uncle charged forward, but another soldier stuck out his foot and he fell. Marta screamed as paper seemed to explode from inside his chemise, sheets and sheets of it, scattering all over the floor in front of the altar, and the dagger went skittering from his hand. He tried to stretch for it, but a third attacker stamped on his hand. Within moments, Aimeric was surrounded on the ground, four swords pointed to his chest.

Marta's head was spinning. She felt giddy and sick. She

screwed up her eyes and looked down at her hands. This time, the blood was real.

'I know him,' one of the soldiers said, delivering a vicious kick at Aimeric's side. 'He's one of de Coligny's men.'

'May God forgive you,' Aimeric said, trying to get up, but a second kick sent him flying back.

'I thought we'd got all the heretics, *mon capitaine*.'

'Here's an eighth for the Devil,' Cabanel spat.

He bent over, grasped Aimeric's hair in his fist, then, in one practised move, cut his throat from ear to ear. Blood pumped over the polished tiles, staining the hem of the white altar cloth red. All over her uncle's papers.

Marta heard herself screaming.

'Stop her mouth,' Cabanel shouted.

The drunk pointed his sword at her. 'Do you want to go the same way? Are you one of them too?' He started to walk towards her. 'Come here, you little whore.'

Marta managed to get to her feet. She started to run towards the open door, but her legs were shaking and she wasn't quick enough.

'Not so fast!' The soldier grabbed her around the waist and spun her up in the air like a trophy. She could feel blood trickling down the back of her neck where she had cracked her head. 'Now what are we going to do with you?'

Suddenly, Marta remembered Louis's words in the rue de Béthisy. She thrust her shaking hand into her pocket and pulled out her mother's rosary.

'One of us,' she whispered.

'What did you say?'

Marta tried to speak again, but now her tongue would not obey her. Everyone paused, then Cabanel waved his hand.

'Are you a Catholic?' Cabanel asked. 'A good Christian?'

Marta hesitated, then nodded.

'Do you live here?'

Terrified, Marta nodded again.

'Whose house is this?' He pointed to her uncle dead on the ground. 'His?'

She shook her head, which made the room spin even more. 'Then whose?'

Marta tried to speak, but all her words had left her. She put her hands together, then made the sign of the cross like she'd seen Great-aunt Salvadora do.

'A priest lives here?' he asked, glancing at the altar. 'Someone important?'

She nodded for a third time.

Cabanel looked around at the opulence, then put out his arms. 'Give her to me. I'll have her taken to my wife until we find out who she belongs to. A wealthy household like this, there's sure to be a reward. Someone will claim her.'

Marta's head hurt. She didn't want to go with this man. But her eyelids were fluttering shut and, though she fought not to, she couldn't stop herself dropping forward onto his shoulders.

As she was carried from the chamber, Marta managed to open her eyes one last time. She saw Aimeric, with his untamed black hair, lying on a bed of scattered papers in a pool of his own blood. His eyes were wide open, but his hand had stopped twitching, so she knew he was dead.

Then, nothing.

CHAPTER FORTY-FOUR

RUE DES BARRES

'My love, I beg you,' Piet pleaded.

'I'm not leaving without my daughter!'

It was nigh on three o'clock, some half-hour after Piet had made it back to the rue des Barres, and the sounds of the battle were getting closer. The Reydon family was gathered in the kitchens at the rear of the house, their most precious possessions about them, ready to flee. Cornelia van Raay was tying the last white cloth armband for Salvadora.

'No! I will not leave. I don't know how you can suggest such a thing!' Minou clutched Marta's blood-stained cap in her hands. 'This proves nothing. What if she comes back here and finds us gone? No.'

Piet grasped her hands between his.

'Listen to me. I don't want to leave either, but we must. Can't you hear them? They're getting closer. I've seen them. They're massacring civilians – men, women, children even.'

Minou banged her hand against her chest. 'If she was dead, I would know it. We have to keep looking.'

'That is your heart talking, Minou, not your head.' He stepped closer. 'We covered every inch of the city, you know that. So many people were looking for her, you know that, too. I did everything, I promise you. We have to accept that Marta is gone.'

She met his gaze. 'I do not accept it. I am not abandoning

my daughter,' she said, in a voice that seemed to come from a long way away. 'You can go if you wish to. I'm staying.' She was gripping Marta's cap so tightly that her knuckles were turning blue. 'This proves nothing.'

'Minou, listen to me!' he begged again. 'We are running out of time. We have to go. It's not safe to stay here. The dead lie butchered in the street. This is as bad as anything I've ever seen. The Catholics have shut the gates and set cannons at the Hôtel de Ville. This is a thoroughly prepared and executed plan. They intend to kill us all, don't you understand?'

Minou shook her head. 'This house is owned by a Catholic. The landlord will vouch for us.'

'Lie for us, do you mean?' he countered. 'Even if he did, it wouldn't matter now! The mob has taken over. Whatever else was intended, it's too late. Paris has gone mad.'

'They have let us alone so far.'

Piet wasn't listening. 'Don't you think our neighbours will denounce us as Huguenots to save themselves? The enemy within, that's how they see us. Catholics – decent people for the most part, people like us – have been given licence to turn on us. Don't you remember what it was like in Toulouse in the early days of the war?'

Minou shut her eyes against the images of Toulouse burning ten years ago. The blood and the barricades, the dying men and women laid out in the refuge, row after row after row.

'I remember,' she said finally in a quiet voice.

Piet clutched her arms. 'Well, this is worse, even. Ordinary men – like our landlord – are blocking the streets with chains. Gangs of youths are targeting the quartiers where Huguenots congregate – Saint-Martin, Saint-Eustache, Saint-Honoré – I saw it with my own eyes.' He pulled at the cloth on his arm. 'A white scarf will not deceive them for long.' He suddenly let his hands drop. 'For the sake of Jean-Jacques, for Salvadora, we have to leave.'

Minou looked into the anguished face of her husband, then at her aunt's face flushed with fear and Cornelia van Raay, pale and serious, listening to every word. Last, at her little son sleeping peacefully in his nurse's arms, unaware of how his life lay in the balance. Finally, her resolve waivered.

'If we leave Paris now,' she said, her voice cracking, 'we will never know what happened to Marta. We will spend the rest of our days wondering. Don't you understand? It will destroy us.'

Piet cupped her chin with his hand. 'My heart is breaking too; I can barely breathe or think. Like you, I want to believe she is alive and that she is safe. But the odds are against it. Marta has been missing for two whole days. The longer we delay, the less likely it is we will escape. Think of Jean-Jacques.'

Minou's eyes brimmed with tears. 'Now you are asking me to choose between my son and my daughter?'

'No,' Piet said quietly, 'I am asking you to choose between the living and the dead. Marta is lost, Jean-Jacques is here. He needs you.' Minou heard him catch his breath. 'I need you.'

For a moment, his words seemed to hang in the air between them. Sharp, painful, terrible words, impossible to take back.

She raised her head. 'You understand that if I come with you now, I may never be able to forgive you for forcing me to abandon our daughter? This moment will divide us for ever.'

Now Piet's cheeks were glistening with tears too. 'I understand we have no choice,' he replied, his voice breaking, 'if we are to save what remains of our family.'

Minou felt her heart crack. She knew Piet was right, but so was she. It might be unjust and unfair, but this choice would stand between them for the rest of their lives. She held his gaze a moment longer, then surrendered.

'Very well.'

Piet sighed. 'Thank God. And as soon as I have got you all to safety – and the worst of this terror is over – I will come back to Paris and keep looking for Marta. I give you my word, Minou. I won't relent until I find her.'

But though Minou saw his lips were moving, she heard nothing and his relief at her surrender sickened her. She turned her back on him and took Jean-Jacques from his nurse's arms.

'My love, look at me,' Piet said. 'Please.'

Minou felt oddly calm now, detached from all that was happening, as if she was looking down at the scene from far away.

'Nurse, will you fetch my casket from my chamber. I would not leave that behind. And Jean-Jacques' spinning top.'

'Minou, please,' he begged, trying to take her hand.

She stepped out of reach. 'Cornelia, will you tell my husband what you told me?'

The young Dutchwoman nodded. 'During my time here, I have been staying on one of my father's barges. If we can reach the river, we have a chance of getting out of the city.'

'Where is the barge moored?' Piet asked quickly.

'Upstream of the Place de la Grève. Opposite the Île de Louviers.'

'But on this side of the river?'

'Yes.'

'You think the guards might let us pass?'

Minou closed her ears to the hope in her husband's voice. It was as if he had already forgotten Marta was to be abandoned.

'My father is as well known in Paris as he is in Amsterdam, Monsieur Reydon. He is known for a devout Catholic, having made several endowments to the Église Saint-Merri. We have our own family pew there. So I am hopeful that, if the watchmen on the towers recognise our ensign, they will allow us to pass. If we can get through the checkpoints, and safely downstream without being searched, there's a chance we can reach Rouen, where my father's cargo fleet is anchored.'

'My love?' Piet pleaded. 'What do you think?'

'I agree,' she heard herself answer. 'This is our best hope.'

'Good, I'm glad you agree.' He exhaled. 'We'll be safe. If we stick together. And I will come back, Minou. I promise.'

Minou marvelled at her husband's naivety. If they made it through the barricades, if they got to the water, if they were allowed safe passage on the river, even so she did not believe that any one of them would ever return to Paris again. In the space of these few hours, on the twenty-fourth day of August, the Feast Day of St Bartholomew, their world had irrevocably changed.

CHAPTER FORTY-FIVE

RUE D'ORLÉANS

'Where is he?'

The Duke of Guise looked with a critical eye around the chamber: at the chaos, the drawers pulled open and the papers strewn about the desk and floor, at the blood splattered on the bottom of the altar cloth, then back to the captain standing nervously before him.

Guise's elation at having avenged his father had faded. The triumph of the early hours – of sinking his blade into de Coligny's chest, the approval of his men roaring in his ears, of the admiral's body being thrown from the window and his severed head held up for all to see – had passed, replaced now by an unease as a mass of people, egged on by the musketeers and militia, had started to rampage through Paris. From a specified number of households as agreed by the Privy Council – to rid the world of the 'war Huguenots' – the attacks had descended into indiscriminate violence. Shops were being destroyed, places of worship, even Catholic homes. The mob was out of control and under no one's command. The killings went on.

It was now a little after four o'clock in the morning, though no one could have heard the call to Matins over the continuing cacophony of the tocsin bell. Wishing to escape the fray, Guise had come to seek absolution from his spiritual advisor. Instead of Vidal, he had found a ramshackle, drunk battalion of soldiers in residence and a charnel house in the courtyard.

'What is your name, Captain?' he demanded.

'Cabanel, my lord. Pierre Cabanel.'

'I will ask you again, Cabanel, and you would be wise to answer truthfully. Where is my confessor?'

In the light of the torches, Guise saw fear flicker in the captain's eyes.

'My lord Guise, I don't know who resides here.' He put his hand to his chest. 'Upon my honour, when we arrived we found the place deserted. It has been so for some days, if I were to make a guess.'

Guise held up his hand. 'Explain.'

'We went first to the stables, my lord. There was no fresh evidence of horses having been there.' One of the soldiers stifled a laugh. Cabanel glared at him.

'Why were you here at all, Cabanel?'

'We were in pursuit of heretics, my lord. They'd fled from a house in rue de Béthisy, adjoining the lodgings of Admiral de Coligny. When their pastor led them in here, fearing for the safety of the inhabitants of this house, we followed, knowing, as I did, that many of the houses in the rue d'Orléans are owned by your noble family.' He swallowed hard. 'When they resisted, in self-defence my men were obliged –'

Guise scowled. 'I saw what your men did in self-defence, Cabanel. Get on with it.'

'Having contained the threat, we searched the rest of the gardens and the outhouses, the servants' quarters, then finally the house itself. There was no one here.'

Guise gestured to the bloodied corpse still lying in front of the altar.

'Then who, pray, is this?'

'One of de Coligny's men, my lord. He must have followed us.'

'Carrying this manuscript?'

'Yes, my lord.'

Guise picked up a sheaf of paper, then another. A wry smile appeared on his lips. He clicked his fingers and one of his personal guard came running.

'Gather these papers. Keep them safe. I fancy the Queen Mother might be interested.' He prodded Aimeric's cold body with his boot. 'And get rid of this heretic.'

Cabanel summoned two of his men, who dragged the body from the chamber, leaving a smear of blood on the tiles.

'And there was no one else? You are sure of it?'

The captain hesitated. 'No, my lord.'

Guise took a final sweeping gaze around the room. He did not look convinced.

'This is the house of Cardinal Valentin – Vidal, by his given name. I would be distressed if anything ill has befallen him. But I would be even more displeased were I to discover that he had – of his own accord – taken himself from Paris without permission. That I would consider an act of gross disloyalty.' He produced a coin. 'Do I make myself clear?'

Cabanel's eyes glinted. 'Yes, my lord Guise.'

'If you procure the information I seek, you will be well rewarded for it. I do not care how long it takes, or how much it costs, I would know where Vidal has gone.'

CHAPTER FORTY-SIX

ÎLE DE LOUVIERS

Minou followed Cornelia through the wild streets in the darkness, cradling her son's warm body hidden beneath the folds of her cloak. She could not think, she could not allow herself to feel. Over the sounds of distant fighting, she could hear the rasping sound of Salvadora's wheezing as she struggled to keep up. Staying close to her side, Piet carried her casket with her journal and other treasures in his arm, dagger drawn in his left hand.

Minou could not bear to look at him.

Every step away from the rue des Barres was a betrayal of her daughter. And though her head told her there was no hope of finding Marta in this terror and chaos, her heart told her she was betraying her own flesh and blood.

Many others were heading for the river, so their little band found themselves caught in a huddled stream of refugees. Someone trod on the hem of her cloak, tightening the ribbon at her neck. An elbow dug into her ribs. She was trapped in a miasma of sweat and the sour breath of strangers.

Twice before, Minou had been caught on the streets when anarchy took over. When she was a child of some seven or eight summers, the age Marta was now, in Carcassonne. She could still remember how tightly her own mother had gripped her hand and made her feel safe despite the roar of the mob. How she averted Minou's eyes away from the bodies lynched and twisting on the gibbet.

Then again, ten years ago in Toulouse at the beginning of the first of the religious wars. On that day in May, Piet had thrown himself into the fray, defending those who could not defend themselves. He had stood tall in the face of danger, not run from it. He had shown no fear.

On that day, Piet had saved her.

But now? Though she did not judge his motive – she accepted he was acting out of love for her and their son – his actions were destroying her.

'Everything will be all right, *mon brave*,' she whispered to Jean-Jacques, trying to anchor herself through the love she felt for her son. 'Maman won't leave you.'

The fierce looks on the faces all around them drove Minou on; the hatred and malice transforming decent people into monsters. In this, Piet was right. Paris had turned on them. She realised they could not stay in the city and hope to survive.

They were now at the easternmost point of the city walls near the Bastille, a quartier Minou barely knew.

'This way,' Cornelia whispered.

They turned to the right and walked fast towards the city walls. Piet went to step forward, but Cornelia threw out her hand to stop him.

'Let me. They know me.'

Minou watched a huddled conversation, then Cornelia pressed a coin into the hand of one of the guards on duty. To her astonishment, he unbolted the gate and ushered them swiftly through.

Quickly, Cornelia led them all the way along the Quai des Célestins towards the wharves opposite the Île de Louviers, where several barges were bobbing in the water. Minou walked faster, more nervous now they had nearly made it.

Then, on a gangway ahead, a single word. 'Heretics!'

Cornelia gestured them back out of sight. They waited,

holding their breath, and Minou saw to her horror a mob had trapped a family on a wooden jetty: an old man – the grandfather perhaps – his daughter and three little girls, their sombre clothing betraying them for Huguenots.

'Traitors! Infecting France with your heresy.'

Words, sharp as thorns, baiting, taunting, jeering. Minou saw a bearded man take hold of the grandfather and shove him into the water, then reach for one of the children. The mother attempted to intervene.

'I beg you,' she screamed. 'They cannot swim.'

'Your God will save them if he sees fit,' the man laughed, then grabbed the smallest of the girls and tossed her into the river as if she was nothing.

'We have to do something,' Piet protested.

'It is terrible, but we cannot. They would turn on us too.'

A roar went up from the mob as the mother and the two remaining children were thrown into the stinking river Seine, already a graveyard for too many. Minou put her hands over Jean-Jacques' ears.

Salvadora was sobbing, 'I am too old for such sights. I cannot go on.'

'We won't leave you behind,' Piet said, putting his arm around her. 'Lean on me.'

Minou turned away.

As soon as the mob had moved on, Cornelia beckoned for them to continue.

'It's not much further,' she said. 'The last wharf.'

They stepped down from the quay and hurried along the wooden jetty where Willem van Raay's barge was moored. Two crewmen were waiting by the gangplank, their eyes darting fearfully to left and right. Minou saw relief in their eyes as they stood to attention.

'*Zeg niks,*' Cornelia said. '*Dit zijn mijn vrienden.*'

The barge was one of the finest Minou had ever seen. Sitting low in the water, there was a large central cabin in the middle of the vessel and curved wooden benches along the sides. There were four oarsmen, two on either side, and at the back of the boat, an ensign with the trading colours of Amsterdam and what Minou presumed was the van Raay family crest.

'I told them that you are my friends,' Cornelia said, as they stepped down into the boat, 'and warned them they are to say nothing if we are stopped. Monsieur Reydon, it would be best if you remained out of sight until we are well clear of Paris. Madame Boussay, you, too, perhaps, might be more comfortable below?'

Piet looked as if he wanted to protest, but he accepted Cornelia's advice.

'Come, Salvadora,' he said, 'let me help you. Minou?'

'I will remain here, if Cornelia will permit me.'

'If you wish it.'

Piet hesitated, then took Jean-Jacques from her arms, handed him to the nurse, then offered his arm to Salvadora and they disappeared below deck.

'*Roeien!*' Cornelia commanded the crew.

They immediately untied the rope and hauled it on board. There was a lurch as they pushed the craft away from the jetty. The oarsmen began to row away from the bank and into the middle of the current.

'Good,' Cornelia said, though her face was drawn and pale with worry. 'If there is no barricade at the head of the river, we have a chance.'

The air was filled with sounds of screaming, of cannon, of death. So many people thrashed in the water, crying out as the river and the weeds pulled them under. The sky was bright with fire, orange flames licking the black night sky. It looked as if whole quartiers, on both sides of the Seine, were burning.

Still they kept going, the oars dipping in and out of the water, until they came level with the last of the towers in the city walls.

Then, just as Minou thought they were safe, a shout went up. She turned and saw a boat chasing through the water behind them.

'In the name of the King, I order you to stop!'

The vessel came alongside them. As well as a captain, in royal livery, she could see four archers and two guards with firearms.

'State your business,' the commander called.

'I am Cornelia van Raay from Amsterdam.' Minou marvelled at how calm she sounded. 'I am in Paris on my father's business.' She waved to their ensign. 'His fleet is anchored in Rouen. In the light of what is happening – no doubt some new outrage perpetrated by the Protestants – I judged it expedient to leave.'

The boat bobbed closer, so near that Minou could see the lines of sweat on the commander's brow.

'Why not wait until morning?'

Cornelia managed to smile. 'I would not risk my father's cargo for the sake of a few hours.'

The captain sent his eyes prying up and down the barge.

'What manner of business has your father?'

'He is a grain merchant, monsieur, and a Catholic benefactor.'

The commander put one foot on the edge of the barge, as if staking a claim, and pointed at Minou.

'Who's she?'

'My father's wife,' Cornelia said quickly. 'My lady has been in Paris to visit her relations. We are returning now to Amsterdam.'

'No one else?'

'No one else,' Cornelia lied. She gestured. 'You are welcome to board and see for yourself, monsieur.'

Minou held her breath, praying he would not come on board and that no one below made a sound. Her heart was thudding so loudly in her chest, she could not believe that he did not hear it.

The commander removed his boot and stepped back. 'That will not be necessary, mademoiselle –'

'Van Raay,' Cornelia said, her voice still as clear as a bell. 'My father will hear of your courtesy. God save the King.'

The commander saluted, then his boat turned in the water and headed back towards the bank.

Cornelia stood watching, then collapsed on the seat beside Minou, breathing heavily.

Minou put her hand on the young woman's arm. 'Thank you, Cornelia.'

Her friend didn't answer, just sat clutching the bench with white knuckles. Then she gave a long sigh, and raised her head.

'*Ga door*,' she instructed the crew. Continue on.

Minou touched the old twine betrothal ring that she had made the day Piet had asked her to be his wife. Since she and Piet had found their way back to one another's hearts in Paris, she had worn it every day next to her silver wedding ring. Minou looked down at the twist of twine in her palm, then hurled it out onto the black waters of the Seine. What need had she for such mementos of affection now?

Minou turned around and watched as Paris got smaller and smaller behind them. She wondered if they were merely postponing the hour of their death and if, at this moment, she even cared.

'Forgive me, *petite*,' she murmured into the darkness, still hoping against all hope that Marta was still alive. And that, somehow, she might hear her voice.

PART THREE

AMSTERDAM & CHARTRES
May 1578

CHAPTER FORTY-SEVEN

Six Years Later

ZEEDIJK, AMSTERDAM
Saturday, 24 May 1578

Minou shook the water from her hands. She stepped forward onto the stone terrace that ran the length of the long building and turned them over to dry in the sun.

They were the hands of a working woman now.

After a particularly hard winter and a dispiriting spring of rain, fog and squalling winds, May had arrived suddenly in Amsterdam with clear skies, white-frost nights and warm bright days. The leaves on the apple trees had turned a pale silver-green and clouds of white blossom filled the boughs. The grass was dotted with clover, yarrow, dog daisies and celandine. As the days grew longer, the garden was becoming beautiful again.

'*Doucement,*' Minou called out, as one of the older boys barrelled into a pale, undernourished girl who had not spoken since she'd arrived. 'Be careful, Frans. *Voorzichtig!*'

The boy waved an apology. Minou looked out over the wooden railing that divided the terrace from the orchard, wondering if she should further intervene. Then one of their longest-term residents, Agnes – a child from Brielle whose entire family had been murdered in the early years of the Revolt – put her arm around the new girl and led her away to sit quietly.

'*Voorzichtig!*' Minou called again. Frans took no notice.

She gave a wry smile. Though she'd attempted to master the language, the hard-edged Dutch words felt uncomfortable to her and the bolder children, like Frans, sometimes pretended they did not understand. Still, Minou persisted – so many of their orphans were from Zeeland or Friesland, occasionally Flanders – though often she had to rely on her own children to help. Both Jean-Jacques, now eight years of age, and little Bernarda, who had turned five last week, spoke Dutch as their mother tongue.

She had high hopes of this year's crop of apples in the orchard, a tiny Eden in the heart of the beleaguered city they now called home. Minou knew she should feel lucky. Mostly, she did. She woke each morning with a roof over her head and in the company of those she cared for. And though the streets were often dangerous as the war against Spanish occupation dragged on – as sailors carried their grudges off their ships and into the city, and there was often not quite enough food – their family's survival was a miracle when so many had died. She was grateful for their lives in a world turned upside down. Though it was not God she thanked for their deliverance, but Cornelia van Raay.

From the moment Cornelia had presented herself at their front door in the rue des Barres six years ago – the day Minou thought of as marking the end of her previous life – the young Dutchwoman had become one of their family. She had a strength and a resourcefulness that belied her privileged upbringing. She had got them away from Paris, when most every other vessel was turned back or attacked. In the grim weeks that had followed the St Bartholomew's Day massacre, and the savagery and mob violence incited against Huguenots had spread to other cities in France, Cornelia had hidden them aboard her father's cargo ship anchored in Rouen until it was safe to move on. And it was

Cornelia who had brought them, finally, in the winter of 1572, to Amsterdam. Salvadora had been suffering from gout and a palsy; Jean-Jacques was a bag of bones; Piet was silent, in conflict with himself and his conscience; and Minou, afflicted by sickness from the quickening of an unwanted child in her womb, was still numb from the loss of Marta and Aimeric.

With little fuss, Cornelia also continued to search for the documents entrusted to Mariken. As the daughter of a respected Catholic merchant, she was able to ask questions that Minou, as a Huguenot refugee, could not. But though Cornelia visited cloister after cloister – in search of the friend to whom Mariken had given the papers pertaining to Piet's birthright – she learnt nothing.

Cornelia had found them lodgings, then persuaded her father to help negotiate the purchase of this modest corner plot from the former monastery of the Brown Friars. Like most of Amsterdam's monasteries and convents on the Oude Zijde, the oldest part of the city, taxes had driven the Brown Friars into poverty and out of business. Only the hated Grey Friars cloister, a stone's throw from Minou's front door, had been spared.

Minou looked at their slim, four-storeyed house with pride. Built at the eastern end of Zeedijk, one of the original dykes of medieval Amsterdam that curved along the northern boundary of the city at the harbour, their plot sat on the far corner of a square opposite Sint Antoniespoort, the main gate into Amsterdam from the east.

The terrace gave onto a small orchard, where the children could play in the afternoons. As their makeshift community grew, they needed more space. Willem van Raay had acquired the Brown Friars' old stable block for them to convert into sleeping and living accommodation.

Their *hofje* – almshouse – was arranged along the same lines as the almshouse for Huguenot refugees Piet had previously worked in, in the rue du Périgord in Toulouse. Anyone in need had been welcome. Now, some sixteen years later in Amsterdam, he and Minou cared for scores of displaced children, innocent victims of the wars in France and the Dutch Provinces, who found their way to Amsterdam. Refugees like them. It gave them a chance to express their gratitude to the city that had offered them sanctuary. For Minou at least, it was a way of assuaging the burden on her heart.

Little by little, they had fashioned new lives for themselves in the city of tears, as Minou had thought of Amsterdam when she'd first arrived, broken-hearted. They became accustomed to eating pancakes and perch and soused herring instead of *pan de blat*, goat's cheese and fresh figs, to drinking sour Dutch beer instead of wine from Tarascon; to wearing close-fitted coif bonnets and plain collars rather than embroidered hoods and ruffs. Minou learnt to care for another daughter, Bernarda, born in the spring of 1573, though to her shame she could never learn to love her. Named in honour of Minou's father, Bernarda was blessed with Piet's russet hair and Jean-Jacques' freckled complexion. She looked nothing like Marta.

In the summer of 1573, word finally reached them that, two months after the St Bartholomew's Day massacre in Paris, Puivert had been attacked by Catholic forces. They learnt that Alis, despite her injuries, had managed to escape and was believed to be in the Huguenot stronghold of La Rochelle on the Atlantic coast.

Minou had waited for further news. But the weeks passed, then years, and there was no word. Gradually, she was forced to accept that Alis, like Aimeric and Marta, was lost to her too.

From then on, Minou tried to close her eyes and ears to the ghosts of the past. So when she thought she saw her daughter's face in the stone colonnades of the medieval town hall on Plaats, she turned away. When she glimpsed a black-haired man like Aimeric taking the air in Oudezijds Voorburgwal, or heard a spirited young woman the spit of Alis bartering with a bookseller on Kalverstraat, she knew not to be deceived. She could not let her tattered heart be ripped open all over again.

In the displacement of so many thousands of people, the wars that ravaged France and the Dutch Provinces, the bloody violence of the Revolt against Spanish rule, the day-to-day battle for survival, the hunger and the fragile peace within Amsterdam, the cautious rebuilding of their lives in a new city, stories of the past were forgotten.

Minou told herself all that mattered now was the present.

Willem van Raay, though reserved and formal, took to accompanying Salvadora to Mass each Sunday. He was a pious man, devout in the Catholic traditions in which he had been raised. He worshipped at the Nieuwe Kerk and was pleased to take Madame Boussay with him. There had been a time when Minou wondered if some autumn romance might flourish between the two but, though they enjoyed one another's company, Salvadora did not take to life in Amsterdam. The language, the customs, the confinement, none of it suited her. Her health was poor and the loss of her great-niece, her niece and her favourite nephew had taken its toll. When the Peace of La Rochelle was signed in July 1573, bringing the fourth war to a close – and the travelling roads through France became passable once more – Salvadora had returned to Toulouse.

Minou had been sad to see her go, and fearful for her undertaking. But Willem van Raay had provided an escort for some of the journey, and Salvadora had made it home without mishap. Though news was sporadic, from time to time a letter from her did manage to make its way from Languedoc to Amsterdam. Now she was no longer in Salvadora's company every single day, Minou found it easier to think fondly of her aunt.

And as France herself stumbled from one conflict to the next, bringing a realisation that they could not yet – perhaps not ever – return to Languedoc, Amsterdam had slowly become home.

CHAPTER FORTY-EIGHT

The winters were less harsh in Amsterdam than in Puivert and the air in spring was softer. The land beyond the city walls stretched out flat and wet, a criss-cross of locks and dykes and waterways, so far as the eye could see. Fields of farmed land, windmills and occasional clusters of houses, a church. It was a landscape as unlike the jagged, grey landscape of the Midi as Minou could imagine. Even the light in Amsterdam was different.

Increasingly, Minou came to think of France as somewhere existing only in her imagination. Carcassonne, Toulouse, Puivert – places she had once known and loved – were only memories existing in old dreams as they faded and lost their colour. So, although she tried to hold in her mind the image of the chapel in Puivert where she and Piet had married, the vast wooden vaulted ceiling and the skylight paintings of Sint Nicolaas were more real to her now. And when she tried to remember the feeling of the wind on her face as she rode her bay mare through the Puivert woods on a summer's day, it was instead the rough salt spray of the IJ on her skin that made her feel most alive.

As the months passed into years, Minou became accustomed to living in a world defined by water rather than forest. She crossed the narrow bridges and explored medieval passageways. She walked the whole world of the walled city along broad canals that followed the line of the medieval moat protecting Amsterdam, from Singel in the west to Sint Antoniespoort in the east, and home to Zeedijk. She stood on Damrak and looked south to Heilige Stede chapel where a fourteenth-century miracle had made Amsterdam one of the most visited pilgrim sites in the north. Even in these difficult times, hundreds of Catholics still flocked to the city each March to honour the Miracle of Amsterdam and walk the pilgrim route. Other days, she went to Damrak and looked north to the forest of masts in the deeper water of the IJ. She came to love the sound of the rigging snapping in the breeze in the floating palisade of tall ships in the harbour and the harsh shriek of the gulls calling the sailors home.

All the same, sometimes, when her spirits were low, Minou failed to stop the ghost of her daughter coming to stand beside her. Marta would have loved the seagoing ships and their promise of adventure, the setting sail for other lands. On those deceiving days, Minou glimpsed girls with long brown hair like Marta everywhere: a moment of hope, and Minou's heart would speed up and she would follow. But the flash of blue stayed always just out of reach, and when the dream passed Minou would find herself bereft again, standing alone on an unknown street.

News of the French wars reached them from the stories of merchants and sailors, from the deserting soldiers and villagers fleeing north: of the concessions granted and rescinded; of the death of King Charles and the accession of his brother, the Duke of Anjou, to the throne; of the foundation of the Catholic League led by the Duke of Guise and the escape of Navarre from his long house arrest in Paris to lead the Huguenot forces. Fragments of information carried on the wind and in the sails of the mighty ships and the hulls of the little boats.

The situation was no less fragile in the Dutch Provinces. Brutal suppression of the Prince of Orange's forces by the Spanish, and the destruction of villages and crops, had left the populace homeless and starving. Amsterdam, the sole remaining Catholic city, was suffering economically, losing trade and financial power as the battle for independence dragged on. It was time for that to change. Many of the Calvinists and Geuzen exiled in the early years of the Revolt had started to return to their land and property in Amsterdam.

Piet had been welcomed into their company with open arms. His many years of supporting Dutch independence meant that he was much sought after, as an ally, a leader, and as a friend. During the course of the previous winter and spring, he had frequently attended meetings in Lastage, the shipbuilding and chandler district outside the eastern gates that was home to many rebel Protestants. Amsterdam was returning to him a purpose and vitality that had been lost. Minou tried to be pleased, though the truth was she was angry at how easily he seemed to forget the past: Aimeric missing, Alis missing, Marta gone.

'Frans,' Minou called out, 'this is the last time I will say this. Be more careful! You are too wild.'

'*Het spijt me.*' I'm sorry.

Minou poured herself a cup of ale from the pitcher, then looked for her own children in the crowd. Just as Aimeric and Alis had sometimes been taken for twins in their childhood, despite their difference in age, so Jean-Jacques and Bernarda, though some three years apart in age, were likewise a match. They favoured their father in their colouring. Neither child looked anything like her, or their older sister.

Marta. Minou felt the familiar twist of her heart. She would have been thirteen this summer.

Six years had passed and she and Piet never talked about Marta now. There was little point. Minou remained convinced that if her daughter's life had been taken, somehow she would have known. Piet believed the opposite and thought Minou's refusal to accept the truth held her imprisoned in the past.

She envied Piet his certainty. When her beloved father had passed away, she had thought death was the greatest loss a heart could bear. Now she realised that not knowing what had happened was a different kind of hell. That tiny treacherous sliver of hope, diamond sharp, that refused to die.

They spent time in one another's company, and they were courteous and respectful of one another's opinions. But they lived now more as affectionate friends than wife and husband. Minou had tried to forgive Piet for making her abandon Marta in Paris and for having stopped looking since. This far after the event, she accepted there was nothing else they could have done – the toll of the dead and the missing confirmed it – yet, unfair as it was, she still blamed Piet for not fighting harder. For giving up.

'Mistress Reydon?'

Minou turned. 'What is it, Agnes?'

'There is a person at the front door asking for you.'

Minou raised her eyebrows. 'A person?'

Agnes frowned. 'A man, I think, though slight. He is unkempt, and his hair is short and wild, but his clothes are . . . strange.'

'Strange?'

'I did say you might not be at home.'

Agnes was right to be cautious. From time to time, a mother or a father, who had put their child out onto the streets, turned up at their door demanding restitution. Seeking payment for a child they'd abandoned.

Minou sighed. 'Did this person give you their name?'

'I asked but—'

Behind them, the door onto the terrace banged back upon

its hinges, and the visitor stood unannounced, swaying under the burden of something they were carrying.

For a fleeting moment, her eyes tricked her into believing Aimeric had come back to her. Minou blinked. Then the visitor spoke.

'I have found you.'

At the sound of the familiar voice, Minou's cup fell from her hands, the ale splashing across the flagstones. With tousled black curls cut crooked and short, the visitor looked like a boy rather than a woman of three-and-twenty years, but there was no mistake.

Minou rushed across the chamber and threw her arms around her sister. 'My darling Alis! Can it be?'

'At last,' Alis said, then collapsed in a faint at her feet.

CHAPTER FORTY-NINE

The setting sun was painting the tops of the towers of Sint Antoniespoort a burning red when Piet rushed into the attic room at the top of the house.

'Is it true? Is Alis here?'

Minou looked up from her sister's bedside and smiled. 'Yes. Salvadora would say it was a miracle.'

Piet glanced at Alis lying still beneath the covers. 'When did she arrive?'

Minou looked out through the small, square window and saw it was nearly sunset.

'Early in the afternoon.'

Piet's face was creased with worry. 'Is she hurt? Ill?'

'She is exhausted. She fainted, so we carried her up here. She's been sleeping ever since.' Minou paused. 'I sent Frans to Lastage to fetch you some hours ago.'

Piet ignored her unasked question. 'And she's said nothing in all that time? About where she has been or how she—'

'Nothing.' Minou put her hand out and touched the tapestry. 'Do you remember this, Piet? Alis managed to carry it all the way from Puivert.'

For an instant, Minou closed her eyes, remembering how the light fell on the tapestry hanging in the solar in Puivert while her family talked and lived beneath its gaze. The colours were faded now, but the vibrancy and movement in the stitching was unchanged. The Reydon-Joubert family in their finest clothes. She and Piet adorned in gold thread and silver and jewelled beads, with two-year-old Jean-Jacques in velvet breeches with his wooden rattle and seven-year-old Marta in her vivid blue dress and favourite cap with red stitching.

She opened her eyes to the Amsterdam dusk. 'Where have you been, Piet? Frans said he couldn't find you.'

Piet looked around, as if fearing to be overheard, then closed the door and the window. But for the expression on his face, Minou might have laughed at the idea that their conversation at the top of the house could possibly be overheard in the street.

'Change is coming,' Piet said, his voice stiff with anticipation. 'Hendrick Dircksz is under pressure at last.'

Minou joined him at the window. 'Is he no longer in charge of the town council?'

'For now, the Stadhuis is still under his control, but his influence is declining. The massacres in Naarden, in Haarlem, the wholesale slaughter of women and children by Spanish troops, these crimes are not forgotten. Dircksz held out for too long against signing the Satisfaction. Even now, he refuses to comply with many of the terms.'

'Why did he agree to sign at all?'

'The "Beggars" forced him to at the point of a sword. But –' Piet was warming to his theme – 'by continuing to support the Spanish occupation against the Prince of Orange – when every other major city in the north and west of the Province has joined the Revolt – Dircksz is destroying Amsterdam's prosperity. Too many ships pass us by these days in favour of Baltic ports. Merchants are moving their warehouses to England and Denmark.'

'Commerce, then,' Minou observed, 'rather than sovereignty or faith.'

'Dircksz and his fellow burgomasters bowed to commercial pressure, yes. But if they continue to deny us our churches, they must go.'

'Us?' she asked lightly. 'You mean Huguenots, refugees like us?'

'Huguenots, Calvinists, Protestants, the word doesn't matter. All of the Reformed faith,' he said. 'Dutch, French, even English; that, too, does not matter. Many of the Calvinists exiled from Amsterdam have now returned. I have known many of these men by reputation for some ten years. To now be of their company and to be welcomed as a brother is an honour.'

'I know that,' Minou replied carefully. 'But, from your expression, something specific is going to happen. Isn't it?'

'You should not fear change, Minou.'

'That's a foolish thing to say.'

Piet met her gaze. 'This situation has dragged on long enough. The Dirckists have ruled Amsterdam for forty years. The world has changed, Amsterdam has changed. We need new leaders, a new Holland led from Amsterdam as its capital city. We need to look forward, not back.'

'Should I be frightened?' Minou asked steadily. 'It seems to me I should. For our friends and neighbours, the children. Ourselves?'

'No, of course not. Our intention is that this change of government at the Stadhuis should be peaceable, reasonable, an appeal to common sense.'

Minou looked at her steadfast, honourable husband and saw the worry lines on his brow. His russet hair was faded and grey at the temples now. He was a good father, a good husband, a man of principle, but she saw zeal in his eyes, the light of adventure, and a naivety. She did not find it reassuring.

'There have been reports of nuns paraded naked through the streets, a Catholic priest found mutilated and hanging from a tree outside Schreyershoektoren,' she said. 'After every hedge sermon, where the Calvinists stir up the blood of the crowd, there are rumours of marauding bands beyond Haarlemmerpoort menacing the local populations.'

Piet frowned. 'They are opportunists, vigilantes, nothing more.'

'Dangerous all the same.' Minou sighed. 'And what will happen if the burgomasters and burghers – the Catholic clergy too, I assume – do not go willingly? What if they do not simply cede office to your comrades?'

Piet screwed his left hand into a fist. 'They will, they must. We have men on the inside who think the tide has turned. They believe the time is right and that religious loyalty is no longer the deciding factor. We will give the old guard no option but to withdraw. For the good of Amsterdam, and for our faith.'

For a moment, Minou was silent. Memories of Carcassonne, of Toulouse, of Paris, overcame her. Blood in the streets, families at war. History proved how rare it was for men to relinquish power readily once they became accustomed to it; how men of ambition did not meekly hand over the keys of a city they controlled to those they despised.

'Should we prepare to leave?' Minou asked, though she was doubtful she could survive another exile. Not now Alis was here, too. She had lost one home, she was not sure she could endure the loss of another. 'Tell me, Piet. Should we leave before this "peaceful coup" becomes another massacre?'

'No!' he cried. 'Minou, I give you my word. There will be no blood spilt by our side. We want to protect Amsterdam as a safe and prosperous city for our children and grandchildren, not destroy it.'

'What about Cornelia and her father? Willem van Raay is a burgher on the town council. He is one of Dircksz's men. What will become of him?'

He held her gaze. 'All will be welcome, provided they accept that things are different. This is for the good of all.'

Minou looked at him with disbelief. 'After everything Monsieur van Raay has done for us, after everything Cornelia does, would you turn your back on them? Piet, you must warn him of what is to happen.'

'Warn him?'

'Give him time to prepare, at least.'

'I cannot betray—'

'It is not a betrayal!' she cried, her voice rising. 'Take him into your confidence, Piet. Without him and Cornelia, we would have nothing. We would not have survived.'

They were interrupted by the creaking of the frame of the bed.

'Minou?' Alis murmured.

Putting their quarrel aside, Minou rushed back to her sister's bedside and looked down on the beloved face. She was thinner, and her black curled hair was hacked short, but the spark in her dark eyes was undimmed. At this moment, she looked so like her brother. Minou caught her breath. How could she bear to tell Alis about Aimeric?

'Minou . . .' Alis said, trying to sit up in the bed. 'I am here? It wasn't a dream?'

Minou laughed. 'It wasn't a dream. Welcome to Amsterdam.'

CHAPTER FIFTY

WARMOESSTRAAT

'You rang for me, Father?'

'Come in, my dear.' Willem van Raay ushered Cornelia into their formal room on the first floor, and closed the door behind him.

Devastating fires in 1421 and 1452 had destroyed most of the wooden heart of the medieval city. At the same time, the tragedies had given the opportunity to the modern city of Amsterdam to find its shape and go from being the poor relation of Antwerp to surpassing it in trading power and influence. At the heart of this new commerce were men such as Cornelia's father, Willem van Raay. Sober, honest, pious, but prepared to drive a hard bargain.

Many of the fine red-brick merchant houses on Warmoesstraat, where they lived, were some five storeys high with elegant neck gables and ornate pediments. Steps led up from street level to a narrow front door, with long leaded glass windows to the side. On some houses, above the door, carved decorative tiles of painted plaster and gilt boasted the year of construction and, often, an indication of the occupation of the householder. The tile set between the stone-arched windows of the van Raay house showed a richly dressed man, standing in front of a cargo ship bearing the family ensign, letting grain slip between his fingers into a basket.

Cornelia disliked the ostentation, though she understood it

was important to her father that his success was visible to others, especially now when so many merchants and tradesmen had been driven out of business by the wars. Even in these troubled times, appearances still mattered in Amsterdam.

To the rear of the houses on Warmoesstraat, warehouses led directly to the quay. Through their long, tall windows Cornelia could see the last rays of the setting sun reflecting on the water. Armies of lighters and barges and shallow-hulled boats sailed up and down Damrak from dawn until dusk, ferrying merchandise to the cargo ships moored in the harbour and the ship-building and repair yards at Lastage: grain, hops, cheese, fish, beer, wine, cloth, soap, hemp, timber, nails, rope. In this great trading city, anything could be bartered and sold.

Willem van Raay gestured. 'You are acquainted with our neighbour, Jacob Pauw.'

She glanced at the corpulent man sitting in an armchair, a pewter tankard on the low table at his side. Wearing a white silk padded doublet with gold buttons and red silk breeches, she knew him for a vain man. Even so, he seemed rather over-dressed for a domestic visit. Her heart sank.

'Of course,' she said, inclining her head. 'Good afternoon.'

'Juffrouw van Raay,' the old man wheezed, as he heaved himself to his feet in greeting.

'Sit down, Cornelia,' her father said.

She noticed he, too, was holding a tankard, though the lid was shut. Was there to be a toast? Some kind of arrangement to be celebrated?

Her confidence faltered. Cornelia despised the affected scorn of the women she'd seen in Paris and the shameless social climbing of the daughters of their neighbours as they preened for a husband, but surely this couldn't be the latest suitor her father hoped to persuade her to wed? She was a kind person by nature, but she doubted she would be able to keep a straight face if Burgher Pauw tried to offer her his hand in marriage.

She sat cautiously on the edge of her chair and placed her hands on her knees.

Cornelia knew she was considered plain, lacking in both the feminine qualities and the domestic ones considered desirable in a good Amsterdam wife. Her brows were heavy, her brown hair was coarse. She had broad, honest features. There was no delicacy in her looks. She was twenty-five, so though not yet quite too old to be a new bride she was certainly old enough for the widows in the pews in the Nieuwe Kerk to whisper about and point at.

But her father was wealthy and she was his only child. He wanted a grandson to whom he might pass on the fruits of his labour. In his calculations, Cornelia chose to think he would also like her to be happy. It was just that she knew a husband would not make her happy.

'Cornelia,' her father began. 'I have something I must tell you.'

He pulled at the sleeves of the long, brown robe he always wore at home and she realised, with a jolt, that he was also nervous.

'You may remember some years ago I asked –' he held up his hand – 'of course, I am being foolish. Of course you remember. They are now your friends.'

Cornelia was surprised by the edge of uncertainty in her father's voice. He was not a talkative man, he always weighed every word carefully before he spoke. He was certain, in his faith and his business dealings, and seemed to have few doubts about what was right. Then again, since burgomaster Dircksz had signed the Satisfaction in February, betraying the Catholics of Amsterdam, as her father saw it, Cornelia had witnessed many changes in him. His faith in those with whom he served in the Stadhuis had been shaken.

'Some six years ago, I sent you to deliver a message to Mariken Hassels, may the Lord rest her soul.'

Cornelia sat bolt upright. 'It was the ninth of June, fifteen-seventy-two.'

He nodded. 'When you returned that day, having discovered the honourable lady was no longer in Begijnhof, do you recall telling me you suspected your conversation with the Mistress was being overheard?'

'I do.' She saw the two men exchange a glance, and something of her father's discomfort started to make her uneasy, too. 'What is it?'

Pauw sighed, his breath whistling in his chest. 'It was me. I was concealed behind the screen.'

Cornelia hid her surprise. 'I see. At the request of the Mistress?'

He shook his head. 'No, though she was cognizant of my purpose.'

'Which was?'

Pauw looked to her father, as if seeking permission to answer. 'Tell her, Jacob.'

Pauw exhaled. 'Juffrouw van Raay, there are many things I have done in my life of which I am ashamed. This, chief amongst them. You have to understand my situation. All of my business interests, at the time the Revolt began, were in the west. In the town of Brielle, to be precise.'

Cornelia nodded. Everyone knew that the taking of the western seaport town by the Waterbeggars in April 1572 had been a turning point in the war between the Calvinist rebels and their Spanish overlords.

'When the Watergeuzen took the town, I lost everything. I

came here to Amsterdam, intending to start again, but it was hard to gain a foothold.'

Cornelia looked at his expensive clothes, considered the fact that he was a neighbour on one of the wealthiest streets in Amsterdam and instantly understood.

'Someone offered to help you . . .'

'There did not seem any harm in it,' Pauw said. 'They offered so many guldens, I could not refuse.'

Cornelia glanced at her father but, warned by the look in his eyes, did not say what was on her mind.

'I am sure you thought you were doing the right thing,' she lied.

'A Frenchman in the service of a most eminent cardinal believed one of the lay sisters at Begijnhof – he identified her by name, Mariken Hassels – possessed information about a Huguenot. An enemy—'

'Piet Reydon,' Cornelia interrupted, 'is a friend.'

'Of course.' Pauw flushed and his breathing grew more laboured. 'Yes, of course.' He faltered. 'The monsieur attempted to speak to Mariken directly, only to ask her the question, you understand. He meant her no harm. But she misunderstood and . . . she left Amsterdam.'

'She *left* Amsterdam?' Cornelia repeated. Surely it couldn't be possible Pauw accepted such an explanation? 'Are you saying she went of her own accord?'

Pauw stumbled on. 'The Frenchman was understandably disturbed not only by this, but also by the fact that he was no closer to acquiring the papers his Eminence believed to be in Mariken's possession. Information that could damage our cause.'

'Whose cause exactly?'

'Our Holy Mother Church,' her father answered steadily.

Pauw was suddenly overtaken by a paroxysm of coughing.

'So he approached Jacob for assistance,' her father continued, while Pauw struggled to catch his breath.

'He offered so many guldens,' Pauw managed to say when the attack had passed. 'Enough for me to buy a warehouse and start again. Enough to join the guild.'

Cornelia looked at him, then at her father.

'After Jacob overheard the conversation between you, Cornelia, and the Mistress of Begijnhof, he began to doubt things were as they had been presented to him.'

'This all happened a long time ago.'

'I believe that Burgher Pauw thought the matter was over. Is that not so, Jacob?'

Pauw wiped his mouth. 'The Mistress had Mariken's cell searched, and found nothing. The monsieur also found nothing. Your father tells me that Mariken was an Amsterdammer, born and bred. She had no sisters or brothers, and her parents were long dead. She had never lived anywhere else. You have to understand, I have been mostly away from Amsterdam. The Revolt, the loss of our markets in the west . . . it is only recently I learnt of Mariken's disappearance.'

Cornelia kept her expression neutral.

'I confided in your father. I made inquiries and learnt there was a nun who had worked alongside Mariken at Sint Nicolaas church, around the same time as the death of Reydon's mother. Of a great age now, Sister Agatha is one of the few nuns remaining at the Convent of Sint Agnes on Oudezijds Voorburgwal. I wondered if it was possible Mariken had left anything with her for safe-keeping.'

Cornelia knew the convent. It was one of the few cloisters to which she had been unable to gain access when looking for the missing documents.

'And were you successful, Burgher Pauw?' she asked, struggling to keep the excitement from her voice.

He put his hand beneath his padded doublet and pulled out a package of papers, wrapped in an old piece of grey cloth.

'Take it,' he said, passing the bundle into her hands. 'I am a good Catholic, but to murder – or hound to death – a good woman, who gave a lifetime of service to the Church?' He shook his head. 'That I cannot countenance.'

Cornelia held his gaze. 'What is the true reason you are sharing this with my father only now? You have had six years to repent of your actions.'

He gave a long, thin sigh. 'I am dying, Juffrouw van Raay. The cankers in my throat and my chest are growing. Soon I will not be able to breathe at all. I have no children living, no wife. I would not go to my grave with Mariken's death on my conscience.'

CHAPTER FIFTY-ONE

CHARTRES

In the blue hour between afternoon and dusk, the nobleman and his fifteen-year-old son walked the short distance between their imposing town house on the rue du Cheval Blanc to the cathedral cloister in silence.

Lord Evreux cut an imposing figure in the early evening light. Tall and lean, a nobleman of distinction, his exquisite clothes shimmered with his status and his wealth. He wore a cambric shirt beneath an embroidered doublet, stitched with gold thread and sequins, a stiff lace ruff collar and matching wrist ruffles, padded short breeches and green hose. Rosettes adorned his shoes, the cork soles lifted by the heels made fashionable by the King. His black beard was trimmed to a point, and his tonsured head covered with a stiffened gathered hat, green to match the rosettes. Beneath his short blue velvet cape, he carried a bag of Spanish leather.

The boy knew not to disturb his father's thoughts, but wondered where they were going and why. Usually, Louis was left behind in their country estate to the west of Chartres when his father came to the city.

Not this time. The air seemed to hum with expectation and intrigue.

Moving quickly, father and son passed the Bishop's Palace and continued along the northern perimeter of the great Gothic cathedral the chroniclers called the 'book in stone'. The whole history of the Old and New Testaments carved on the portals, the stained glass to rival even the Sainte-Chapelle.

Louis had only been inside once before, slipping in to look at the celebrated pavement labyrinth.* He'd watched the pilgrims following the Chemin de Jerusalem – some on foot, some on their knees – and had felt a violent revulsion and contempt for a religion that reduced human beings to such unthinking, dumb creatures. Chartres, Paris, Saint-Antonin, the mass of the faithful duped by the mirage of an afterlife, by the false promises of pilgrimage given by self-serving peddlers of lies and hypocrisy. He was unmoved by the Sancta Camisia, the robe supposedly worn by the Virgin Mary and said to have been presented to the cathedral by Charlemagne himself.

But the labyrinth itself was beautiful, mysterious. Carved into the stone floor of the nave, eleven concentric circles curled ever inwards to where a copper plaque of Theseus fighting the Minotaur glistened in the centre. It had pierced his heart like nothing else ever had.

Louis hated it. It made him weak.

'This way,' his father commanded, sweeping into the north transept of the cathedral.

It was the time between Vespers and Compline and the stone spaces were quiet. All the same, Louis could see a priest in a black cassock standing in the shadows outside the door into the vestry.

'Wait here. If anyone approaches, do not let them pass.'

Louis bowed his head. 'Very good, my lord.'

'The matter will not detain me long.'

Louis obeyed just until his father disappeared into the vestry with the priest, then he followed. The door was ill-fitting so,

---

*Labyrinth (2005)

though he could only see a strip of light coming from the room, he could hear.

'Do you have it?' his father was asking.

'Lord Evreux, I do, although . . .'

'Yes?'

'Were it not for your lordship's reputation for fair and honest dealing, I would not mention it. But I fear the expenses which I have been forced to incur, in the acquiring of this object, are in excess of the monies you have made available to me.'

'Is that so?' Evreux replied coldly.

'It is, my lord. The craftsman required the finest thread, which regrettably was not available in Chartres. Not even in Paris. I had to send to Spain.'

'To Spain, indeed! I am impressed by such diligence.'

Louis felt a shiver go down his spine. He remembered what happened when his father used that tone of voice. In an instant, he was back in the ruins of the old monastery in Saint-Antonin.

Evidently the priest heard it too, for he started to stammer.

'It was an honour. I meant no complaint, no—'

'It is incumbent upon me to ensure you receive what is due to you.'

'I am grateful for your—' the priest fawned. His last words were lost in a gasp and a long, painful exhalation. Then Louis heard something thump heavily to the ground.

He moved quickly away. By the time his father emerged some minutes later, Louis was back in his assigned place guarding the approach to the vestry. Evreux was holding a length of yellowed cloth in his hands. Louis fell into step behind him.

'Is all well, my lord?'

Evreux folded the material and put it beneath his cloak. 'Mankind's desire to be deceived is constant. All men are fools. The right words uttered in prayer, enough coins thrown onto the offertory plate, the worshipping of a relic, investing it with power to transform miserable, base lives. All the same, what might be achieved . . .'

He suddenly stopped, as if regretting having shared his inner thoughts, then put the cloth into his leather bag. 'This is to be an addition to my collection.'

Louis didn't understand. 'Your collection, my lord?'

His father paused, then he smiled. 'Our collection.'

CHAPTER FIFTY-TWO

ZEEDIJK
AMSTERDAM

'Here,' Minou said, handing her sister a kerchief to wipe her eyes.

'But they could be alive,' Alis insisted. 'You thought I was dead, but I'm here now. You cannot be sure.'

It was dusk. The sisters were now settled on the bench on the long stone terrace, looking out over the darkening orchard. Minou had told Alis everything that had happened in Paris, and their lives since.

'It is hard to describe what it was like in Paris during those August days,' Minou said, choosing her words with care. 'On the surface, everything was agreed. The wedding would go ahead, the alliance would bring together the Catholic and the Huguenot factions. But beneath the civility the old hatreds were, if anything, even stronger.' She sighed. 'Aimeric was always in de Coligny's company. It is almost certain he would have been there on the night of the admiral's assassination. This, and the massacre that followed in the early hours of St Bartholomew's Day, were part of a deliberate attack on the entire Huguenot community, Alis. Whoever gave the order – the late king, or Guise or Anjou or the Queen Mother – they were united. I do not believe Aimeric can have survived. It was too well planned.'

'Aimeric might have escaped,' Alis sobbed. 'A few did.'

'Most did not. Thousands of people died that night, and thousands more in other cities in the weeks that followed.'

Tears came again to Alis's eyes. 'It seems impossible I will never see him again. How do you accept it?'

Minou took a deep breath. 'I can't, but I have learnt to live with it. There was no choice. It gets easier as time passes.'

Two lamps hung either side of the door and, from time to time, the wings of moths flapping towards the flame was the only sound in the gardens. The children were in their dormitory, the kitchen was silent.

Since waking, Alis had bathed and put on fresh clothes. She had eaten a plate of pancakes and drunk her fill of ale. She'd winced at her first sip of Amsterdam beer, accustomed as she was to the distilled burnt wine drunk in the refugee camps in and around the Huguenot stronghold of La Rochelle, but she had quickly finished a gage and asked for another. She had been introduced to her niece, Bernarda, and reintroduced to Jean-Jacques, who did not remember her. Only then had Minou told her that Aimeric and Marta were gone.

Alis handed back the kerchief.

'Do you feel better?' Minou asked gently.

Alis shrugged. 'It is the strangest thing. Since fleeing Puivert, there wasn't a day when I didn't think of you and Aimeric, of the children. The belief that we would all one day be together again gave me the courage to keep going. So to learn now that Aimeric is most likely dead – and Marta . . .'

Minou squeezed her hand. 'I know. It is too much to take in.'

For a while, the sisters sat in silence. Beyond the walls, the city continued about its business. Minou knew not to rush her sister.

'It is good to hear such normal, domestic sounds,' Alis said eventually.

Minou smiled. 'Amsterdam is a city that never sleeps. Day and night, one hears the sound of carts transporting goods to the harbour, the wind in the ships' rigging. The guilds patrolling the streets and waterways at night. You grow used to it.'

'I like it. It speaks of life going on.' Alis smoothed her borrowed skirt. 'I'm not sure I'll ever get used to the feeling of this.'

'While you were on the road, you always wore breeches?'

She nodded. 'After I fled Puivert, I realised it was safer to be taken for a boy. Travelling from place to place, a woman alone, drew unwelcome attention. So I cut my hair, exchanged my skirts for a jerkin, hose and breeches, and hid myself in plain view as well as I could.'

'That was wise.' Minou patted her sister's leg. 'Has the wound healed? The last letter I received from Monsieur Gabignaud, albeit many years ago, said you were making slow progress.'

Alis's face grew sombre. 'Dear Dr Gabignaud. He was killed in the attack on Puivert in the autumn of 1572.'

'Oh no! As a Catholic, surely he should have been safe?'

'He died protecting his Huguenot friends and neighbours.' Alis frowned. 'Gabignaud was by nature melancholic. He feared that I would find it hard to accept I would be lame in my left leg. I, on the other hand, was concerned only with what I might be able to do. I was determined to recover. Fresh air, walking for an hour each day in the *basse cour*, regaining my strength, I drove the poor doctor to distraction.'

Minou laughed. 'I'm sorry he's gone.'

'He was a good man. After Puivert fell, I fled taking only what I could carry. When I had nothing left to sell, I worked my way from village to village, reading and writing letters in exchange for a bed for the night.' She looked down at her skirts. 'I made a good boy. You always said I would!'

Minou laughed. 'You were so jealous of Aimeric and his freedom. You always copied him, even when your health was poor, trying to climb the trees in Place Marcou, racing after him through the alleyways of La Cité or the road outside father's bookshop in the Bastide. I was forever having to stitch yet another tear in your skirts, or send you back to the river to find a lost shoe or bonnet!'

At the mention of Aimeric's name, the shadow fell again.

'Do you think he truly is dead?' Alis asked quietly. 'Not just missing? So many people are missing.'

'He would have found a way to get word to us, Alis.'

'But your little girl . . . our Marta. Is there no hope for her being found?'

For a moment, Minou did not answer. 'On the day of Admiral de Coligny's assassination, Piet found her cap, stained with blood, in the street. She had been missing for two days by then. He took it to mean the worst.'

'But what about you?'

Minou hesitated; having held her thoughts to herself for so long, it felt dangerous to bring them out into the light. But this was Alis. Alis would understand.

'If Piet had not been so sure Marta was dead, he would not have left Paris that night, nor forced me to go with him. I didn't want to. Even now, all these years later, I wake up in the night cold with guilt for the fact that I abandoned her. Several times, I thought to pray for her soul. Or to make a tombstone with her name on it, to persuade myself she was gone. Every time, I stepped back. I can't give up on finding her, Alis. I will never accept she is dead until I hold her body in my arms.'

Alis's eyes narrowed. 'You don't believe she is dead?'

Minou shook her head. 'In my heart, I feel Marta is alive, that she's still somewhere out there in the world. And although

I know it goes against every possibility or reason, I pray for her each night, pray that she is flourishing and is cared for and happy and – that she hasn't forgotten us.'

'My dear sister . . .'

Now a different silence filled the air.

'Do you realise Marta would be thirteen now,' Minou said quietly. 'A young lady.'

Alis laughed. 'Marta considered herself a lady at the age of seven! Do you remember how she loved her birth-date celebration, the fuss, the gifts?'

'She relished being the centre of attention.'

'And didn't that vex Salvadora! She was always reprimanding Marta for "making an exhibition" of herself.'

Minou smiled. 'Salvadora is of the generation that believed girls should be seen and not heard.'

'She used to say the same things to me, don't you remember? Instructing me to behave more like a lady, to be quieter and less uncouth. For all the good it did!'

Minou nodded. 'It was Aimeric she held closest to her heart. The loss of him was more than she could bear.'

Alis sighed. 'I understand why Piet feels the way he does, but you have a mother's intuition. If you believe Marta is alive, then perhaps she is.' She raised her hands. 'Is there to be a limit on miracles? Look at me, am I not proof that miracles can happen?'

Minou felt a wave of gratitude and love for her sister. 'Yes. Despite everything, against all odds and the dangers, you found your way back to us.'

'A mother's intuition,' Alis repeated firmly.

And, for the first time for as long as she could remember, Minou felt her heart ease a little.

CHAPTER FIFTY-THREE

WARMOESSTRAAT

Cornelia looked down at the package on her lap.

Burgher Pauw had stayed late into the evening. A man who had been ruined, and risen again, he was, all the same, someone who had paid too high a price for the restoration of his fortunes. No wife, no children, just the fading of the light as the cankers took hold. All he had now was fear of the judgement to come when God finally took his soul.

For her father's sake – and out of pity for the dying man – Cornelia had stayed with them until the lamps were lit and, finally, Jacob Pauw had taken his leave. Only then had Cornelia been able to repair to her own chamber with the package Mariken had left with Sister Agatha so many years ago.

Her curious fingers hovered over the scrap of grey cloth, faded around the edges. A knotted piece of string was wrapped several times around it like a belt. It didn't look as if it had been touched in the many years since Piet's mother had died. All the same, there was no seal. Cornelia was desperate to know what was inside.

'Except Piet is your friend,' she told herself again. She had no right to pry into his private correspondence, nor to learn his secret before he did.

As the ten o'clock bells echoed into silence, she came to a decision. If she took the package to Piet now – tonight – at least she might learn what it contained. After all, this was the matter that had brought their friendship into being in the first place.

Cornelia took her plainest brown cloak from her wardrobe and, making sure the servants didn't hear her, she crept down the stairs and into Warmoesstraat. Walking in her usual, steadfast way, Cornelia crossed the canal opposite the Sint Nicolaas onto Oudezijds Voorburgwal and over the next canal into the network of crowded alleyways leading to Zeedijk.

Luck was on her side. It was a quiet night, no *schutterij* with their muskets demanding to know where she was going, no sailors stumbling from taverns or bawdy houses to accost her, or starving beggars with their hands outstretched as she hurried through the streets towards her friends' house on Zeedijk.

ZEEDIJK

When night had fallen, and the blizzard of tiny insects that hovered over Amsterdam's waterways had come out in force, Minou and Alis had been driven inside and had settled in the family's private living quarters, where Piet joined them at ten o'clock.

It was a plain but pleasing room. What gave the chamber its particular character was a printed copy of the celebrated map of Amsterdam by Cornelis Anthonisz which hung above the fireplace. Commissioned by the city fathers in 1538 for the visit of the Emperor Charles V, it had instead been placed on display in the Stadhuis, the town hall, on Plaats as a symbol of civic pride. The cartographer had started to produce print versions of his illustrious map, selling them from his studio behind the Nieuwe Kerk. Willem van Raay had bought Piet a copy as a generous house-warming gift.

In the streets outside, the lamps were lit, sending golden halos of light onto Zeedijk and the square in front of Sint Antoniespoort. As the three had talked, they heard the closing of the gates and the arrival of the night watch. They heard the bells of the churches calling to one another across the rings of water. Minou and Piet talked of their settled lives in Amsterdam, the life they had made for themselves. Alis told them about living under siege in La Rochelle, her long and circuitous journey north, making her way from port to port. Of the cruelties she'd witnessed. Nearly six years of moving from place to place, never sleeping in the same bed for more than a few days at a time, only the thought of finding her family again – and praying her instincts they might be in Amsterdam were right – giving her a reason to carry on.

'I'm astonished you thought to take this with you when you fled Puivert,' Minou said, running her fingers over the heavy threads of the tapestry. 'And you never sold it. That's another miracle!'

Alis grinned. 'I was tempted to – it's heavy and it's bulky and it would have fetched a good price – but it gave me courage. It helped me believe that you all were safe somewhere and waiting for me.' She grinned. 'And I admit it served me well in other ways. As a cloak in the winter, as a saddle rug, as a bed or a cover. It became a talisman, I suppose, rather like that old dagger of yours, Piet. You gave it to Aimeric the day he left Puivert.'

He nodded sadly. 'I did.'

'My wooden casket was the same.' Minou smiled. 'I couldn't bring myself to leave it behind in Paris. Some things from it have been mislaid – our mother's rosary, chief among them – but I still have my papers, the chalk map of Carcassonne –'

'I remember it!' Alis cried.

'And my journal, I still have that, too.'

'Do you still write?'

'Not really.' Minou shrugged. 'These days, just to live is enough.'

For a while, the three sat in companionable silence. There was both too much to say, and no need to talk. Then Alis put down her tankard and Minou noticed another way in which her sister's years of living in disguise had changed her. She sat like a man, her knees apart and her hands set firm upon her legs.

'There is something else, though I am not certain if you will wish to hear it, Piet.'

His eyes narrowed. 'What is it?'

'In the early months of this year, I found myself in the region of Champagne, travelling through lands owned by the Duke of Guise –' She broke off. 'Did you know, since Guise was injured in the Fifth War they call him le Balafré – Scarface – like his father?'

'I've heard it said, yes,' Piet nodded.

Alis continued. 'I was heading for Flanders, and from there to Amsterdam.'

'How did you know we might be here?'

Alis shook her head. 'I didn't, not for certain. When word reached Languedoc of the Paris massacre, I was desperate for news. No one knew anything. Then the slaughter spread to Toulouse and Puivert, so I realised you wouldn't be able to come home. After the siege was lifted at La Rochelle, and the ships started to sail into the harbour again, the common talk was that Amsterdam had taken in many Huguenot refugees. Given Piet's Dutch birthright, I thought it was possible you might have been among them.'

'It was bold to make the journey on the basis of so little,' Minou said.

Alis shrugged. 'I had nowhere better to go. Anyhow, it was March and I was passing through the lands of Champagne. It was approaching Eastertide, so there was even more fervour than usual for Guise's Catholic League. Then one night in a tavern in Reims, I overheard a conversation between two soldiers about Guise's personal confessor.'

Piet swallowed. 'Vidal?'

Alis nodded. 'It seems he disappeared on the night of the Paris massacre. Did you know?'

Piet now turned white. 'You mean he was killed? Vidal is dead?'

'No one's certain. The house where he'd been lodging was found deserted. He might have been caught up in the mob violence of St Bartholomew's Day, or taken hostage, or murdered. What is known, however, is that Guise has spent a great deal of his fortune over the past five years trying to find out.'

Piet sat back in his chair. 'Is it possible Vidal has been dead all this time, Minou, and I didn't know it?'

'If Guise is searching for him, it suggests he doesn't think so.'

Piet was on the point of answering when a sharp knock at the front door silenced their conversation. He was instantly on his feet, his hand on the hilt of his knife.

'Who would call at such an hour?' Minou asked.

'I'll go down,' Piet said. 'More than likely it will be for me.'

Alis waited until the sound of his footsteps had died away. 'Why is Piet so uneasy?'

Minou hadn't wanted to alarm her sister by admitting that Amsterdam might turn out to be no safer than the ravaged French countryside through which she had travelled. So she had mentioned nothing to her of the political situation in Amsterdam.

'Piet fears there may soon be some kind of coup in Amsterdam,' she began carefully, seeing the look of horror on Alis's face. 'He is convinced it will be peaceful, but—'

Minou broke off as Piet walked back into the chamber accompanied by their visitor.

'Cornelia?' Minou said in astonishment. 'How now?'

'Forgive me for calling at so unreasonable an hour and when you have company—' Then she saw Alis's face and broke off.

Minou smiled. 'This is my sister Alis, Cornelia. She reminds you of Aimeric, I'll warrant. After six years, she's found her way back to us. Alis, this is our dear friend, Cornelia van Raay.'

'It is my pleasure to meet you, Mademoiselle van Raay,' Alis said warmly. 'Minou has told me how kind you and your father have been.'

Piet held out a small package tied round with string. 'Minou, Cornelia has found it.' His voice sang with anticipation. 'After all this time, Cornelia has found what my mother entrusted to Mariken before she died.'

CHAPTER FIFTY-FOUR

Minou took the two candlesticks from the mantel and put them in the middle of the table.

'Bring the package here,' she said. 'It will be easier to see.'

'Would you like me to go?' Cornelia asked. 'I am curious to know what's inside, but if it's a private matter . . .'

'Since you found it, Cornelia, I think you should stay. What say you, Piet?'

'Of course.'

The three women gathered around the table, watching as Piet placed the package carefully on it. He took his dagger, then gently cut through the string and slipped it off the cloth.

'What is this fabric?' Alis asked.

'I think it's a piece cut from a *falie*,' Cornelia replied.

'What is a *falie*?'

'It's the head covering the sisters of Begijnhof wear,' Minou answered. 'Mariken Hassels was with Piet's mother when she died.'

'Mariken, of course.'

Piet unfolded the fabric gently, as if worried it would turn to dust in his hands.

'What's inside?' Minou asked. 'Can you see?'

'A letter,' Piet replied. 'No, two letters. This one is sealed and written in a formal hand.' He put it back on the table. 'In the second, the ink is more faded and hastily transcribed.' He put it next to the first, then stepped back. 'I can't bear to look.'

Minou put her hand on his arm. 'There is nothing here that can hurt you now.'

'You don't know that.'

'These are old words. We are here, and together. Nothing matters more than that.'

His face softened. 'All the same, will you read the letters for me? I swear I cannot.'

'If that is what you wish, then of course I will.'

Piet pulled up his chair and sat down. Alis and Cornelia did the same. Minou was acutely aware of the scraping of the wooden chair legs on the tiles, the settling into position, the sense of held breath. All eyes were on her.

She picked up the letter. 'It is in Dutch, Piet. I cannot read it. I'm sorry.'

'I can translate, if you would like me to?'

Piet hesitated, then nodded. Minou handed Cornelia the letter and sat at her husband's side.

'It is from your mother, written to you on the eighth of March in the year 1542.'

'That was the month she died.'

Minou held Piet's hand tightly as Cornelia began to read.

'*Mijn lieveling,*' she began. '*My little darling. I write in haste, and with the help of my dear friend Mariken, for I have little strength. The sickness has hold of me. I do not think I will live to see the month out. By the time you are old enough to read this, I will have been long in the ground.*'

Cornelia paused, as if unwilling to intrude at so personal a moment.

'Go on,' Minou urged quietly.

'There is little I will miss of this life, save you, my beautiful son. My life, these past seven years, has been a Calvary. Your father loved me. We went through the red door together on the twelfth day of May in the year 1534. Excepting the day of your birth, when you made a healthy and quick arrival into the world, it was the happiest day of my life.'

'What does she mean by going through the red door?' Alis asked.

'The door of Sint Nicolaas church is red,' Minou explained. 'It means that they were married there.'

'Married?' Piet said sharply. 'But I have always thought—'

Minou remembered how Piet had first told her, with a mixture of shame and pride, how his mother had been reduced to selling herself on the streets of Amsterdam to provide for him.

'*Mon coeur*, let us listen. Cornelia, please.'

'Philippe could not stay with me in Amsterdam beyond the summer, for his duty and responsibility to his father and his estates drew him home to France. We chose Reydon as the name to be spoken before the priest, in honour of his family estates. We knew that until Philippe had asked for – and received – his father's blessing, so I could be acknowledged as his wife, we needed a name of our own to share.'

Alis shifted in her chair. 'What does she mean?'

'I assume that because Philippe entered into the union without permission,' Minou answered, 'he could not confer his family name upon his new wife until he had spoken to his father.'

'But wishing to protect her, he chose a name that linked her to him?'

'I think so.' Minou glanced at Piet, but he was locked in his own thoughts.

Cornelia continued:

'Philippe gave me his solemn word he would return for me, that he was desperate to meet his son and promised to send monies in the meantime. He left with me a testament — to prove the truth of our marriage and your legitimacy — which I herewith enclose.'

'The poor, poor woman,' Minou whispered.

'Autumn arrived, then the winter. I waited, and I waited, but nothing came. He never returned and sent no word. So, with no means of support, I was obliged to return to Sint Nicolaas, no longer as a bride but . . .'

Cornelia blushed and stopped reading. 'The next few lines are hard to decipher.'

Minou smiled. 'You are gracious, Cornelia, but there is no need. Piet knows how his mother was obliged to live. It is how she made the acquaintance of Mariken.'

Cornelia gave an abrupt nod.

'Lieveling, you are your father's son and heir. I pray that you will have a good life, a better life without me. I entrust you into Mariken's care. She will find a good and pious family to take you in. You are quick-witted and able, a son any man in Amsterdam would be proud to call his own. I

entrust my soul into God's care and pray he will keep you in His good grace. Je liefhebbende moeder, your loving mother, Marta Reydon.'

As Cornelia placed the letter gently on the table, Piet covered his face with his hand and sobbed.

CHAPTER FIFTY-FIVE

For a moment, the air in the chamber seemed to vibrate with the dusty words of love from a long-dead mother to her son.

Finally, Piet spoke. 'Thank you, Cornelia.'

She bowed her head. 'It was my honour to read such a letter.'

'Shall I go on?' Minou said softly, not wanting to rush him until he was ready. Piet nodded, so she took the other document from the table. 'This must be the testament she refers to. Do you want me to open it?'

Piet passed her his dagger to use as a paper knife.

'Please, yes.'

Minou slid the point under the unbroken seal and snapped it open, sending shards of red wax splintering across the surface of the table. She unfolded the heavy parchment and smoothed it flat.

'This is written in French, I assume by your father's hand. It is an official testament confirming that on the twelfth day of May in 1534, in the church of Sint Nicolaas in Amsterdam, Marta Franssen, spinster of the parish, was married to Philippe du Plessis, the Lord of Radon and Forges.'

Piet stood and sent his chair flying back.

'*Mon coeur*, whatever is it?' Minou said, alarmed at the look on his face. She stood up too. 'What's the matter?'

'That name,' he said, his eyes flashing. 'It's not possible that this could be—'

'The spelling of Reydon rather than Radon, is that what you mean?'

'No! Du Plessis. Philippe du Plessis.'

Minou shook her head. Piet picked up the testament, as if needing to see it for himself, then tossed it across the table.

'Piet, what does the name matter? Tell me.'

She watched him run his fingers through his hair, then take a deep breath.

'Philippe du Plessis was a man who took in his young nephew, after the boy's father – his brother – was executed for treason. He was the man who paid for his nephew's education in Toulouse. The man who bought his nephew his first living in Saint-Antonin and raised him as his own son.'

Minou felt the ground go from under her. 'It cannot be.'

Alis and Cornelia looked at one another. 'I don't understand,' Alis said. 'Who is du Plessis' nephew?'

'Vidal,' Minou replied, in a voice that seemed to come from a long way away.

Alis's colour drained away too.

'Which means you and Vidal are blood cousins?'

Piet nodded, but did not speak.

'We always suspected he was the cardinal who wrote to Mariken,' Minou said, 'though we didn't know why. Now we do.'

ZEEDIJK

'Boy! Yes, you. Boy.'

Frans jolted awake. After opening the door to Juffrouw van Raay – she was a regular visitor to the Reydon household, so he'd had no qualms about admitting her – he'd sat down, thinking to have a few minutes of peace and quiet. The boys' dormitory was airless and crowded, too much sniffing and farting and, when the candles burnt out, sometimes crying too.

Frans scrambled to his feet. 'How now?'

A man with a mouthful of blackened teeth stepped out from the shadows. 'Is this the Reydon house?'

'Who wants to know?'

The next moment, he was pinned up against the wall with the man's hand on his throat.

'Let me go!'

'I'll ask you again, boy, and this time you will answer.' Frans tried to nod, but the man had tightened his grip. 'Understand?'

'Yes, sir,' he croaked.

'Good. Is this the house of Piet Reydon?'

'Yes, sir.'

'I have a message for him – his ears only – from his comrades. Tell him that it is to happen the day after tomorrow. You tell him that.'

'The day after tomorrow,' Frans repeated, struggling to breathe.

'That's it.'

The man gave a final clench of his hand, then let him go. Frans fell to his knees, clutching his throat.

'Don't forget,' the man said, then melted back into the shadows of the street.

Frans bent over and vomited. Now he remembered the man's name – Joost Wouter, one of Houtman's men.

He knew Houtman all right. On his knees at the Calvinist service on Sundays, but on his knees in a very different position every other day of the week. And him a married man with six children to support.

Piet was pacing up and down the chamber.

'Vidal must know that we are cousins, it's the only explanation.'

'And was seeking confirmation from Mariken?'

Piet snatched up the testament. 'Or he knew this existed and wanted to destroy it.'

'Is Philippe du Plessis still alive?' Alis said.

Piet shrugged. 'I don't know.'

'There must be a reason this all began when it did after all this time,' Minou reasoned. 'The letter to Mariken, the attack at Puivert. Vidal had let us alone for ten years. But if du Plessis was dying, he might well have confessed his sins – and indiscretions of his youth – on his deathbed.'

Piet paused. 'Yes, which means it might have only been then, that winter or spring of 1572, that Vidal realised there was someone who had a better claim on his uncle's estates.'

'And to learn that man was you, Piet. Can you imagine his shock?'

'When we were students, Vidal told me his uncle had never married and so, as his sole heir, he stood to come into a significant fortune.'

'It should be possible to find out if du Plessis is dead. We know where his estates are; the letter tells us. We should start there.' Minou snapped her fingers. 'And if Vidal became very wealthy overnight, then what need would he have to stay in the service of the Duke of Guise? That also makes sense of why he disappeared. If we assume Guise refused to release him, Vidal might have taken his chance during the chaos of the St Bartholomew's Day massacre to vanish.'

Piet's eyes blazed. 'You think Vidal is alive?'

'If the conversation Alis overheard in Reims can be believed, it seems likely.'

'Why would Guise not release him?' Alis said.

Minou frowned. 'Vidal was Guise's personal confessor. He will have heard many things of great privacy and discretion:

his litany of faults and sins – we know what manner of man Guise is. Especially now he leads the Catholic League, he would not want the possibility of Vidal betraying him or revealing his impieties.'

'And Guise is a vengeful man,' Piet added. 'He would punish Vidal as an example to others that no one, however exalted, is beyond his reach.' He frowned. 'Vidal cannot be on his uncle's estates. Guise would have found him long ago. So where is he?'

CHAPTER FIFTY-SIX

'Excuse me, Madame Reydon.'

Minou turned round. 'Frans, you startled me! You should be in bed.'

'I have a message for the master.'

'Can't it wait until the morning?'

'I don't think so.'

Piet waved his hand. 'Let him come in.'

Frans glanced at the women.

'It is for your ears only.'

'Don't be ridiculous,' Piet said. 'Out with it.'

Frans edged further into the chamber. 'He told me to tell you that it is to happen the day after tomorrow.'

Piet's demeanour changed. 'He? Who brought this message?'

'A man just a few minutes past. He didn't give me his family name, but I know him. Joost Wouter. He's one of Houtman's men.'

Slowly, Piet put his dagger back into his belt and turned to Minou, the momentous events of the evening seemingly forgotten.

'I must go.'

'Now?' she said. 'At this time of night?' Minou gestured to the documents on the table. 'After this?'

He took her hand. 'I won't be long.'

'What's happening?' Alis asked, the moment Piet had left the chamber.

In the excitement of Cornelia's discovery, Minou had allowed what Piet had told her earlier about the planned coup to slip from her mind. Now her fears came storming back. She dropped her hands to her sides.

'Do you know where Piet is going?' Alis persisted.

'No,' Minou replied, more sharply than she intended.

'But you do know what the message means, I can see it in your expression.'

'Do you?' Cornelia asked.

Minou hesitated, caught between loyalty to her husband and gratitude to her friends who had saved their lives not once, but many times over. Her heart started to thud at the thought that she was about to betray her husband. She didn't see it in such a way, but would Piet? Until Cornelia had arrived, the dilemma about whether to speak had preyed endlessly on her. She didn't challenge the justice of his cause, only his willingness to put all ties of friendship and family obligation to one side in the service of it.

Minou did not know Willem van Raay well – he had always kept a respectful distance. But from Salvadora, Minou had gathered fragments about his character: that he loved his city and did his duty; that he had a beautiful singing voice, deep and sonorous; that he was pious; that he always attended Mass and went to Confession every Friday without fail; that he remained devoted to the memory of his dead wife.

That he had raised an exceptional daughter.

Minou knew how much she had owed to her own beloved father, and how she would have done anything to protect him. Did she not owe as much to Cornelia? It was not a matter of betraying her husband, but rather of honouring their friendship.

'Cornelia, will you take me to your father?'

Cornelia's eyes widened. 'At this hour of the night? He will long be in bed.'

'I am aware it is late. All the same . . .'

Cornelia met her gaze, then nodded. 'Very well.'

'What about me?' Alis said. 'What shall I do?'

Minou's face softened. 'You should go to bed. It has been a long day. You must be greatly fatigued.'

'What shall I tell Piet if he comes back before you return?'

'Tell him I have escorted Cornelia back to Warmoesstraat. He knows how dangerous the streets can be at this time of the night.'

'It was a pleasure to make your acquaintance,' Cornelia said, holding out her hand. '*Tot ziens.* That's to say, goodnight.'

'*Tot ziens*,' Alis repeated, and both women smiled.

Minou kissed her sister on the forehead. 'Do not worry, sweet Alis. I'll be back before sunrise.'

CHAPTER FIFTY-SEVEN

Rue Vieille du Temple, Paris

'What do you mean, nothing?' demanded Guise. 'For six years you have lived at my expense, Cabanel. In that time you have brought me fragments of rumours, but no useful information whatsoever.'

Cabanel had been summoned to Guise's presence unexpectedly and had not had a chance to prepare his report. He was tongue-tied and nervous. He tried not to stare at the vivid scar on the duke's face.

'My lord, I have not been idle—'

Guise interrupted. 'Nor have you been successful.'

Cabanel held his ground. 'Even now, there are so many people unaccounted for after the massacre and the records—'

'St Bartholomew's Day massacre!' Guise raged. 'How much longer is that to be used as a justification for every failure! Someone of Cardinal Valentin's importance does not simply disappear.'

'These past five years, I have searched every cloister, every religious house, every monastery, scoured the records of the smallest of churches as well as—'

'I don't want excuses, Cabanel. I have charged you to find my confessor. If truly you have searched all of Paris, then clearly he is not in Paris.'

'I have travelled to Saint-Antonin, to Toulouse, to his late uncle's estates.'

'Then look harder. Vidal is not unknown to the common people. He has characteristics that make him distinctive.'

Cabanel paused. 'But if he is dead, sire?'

The Duke of Guise stepped towards him. 'Then bring me his body, Cabanel. I have rewarded you well for your service, but I am running out of patience. Do you understand?'

'Yes, sire. And if – when – I do find him?'

Guise held his gaze. 'Those who do not keep their vows, who betray their betters who have raised them to higher things, they should suffer the same fate as heretics and traitors. Is that clear, Cabanel?'

At a noise in the lobby, Guise drew his dagger. Cabanel was aware the duke lived with the constant threat of assassination. He had many enemies on his own side, as well as within the Huguenot camp. Guise's personal bodyguard was said to be even larger than that of the King himself.

'Who goes there?'

A guard pushed a pretty girl in an indigo dress into the chamber.

'I found her wandering around in the corridor, my lord Guise.'

Cabanel felt his bowels turn to water.

'My lord, forgive me. This is my daughter. She was in my company when you summoned me, but not wishing to keep you waiting, I brought her with—'

'Enough.'

Guise put his poniard back in its sheath and beckoned her forward.

'What is your name, girl?'

'Marie Cabanel.'

'Show due respect,' her father hissed.

'My name is Marie Cabanel, my lord Guise,' she said quietly, dropping a curtsey.

To Cabanel's relief, Guise appeared to be charmed.

'How old are you, Marie Cabanel?'

'I have seen thirteen summers, my lord, but I am advanced for my age.'

Cabanel started to apologise. 'My lord, she—'

Guise held up his hand. 'Be quiet, man.' He lowered his face to her level. 'You are bold, child.'

Marie did not look away. 'I have been raised to tell the truth, my lord.'

Guise smiled. 'Have you indeed.' He pinched her chin between his thumb and forefinger. 'Are you a good Christian? Do you serve God in thought and deed?'

'I go to Confession on Friday, Mass on Sunday, and say my prayers every night.'

Cabanel was terrified that Marie would offend the pious and devout Guise with her impertinence. She never had learnt to mind her tongue.

'How did you get that scar?' she asked, touching the duke's face.

'Marie!' Cabanel exclaimed. To his astonishment, Guise laughed.

'Extraordinary eyes,' he muttered, then released her. 'Cabanel, take your daughter away. And do better. I want the cardinal found, and dealt with. It causes a sickness in me even to suspect that he still lives.'

'Yes, my lord.'

Cabanel bowed, then grabbed his daughter roughly by the arm and marched her from the chamber.

CHAPTER FIFTY-EIGHT

LASTAGE, AMSTERDAM

It was nigh on midnight when Piet approached the meeting house in Lastage. He heard footsteps ahead in the dark, so he stepped back out of sight until he saw who it was.

'Le Maistre,' he cried, advancing on his old friend, 'by all that's holy! I had not known you were in Amsterdam.'

Piet had not heard word of Antoine le Maistre for more than six years. The last time he had seen him was when he and Minou had broken their long journey in Limoges en route to the royal wedding in Paris.

The two men embraced.

'Reydon, by all that's holy! I am delighted to see you.'

'How goes it with you?' Piet asked, dismayed by the change in his friend. Time had been cruel. Now bone thin, le Maistre's skin was sallow and scored with lines. His hair was as white as snow. As they pulled apart, Piet could feel his friend's ribs beneath his clothes. Melancholy seemed to hang about him like mist.

Antoine raised his hands. 'As you see, I still walk this earth.'

'How fares your family?'

Le Maistre shook his head. 'I have no family now. Our lands were besieged during the last war.' He sighed. 'I was not there to defend them. They left no one alive.'

'My friend, I'm sorry.' Piet thought of le Maistre's sweet-faced wife and his apple-cheeked children and the happy days they had spent in Limoges that July.

'We live in troubled times, Reydon,' le Maistre said quietly. 'After that tragedy, there was nothing to keep me in Limoges, so I came north to offer my sword. What of you?'

'We live here in Amsterdam now. Puivert was taken, so after what happened on St Bartholomew's Day, we could not return home.'

'Are your wife and children with you?'

A shadow passed over Piet's face. 'We lost our eldest daughter, Marta, in the Paris massacre. Missing, rather than dead, but all the same. My brother-in-law, also.'

'I am sorry, too, for your loss.'

Piet nodded. 'But Minou is well, our son thrives and our youngest daughter, Bernarda. Named for Minou's father, of course. And just today, Minou's sister, Alis, who we had not heard of since the raid on Puivert, arrived in Amsterdam to join us.' He slapped le Maistre on the arm. 'I have much to be thankful for.'

For a moment more, the two men stood in silence with their ghosts.

'So here we are again,' le Maistre said finally. 'For better or for worse, brothers in arms.'

'Brothers in arms.' Piet gave a wry smile. 'And once again called upon to serve. Shall we go up?'

As they climbed the steep stairs to the top of the house, Piet noticed with sadness how laboured Antoine's breathing was. When he suggested they should pause, his old friend waved his concern away.

They stepped into a fuggy room, the air thick with the smell of herring and wood smoke.

'Reydon!'

One of the leaders of the Lastage faction of Calvinist rebels was Jan Houtman – a hard-drinking, uncompromising soldier whose parents and siblings had been massacred by the invading Spanish troops at the siege of Haarlem.

He stood up. 'I was not expecting to see you.'

Piet's heart sank. Although most of Amsterdam's Protestant community had welcomed him, and all who shared their commitment to building this new Protestant nation, there was a hard core of Hollanders and Zeelanders who resented anyone who did not hail from the Dutch Provinces.

'A messenger was sent to my house this evening.'

In the corner of the room, Piet noticed a rough-looking man picking dirt from beneath his nails with a knife. He matched precisely the description Frans had given of the man who'd accosted him.

'There was no need for you to come in person,' Houtman said roughly.

Piet met his gaze. 'Since the message was not given to me in person, I thought it wisest to make sure that it had been delivered correctly.'

Houtman threw a furious glance to the man in the corner. 'I told you! Who did you speak to?'

'Some kid hanging around outside.'

'You're a fool, Wouter.'

Piet forced Houtman to meet his eye. 'I would be sure of what was planned, the better to fulfil any duty assigned to me.'

Houtman hesitated, then gestured Piet should sit. 'You must be Antoine le Maistre,' he said, his voice considerably warmer. 'You are most welcome, your generosity these past months has been appreciated, monsieur.'

'At your service.'

Antoine cast a look at Piet before sitting down, as if to apologise for not having confided the extent of his involvement with the group.

Piet looked around. It was a smaller gathering than usual, and he recognised few, a mixture of Calvinist rabble-rousers, the kind who preached on Plaats whenever the town council was sitting – herring sellers, traders, bookkeepers, chandlers, shoemakers. Ordinary working men.

'Is it true the date has been brought forward to the twenty-sixth?' asked Piet.

Houtman glared at his bluntness. 'It is.'

Piet wasn't sure why events had accelerated, nor why the atmosphere seemed so charged. Given the extraordinary personal revelations of earlier in the evening, it was possible he was reading more into things than warranted. But, at the same time, here was proof that the plans for Amsterdam's becoming a Calvinist city had been agreed. Yet there was an air of dissent in the chamber. He didn't think he was imagining it.

'You find us in the middle of a discussion,' Houtman said carefully. 'About how precisely matters should proceed.'

'I thought the decision had been made?'

Houtman gave a cold smile. 'It is more a matter of how we shall proceed, not when.'

'And we don't have time to go through it all again for the benefit of foreigners,' another of the other men growled, a Zeelander by his accent.

'We are all brothers in the Reformed faith,' Houtman said quickly, glancing at le Maistre, not wanting him to feel offended.

Antoine raised his hand. 'I understand. It is the times we live in that make us inclined to trust only our own kind. I sympathise.'

'Wouter believes,' Houtman continued, 'that the Dirckists will not yield except at the point of a sword or a musket. I do not.'

'We cannot trust them,' Wouter complained. 'They signed the Satisfaction, ratified the terms, then paid no heed.'

'There are many moderate Catholics on the council,' Houtman countered. 'They will see sense.'

'You're easily duped if you think so!'

The room burst into argument. Piet had been party to many such conversations over the years – in Carcassonne, in Toulouse, in Amsterdam. The issue was always the same: whether to act in good faith and assume the other side would do the same, or to assume the worst and strike first.

'Hear me out,' Houtman shouted into the mayhem. 'There are as many Catholics who wish to reach a compromise, as there are moderates on our side who work for peace and justice.'

'They're papist vermin!' Wouter said, banging his hand on the table.

Houtman ignored him. 'Monsieur le Maistre, what do you think? You are free to speak. You are amongst comrades.'

Antoine raised his hand. 'I could not possibly put my view. I have been in Amsterdam but a matter of weeks.'

'What of you, then, Reydon?' Wouter sneered. 'You are part Amsterdammer at least, though on the distaff side.'

Piet felt the air sharpen. How tangled were the ties of blood and loyalty and birth. In his fighting youth in Carcassonne and Toulouse his allegiance to Languedoc had often been questioned because he was only part French. More than fifteen years later, and now he was mistrusted because of having too much French blood in him.

'Like le Maistre, I would not presume to speak for Amsterdam. As my friend here points out –' Piet gestured to Wouter – 'I am but half Dutch. But by your leave, I will say this. This glorious, magnificent modern city – which has accepted so many of our faith as brothers – I believe should, and will, form the heart of a new Protestant nation. That being the case, do I think our cause to win hearts and minds might be damaged by effecting the transfer of power from them to us through aggression? Yes, I think it would. If you ask how to prove our worthiness as the new leaders of this city, then I would say that our arguments should prevail without force. There has been enough blood spilt.' Piet looked around the room, taking in each man with his gaze. 'We deserve to be in power. We should respect the terms of the Satisfaction that Dircksz agreed with the Prince of Orange, even though he and his followers failed to honour it. We should prove that our cause is so unshakeable that we do not need to resort to violence to prevail.'

For a moment, the chamber was silent. No one spoke, no one moved. Then, one by one, eyes shifted to Jan Houtman.

'You speak well, Reydon. But words may not be enough.'

'We have the people on our side,' Piet countered.

Houtman frowned. 'As well as many of our number in the armed guilds.'

'And men on the inside,' another said. 'If they can persuade their fellow burghers . . .'

'Exactly so,' Piet agreed.

Houtman was nodding now. 'A peaceful transition would give us – our new administration – influence to implement quickly the changes we desire.'

'And if they do not go quietly?' Wouter countered. 'Then what? Would you have us down on our knees, like nuns, to beg for the keys to our own city?'

'It will not come to that,' Piet insisted. 'They will see their time is over.'

As he watched the expressions on their faces, he was taken back to another such conversation, in another such room in Carcassonne on the eve of the French wars. A similar debate between men – some of them traitorous, as it later transpired

– a number of whom wished to press for peace and others who believed that only force would triumph.

Piet remembered his younger self – the man he'd been before love and war and loss had exhausted him – taking a battered leather satchel from his shoulder and laying it carefully on the table. He remembered unfastening the buckle and reaching inside, the way the light caught hold of the delicate fabric within and how the pale cloth of the Shroud of Antioch seemed to shimmer, transforming the grey gloom of the modest room into a place of light.

His thoughts tumbling now, Piet suddenly saw himself standing in the Sainte-Chapelle in August 1572, on the day Marta went missing, hearing the guards say that there had been an attempt to take the Crown of Thorns from its reliquary. Now, the memory of those terrible hours of scouring Paris for his lost daughter washed over him like a wave.

And in its wake, a sudden realisation of why Vidal might be amassing so much wealth. Vidal, his cousin. All the time he and Minou had been talking, it had been rubbing away at him as to why Vidal would trade status and power for a life of obscurity. Maybe this was the answer? His obsession, his ambition, his greed. The lengths to which he was prepared to go. He was a hunter, but not of people or animals.

Of relics.

CHAPTER FIFTY-NINE

WARMOESSTRAAT

Leaving their house on Zeedijk, Minou hurried with Cornelia along the street, her heart thudding with the lateness of the hour.

Over the medieval canals of the Oude Zijde, avoiding squads of civic guards at every turn, concealing themselves in doorways and the shadows until each new patrol had passed by. Minou wondered on whose side the crossbowmen, the young soldiers so vain with their firearms, would be if the coup went ahead.

She pulled herself up. Not if, but when.

It was a little shy of one o'clock in the morning when they entered the van Raay house in Warmoesstraat and established themselves in the same chamber where Pauw had made his confession some few hours earlier. As they waited for Cornelia's father to join them, their conversation ebbed and flowed. The candles guttered, the pale wax pooling on the round brass base.

'Do you think Piet will now try to find Vidal?' Cornelia asked.

'I do not know.'

As friendship and trust between them had grown, Minou had confided in Cornelia not only how she had come into her unexpected inheritance and become châtelaine of Puivert, but also how Vidal had nearly succeeded in destroying their family.

'You have to understand that Vidal is always present in Piet's mind. Like a malignant shadow. To discover that they are cousins, well – Piet has never thought it safe for us to return to France, even though there is a truce at present. But this new knowledge might change things.'

'Because if du Plessis did die without further issue, then it is Piet rather than Vidal who is the legitimate heir to his estates.'

'Exactly.'

'Will Piet's affection for his mother be changed because of what he's learnt tonight?'

Minou smiled. 'No, despite the manner of her life and the tragedy of her death, Piet loved her without reservation. To discover she was married after all, that will only reinforce her goodness in his mind.'

'And blacken the memory of his father?'

'Piet never had any regard for his father. He'd assumed that he was . . . he despises men who seek to buy women in such a way.'

Cornelia raised her eyebrows.

Minou laughed. 'Piet would close all the flophouses. He'd regulate taverns and taphouses by the harbour where the sailors congregate, and monitor the muster points where the civic guards finish their night watch and then go seeking company.'

'Marriage or nothing?'

'Marriage or nothing,' Minou agreed. 'You are surprised?'

Cornelia considered. 'I suppose I associate such rigorous morality with the Calvinists. Their austerity of worship and their absolute adherence to living by God's commandments every second of every day seems to take much of the joy out of things. Piet has never struck me as sharing those views.'

'After the massacre in Paris, attitudes of both Catholics and Huguenots hardened. Moderate voices were shouted down as their leaders moved away from a belief that compromise was possible, to a black-and-white view of the world.'

Cornelia sighed. 'You are either my friend, or my enemy. Nothing in between.'

Minou nodded. 'I would not say Piet is like that, but he now defines himself first and foremost as Protestant. Before, though he was proud to be a Huguenot, he was also a landowner, a husband, a man of Languedoc, a father.'

Cornelia nodded: 'Will Piet challenge Vidal over his inheritance?'

Minou thought for a moment. 'There was a time when I would have known how to answer. Now, I'm not sure. We survived the first three wars, only to lose everything after the Paris massacre. Land, wealth, our children's inheritance, our home. My brother and daughter most of all. Without you and your father, Cornelia, we still would have nothing. Thanks to you, we have been able to rebuild something of what was lost. But Piet will never stop worrying and I fear the roots of that are in his own childhood – the memory of sitting at his mother's bedside in Kalverstraat and, even though he was so young, understanding she was dying because they were poor. They had no money to pay for lodgings, no food to eat, no way of hiring a doctor to ease her symptoms. So, yes. It is possible that Piet will attempt to gain some of what is – what might be – rightfully his if he believes it could secure our children's future.'

'I understand that,' Cornelia said. 'But what of you?'

Minou sighed. 'I do not want Piet to seek Vidal out. For all that I try to reassure him that he cannot harm us now, I fear him.' She hesitated. 'On the other hand, if Piet's petition to prove himself du Plessis' heir was successful, we would have the resources to renew our attempts to find Marta. We never did that, we couldn't afford to. We did what we could, we asked questions and sent letters, but we never launched a proper search. We gave up trying, and that is always on my conscience.'

'But Minou, after all this time – is there any hope?'

'At least I would know we tried.'

Again, they were quiet. Cornelia trying to imagine how it would feel to be so haunted by a child you had lost. Minou trying to imagine – as she had every day since her daughter's disappearance – what her child would look like now.

'Marta's eyes are like mine. One brown and one blue. It's very rare.'

'From the tapestry Alis brought with her from Puivert, Marta seemed to favour you in other ways too.'

'In appearance, she did. In her character, there was more of Alis, if anyone, in her. Marta was forever rushing, forever impatient and quick-tempered, ready to answer back.'

Cornelia smiled. 'Alis was exactly as I imagined from your descriptions of her.'

'In the refugee camp outside La Rochelle, and during her time on the road, she disguised herself as a boy!'

'Perhaps, as you realised, as she so strongly reminded me of your brother, that does not seem so outlandish.'

The tiny counter clock began to whir and shift its weights and click as its single hand found the top of the hour.

'One o'clock,' Cornelia said. She glanced up, listening for signs of life from her father's chamber, but the floorboards remained silent. 'He retires early and is a heavy sleeper. It might be better to return . . .'

'It should be tonight.'

Minou shivered and pulled her shawl around her shoulders. She had not told Cornelia why it was so urgent to speak to Willem van Raay. And her friend, knowing her well, had not pressed her.

'Then we shall continue to wait,' Cornelia said.

CHAPTER SIXTY

ZEEDIJK

Piet stopped outside his own front door and heard the bells strike one o'clock. The house was dark. He assumed all had gone to their beds.

Just as Frans had done earlier, he sat on the step, reliving the events of the evening in his head: the confirmation of his fears about Vidal's continuing meddling in their lives, the identity of his father, the words of love from his mother heard only now across the years. All the same, Piet knew that for the next forty-eight hours at least he had to put all personal feelings to one side.

He'd told Minou in good faith that the coup was to be a peaceful changing of the order, from the old way of doing things to the new. No longer a vassal state under the Spanish heel, but Amsterdam at the heart of the new independent country led by the Prince of Orange. A Protestant state in its own right, nothing less.

But after listening to Jan Houtman and his followers, he was less confident. He saw the same belligerence in their eyes that he'd seen in the eyes of Guise's men on the streets of Paris in 1572 as bloodlust stripped all human emotion from their hearts. The same brutality he'd seen sweep through Toulouse on that first night in May 1562 when the city started to burn.

Then Piet remembered what good had come out of those dark times, for that night in Toulouse was when he'd led his injured comrade into the sanctuary of a house – Salvadora's house – and found Minou again. A courageous girl, a girl of principle and honour. The girl who would later do him the honour of becoming his wife. Even in the worst of times, it was a miracle how the human heart kept beating.

Love and hope.

'My lady of the mists,' he whispered into the night air.

The smile faded from his lips. He had promised Minou that Amsterdam would pass peacefully from its past to its future. Houtman wasn't the worst of them by any means. He was an intelligent man, and a man of his word, despite his dislike of foreigners. Had Piet done enough this evening to convince Houtman that their best chance was to behave as politicians not soldiers?

If he had not, what would happen to them all?

Without Willem van Raay, they would have nothing. So the question Piet had to ask himself was did he owe his loyalty more to an ideal, to the Huguenot cause, or to those who'd cared for them when they needed it most?

Piet stood up. Minou was right. He owed it to their friends to warn them. Van Raay was a sombre and dutiful man, he was devout. But for all that, Piet knew that he found the excesses of the Catholic forces troubling. He had to gamble on the fact that van Raay loved Amsterdam more than the men who currently ruled it.

He had to tell Cornelia's father what was intended and pray to God that he did not alert the authorities. Otherwise, Piet was as likely to meet his reckoning at the end of a Calvinist sword as a Catholic one. Condemned as a traitor to both sides.

WARMOESSTRAAT

'And this coup is due to take place in two days' time?'

'My husband assures me the intention is for there to be no bloodshed. He gave me his word on that.'

Van Raay met her gaze. 'And you believe him, Madame Reydon?'

'I believe that is what Piet believes,' Minou answered carefully.

Van Raay gave a tired smile. 'But there are no guarantees.'

'In such situations, there never are.'

'No.'

Cornelia leant forward. 'Father, what do you think? Might Burgomaster Dircksz concede? You have served alongside him for many years.'

Van Raay rested his hand on his daughter's shoulder. 'We are old men, my dear. We are prisoners of our own experience and, dare I say it, our traditions. Hendrick is a devout Catholic, somewhat unyielding, and a true Christian. It is hard for him to imagine a different order of things.'

Minou glanced at her friend, then back to their host. 'Piet believes there are within the town council, a significant minority of men – also pious Catholics – who have lost faith in Dircksz's leadership. The Calvinists say there are men on the inside who believe Dircksz's intransigence is damaging Amsterdam almost beyond the point of no return. That it is no longer a matter of faith but rather a betrayal of Amsterdam's economic future.' She met his eye. 'Would you say that was true?'

Minou could see that Willem van Raay was perturbed by her question. For years she had been his daughter's friend and Piet Reydon's wife. That she should have views of her own confused him.

Cornelia noticed his consternation, too. 'Minou was – is –

Châtelaine of Puivert in Languedoc, Father. She ran the estate for many years on her own.'

Willem van Raay coughed. 'I did not mean to suggest otherwise.' There was another silence while he weighed Minou's question. 'Yes, I would consider what you say is a fair assessment of how things stand.'

Minou breathed a sigh of relief. 'That is good.'

'Answer me this, Madame Reydon. Do you believe in the inherent goodness of mankind, or that we are all fallen?'

Minou hid her surprise at the nature of the question. 'I think perhaps that is the difference between us, Burgher van Raay. You believe in original sin, that man is fallen. We believe that man will be saved through God's grace and God's grace alone. We do not need intercession, only our own true spirit.'

A spark lit the old man's eyes. 'I fulfil my Christian duty through alms and charity, as do you, Madame Reydon. Your *hofje* is fashioned on the very model of a Catholic almshouse.'

Minou smiled. 'Exactly. We both believe it our Christian duty to help those in need. Perhaps it matters not where we pray on Sunday for our work to count?'

Van Raay raised his hand. 'You cannot expect me to accept that. I fear for the souls of those who have turned away from the true Church.'

'You would call us heretics?'

'I prefer to call you misguided. I pray that you will return to God's grace and the forgiveness of sins, to the faith of your esteemed aunt.'

Minou inclined her head. 'As in my conversations with Salvadora, we must agree to differ.'

There was another heavy pause. 'Tell me this, madame. Will we be allowed to worship in peace? Will our churches be taken?'

Minou felt a stab of doubt. She felt Cornelia's eyes on her.

'In truth, I do not know,' she replied.

Willem van Raay nodded at her honesty. 'The hour is late. What precisely are you asking of me?'

'I wanted to warn you. And thank you for all you have done for us over these years.'

Van Raay waved away her gratitude. 'Yes?'

'What I am asking is this – if the Calvinists behave with honour, is it your opinion that their voices might be heard and their conditions accepted? For the good of Amsterdam and its people?'

Van Raay pressed his fingers together. 'If your husband's conviction that the Geuzen genuinely want a peaceful transition is correct – and if we can mobilise enough voices of moderation within the chamber to support such a move – then, it is possible that Amsterdam can show the world how things might be done.'

At that moment, the door opened and a flustered servant entered, followed instantly by Piet. Dishevelled and breathless, he blinked in astonishment to see his wife.

'Minou?'

'So late and yet another guest . . .' Willem van Raay observed wryly.

'Burgher van Raay, forgive my intrusion at this hour, but there is something urgent I must tell you.'

Van Raay began to laugh.

'Father?' Cornelia rushed to him, astonished by his behaviour. He waved her away. 'Bring wine for our visitor.'

'But it is half past one in the morning!'

'The sun is over the yard arm somewhere,' he exclaimed, falling into another bout of laughing.

Cornelia started to laugh too, then Minou joined in. Piet looked on, bewildered.

The hand of the clock clicked and rang its hesitant chime, moments before the bells of Sint Nicolaas came clamouring into the chamber and drowned them all out.

CHAPTER SIXTY-ONE

EVREUX ESTATE, CHARTRES
Sunday, 25 May 1578

Louis felt the cover being dragged from his bed. Instantly, he was on his feet, his heart pounding, back in the days of the orphanage. Then he remembered. Those days were dead and gone.

'Get up!' Xavier shouted. 'Lord Evreux requires your presence.'

Louis was as tall as Xavier now, no longer a helpless child who could be beaten into silence. And, these days, he was confident in his father's regard. Didn't the fact that Lord Evreux had taken him to Chartres yesterday prove it?

Louis reached for his jerkin. 'You should not talk to me like that.'

Xavier poked him in the chest. 'I'll talk to you any damn way I choose, boy. You might have him fooled, but not me. He is at the jetty.'

'Down at the lake?'

Xavier was already striding from the chamber. 'Hurry,' he shouted over his shoulder. 'Don't keep Lord Evreux waiting.'

Louis watched him go, hating him with every sinew of his body. He shivered. It was early. The first glimmers of light were only just coming through his window. He scooped cold water from the bowl on his chest of drawers, washed his face and his hands, then dressed and hurried down the corridor.

Outside, the dawn was breaking.

CHARTRES CATHEDRAL

No one worried when the priest failed to observe Matins. On days of no particular religious significance, even on a Sunday, the Chapter was prepared to turn a blind eye to an occasional absence.

When dawn came creeping through the stained glass of the cathedral, a few eyebrows were raised when his stall was still empty at Lauds.

Now it was six o'clock and the prayers for Prime were nearly over.

'Perhaps he has been taken ill?' whispered one of the novices. He was a new recruit from Brittany, pale and brimming with religious fervour, uncompromising and zealous. He was yet to learn the customs of the Chapter.

'He's likely overslept,' a voice beside him countered, aware that the absent priest was just as likely to be found in the arms of a woman in the rue du Cheval Blanc than on his knees in the cathedral. 'We all need a little help getting up,' he added, then laughed at his own joke.

The novice frowned and resumed his murmuring of the office until the prayers were done. '*Sancta Maria et omnes sancti. Amen.*'

He crossed himself and genuflected before the altar, then went to the north transept to hang up his surplice.

The sun had not yet fully risen, but there was light enough to see something on the flagstones. He stopped. His father was a butcher; he knew the smell of blood. Holding up the hem of his cassock, he knelt. A viscous ribbon of red led his eye across the stone floor and under the door of the vestry. His heart thudding, the novice pushed open the door.

At first, he couldn't make sense of what he was seeing. A

black cloud of buzzing insects. Then, the sacrilege became clear – flies swarming around the body, the jagged skin of a throat cut from ear to ear, the halo of blood around the priest's head, his blue-veined hands clutching a leather bag to his chest like a shield. The key to the reliquary of the Sancta Camisia was lying by his side.

Despite his childhood spent in the slaughterhouse, the novice staggered back, then screamed.

EVREUX ESTATE

Louis emerged into the sunrise.

From the top of the gardens by the manor house itself, he could see all the way down across the sweeping lawns to the lake that sat at the heart of the estate. The ornate white crenellations of the Italianate tower on the small island were just visible through the early morning mist rising off the water.

Then Louis spied his father standing by the jetty down at the water's edge, and he ran.

His father removed the damp cloth he was holding to his temple. 'You have kept me waiting.'

'Forgive me, I came as fast as I could.' Louis looked at his father's pale face. 'Are you quite well, my lord?'

'A headache, nothing more. Come.'

His father's headaches had been more frequent of late. The apothecary had bled him, but so far as Louis could tell, it didn't seem to have done any good.

Louis followed Vidal onto the jetty, where a boatman waited. 'Are we to go across to the island?'

Evreux didn't answer, simply gestured that he should get into the flat-bottomed boat and sit at the front. Louis was a strong swimmer, but he disliked the way the craft rocked low in the water, so he climbed over the wooden benches to the bow and clasped his hands tight to the gunwales.

The craft lurched again as his father got in and settled himself in the stern. The boatman pushed out and jumped in, then reached up to the heavy iron chain that hung from a pole connecting the shore to the island. Slowly, hand over hand, he began to pull them across the water.

As they drew closer to the white rectangular tower, Louis felt a stab of excitement. His father had never brought him to the island before.

'Why are we here, my lord?' he asked, turning around in the bow.

'You ask too many questions.'

'Forgive me,' Louis apologised again. 'I'm sorry.'

His father laughed. 'Thrice before the cock has crowed. Should I call you Peter?'

'Peter, my lord?'

Vidal raised his eyebrows. 'For a child raised in a monastery orphanage, your spiritual education is woefully poor. We must remedy that.'

CHAPTER SIXTY-TWO

Zeedijk, Amsterdam

Outside, the first rays of sun were rising over Amsterdam, painting the walls of the city bright with morning. Inside Minou's bedchamber, the light was still dim.

'The children will wonder where I am,' said Minou, rolling over to face her husband.

Piet moved closer, so that their noses were almost touching.

'I should get up,' she said.

'You can grant me a few more moments of your company,' he replied softly, winding his fingers through her long brown hair, which lay fanned upon the pillow. 'Agnes can manage. And Alis is here now.'

Minou smiled at him. His beloved face, his russet beard and hair flecked with grey. When they had first met, he'd taken a great deal of trouble to darken the colour. His pale northern looks and red hair had stood out among the darker skinned, dark-haired men of Languedoc. In Amsterdam, he looked like a native.

'Did you sleep?' she asked.

It had been three o'clock when they'd finally taken their leave of Cornelia and her father. Almost four before they were in their bed, holding hands and talking in the dark. Minou supposed she must have slept, for the day was seeping around the edge of the shutters, but she had no memory of having done so. Her limbs felt heavy and she had a sick feeling in the pit of her stomach.

'Not much.' He stroked her cheek. 'Did you?'

'A little. Every word of our conversation was going around in my head until I felt quite mad with thinking.'

Piet propped himself up on his elbow. 'Me too. The situation is so fragile. One wrong word, from either side, a stone thrown or a guard with a grudge, and that will be that. Until last evening, I truly believed there was no intention to violence. But Houtman . . .'

'I know,' Minou said, realising how much it mattered to him that she believed he had been acting in good faith. 'You did the right thing, *mon coeur*. You did not sacrifice our friends for an idea. You gave them fair warning.'

'No, *you* did.'

She kissed his lips. 'What do you think he will do? Can he be trusted?'

'I don't know Burgher van Raay well,' Piet replied. 'He is known to be a man of principle and piety but, above all, he is a man of commerce. I pray that will guide his actions. I hope he will go into the chamber and speak for moderation.'

'He will not flee?'

Piet considered. 'I don't think so. If van Raay's voice prevails, we just need to make sure that Houtman's men follow their orders.'

The silence closed around them. Everything that could be said had already been said. Now, it was only a question of waiting.

For a while, they lay gently in one another's arms. Minou realised how long it had been since they had last done so. The loss of Marta had taken their intimacy from them, like so much else.

Minou could remember vividly the last time they had lain together as true husband and wife. The morning of the royal wedding, the August heat, the illicit knowledge that they should be dressing, but yet remaining tangled beneath the covers for another kiss. Bernarda had been conceived that day, though Minou had not known it until they were many leagues away from Paris.

One daughter for another.

Minou was fond of her youngest child, of course, though she could not help but find her timidity tiresome. And in her most private moments she knew she would never forgive her for not being Marta and felt guilty for that.

'Do you love me still?' Piet whispered.

The doubt in his voice made her heart crack. 'My love, how can you ask such a thing?'

'Do you?'

'Of course.'

'I have been a poor husband. I have been neglectful, I—'

Minou put her finger on his lips. 'No more of this. You are a good man, Piet, a good father. You have done the best you could. As have I. No one could ask more.'

She leant forward, allowing her hair to fall across his bare skin like a veil, and kissed him on the mouth.

'Sandalwood, as it ever was.'

He looked up at her with desire in his eyes. 'Are you sure?'

'No more words, my lord,' she said. Minou eased her chemise from her shoulders, then lay back down alongside him. She could feel the heat of his skin.

'Minou.' The word slipped from between his lips, as he turned back towards her.

She placed her hands on his back, her fingers splayed wide in the shape of stars, and welcomed the force in him. He was breathing faster now, harder, driven by the memory of all they had lost, until finally he cried out her name once more. He shuddered, then was still.

Gradually, the roaring in her head faded away until nothing remained but the hushed silence of the room and the sounds of Amsterdam awakening in the street outside. They knew nothing but each other, lovers once more. Piet moved his head to her shoulder and rested it there, his tears damp on her skin. She felt him growing heavy in her arms as he slipped into sleep.

Reconciled. At peace.

CHAPTER SIXTY-THREE

EVREUX ESTATE, CHARTRES

As they drew closer to the island, Louis could see the tall, white rectangular tower was far bigger than it looked from the shore, and even more magnificent.

Built in the Italian style he remembered from the Guise house in Paris, the façade was perfect and smooth, the pediment precisely in its centre, the angles identical, the pilasters undamaged. At each corner stood an ornamental square turret.

Louis wondered what it was. A folly? Or a chapel? He dismissed the idea. There was a place of worship within the house for their private use and a small church on the outskirts of the estate for the labourers and their families.

The boat rocked as the pilot jumped out, secured the craft to a wooden pole set into the water, then offered his hand to Lord Evreux. Louis followed.

'This is all reclaimed land,' his father explained, as if showing a prospective purchaser around. 'Beneath the tower and antechamber, there's a channel with a sluice feeding into the lake, in case the water gets too high. As you can see, the lake is in a dip – on the site of an ancient dew pond, in fact – so the building is at risk of flooding.'

'Has it ever flooded?'

Vidal shook his head. 'Never. I hired Dutch engineers from Amsterdam to build the chamber beneath with a sluice to control the water. Their knowledge of such engineering is second to none. The tower is the work of Italian stonemasons I had brought here from Venice.'

'It must have cost a great deal.'

Vidal smiled. 'Indeed, but you will learn in time that the best craftsmen are worth paying for.'

They walked from the landing platform across stone tiles in silence. In the centre of the white tower was an ornately carved wooden door, with a smaller door set within it. The door was accessed by stone steps sweeping up from the left and complemented by a running balustrade in front. A single round window was set in the middle of the building below the gable, like a giant eye, reflecting the rays of the rising sun.

Louis squinted up at the stone carving on the tympanum, shielding his eyes, and realised it was a scene from the Passion of Christ. So was it a church after all?

'My lord, what is this place?' he ventured to ask.

His father smiled. 'You will see soon enough, boy. Come.'

Vidal opened the door with a heavy iron key. For a moment, they stood at the entrance with the sun behind them, their shadows elongated and monstrous, then they stepped inside.

Instantly, Louis's senses were assailed by the smell of incense and wax and confined air. Along one side of the narrow corridor, black wrought-iron double sconces were set into the wall at intervals. All the candles were burning, their flickering light casting shadows onto the vivid frescoes painted in the alcoves set in the opposite wall: Christ on the Cross at Golgotha, the Roman centurion piercing his side with a lance; Saint Louis in the humble robe of a penitent, bearing the Crown of Thorns through the gates of Paris to the Sainte-Chapelle; Mary Magdalene in the garden of Gethsemane weeping with the Shroud in her hands; Mary, Mother of God, in her sacred robe with the Christ in her arms; a woman wiping Christ's brow with a cloth; Charlemagne holding a vial of royal blood; Constantine, with his sword in his hand and the mark of the Cross painted in the sky above him.

Louis couldn't help himself reaching out and tracing the lines.

'*In hoc signo vinces*,' Evreux said. 'By this sign, wilt thou conquer. The Emperor Constantine was said to have witnessed a portent in the sky before a major battle. Against the odds, he was victorious. That day, in grateful thanks for his deliverance, he converted to Christianity.'

'And this?' Louis asked, pointing to an illustration of the labyrinth of Chartres Cathedral.

'Some say that the bones of Mary Magdalene are buried beneath it.' Evreux raised his hands. 'I have yet to be convinced of that.'

'Why is there a goblet in the painting?'

'Ah, the legend of the Holy Grail, the cup in which drops of Christ's blood were caught. That is also associated with the cathedral.' He gave a wry smile. 'That stretches my credulity, but the labyrinth itself is a work of exceptional quality. There is transcendence there.'

His voice trailed off. Louis nodded, not wanting to break the spell. He had not seen his father like this for some time. From the moment he had put aside his red cardinal's robes for those of a nobleman and landowner, his father's eyes had seemed set on the workings of the earth not those of Heaven. Vidal, honoured confessor to the Duke of Guise, had become Lord Evreux, a wealthy recluse living deep in the Chartres country-side.

Louis had always assumed it was not a love of God that had driven his father's piety but rather the power conferred on him by his office. His father's ambition had ultimately been held back by his service to the Duke of Guise rather than helped by it, and Louis understood why he had been forced into hiding – Guise was not a man accustomed to having his wishes ignored or flouted. All the same, Louis had wondered why Vidal had been prepared to give up so much to live like a hermit.

Now he understood.

'It's a reliquary,' he said, glancing up at his father.

Vidal nodded. 'It has taken many years to complete. I waited ten years before I could transport the first of my treasures, the Shroud of Antioch, from its temporary home to its final resting place here, and begin my life's work – the glorification of God's kingdom on earth through the power conferred in me by these holy objects. This heralds a new age of Christian faith based here in Chartres, not Rome.'

'You're a relic hunter . . .'

Vidal smiled. 'Some would say so. Come, boy.'

They walked a few steps more and came to a halt at the end of the passageway. Evreux pulled back a heavy red curtain to reveal a door with a brass key set waiting in the lock.

'"For the Lord thy God bringeth thee into a good land, a land of brooks of water, of fountains and depths that spring out of valleys and hills",' he recited as he turned the key. 'The Book of Deuteronomy. Chapter eight, verse seven. For although we have few hills in Chartres, we do have brooks and fountains and this, our island in the lake!'

Louis felt his father's hand in the small of his back and he was ushered forward into a long and cavernous chamber.

At first sight, it seemed plain after the lavish colours of the passageway. There was a table serving as an altar, and two chairs set in the middle of the room. Two candelabra with pure white candles stood on the floor. There were no windows, only a small door at the far end of the chamber that seemed to lead into an anteroom beyond, but a vast lantern skylight, set into the white plaster and wood ceiling, flooded the chamber with dazzling morning light.

In genuine awe, Louis turned slowly around and around, aware of his father's eyes upon him.

'Is this not how we should worship God?' Vidal said.

'I have never seen anything like it, my lord,' he replied honestly.

As Louis's eyes became accustomed to the dancing light and shadow, he could see the frescoes in this inner sanctum covered the entire left-hand wall. In front of each, on a pedestal, was a gold casket with glass sides.

'We shall begin your religious education here,' Vidal said. 'Come closer. What do you see?'

'That these paintings were done by the same hand?'

His father nodded. 'That is true, but I meant rather what they depict.'

'They are the Stations of the Cross,' Louis replied, remembering the walls of the church in Saint-Antonin before the Huguenots razed it to the ground.

'So you know some things, good. Originally, the stations were actual places for pilgrims to pray on the Via Dolorosa, the Road of Sorrows, the route along which Christ walked to his Crucifixion at Golgotha. Over time, painted illustrations of each of the seven stations began to grace the walls of churches and cathedrals too.'

'Why seven?'

Vidal signalled his approval. 'That is a question that theologians and learned men have debated for centuries. Rome considers these seven scenes to be the most theologically significant. I, however, believe that if we wish to bring believers back to the one true Church, then there should be more – twelve, or even fourteen stations – telling the whole story from Pontius

Pilate sentencing Christ to death all the way to Christ's Ascension into Heaven to sit at the right hand of His Father.' Louis saw how his father's eyes glinted with zeal. 'One day it will happen. Change is coming.'

He beckoned Louis forward. 'This is the first station. After being condemned to death, Christ takes up his cross. And this relic, the first in my collection, purports to be a piece of the True Cross.'

Louis looked into the casket to see a piece of blackened wood the width of a man's hand lying on a cushion of white satin.

Vidal moved to the second tableau. 'This next is where Jesus falls.'

The casket beneath was empty. 'You have no relic for this?'

'Not yet,' he replied, moving to the third station.

'This casket is empty too.'

'This is why we are here.' Vidal removed the lid and handed it to Louis. 'This fresco of the third station shows the moment when Jesus meets his mother, Mary, on his way to Golgotha.' He put his hand beneath his doublet and pulled out the length of material he had taken from the cathedral.

Despite himself, Louis was caught up in the mystery of the moment. 'What is it, my lord?'

'The Sancta Camisia. Formerly of Chartres Cathedral and now so much safer in our reliquary, away from the thieving hands of greedy priests. It is said to be a fragment of the Holy Tunic worn by Our Lady at the moment of Christ's birth.'

Louis watched his father carefully drape the delicate fabric over a small wooden frame.

'Replace the lid.'

He obeyed. 'But will not the priests see it is missing and raise the alarm?'

'Ah, an exchange was made well before yesterday afternoon.

A copy of the Holy Robe, an excellent one, has been displayed in the reliquary in Chartres Cathedral since Whitsun. Yesterday was merely a matter of payment for that earlier sleight of hand and to take possession of the original.' Vidal tapped the lid of the casket. 'It is a trick I learnt from an old friend, Piet Reydon. It was he who was responsible for helping me acquire the very first of the treasures in my collection, the Shroud of Antioch.'

With a jolt, Louis suddenly thought of the girl with the mismatched eyes. He had never told his father about following her to Admiral de Coligny's lodgings, then imprisoning her in the blue room.

'The man you sent me to watch in the rue des Barres?'

Vidal raised his eyebrows. 'I had forgotten you'd had sight of him. Yes. It was Reydon who taught me that if the copy is fine enough, an accurate match for what the common people expect to see, then they will accept it. Faith in its properties is more important than the object itself.'

'Monsieur Reydon sold you the relic?'

Vidal laughed. 'It was not quite how the transaction took place.'

His father walked past the fourth fresco, gesturing at another empty casket. 'This is awaiting the Sudarium, the Veil of Veronica. There are several claiming to be the original cloth with which St Veronica wiped Christ's face on the Via Dolorosa, lost during the Sack of Rome in 1527. Some say it never left Rome, others claim it was taken to Vienna. I consider Alicante more likely, but I have had no success finding it yet.'

He continued past the next two stations without pausing, then stopped in front of the seventh and last casket.

'This is what Reydon brought me,' he said. 'The Shroud of Antioch.'

Louis peered at the shimmering cloth, studied the ornamental stitching and the strange writing, and felt something stir in his chest. It was an uncomfortable sensation.

'What are those letters?'

'Kufic. It's one of the oldest forms of calligraphy in the world.'

'It is beautiful.'

Vidal nodded. 'It is.'

Wanting to slip out from under the Shroud's spell, Louis moved quickly back along the wall to one of the frescoes they had missed.

'What about this one?'

His father raised his eyebrows. 'I believe you know. At least, Xavier always told me you did.'

'My lord?'

'When we rested the horses overnight when I first brought you to Chartres, on the eve of the Paris massacre, he accused you of looking inside the chest we'd brought with us, against his express orders.'

Louis felt himself blush, remembering how he'd taunted the steward and kicked a piece of wood across the refectory floor to distract him for long enough to lift the lid.

'Xavier wanted to beat you for it. He thought then – and still thinks – that you are disobedient, that you are dangerously disloyal.' His father's hand was suddenly on the back of his neck, his fingers pinching into Louis's skin. 'Are you disloyal, boy?'

'No, my lord,' Louis said, trying not to flinch or look away. 'But I owe my duty and loyalty to you, no other.'

Vidal held his gaze. 'Well answered. But remember this. Xavier has served me faithfully for more years than you have spent on this earth. Do not make an enemy of him.'

Then as if the conversation had never happened, Vidal released him. Louis swallowed a sigh of relief.

'Come and look upon what my steward did not want you to see.'

Inside the casket in front of the sixth station, a single thin evergreen thorn, as long as Louis's hand, lay on a fold of white silk. Unexceptional. It could have been cut from any bush or tree on their estates.

'A holy thorn from the Crown relic.'

Vidal nodded. 'If I could have found a craftsman capable of reproducing the entire Crown, I would have done so. I expended too much time and a great deal of effort attempting to find such a craftsman – in France, in the Levant, in the Holy Land – but there was no one. In the Sainte-Chapelle, I visited the *grande châsse* itself many times. The Crown is so delicate, and never unaccompanied, that it was impossible to observe it for long enough, closely enough.' He tapped the glass. 'For now, this single spine must suffice, but one day the Crown of Thorns will sit here.'

His father's words in his ears, Louis looked at the caskets.

'My lord, does it matter if it is the actual relic rather than a copy?'

Vidal turned to look at him. 'All things must be true and valuable of themselves in the service of God, Louis. A relic touched by Notre Dame or our Lord, these are things beyond price.' He paused. 'However, if the people believe and invest their faith and trust in an object, even if it might be a copy rather than the true relic, then God's purpose is also fulfilled. As I said, Reydon taught me that, too.'

Louis threw his mind back, remembering all those hot August days crouched on the platform of the mighty reliquary of the Sainte-Chapelle, looking down on the tiny people below. He closed his eyes and pictured the dimensions of the Crown.

'I could draw it, my lord.'

The atmosphere sharpened. 'You consider yourself more gifted than the finest artists in France? Are you so proud?'

'No, my lord, but I believe I could sketch it well enough for an expert forger to copy.'

Now he knew he had Vidal's entire attention.

'How so, boy?'

'During our time in Paris, I was much in Xavier's company. When he went to the Sainte-Chapelle, on your service, I accompanied him. I passed many hours in the company of the Holy Crown.'

'How could you observe it at close quarters when I could not?'

Louis hesitated. 'I climbed onto the narrow ledge at the top of the *grande châsse*, my lord, and hid there. No one saw me.'

A long, slow smile broke across Vidal's face. 'Well, well, well, Volusien known as Louis.' He paused. 'You remember, that was how you were first presented to me?'

'Yes,' he replied, delighted that his father had not forgotten. 'Though if it pleases you, I prefer Louis.'

Vidal raised his hand. 'Let us return to the house, Louis. Then you will show me what you can do. I hope, for your sake, you have not exaggerated your talent.'

CHAPTER SIXTY-FOUR

ZEEDIJK, AMSTERDAM

When Minou next awoke, the chamber was empty. For a moment, she felt like a young bride again, remembering the pleasure of being loved for the first time. But when she sat up, against pillows that held her husband's scent, Minou felt the creak and ache of age in her bones, and laughed.

She threw the sheets back and got up. She used the pot, then splashed cold water on her face and dressed quickly. A thin canvas corset over her smock and a light farthingale beneath. Though the burghers' wives wore rigid hoops beneath their skirts, Minou had long since forsaken fashion for practicality. She dressed now for days of physical labour.

Minou took her favourite green dress from the wardrobe, laced it up the front and attached an open collar. Stockings, and shoes with red soles, were her only concession to the changing times.

Having opened the shutters, she went to the dressing table and began to brush her hair. One hundred strokes morning and evening, as her mother had taught her so long ago in Carcassonne and as she had taught Alis and, later, Marta. Now, Bernarda. As she counted, her eye drifted to the enamel box given to her by Antoine le Maistre's wife all those years past – Piet had told her last evening that he was a widower now and living in Amsterdam, a major financial donor of the Calvinist rebels.

Next to it was her wooden casket, the one significant object not lost to her from Puivert and the flight from Paris. Minou opened the lid: the plain Bible, the only heirloom from her birth mother; the chalk map of Carcassonne Alis remembered too; her tourmaline birthstone ring set in silver, which she rarely wore now. But she no longer had the wooden rosary with a silver cross, a relic of her previous Catholic life. Minou hadn't even noticed it was missing until they'd reached Amsterdam.

Minou looked down at her ring finger, remembering how she had thrown the twine betrothal ring she had made into the dark waters of the Seine. A gesture, she supposed, of how the trust between them had been broken. Did she feel the same now? Could last night begin at last to repair the damage done between them?

She hoped it could. Minou caught her breath, realising that without even noticing it happen, finally she had forgiven Piet. He was still the love of her life. Smiling, she picked up her journal. Alis's words last evening had reminded her of how much she had enjoyed writing, another pleasure that had been stolen from her by the senselessness of the wars. But Alis was safe now and Minou realised she was free to remember with pleasure those long, summer writing afternoons spent on the roof of the keep. Once, writing had helped her make sense of what she felt. It had been her daily conversation with herself. Then the keep had become the place where Alis had nearly been killed, and Minou had lost heart.

She unknotted the leather tie and opened the journal, releasing the scent of Languedoc and the Puivert woods. Pine and beech and the heat of the Midi. She turned to the last entry – Friday, the sixth of June 1572 – almost six years ago.

Minou exhaled, remembering how she'd passed that afternoon wrestling with her conscience and trying to decide if they should accompany Piet to Paris or not. If only she had chosen otherwise, how different their lives would have been.

Then she pulled herself up. They would not have lost Marta, that was undeniable. She would not be living every day with a hole in her heart, wondering if her daughter was alive. But Aimeric would still have been in Paris, and Piet alongside him. They would have been caught up in the massacre. And months later, Puivert would still have been attacked too.

What if.

Minou felt a wave of sadness wash over her. There was no sense in regretting the decisions of the past. She couldn't go back. All she could do was to make the best of the present and cherish what they still had.

Alis was here. She had survived.

Today, she would show her sister the city Minou had come to love. They would go to the cloth merchants on Rokin and buy fabric to make Alis some new clothes. Then, she would take her to Kalverstraat, where the artists' ateliers and book binders had their studios, and buy herself a new quill and inkwell. After tomorrow – God willing, if all went peacefully – Alis would start to settle into life in Amsterdam, and she would begin to write again. Minou took a final glance at the empty page in the journal and imagined inscribing today's date: the twenty-sixth day of May 1578.

A red-letter day.

Then she thought of how much might go wrong in the coup – all it would take was one nervous boy with a rock in his hand – and her thoughts clouded.

There was a sound behind her as Frans came into the chamber. 'Madame, the master wants to know if you will join him below?'

Minou shut the lid of the casket. 'Tell him I will.'

Rather than taking his leave, the boy sauntered over to the window.

'Are you recovered?' she asked kindly.

'I can take care of myself,' he said with bravado. 'I recognised him – one of Houtman's men. Joost Wouter. He's an idiot. I'll kick him up the arse next time I run into him.'

She laughed. 'You will do no such thing!'

'Speak of the Devil,' Frans said, peering out of the window.

Minou moved to join him. 'Is that the man who hurt you? Wouter, did you say?' She followed the line of his gaze to Sint Antoniespoort opposite.

'Nah, that's Jan Houtman. He's in charge.' He sniffed. 'Mind you, there's a few tales I could tell about him.'

'What kind of tales?'

'Tales he wouldn't want getting about, I'll tell you that for nothing.'

Minou had the glimmering of an idea. Firmly, she put her hands on his shoulders and turned him to face her.

'Frans, this might be important. Tell me everything you know about Jan Houtman.'

CHAPTER SIXTY-FIVE

PLAATS
Monday, 26 May

At the beginning of the day in which Amsterdam crossed from the past into its future, the air was muggy, greasy with the smells and sounds of an overcrowded city. The wind blew briskly over Op 't Water towards Damrak, setting the ensigns and flags snapping. There was a whispering in the rigging of the ships on the IJ, as messages were passed between the lighters and the barges. There was a shimmering in the sky as the sun went in and out of the scudding clouds.

When Minou looked out of the top-floor casement, she noticed a group of men clustered at the corner of Zeedijk. She turned her head to the right and saw that the gates of the Grey Friars monastery, a few paces from their little house, were still closed even though the sun had risen. Opposite, outside Sint Antoniespoort on the far side of the square, she realised some soldiers were still at their posts despite the night watch having finished some hours ago.

The action – if all went ahead according to plan – was to take place in Plaats in the afternoon when the council was in session.

Her nerves taut in her chest, Minou turned away from the window, hoping that what Frans had told her about Houtman might be the leverage to force him to keep his word. Houtman was the key. His men would follow his lead. If he ordered them to attack, they would. If he ordered restraint, they would obey.

But a little after midday, Minou heard a musket shot ring out from Sint Antoniespoort. She rushed to the front door and saw a man running across the square, waving rebel colours.

'Any who love Orange, show heart and follow me!'

The action was supposed to begin at Plaats, but yet something was happening here. It was too soon. She watched nervously as the gates of Sint Antoniespoort were thrown open and men staggered out with hay bales, then others started to roll cannons across the bridge over the moat into the square.

'What's happening?' Alis asked anxiously, appearing at her side. 'Is it starting?'

'I'm not sure. I must tell Piet.'

'I'm coming with you.'

Minou hesitated. 'Very well. Tell Agnes to lock the doors and keep the children inside until we return.'

As Alis went, Minou turned back to watch. On the far side of the square, she could now hear the sounds of fighting – the *schutterij* and the men of the night watch – and it was impossible to know on which side any man's loyalty might lie.

They hurried over the canals towards the main square. It was market day, so the streets were crowded. So far, the disturbance at the eastern gate didn't yet seem to have spread into the heart of the city.

But when they arrived at Plaats, Minou saw how the rebels had closed off all the entrances into the square. The small streets leading into the main square from the north and the west were already blocked. A line of men was standing at Damrak.

'Are they Catholic or Protestant?' Alis whispered.

Minou remembered the white armbands and painted crosses upon the doors of Catholic houses on the night of the St Bartholomew's Day massacre, and realised how much more complicated things were in Amsterdam.

'It's hard to tell. There are men of both denominations within all of the *schutterij* guilds and the Watch.'

The Stadhuis stood impassive in the overcast day. Once one of the city's finest medieval buildings, the passing of time and fire had tarnished it. Slogans supporting the Revolt had been daubed on the peeling plaster. The weathervane atop the tower had fallen to one side, giving the impression the wind was coming up from the cobbles of the square rather than from the west.

'Is Piet here?' Alis asked.

'Somewhere.'

As Minou scanned the crowd, looking for sight of him, she realised that there were very few women about. And all around the square traders were attempting to leave: closing up their wooden shelves with a snap, loading their goods onto carts to be wheeled away from Plaats and trouble. Without an order being given or a shot fired, the Stadhuis had become a muster point. Members of the watchmen and *schutterij* sympathetic to the Calvinist cause, would protect the gates. The leaders of the Geuzen would go into the chamber to disrupt the session. The aim was to intimidate Dircksz and the burghers into submission through force of numbers.

Piet had explained that Houtman and his men would approach from the direction of Sint Nicolaas. Minou kept looking until, finally, she saw her husband standing in the middle of the three wide stone arches in front of the council house. He was with Houtman, who was on the point of mounting the steps.

'There,' she said urgently to Alis. 'Come.'

Quickly, they made their way across the square until she was close enough to catch his eye. Piet nodded, then, as arranged between them the previous evening, he slipped away from Houtman's side so that Minou could take his place.

'Meneer Houtman?'

'Not now, woman.'

'Meneer,' she insisted, in her careful Dutch. 'I would speak with you.'

Houtman ignored her. Minou darted up the steps to stand directly in front of him. She had to make him listen.

'Get out of my way.'

She held her ground. 'I know you are a man of honour.'

'Get out of my way.'

He tried to move past her, but again Minou blocked his path. 'Go into the chamber armed with words, not weapons.'

He hesitated. 'What!'

'We want no bloodshed. We have seen enough.'

Houtman went to push Minou aside, but Alis grabbed his wrist and dragged his arm up behind his back. One of Houtman's men moved to intervene, but Piet blocked him.

'Let him go, sister,' Minou said quietly.

Alis jerked his arm up between his shoulders, then released him.

Houtman rubbed his wrist. 'Who do you think you are? I've no time to listen to the prattling of women.'

Minou met his gaze. 'Indeed, I heard the opposite. That, in fact, so much do you enjoy the company of women that you have not one but two wives, and two households. The question is do the ladies know about one another? Do our Calvinist ministers know?'

Houtman's face turned puce. 'It's a lie.'

'A pretty house near Heiligeweg – there's a line of blue tiles above the lintel – and the other, rather less salubrious, by Sint Olofspoort.'

Houtman brought his face close to hers. 'Who told you that?' he spat. 'Whoever it was, they lied.'

Minou smiled. 'Perhaps it is a misunderstanding, but men will talk and common gossip spreads so quickly, true or false.'

'If I do support any residence in Sint Olofspoort, it is for charitable reasons alone. All good citizens should know their Christian duty.'

'That is honourable.' Minou smiled to mask her true feelings.

Houtman turned on Piet. 'Is this your doing, Reydon?'

'Listen to what my wife has to say, Houtman.'

'What is it that you want, woman? Speak. I cannot wait.'

'Only that there should be no bloodshed.'

He laughed. 'And you think I can prevent it?'

'I think that you have the respect of your men,' Minou replied in a level voice. 'Where you lead, they will follow.'

Houtman paused. 'And if I do speak for moderation, you will not utter a word of this heinous gossip?'

Minou held his eye. 'If you do your best to ensure that this transition will be peaceful, then I will keep what I know to myself. Use your influence, Meneer Houtman. No weapons, no mock trials, no executions.' Then she bent down and whispered the final damning piece of information in his ear.

Houtman pulled back in fury. 'I will do all I can,' he said, 'you have my word.' Then he swept up the steps and into the town hall.

Minou signalled to Piet, waiting now on the corner of Kalverstraat, letting let him know the message had been delivered, then took Alis's arm and walked away from the Stadhuis. It was in Piet's hands now.

'Alis, are you all right?' she asked, realising her sister was struggling to keep up.

'I walk a little slower these days.'

'I didn't think, forgive me.'

Alis took a couple of deep breaths. 'Do you remember, when I was little, I used to be able to outrun even Aimeric.'

'Yes. And just now you were courageous – my thanks. Tackling Houtman like that.'

'Old habits.' Alis pulled a wry smile. 'These past years, I've picked up one or two tricks to discourage men with straying hands. Strike first, ask questions later.'

Minou laughed. 'I can't imagine what Aunt Salvadora would have to say about that. Strange to say, I miss her company.'

'We'll see her again. We'll see Toulouse again.'

Alis looked around at the crowds that were gathering. Some were shouting, but most were quiet. 'What are they waiting for?'

'To see what happens next.'

'What should we do?'

Minou wasn't sure. The cannons dragged from Sint Antoniespoort and elsewhere were now lined up near Damrak. Close to Oudezijds, the dam was blockaded with hay bales and in the water below two barges, guarded by *schutterij*, were moored and waiting. If there was trouble, then she and Alis would be trapped.

'At the first sign of trouble, we'll leave,' Minou said in a low voice.

Her heart was racing now, with hope or with dread, she couldn't tell. How long would it be before there was news from within the chamber?

'Why would Houtman be so worried about such a secret?' Alis asked. 'There was barely a man in La Rochelle who didn't have a mistress tucked away somewhere.'

'Amsterdam is a city that thrives on order. The Calvinists are very austere in matters of morality. They judge men's venial habits almost as harshly as they do those of women. If Houtman wishes for advancement in the new regime, he cannot afford to have a scandal against his name.'

'It seems such a trivial matter. Not to the women themselves,' she added quickly, seeing the look on Minou's face. 'But, to me, it seems so little with which to bargain with a man like Houtman, that's all.'

'Frans – he's the oldest of our boys in the *hofje*, you met him last evening – he told me that Houtman's new wife in Heiligeweg is wealthy, an elderly widow with no children. His first wife, on the other hand, is young – and has given him three sons in so many years – but as poor as a church mouse.'

Alis raised her eyebrows. 'So he married again unlawfully to support them. I see.'

Minou nodded. 'It seems so. Amsterdam is not like Toulouse, where only men from the oldest families are allowed to serve in civic positions. But to advance, Houtman will need money. Without it, he has no chance of reaching high office.' Minou gestured to the new warehouse buildings, the freshly painted shutters, the keystones above the doors, the gleaming brass door knockers reflected in the surface of the still water. 'Look around you. All this respectability comes at a price.'

'And this is the kind of man you put your trust in? If our leaders are dissemblers, dishonest, then what hope for the rest of us?'

Minou's expression grew grave. 'I know. I only hope it's enough.'

'Do you really think one man's word can make the difference?'

'In my experience, it is always one man's voice that makes

the difference. For good or for ill. If Houtman makes his case well, others will follow.' Minou sighed. 'And it's to be hoped it isn't just me. In Amsterdam, as true as we stand here, there's an army of women using their powers of moderation and persuasion to the same end. To persuade men to lay down their weapons.'

'A regiment marching to peace not war.'

Minou looked down at her own reflection in the water. With her white coif, her modest gown and matron's collar, these days she looked quite the Dutch housewife. She smiled.

'Exactly so.'

CHAPTER SIXTY-SIX

Plaats

Piet found a place in the balcony that ran high up around three sides of the debating chamber.

The Calvinists had taken possession of the Stadhuis with little resistance. Though the crowds outside in Plaats were noisy, they had been orderly, as if there was no question of dissent and the Geuzen had walked unchallenged into the building, flanked by armed civilians and soldiers.

When the leaders had continued into the courtroom itself – sparking fear and outrage amongst the council members – their supporters had remained in the hall to ensure the official guard had no reason to intervene.

Sitting in wooden stalls, far below Piet, were the burghers, magistrates, councillors, court officials, with their flat, black hats and fur stoles of office. Some were on their feet objecting to the occupation of the chamber, most were waiting in silence to see what would happen.

On the raised dais at the west end of the chamber stood Hendrick Dircksz, burgomaster and leader of the council for forty years. His closest allies sat behind him in two rows of high-backed oak chairs. In front of the dais, two scribes and the council Recorder were positioned on high stools at a long narrow desk, their quills poised in their hands as if paused in the act of some official business that might never now be concluded.

Piet was assailed suddenly by a memory of his younger self

stealing his way into another such meeting in Toulouse in the early days of the wars. On that day in April in 1562, the wrong decision had been taken, resulting in a massacre that lasted five days and destroyed whole sections of the ancient city. Many thousands of Huguenots – Catholics too – had been slaughtered, all because their leaders had been unable to agree a compromise. Piet caught his breath. Pray God, that would not happen again.

This was Amsterdam not Toulouse.

Standing in front of Dircksz was the leader of the Calvinist Geuzen, flanked by his comrades. Piet could see the glint of the silver crescent medals on his black doublet, so although Piet didn't know who he was, he knew he must have done great service to the rebel cause to have acquired himself such ornamentation.

Piet cast his eyes around the chamber, picking out those men he knew from his own side and on the council: Willem van Raay, standing to one side; Burgher Jansz, a soap merchant on Warmoesstraat; the van Raays' neighbour, Jacob Pauw; Joost Buyck, one of the most successful grain merchants in the city. On the opposite side of the chamber, stood Jan Houtman with Wouter at his side.

Like the calm before a summer storm in the Pyrenees, the atmosphere in the chamber crackled with expectation and menace as the two opponents, enemies for many years, at last found themselves face to face.

'These are our demands,' the Calvinist leader said, holding out a document.

Piet watched Dircksz take it. Calmly, his hand appearing steady, he began to read. It seemed to Piet that every man in the chamber, however he worshipped God, was holding his breath.

Dircksz read the document through a second time, then raised his head.

'I regret that, without better safeguards, I cannot agree to these terms.' He slapped the paper with the back of his hand. 'We need guarantees that you will abide by what you say. How can we be certain you will honour these conditions in return for our agreement to step down?'

Piet had expected Dircksz to refuse to negotiate point blank, even to summon the guard, but yet he appeared to be suggesting there was some kind of negotiation to be had. Was there reason to hope? Gripping the wooden balustrade, he leant further out.

'Are you doubting my good faith?'

'I am asking for proof of it,' Dircksz replied.

Then someone from the floor uttered an oath and the chamber erupted. In an instant, everyone was arguing, fingers jabbing at the air, a priest raising his hands as if to Heaven. Several of the Calvinists turned and shouted insults until, at a sign from Dircksz, a sharp rap of a gavel cut through the commotion.

'I will have silence!' the Recorder shouted. 'Burgomaster Dircksz will speak!'

But the Calvinist leader stepped forward. 'You insult the Prince of Orange, and our nationhood, by refusing to comply with the terms of the Satisfaction. He is the rightful ruler of these Provinces, not a Spanish king who shores up his debt-ridden Empire from Madrid on the back of our taxes.'

'A king rules by divine right.'

'Not in Holland, he doesn't. He's no more than a man.'

Dircksz crossed himself. 'You offend God by your blasphemy.'

The Calvinist turned away. Again, his followers burst into noisy objection.

'Order! I will have order!' the Recorder shouted. 'Members of the town council, my noble lords, gentlemen all, respect the traditions of this chamber.'

As the debate raged on, Piet noticed Houtman walk up and

whisper something to the Calvinist leader. At the same time, he saw Willem van Raay step out of his stall and approach the dais to speak to his colleagues.

Piet's heart caught in his throat. Might their plan work? Dircksz seemed to be shaking his head. Houtman put his hand on his leader's arm and was shrugged off.

Then the doors were flung open and a messenger came running, pushing his way through the mass of men crowding in the aisles until he reached the dais. Red-faced and out of breath, he passed a note to the official Recorder, who stepped onto the dais and gave it to Dircksz himself.

The chamber fell into an expectant silence.

'There is no doubt of this?' Dircksz asked.

'None,' the messenger replied, his voice as clear as a bell.

Dircksz read the message one last time, and then nodded. He seemed to have aged ten years in as many minutes, as if his forty years of responsibility had suddenly taken their toll. His shoulders dropped, though whether in relief or despair Piet couldn't quite tell.

'I see,' Dircksz finally said, turning first to his allies, sitting behind him, and then to the mass of councillors sitting below. '*Mijn vrienden*,' he said. 'My friends and loyal colleagues, for the good of Amsterdam, I concede.'

A murmur of disbelief spread like wildfire through the chamber. Men looked at one another, whispering frantically, no one quite sure what was happening. The Calvinist leader hesitated for a moment, then he spoke.

'By the authority invested in me, I hereby attest that on the twenty-sixth day of May, in the year of our Lord 1578, in the presence of all its members, we take control of this chamber in the name of the Prince of Orange.' He turned around. 'Will you escort these gentlemen from the chamber?'

Piet realised he'd been holding his breath. Could it be possible that power could be taken so easily and without a shot being fired?

With great dignity, his head held high, Dircksz stepped down from the dais. After a moment of stunned disbelief, his fellow burgomasters and burghers followed, progressing in silence through the chamber and out through the main doors.

For a moment after they'd gone, there was silence. Then, pandemonium. Calvinists were slapping one another on the back, some even occupying the seats in the stalls just left vacant.

'Long live Amsterdam!' went up the cry. 'Long live the Prince of Orange!'

The remaining councillors headed for the doors, pushing and elbowing one another aside in their haste to return to their businesses and their ships, their warehouses and hearths. Their leaders had gone, but they had no idea what this would mean for the common man. Only time would tell.

Up on the balcony, Piet leant back against the wall, trying to make sense of what he had witnessed. Was it possible that forty years of uninterrupted power had been brought to an end just like that?

He knew what the note had said – that all the gates into the city were now in the hands of Calvinists, control of the harbour too. Dircksz had no choice but to concede. He, and his fellow burgomasters and burghers, would be escorted to exile beyond the boundaries of Amsterdam. Two barges were standing ready at Damrak to transport them, along with leading members of the Catholic clergy and friars. It was a sensible precautionary measure to prevent them organising opposition to the new council. Since many Calvinists had themselves been exiled from the city during the wars, it was no wonder they wished to impose the same penalty on the men they had finally defeated.

Piet also knew the note presented to Dircksz promised that all best attempts would be taken to protect the exiled men's homes from looters, and that their families would be allowed to join them in exile.

They would now have their churches. Their Protestant churches. But Catholics, too, would be free to worship in peace. Amsterdam would be a modern city, a tolerant city.

Piet shook his head, still not quite able to accept the evidence of his own eyes. Was it truly possible that not a single man, on either side, had raised his firearm or let his hand slip to his knife? He hesitated, feeling an unwelcome stab of doubt. What if there was some kind of ambush waiting outside the building? What if it had all been a trick, a show of smoke and mirrors? What if the barges were attacked or an assassin was waiting in the square? All it would take was for one shot to be fired or one man to draw his sword, and diplomacy would be dead.

Piet leapt to his feet and ran for the stairs.

CHAPTER SIXTY-SEVEN

PLAATS

Alis looked back towards the Stadhuis.

'Minou, I think something's happening.'

Half an hour had passed since the Calvinists had gone into the town hall. Minou could hear the shouting too, but could not see what the crowd was reacting to. The atmosphere was unlike anything she'd ever experienced. There was anger and protest, but none of the smouldering resentment that so easily turned a crowd into a mob.

'Isn't that Cornelia?' Alis said.

'Where?'

Alis pointed. 'There.'

Minou looked towards Kalverstraat, then waved. Cornelia quickly pushed her way through to join them.

'What is happening?' she asked quickly. 'Could you see?'

'The Geuzen are bringing out the burgomasters and some of the burghers. They're taking them to the barges.' She clasped Minou's arm, her face white with fear. 'Minou, what if my father is one of them? If he's taken away, what will I do? He won't survive exile. Our business won't survive.'

'Piet has done what he can to protect your father,' Minou said, praying Houtman would keep his word. 'No harm will come to him.'

'The leaders in the chamber might have agreed,' Cornelia said desperately, 'but what of them?' She gestured to the crowd.

'What about all those who've resented Dircksz's control of the city for so long? They hold him and his associates responsible for their hunger and suffering, how are *they* to know my father is a good man?'

Minou couldn't ever remember seeing Cornelia lose control of her emotions before. During their flight from Paris and their perilous journey north, she had never been anything less than steadfast.

'Even if your father is obliged to leave the city for a while, you can manage his affairs in his absence. We will help.'

Alis nodded. 'Whatever happens, your father will be safe, Minou and Piet will make it so. I cannot think your father would want you to be distressed.'

Cornelia exhaled. 'That, at least, is true.'

Abruptly, the crowd parted to let through three or four of the Geuzen, followed by two lines of heavily armed citizen soldiers escorting Hendrick Dircksz and his fellow burgo-masters. The council Recorder and other burghers walked in pairs behind them, followed by leading Catholic clergy and the hated Grey Friars, who had been the eyes and ears of the Spanish in Amsterdam.

'Why have they capitulated?'

Minou looked at Cornelia. 'The Calvinists are too well organ-ised, they have the people on their side.'

'There's our priest from the Nieuwe Kerk,' Cornelia said in distress. 'I pray they will not harm him.'

Only the Grey Friars showed signs of violence: torn robes and bloodied faces. As soon as the crowd saw them, they started to jeer and shout abuse.

Cornelia let out a sob when she saw her father near the back of the line, moving slowly with his arm supporting Jacob Pauw, who could barely walk.

When the prisoners reached the water's edge, the taunting and the yelling stopped. A hushed silence fell over the crowds watching near Damrak and the Nieuwe Zijde.

Dircksz was the first to be put into the boat.

He hesitated a moment on the wharf, turning back as if to bid a final farewell to his fiefdom. Then, ignoring the proffered hand of a soldier, he stepped down unaided into the barge. The council Recorder followed, the craft rocking on the water as the burgomasters joined them.

Then, it was Willem van Raay's turn to be brought forward to the wharf. Minou looked around, desperately trying to find Piet in the mêlée.

'I can't bear it,' Cornelia cried. 'I have to speak to him! I can't let him go without a word.'

Minou held her back. 'I know it's hard to watch and do nothing, but you will make it worse for him. We have a plan. Try not to worry.'

She looked anxiously back across the square, in time to see a man running from the direction of the Stadhuis, pushing his way through without regard. Only when he reached Damrak, did Minou realise it was Houtman himself.

'Stop!' he shouted. 'This prisoner is to be given into my care,' he panted, gesturing to Willem van Raay.

Minou breathed a sigh of relief.

'On whose orders?' a soldier demanded.

Houtman held out a document. 'Here, in black and white. The prisoner is to be taken to Sint Antoniespoort.'

'No!' Cornelia cried. 'If they take him in there, I'll never see him again. Prisoners don't survive in that place, you know it. Let me go.'

'Cornelia, you have to trust me,' Minou whispered urgently. 'No harm will come to your father, I give you my word.'

Willem van Raay was dragged out of the line, his arms pulled up behind him, and was instantly surrounded by Houtman's men.

'No!' Cornelia shouted again. 'Let me go!'

Again, she tried to get free, but the soldiers were already marching her father across to the Oude Zijde. The fight suddenly went out of her. Her body slumped. She dropped her head onto Minou's shoulder and started to weep.

'All will be well, my friend. Everything will resolve itself.'

Except it might not, whispered the spiteful voice in her head. What if Houtman went back on his word? What if something had happened to Piet so he couldn't intervene? What if the price for averting widespread conflict turned out to be the life of Willem van Raay?

'All will be well,' Minou said again, and prayed she was right.

Now the second of the barges, this one with Jacob Pauw on board, pushed away from the quay and began its journey to the IJ.

'How can you be sure?' Cornelia sobbed. 'Men rarely keep their word.'

'Follow them,' Minou whispered to Alis. 'Make sure they indeed take Willem to Sint Antoniespoort.'

A look of panic flashed across Alis's face. With a jolt, Minou realised her sister had no idea how to get there. It felt so natural to have her by her side, she had forgotten Alis had only been in Amsterdam a matter of forty-eight hours.

'We'll go together,' Minou said quickly.

The three women followed Houtman's men across the canals and alleyways to the east of the city. Behind them on Plaats, Minou could hear sounds of cheering and celebration, but she kept her eyes focused on Willem van Raay being walked to the east of the city. Her nerves were strung tight for fear their plan would fail.

They hurried across Oudezijds Voorburgwal, along Kloveniersburgwal and in the direction of Zeedijk until the familiar red towers of Sint Antoniespoort came into view. As she stood at the periphery of the square, she could see their own house calm and undisturbed in the May afternoon sunshine, but the doors of the Grey Friars cloister were wide open and she suspected the looters were already inside. The people despised them.

'Wait,' Minou said.

They could only watch as Willem van Raay was taken onto the footbridge over the moat, and into the gatehouse.

Cornelia let her hands drop to her side. 'He's gone.'

'This is what we planned. Go with Alis to our house and wait there,' Minou said firmly. 'I will join you as soon as I can.'

'What are you going to do?'

'Piet and I promised to look after your father.'

'But it's impossible to get inside!'

Alis put her arm around Cornelia's shoulder. 'Come, Minou knows what to do.'

Minou pulled her bonnet low on her brow and walked quickly across the square towards Sint Antoniespoort. Contrary to Alis's assurance, she had no idea what she was going to do next, only that it would be better to be close at hand for when Piet came. He should have been here already.

The gatehouse was surrounded by a moat, with a small flat bridge leading to the entrance. On the town side were four bulky defensive red-brick towers, with turrets like grey pointed hats. There was another gate with two towers facing towards the countryside beyond and a subterranean sluice gate, so the singing of the rushing water was always just there beneath the everyday sounds of the changing of the guard and the rattle of wooden wheels on cobbled stones.

The narrow door in the tall hexagonal tower was being guarded by the *schutterij* as usual. That was reassuring. Nothing in the soldiers' demeanour gave any indication that something particular was happening inside.

Suddenly, the door was thrown open. Minou heard voices, then the younger of the two guards raised his firearm and disappeared within. In those seconds, she saw a man standing in the courtyard. Minou's gaze took in a torn doublet, the russet-coloured hair, the prisoner's bloody hands tied behind his back. Then the soldier jabbed the man with his musket and he turned, revealing his face to be a mass of bruises and cuts.

'Piet!'

The door shuddered on its hinges and was bolted shut, leaving Minou standing distraught on the wrong side of the gates.

CHAPTER SIXTY-EIGHT

Many hundreds of leagues from Amsterdam, a grey afternoon in the Chartres countryside, Vidal sat and watched his son paint.

As soon as they had returned from the reliquary the previous day, Louis had provided a list of the materials he would need for Vidal's servants. All afternoon, packages kept arriving.

Early this morning, they had repaired to Vidal's private rooms in the manor house, where the light was good, and Louis had begun to work.

High windows from floor to ceiling ran all along one side of the rectangular chamber. On the opposite wall, paintings and gold mirrors reflected the polished oak and walnut furniture, with curtains of pale green satin and matching upholstery. It was a room for entertaining honoured guests, not an artist's studio. All the same, it was here that Louis had asked to be allowed to work. For once, Vidal had indulged him.

'Where did you acquire your skill?' he asked, genuinely curious.

Louis looked up. 'In the scriptorium of the monastery in Saint-Antonin. The monks made use of some of the older boys who showed any aptitude with a quill to save their own hands.'

'What did they teach you?'

'To prepare the pigments – slow, laborious work – and how to copy the letters just so.' His face clouded over. 'It was the only warm room in the monastery.'

'You made yourself indispensable?'

'It was a safer place to be than – elsewhere,' Louis said simply, a frown flitting across his face. 'I was allowed to have any scraps of spoiled parchment for my own.'

Vidal drained his wine, seeing his bare-headed reflection in the bottom of the empty goblet. He placed it back on the table.

'Why did you not mention this before?'

'I never thought it a skill worth having.'

'Until now.'

'Yes, my lord.'

'Though you continued to practise in secret.'

Louis hesitated. 'Was that wrong?'

Vidal smiled. 'Quite the opposite, especially when your talent is now used to the glory of God.'

Louis gave a half-smile, then picked up his brush again.

Vidal poured himself another cup of wine and drank deeply, his thoughts far away.

God had stopped listening to him many years past, a voice becoming fainter and fainter until it disappeared altogether. Possibly God had never been listening. But soon things would change. Vidal was aware how his faith, so often compromised and questioned and broken, was growing stronger again the closer he came to the grave. With the power conferred on him through his acquisition of the holiest relics, he would fulfil his ambition of creating a new Catholic order in the heart of the ancient diocese of Chartres. When it was safe to come out of the shadows once more – when Guise was dead or reduced in power – Vidal would emerge as God's true representative on earth, without the shackles of the moribund Catholic Church. Vidal smiled. He would force God to accept him back into His grace once more.

A devout student in Toulouse twenty-five years ago, Vidal

had quickly learnt that it was wealth and knowledge that mattered in the service of the Holy Mother Church, not piety. It was power that gave a man advancement. He had been quick to learn: Latin, Greek, Italian, English, Spanish, a little Hebrew. A desire never to be at the mercy of other people's interpretations – so to be able to read scripture and holy writ for himself – made him one of the hardest-working scholars at the Collège de Foix.

Vidal had always known he was unsuited to the rigours of a life in the service of the Church but, as the son of a traitor whose assets had been seized, his prospects were poor. Vidal's only support came from his pious uncle and without his patronage, his life wouldn't have been worth the candle. So when his uncle expressed a desire for him to take holy orders when his studies were completed, Vidal knew he had no choice.

In those first months of his first ministry in Saint-Antonin, he had served God with sincerity and belief, though his eye was always caught by a pretty face or the illicit glimpse of an ankle. The life of the soul was considerably less appealing than the pleasures of the flesh. In those days, his conscience had troubled him. After each new transgression, he prayed for forgiveness. He chastised himself and confessed his sins. He vowed never to fall again, he made penance and renewed his vows. He imposed on himself the harshest of physical penalties and confined himself to the narrow path of virtue. But however long it lasted – until this feast day or that, sometimes longer – he'd always found himself back in a warm bed in the end.

Now, at last, his blood had grown cool.

Vidal drank another measure of wine, hoping to dull the throbbing in his head. The pain was bad today. The physician had bled him and given him powders, but neither measure had worked.

Vidal had always accepted that he could not stray from the Catholic Church until his uncle died, not without risking his legacy. He had bided his time. But all the while, he was planning and building up a hidden fortune of his own. Selling indulgences, accepting gifts from grateful widows, his stratagems were various and varied. Finally, he had been in a position to buy this ruined estate outside Chartres, ready to step into his new identity when the time was right.

Finally, in August 1572, some five months after his uncle's death, the stars aligned. The attack on de Coligny and the plot to assassinate the Huguenot leadership on St Bartholomew's Day had given him the chance to disappear.

Cardinal Valentin had become Lord Evreux.

But Reydon continued to prey on his mind. In time, Vidal had learnt he and his family had survived the massacre in Paris and had fled to Amsterdam. However, since Xavier had been adamant no proof of his uncle's ill-advised union or Reydon's legitimacy existed, Vidal had decided to let him alone, though he had spies keeping an eye out in case things changed. But Reydon was always there in his thoughts, like a splinter beneath his skin. His uncle's deathbed confession that he had fathered a child had made sure of that.

Vidal also knew the Duke of Guise had not given up looking for him. Even with the demands of leading the Catholic League, even with the never-ending spiral of wars and treaties, Guise managed to maintain a large network of spies. His tentacles spread into every province of France and, by leaving the duke's service without permission or his blessing, Vidal had turned his former patron into a dangerous enemy.

Until recently, his precautions had held. His identity remained secret. But with the eight months of relative peace after the end of the Sixth War, Guise evidently had more time to turn his attention back to his errant confessor. In past weeks, Vidal had received word from several well-trusted informants about a man in the Duke of Guise's household – a Parisian by the name of Cabanel, formerly a captain in the militia – who had been asking questions in Reims and in Blois.

For the first time since his disappearance, he felt the breath of Guise's hounds snapping at his heels. Vidal hadn't yet decided on his course of action. The temptation to send an assassin to hunt an assassin was strong. It was not conscience that held him back. Vidal had the blood of many on his hands. He had been a feared and effective Inquisitor in Carcassonne and Toulouse in the early days of the wars. In God's name, he had ordered bodies stretched and flagellated and hanged. He had tracked down heretics and blasphemers with a complete lack of mercy. There had also been other killings of course, for advantage and for revenge, that could not be laid at God's door.

But Vidal was also aware that sometimes a trail went cold and also that, by acting too soon, one could end up inviting attention rather than avoiding it.

For the time being, instinct told him to wait.

'Wait and see,' he said.

'My lord?' Louis said.

Vidal was surprised to realise he had spoken out loud.

The clock chimed three. Vidal realised that the boy had been working for hours without stopping to take sustenance. His concentration was absolute.

Louis pushed back his chair and stood up.

'There. It is done.'

Vidal felt an unaccustomed quiver of excitement. As he walked over to the table, he was conscious of how much he wanted the boy to have done well.

Louis flexed his fingers, then stepped back. 'It is not perfect, my lord, but I can do no better.'

In the overcast Chartres afternoon, the image seemed to glow and shimmer and dance in front of Vidal's eyes. Vidal examined the shining halo of colour painted on the simple board, twists of rushes held within a crystal circle. At the top a blue shield showed Christ upon the Cross. Two other smaller discs in the same cobalt blue were equally exquisite, one depicting Saint Louis entering Paris with the relic in his hands and the other the gates of Jerusalem.

'The representations on the shields may not be accurate,' Louis said. 'I never got close enough to see properly. I had to guess at the detail of what each might show. I've done my best.'

Vidal straightened up. He could hear the fear in his son's voice and realised the boy was mistaking his silence for displeasure.

'This is the greatest gift you could have made me.'

Louis's face brightened. 'It pleases you, my lord?'

'It does. This is the Crown of Thorns in every particular. It is a match for its size, its shape, the beauty of its design.'

Louis exhaled. 'It is good enough to place it in the reliquary?'

Vidal stared, surprised by the boy misunderstanding. Then, aware of a sense of pride in his son's work, he smiled.

'That is not its purpose, Louis. What we will do now is to find a craftsman capable of making a fair copy of the Crown itself. Then we will return to the Sainte-Chapelle. Paris is safe for now, but the threat from the heretic Navarre, and his fellow iconoclasts, is ever present.'

He watched Louis's features change as he understood. 'As with the Shroud of Antioch and the Sancta Camisia.'

Vidal smiled. 'The holiest of relics should be kept safe and well away from the hands of those who would destroy them.

All the better to glorify God's purpose.' He paused. 'You have a great talent, Louis.'

The boy blushed.

For the first time since the death of the only woman he had ever loved – he held Reydon responsible for that – Vidal felt his heart moved. For the first time, he put his arms around his son's shoulders and embraced him. At last, he was claiming him completely as his own.

CHAPTER SIXTY-NINE

SINT ANTONIESPOORT, AMSTERDAM

Frantically, Minou looked around, trying to see if there was any possible way for her to get into Sint Antoniespoort.

She patrolled the moat, but all the wooden gates set within the stone arches were bolted with heavy iron bars and latched, and the main gate was guarded by two armed sentries. There was also an iron grille across the sluice gates to stop any trying to approach the tower through the sewers. There was no possibility of her gaining admittance without being seen. Minou looked up at the windows. All were shuttered and, again, in full view.

Then she had the glimmering of an idea. If she could not find a way to get in unseen, then she would have to do so in plain sight. She cast her eyes around the square until she lighted upon an old woman. Wearing a threadbare worsted cloak with a brown hood, nondescript and commonplace, she carried a wicker basket with a red-and-white cloth across the top. That would do well for Minou's purposes. Better still, the woman looked to be heading towards Sint Antoniespoort itself – perhaps delivering bread and herring to a son or husband stationed within the tower? Even on a day like today, ordinary life went on.

Quickly, Minou fell into step beside her. 'How now, Mevrouw, it is a fair afternoon, is it not?'

The old woman turned, her eyes suspicious. 'I've known worse.'

'I hope you will forgive me for intruding upon your peace, but I have a proposition. A friend wagered me – you know the way of these things – that I could not find someone willing to exchange her cloak for mine. I told him he was wrong and accepted the wager.'

The woman stopped. 'Why should you wish to? Is your cloak of so poor a quality?'

'No indeed, the opposite is true,' Minou replied, offering the fabric of her own softly spun wool. She twitched it open, revealing its rich silk lining, the colour of cherries.

The old woman rubbed the cloth between her fingers. 'This is not from Amsterdam.'

'No. I am charged with exchanging my garment, fine as it is, with one of local provenance. Such as yours, Mevrouw. That is the wager.'

'Such as mine?'

'Yes. It is foolish, I know, but I would not have my friend think I have failed in the task with which he charged me.'

'He?' she snorted derisively. 'It's like that, then. Aren't you a bit old for that kind of a game?'

Minou shrugged. 'What can I say? He would make a good match. I am a widow. I have no father or brothers. No sons either,' she added, feeling uncomfortable with the lie.

The woman sneered. 'How old are you?'

'Already into my fourth decade.'

'Not a good age to seek a new match.'

'No,' Minou agreed. 'My first husband was killed in the siege of Haarlem.'

'By Catholics?' Minou was trying to decide where the woman's allegiance might lie, when she spat on the ground. 'Two of my sons died when those Spanish dogs took the city.'

'So many good men dead.'

For a moment, the old woman was silent. Minou prayed she was weighing up the bargain.

'I'll think about it,' she said, suddenly sly. 'I am delivering this to my nephew in Sint Antoniespoort. If you are still here when I come out, we'll see.'

'Why don't I do that service for you after the trouble there today?' Minou said quickly. 'There was a shot fired, before all the trouble in Plaats began. Or so I heard.'

The old woman glanced over her shoulder to the looted Brown Friars cloister, and spat again. 'Amsterdam's better off without them. They should be strung up, the lot of them.'

Minou refused to be diverted. 'My cloak for yours – a straight exchange – and a chore completed on your behalf.'

The woman narrowed her eyes. 'Your bonnet looks to be linen.'

Minou held her gaze. 'It is.'

'A straight exchange. My cloak for your cloak and bonnet?'

'A straight exchange.'

The woman sucked her teeth. 'What about my basket? I would not wish to lose that.'

'I will return it to your door if you tell me where you live.'

'You could do, I suppose.'

Minou held her breath. The tough old woman knew her cloak was worth a fraction of Minou's, but she wanted to drive a harder bargain.

'Your voice. You're not from here. How do I know I can trust you?'

'I was born here,' Minou answered quickly, stealing Piet's history for her own. She'd learnt how suspicious Amsterdammers could be of anyone from outside Holland. 'But my mother died, so to my ill fortune I was taken to be raised by my grand-mother in Flanders.'

'That is bad luck.' The woman sucked her teeth again. 'My nephew is in the gatehouse. You'll have to climb right up.'

'I can do that.'

Finally, the woman nodded. She untied her shabby cloak and handed it over with the basket, then accepted Minou's cloak and bonnet in return. She tied the ribbon firmly beneath her sagging chin.

'His name's Joost. Joost Wouter. He's usually stationed at the top of the tower. There are three pass doors. Make sure you give the basket only to him, they're all thieves.'

'I understand.'

'It's done. No buyer's remorse. No changing your mind. It's not how we do it here.'

'A deal is a deal,' Minou said quickly. The easy part was done.

CHAPTER SEVENTY

SINT ANTONIESPOORT

A hessian hood was being dragged over Piet's head. He struggled, but there was nothing he could do.

With his arms tied behind his back, Piet was pushed forwards at the hard end of a musket. Unable to see, he stumbled and slipped on the stone steps. He didn't understand what had gone wrong. Everything had seemed to be going to plan. When Houtman's men marched Willem van Raay away from Plaats, Piet had followed, as previously agreed. But as soon as he stepped through the gatehouse into the courtyard, rather than finding Willem and Houtman waiting for him, he'd been seized. Piet had landed a few good punches, but it had been four men attacking him. One of them had been Wouter.

'*Naar beneden*,' a voice commanded, ordering him down the stairs.

The lower they went, the more the temperature dropped. Piet could sense the dripping moisture on the brick walls. Through the muffled hessian, he could hear the rushing of the water through the sluice gate. The stench grew worse as they descended, a poisonous stew of fear and excrement and blood. Piet had heard rumours of a hidden prison beneath Sint Antoniespoort, but had thought it a fiction. In this city of canals and dykes, there were few cellars and, in the end, the water always won. Yet here he was, being taken to a hidden Amsterdam he had not wanted to believe existed.

With a final jab in the back from the guard, Piet stumbled on a slimy step. As the hood was ripped from his head, he heard a heavy door being shut and bolted behind him.

Piet blinked, letting his eyes acclimatise to the cramped, dark chamber. There were no windows and no other way out save the door through which he had entered.

Then he felt bile rise in his throat. Bloodstains covered the ground and the walls. Two leather straps hung from metal rings set into the brickwork. A *chatte de griffe*, the spikes stiff with dry brown blood, lay on a table next to an ink horn and a quill. Piet remembered such torture chambers below the streets of Toulouse, where the Inquisition interrogated their prisoners. Minou's beloved late father had suffered in such a place. Many of his former comrades had died in such a place.

But that was France some fifteen years ago. This was Amsterdam.

'On whose order am I here?' Piet demanded.

Now he could just make out the outlines of two men, their faces masked by the shadows. One with the silhouette of a soldier, jerkin and breeches. The other in longer robes.

'Why am I here? Tell me.'

From the shadows, he heard a counter question. 'Why do you think you are here?'

Piet's heart sped up. He knew that voice – formal, precise, measured – but yet, it couldn't be. He had to be wrong.

'Do you know where you are?'

'Monsieur,' Piet said, 'will you identify yourself?'

'Monsieur?' the second man sneered. 'You are in Amsterdam now. You foreigners are all the same.'

Piet's stomach clenched. This voice he recognised for certain. 'Houtman! What in the name of God is going on?'

Clapping slowly, Houtman stepped out of the shadows. 'Are you as much of a fool as you seem, Reydon?'

As Houtman shifted position, Piet had a clear view of his companion's face behind him. The confirmation of what he'd been unwilling to believe hit Piet like a blow to the chest. Willem van Raay. The man who had helped his family, who'd acted on their behalf, the man he'd therefore warned of the coup, this was the man standing in front of him as if their friendship meant nothing.

'Willem?' Piet said in disbelief. 'I don't understand.'

Van Raay said nothing.

Houtman poked Piet hard in the chest. 'Can you imagine my surprise, Huguenot, when Burgher van Raay informed me that I had a spy within my ranks.'

Piet turned cold. 'I don't know what you mean.'

Houtman gave a bark of laughter. 'What kind of vermin leaves his comrades, having sworn an oath of loyalty and of silence, then goes instantly to someone whose allegiance is to our enemies?' He jabbed him again. 'What kind of traitor does that?'

'I can explain.'

Van Raay raised his hand. 'There is nothing to explain. It was an act of treachery.'

Houtman laughed. 'We are Amsterdammers, Burgher van Raay and I. Do you really think we intend to let foreigners instruct us on how to run our city?'

'What of our shared cause?'

Houtman was now standing eye to eye with Piet. 'Don't you understand? There is no shared cause. The new Amsterdam belongs to us. To Holland, not to a ragtag alliance of refugees. Certainly not to you, Huguenot.'

Piet was desperately trying to see a way out of his situation.

Words not weapons, as Minou had said. The thought of his beloved wife renewed his determination. After everything they had endured, it couldn't end like this. He had to keep them talking.

'Houtman, you have no regard for me, that I know. I also know you don't trust me, though I give you my word my motives for speaking to Burgher van Raay were honourable. I owe him as much loyalty for his steadfast support of my family and our *hofje* as I owe loyalty to our cause. Our *shared* cause, as I'd thought. You also know that I have served Holland well. What has been achieved in Amsterdam today is nothing short of a miracle. The peaceful transfer of power. History will judge you as playing a crucial part.' He looked around the prison chamber. 'Don't jeopardise your reputation.'

'And there it is,' Houtman snarled. 'That familiar French arrogance. Can you truly think that the unfortunate death of one man will change things? You put too high a value on your own head.'

'How would my death benefit you, Houtman?' Piet asked wearily, then turned to the man he'd thought his friend. 'Or you, Willem? For the sake of the friendship between our two families, I beg you not to be party to this. This is a personal matter between Houtman and I.' He turned back. 'Isn't that so? This is nothing to do with loyalty or commitment to our cause, and you know it.'

Without warning, Houtman punched him in the stomach. Piet staggered back, the air struck out of him, but stayed on his feet.

'A Huguenot dog who spills his guts like a virgin in a flop-house is of no use to us.'

Piet heard the rasp of the knife being drawn out of its sheath, and turned cold.

'Let's have one less foreigner in our city,' Houtman said, lunging forward with his dagger.

This time, Piet was ready. Shifting his weight to his right leg, he kicked out with his left, slamming his boot into Houtman's wrist. The dagger went skidding across the flagstones.

Houtman screamed, the sound reverberating off the damp walls, then dropped to his knees, his eyes wide in surprise. Piet didn't understand; he might have broken the man's wrist, but nothing worse. But now Houtman was toppling sideways, making no attempt to break his fall. His head hit the ground with a crack but, this time, no sound came from his lips.

'God rest his soul,' said van Raay, wiping a bloodied dagger on his sleeve.

'Willem?' Piet stared in disbelief at the knife. 'My friend, I beg you—'

Van Raay sighed. 'You have nothing to fear from me.'

Piet stared at the man sprawled dead at his feet. 'I don't understand.'

'It was the only way to get him off guard.'

'So you and Houtman were not in league?'

'No.'

'Then how did he know I had told you of our plans?'

'I suspect Houtman had you followed to my home after you left the meeting in Lastage on Saturday night. The following day, Houtman presented himself at my door, claiming he had information pertinent to you and your family, and offering to share it provided I might participate in –' he looked around the prison chamber with a glance – 'this charade. Given what was at stake – for you and for Amsterdam – I had no choice but to accept his proposal.'

Piet looked back down at Houtman. 'Why would he want to kill me, when there is so much more? It makes no sense.'

Van Raay sighed. 'Are you not an Amsterdammer yet, Reydon? Have you not learnt the lengths to which men will go to buy respectability? Houtman had ambitions to sit on the new council. The Calvinists might be all for shaking off the Spanish yoke but, in their different way, they are as hidebound as the Catholic burghers they claim to despise. For a common soldier like Houtman to have any chance of being invited to take a seat in the Stadhuis, he needed money.'

'Hence the rich widow in Heiligeweg.'

Van Raay nodded.

'Minou and I had only thought to use that information to encourage Houtman to keep to his promise not to allow his men to turn to violence. We would not have used it against him.'

'Ah, but Houtman couldn't be certain of that. He wanted to be sure you couldn't talk.'

Piet frowned. 'Did he tell you what information he had about my family?'

'No. He said only that there were spies in Amsterdam, asking questions about you, on behalf of a French nobleman.'

Piet turned cold. 'Did Houtman know the name of this noble gentleman?'

'He didn't say. It might have been a fabrication. Houtman was looking for any excuse to act against you.'

'And Amsterdam is thick with spies,' Piet said, trying to persuade himself it meant nothing. He shook his head. There'd be time enough to think about what this might mean, but now was not the moment. He looked down at the dead man. 'We have to get out of here. It won't be long before someone notices Houtman's missing.' He offered his bound wrists to van Raay. 'Can you cut me free?'

Van Raay gave an apologetic shrug. 'Since Houtman's men

are everywhere, it might be safer to extend this performance a while longer. If they believe you are still a prisoner, but now in my charge, they might not challenge me.'

For a moment, Piet simply stared, amazed at the transformation in the sombre, pious man he had thought he'd known.

Van Raay saw his confusion and smiled. 'I was not always a grain merchant, Reydon.'

CHAPTER SEVENTY-ONE

There were still two soldiers on duty outside the main entrance into Sint Antoniespoort.

Minou took a deep breath, then walked across the bridge holding the borrowed basket with its red-and-white-striped cloth in front of her.

'I have brought victuals for Joost Wouter!'

The younger of the sentries waved her in without even checking, but the second – a man with a face disfigured by smallpox – went with her into the courtyard, closing the heavy door behind them and shooting the bolt.

'Wouter's up the top.'

With a sickening lurch, Minou realised she'd been thinking so hard about how to gain admittance, she had neglected to consider what she might do once she was inside. Piet could be anywhere.

'Look, are you going or not?' the sentry growled. 'You can't stay here.'

'I'm going,' Minou mumbled, keeping her face hidden. '*Dankuwel.*'

She headed towards the tower, but had only taken a couple of steps, when she heard a shout from somewhere below.

'Now what,' the soldier grumbled, dropping his hand to his weapon.

Minou slipped into the shadow of the stairwell.

'Who goes there?' the soldier called down.

There was no answer. Minou watched the man hesitate, then

walk towards the stairs. Then, just as quickly, he seemed to stagger back in alarm, catching his boot and stumbling, as two men came storming up the steps.

'This prisoner is to be transferred to the garrison at the Schreyershoektoren without delay. Unbolt the gate.'

The soldier leapt to attention. '*Zeer goed.*'

Minou felt the ground shift beneath her. Everything seemed to be moving slowly, as if in a dream: the sentry with his pock-marked skin rushing to obey the command; Piet, with his bruised face and hands still tied behind his back; the man in a distinctive flat black burgher's hat holding a knife to Piet's back.

Cornelia's father.

The basket fell from her hands, tumbling down the step into plain view. The earthenware jug rolled free, shattering on impact. For a moment, Minou held Piet's gaze, then time came rushing back.

The sentry spun around to face Minou, just as a fellow soldier, bleeding copiously from a gash on his forehead, staggered up the stairs behind Willem van Raay.

Van Raay drew a knife and leant towards Piet. Minou screamed.

'Piet!'

'It's all right!' he shouted back, holding up his wrists with the rope now hanging from them.

'Sound the alarm!' the sentry ordered.

But before he could shout again, Minou threw herself at him. Taken by surprise, his weapon went flying from his hand. Willem van Raay turned to deal with the wounded soldier coming up the stairs behind them, while Piet punched the sentry on the jaw, laying him out flat.

Minou heard the sound of men's boots on the floor above them.

'More soldiers are coming!' she shouted.

'Minou, go while you still have the chance,' Piet shouted, trying to help van Raay. 'We can hold them off.'

'I'm not leaving without you.'

The guard was dazed – Piet had broken a stool over his head when they'd stormed out of the prison – but the man was roaring and as wild as a bear. He slashed out. Piet parried the strike, but the tip of the blade caught his arm. A red seam of fresh blood opened on his skin.

Minou felt herself being dragged off her feet. She clawed at her throat, trying to stop herself from choking as the borrowed cloak dug into her skin. Then, the air was knocked out of her as she was slammed back against the wall. A man with blackened teeth put a filthy hand across her neck.

'What have we here?'

Piet spun round. 'Take your hands off her, Wouter!'

'Now I've seen it all!' Wouter sneered. 'Bringing your wife to do a man's job.'

In the chaos of the next few moments, Minou didn't see what happened on the stairs. But she heard the shout, next the sound of the guard tumbling down the stone steps, and the thump of his body when he hit the stone flagstones at the bottom. Then silence.

Piet sprang at Wouter, forcing him to release her. Gasping, Minou darted up the stairs to the next floor of the tower and shot home the bolt of the pass door to prevent anyone else getting through.

Piet and Wouter were now circling one another, each with a dagger drawn, each waiting for the moment to strike. Minou could see Willem van Raay was in trouble too. The colour had drained from his face and his breath was coming in short bursts.

Now other soldiers were hammering on the pass door above.

Even if they couldn't get through, Minou knew it wouldn't be long before they attracted the remaining sentry outside, and that would be the end.

She had an idea. Crouching down, she stretched out her hand to where the basket lay on its side by the wall. She couldn't quite reach it. She extended her fingers a little further, desperate not to alert Wouter or distract Piet, then a little more until she managed to get some purchase on the side of the basket. Carefully, she pulled it towards her as the combatants continued to circle and parry.

Minou waited until Wouter was closer to her, then she threw the basket between his feet. It didn't bring him down, but it was enough to make him lose concentration for an instant and stumble, long enough for Piet to thrust his poniard into his enemy's leg. Wouter shrieked like a stuck pig, and went down. His eyes were wide open. Piet rolled him over. Minou's hand flew to her mouth. His belly was sliced open, guts and blood spilling out. He'd fallen on his own knife.

'Don't look,' Piet said quickly, taking her hand, then called to van Raay.

'We must go!'

'You go, Reydon. I'll follow.'

Minou could see the sheen of sweat on his brow. 'Are you hurt, Burgher van Raay?'

'A little short of breath, my dear, nothing more.'

'Can you walk?' Piet asked. 'If we do as you originally suggested, there is still a chance we can get out.'

Van Raay nodded, though Minou saw how much it cost him to do so.

'Minou, you distract the sentries' attention while we pass. Our plan had been to say Willem was taking me to another gatehouse. They often move prisoners between the towers.'

'I'll do my best.' She glanced down at the unconscious sentry. 'There should be only one man on duty outside. This man accompanied me in here.'

Piet nodded. 'Can you tie the rope?'

Minou wrapped the severed cords around Piet's hands, this time in front of him so he could hold the ties in place, then, averting her eyes from Wouter, fetched the basket. She draped the red-and-white cloth across it, adjusted the heavy cloak to hide the red marks on her neck, then stepped through the heavy outer door leaving it ajar.

To her relief, the young sentry was alone. He gave no impression of having heard the fracas behind the thick walls.

'Wouter bids me thank you for allowing me entrance,' she said.

'He'd do the same,' the boy replied. 'Besides, there's a beer in it for me.'

'That's only fair,' Minou said. 'One good turn deserves another.'

Out of the corner of her eye, she saw Piet and Willem van Raay standing ready. She pretended to stumble and grasped the sentry's arm, then beckoned them to start moving.

'Be careful, Mevrouw,' the boy said.

'I don't know what's come over me. I'm all at sixes-and-sevens today. It must be all that business over at the Stadhuis.'

'You heard about it?'

'I was there. I saw Hendrick Dircksz being marched away.'

'Did you! Better times are coming. Holland should stand alone.'

'Will you walk me across the bridge, young man?' Minou said, pressing home her advantage. She gripped his arm even harder. 'Not for anything would I fall into that water. I heard the trouble started here?'

'It did,' he said proudly. 'All men of sound heart follow the Prince of Orange.'

'I don't understand politics,' Minou said, while surreptitiously waving Piet and van Ray out behind his back. 'And look over there.' She pointed across the square, in the opposite direction from where Piet and Willem were heading. 'They've sent the Grey Friars packing at last.'

'Good riddance!'

Minou could see Piet had wrapped his hands into his sleeves, leaving the tail of the rope dangling as if he was still bound. Willem van Raay had his hand on Piet's shoulder as if forcing him forward. If they could just keep going.

'Though politicians are all as bad as each other,' Minou added, rambling to keep the guard's attention. 'It's always us common people who suffer, whoever sits in the Stadhuis. They've no care for the lives of ordinary people.'

'Holland will be better alone. We don't need those Spanish dogs telling us what to do. Deciding our taxes, writing our laws, denying us our churches.'

Minou could see they were almost clear. Just a few steps further. But there was a sudden loud noise, and the sentry turned towards Lastage. At the last moment, he noticed them.

'Hey!' he shouted. 'You, there!'

Willem van Raay looked back over his shoulder. 'Transfer to Schreyershoektoren,' he shouted, though Minou could hear his voice was weak. 'On the orders of Jan Houtman.'

The sentry started to go after them. Minou stepped in front of him and blocked his way.

'Schreyershoektoren!' she tutted. 'I wonder what crime he committed. Must be bad to be taken there, don't you think?'

'Did you say on Houtman's orders?' the boy shouted over her shoulder.

'*Ja*,' van Raay replied but, this time, he did not turn.

'I order you to stop!'

Minou pulled at the young man's sleeve. 'How fortunate we are to have such fine soldiers as you keeping us safe. I tell you what, next time I come, I'll be sure to bring a little extra.'

The sentry took a last look at the two men disappearing into the distance at the north side of the square, then he shrugged. Minou offered up a silent prayer of thanks.

'Well, I'd best be getting on. Thank you for your assistance, young man.'

He bowed his head, then turned back to Sint Antoniespoort, while Minou walked towards Zeedijk, forcing herself not to break into a run. Only then, did the sentry see someone waving frantically from an upstairs window.

'What's that?' he called up.

'The pass door's bolted. We're locked in!'

Minou didn't stop until she was well out of sight.

She found a quiet corner and took stock. Leaning against the tavern wall, she took several deep breaths. Her hands were shaking and sweat was pooling in the small of her back. The fear and anger that had given her the strength to fight was already draining away.

Minou closed her eyes. She could not believe how close they had all come to being arrested. Piet had been badly beaten and Cornelia's father was clearly exhausted, but God willing they were safe now. She assumed they would double back into Zeedijk once they were sure they weren't being followed.

But they had done it. They had defeated the guards and got away. She turned cold at the thought they had killed at least one man, and Wouter was dead too. What would happen when the bodies were found? She'd kept her hood over her head, but

Piet would be recognised. Willem van Raay as well. Pushing the thought from her mind, Minou forced herself to concentrate on the matter at hand. There'd be time enough to decide what to do once they were in the safety of their own house.

As she turned into Zeedijk, she saw Piet and Willem van Raay approaching from the other direction. Minou hurried to meet them.

'*Mon coeur*, you're safe. Thank God.'

'Willem is hurt,' Piet said in a low voice. 'I think his ribs might be broken.'

'The blow knocked all the air out of me,' van Raay gasped. 'I only need a few moments to catch my breath.'

Minou looked at him. His skin was the colour of milk and his breathing was laboured.

'Cornelia and Alis are waiting for us inside,' she said. 'Let me help you, it's not much further.'

Minou put her arm around Willem van Raay's waist and, with Piet on the other side taking his weight, together they walked him towards the corner house. It was slow going. Then Minou moved position and realised her hand was sticky. She looked and saw fresh red blood staining her fingers. It hadn't been a fist at all, but the blade of a knife slipping between his ribs.

'Piet,' she whispered urgently. 'Hurry. He's been stabbed.'

CHAPTER SEVENTY-TWO

ZEEDIJK

Minou and Piet staggered inside, holding van Raay between them. He was barely conscious now. With each step, Minou felt a new gush of warm blood seep through her clothes.

'Frans!' Piet shouted into the empty hallway. 'Frans!'

'We'll take him in here,' Minou said, gesturing to the chamber on the ground floor that gave onto the orchard. 'We don't have time to take him to a bedchamber. He needs to be kept still.'

Piet pushed open the door with his boot. 'Is the wound still bleeding?'

'Yes.'

'Will that do?' he asked, nodding at the oak settle.

Minou shook her head. 'It's too narrow. He needs to lie flat. We'll lift him onto the table. Put your cloak beneath him, and we'll put something else under his head.'

Together, they managed to lean van Raay against the edge of the table, then Piet raised his legs and laid him down gently. More blood gushed from the wound and started to drip from the oak surface down to the floor.

Outside in the garden, Minou could hear the voices of the orphanage children playing. Such innocent and incongruous sounds compared to the horror of the day.

'Piet, ask Agnes to bring water and bandages. We need to clean the wound and bind it. Then find Cornelia.'

'I will. How bad is it?'

'Until I look, I cannot tell,' Minou replied, though she feared from Willem's colour and the amount of blood he had lost, that it was already too late. 'Tell her to bring brandy and valerian root, too. It will help with the pain. There is some in the bottom drawer of the cabinet in our bedchamber.'

As Piet rushed into the hall, Frans came in from the gardens, then stopped dead when he saw Willem van Raay.

'The Devil preserve us –'

'Frans, is Juffrouw van Raay here?'

The boy was looking at the blood pooling on the floor beneath the table.

'Frans!' Minou snapped.

'Sorry. Yes, she's on the terrace. What happened to him? We've been hearing all sorts of rumours all day and they're looting the Grey Friars monastery.'

'Is Alis with her?'

'No. She went to Warmoesstraat to fetch something.'

Minou frowned. 'Without alarming Juffrouw van Raay, go back into the garden and ask her to join me here.'

With a final glance at the dying man, Frans ran back outside.

Minou turned back to her patient. There was a terrible plashing in his chest as he tried to catch his breath. She could see there was no hope.

'How goes it with you, Burgher van Raay?' she asked, relieved that his eyes opened at the sound of her voice.

'Ah, Minou.' His hand reached out and took hers. 'A priest . . . I must confess my sins and take communion. I would see my Lord with my soul shriven.'

'You're not going to die, Willem. I won't allow it.'

He managed to smile. 'Ah, but I am. And if that is God's will, then so be it. I have lived a good life. I have done my duty.'

Minou choked back her tears. 'You have. You are a good man.'

Agnes slipped into the chamber carrying the medicines Minou had asked for. Her eyes also grew wide at the sight of van Raay.

'They said no one was injured in Plaats.'

'This happened elsewhere.' Minou took the bandages from Agnes's arms, though she knew there was now no point. 'I need you to go to the Nieuwe Kerk and—' Minou broke off, suddenly remembering how the priest and his fellow clergy had been among the first to be put on the barges. 'Go to the nearest cloister and find a priest. Burgher van Raay would have the last rites. Make haste.'

Agnes gave a brief curtsey then left. Seconds later, Minou heard the sound of the front door open and slam shut, then silence. The air seemed to reverberate and echo and then settle again.

Minou dropped a few pearls of valerian on Willem's lips and then held his hand, listening to the rattling in his chest. She feared the blade had pierced his lung.

'Father!' Cornelia cried, rushing into the chamber. 'What happened?'

'You need to prepare yourself, Cornelia,' Minou said softly.

At the sound of his daughter's voice, Willem's eyes flickered open. 'Ah, you are here. I am glad. The priest is coming.'

'You have no need of a priest,' Cornelia said desperately. 'You're going to be all right. Tell him, Minou.'

Full of pity for her friend, she took Cornelia's hand. 'It's nearly time. I have sent for a priest, but—'

Van Raay's pupils seemed to grow dark. 'Is that you, Cornelia?'

She looked wildly at Minou, then seemed to accept the situation. Her voice grew calm, gentle.

'It's me, Father. I'm here.'

He coughed, blood pooling in the corner of his mouth.

'What if we are wrong, Cornelia? What if there is nothing waiting for us on the other side? Only darkness?'

Cornelia shook her head. 'God is waiting for you. He is waiting to bring you home.'

'Ah.' A sigh slipped from his lips, then he smiled. 'I would see His face. And your dear mother, how I have missed her.'

Cornelia was biting back her tears. 'You have been both mother and father to me. I have lacked for nothing.'

'Live a long and happy life, my dear. And when your time comes, we will be waiting for you. Your mother and I. Take care of this fine city of ours.' He smiled again. 'Will you pray with me, my dear. One last time.'

Minou stepped back, knowing the moment had come. She watched Cornelia take both of her father's hands between hers, then she began to pray.

'*Pater noster, qui es in caelis, sanctificetur nomen tuum . . .*'

And, though for fifteen years, Minou had spoken the words of the Lord's Prayer in French rather than in Latin, the old words came easily to her lips too: '. . . *et ne nos inducas in tentationem, sed libera nos a malo.*'

'Amen.' Cornelia, tracing the sign of the cross on her father's forehead, then leant forward and kissed him.

For a moment, colour seemed to come back into Willem van Raay's face. He turned his head towards Minou.

'Tell Piet . . . I remembered something else Houtman told me.'

Cornelia squeezed his fingers. 'Hush, Father. Don't try to speak.'

'It's important.' Willem grasped Minou's hand more tightly. 'The relic hunter – the priest, the same –'

'A priest is coming,' Cornelia said desperately.

'No, the French cardinal – Tell Piet that he—' but his words were lost in another bout of coughing.

'Father!' Cornelia sobbed. 'Father!'

At the last, Willem's eyes widened, as if he had seen something of wonder in the far distance, then a look of great serenity lit his face. 'He is waiting. He is waiting in the company of His saints.'

Then van Raay's eyes closed for the last time.

As he took his final breath, Cornelia sank weeping to the ground. Minou put her arms around her friend and held her as she cried. They were still there, in one another's arms, when the priest arrived from the cloister half an hour later with his rosary and his holy oil.

In the distance, Minou could just make out the roar of the crowd on Plaats and the bright fanfare of trumpets as Amsterdam celebrated its bloodless revolution.

PART FOUR

AMSTERDAM & CHARTRES
July & August 1584

CHAPTER SEVENTY-THREE

Six Years Later

Minou stood in their War Room – as she and Piet had christened the ground-floor chamber they'd made their centre of operations for tracking down Vidal – and stared at the wooden board propped against the white-plaster wall. Papers, missives, documents pinned low to high, there was barely any space remaining.

Minou reached up and added the letter they'd received from Antoine le Maistre to the board, wondering when they would hear more. Piet's old friend and comrade had promised to write the instant he had further news. After years of searching for Guise's missing confessor, this was the most promising lead they'd had.

It was a hot afternoon. As Minou leant to open the window to let in a little air she saw her son, Jean-Jacques, in the orchard beyond the terrace, lift one of their newest arrivals onto the wooden swing and begin to push. Gently at first, until the little boy started to trust him and smile. Minou knew it was often the simplest things that helped a war orphan to recover: a spinning top; bright chalks and a slate; a pancake with cinnamon, hot from the pan; apples from the tree.

Russet-haired like his father had been, Jean-Jacques at thirteen years of age was of average height but broad in the shoulder.

His appearance spoke to his virtues. He was steadfast and reliable, slow to anger, hard-working and loyal. He never spoke unless he had something of value to say. Few vestiges of his French heritage remained and, though she and Piet still spoke in her mother tongue in the privacy of their own chambers, the language of the *hofje* was now wholly Dutch. Now that Jean-Jacques had come of age, particularly with the growing anti-French sentiments in Amsterdam, he had taken to using the Dutch form of his name, Johannus. She thanked God every day that he had not yet been called upon to join the Prince of Orange's army to fight.

Despite the challenges of the past six years – as the Calvinist Revolt against the tyrannical Spanish occupation continued in the Provinces – their lives in Amsterdam had remained relatively peaceful. There was much to be thankful for, not least that she and Piet had remained free.

Minou no longer feared they would be brought to account for the deaths of the hard-line Calvinist leader, Houtman, and his henchman, Wouter, in Sint Antoniespoort. For months after the events in the tower in May 1578, she had lived in dread of soldiers arriving to arrest them.

On the night of the Alteration, there had been widespread looting as churches, cloisters and the few remaining monasteries were ransacked. Days passed, then weeks, and Minou started to wonder if the events in Sint Antoniespoort were to be forgotten in the face of the bigger battles raging elsewhere in the city. Had the deaths of Houtman, Wouter and the two guards been put down to a falling-out amongst thieves? Or a grudge between the Lastage faction and more moderate rebel factions? And the young sentry had either never told anyone of the two men seen leaving the gatehouse that afternoon, or he'd been unable to identify them.

For those last days in May 1578 the streets had been dangerous. Calvinist mobs roamed unchecked. But then, little by little, Amsterdam settled into its new order. A moderate council was formed, consisting of both Protestants and Catholics, though under Calvinist control. The church of Sint Nicolaas was taken over to the Protestant faith, but the Nieuwe Kerk had remained as a place of Catholic worship for some time. A Protestant mob had attacked the Heilige Stede chapel, destroying everything that reminded them of the cult of the Miracle of Amsterdam. But the women of Begijnhof had been left alone, as promised, and granted permission to take over celebrating the Miracle, so it continued to bring many visitors to the city each March, spending their money in the taverns and boarding houses.

At every step, the priority of the new council had been the expansion of the city and its trade. Within months, the harbour around Lastage was enlarged – its workers building bigger bleaching houses, vast warehouses and elegant new guild halls. The city defences were strengthened with the Nieuwe Gracht in the east and, little by little, even the Catholic burghers started to creep back from their exile in Haarlem and Leiden.

Outside the city walls, on the wide expanses of green plains and fields, new communities were springing up, too. More Huguenots arrived from France and settled in the west. Marrano and Sephardic Jews, escaping the horrors of the Inquisition in Spain and Portugal, settled on land beyond Sint Antoniespoort to the east.

Ships began to sail into the harbour again. Amsterdam was open for business, welcoming refugees from Ghent and Bruges, Brussels and Antwerp. Merchants, musicians, artisans, artists, bankers, lawyers – people of education and skill – seeking safety and a place to lay their heads. Such a lot had changed in six years.

Minou closed the window, to keep out the flies that plagued the city in the summer, and caught sight of her reflection in the glass: an elegant woman in her middle years, her brown hair still thick and untouched by grey, a few lines around her eyes. Minou did not regret the loss of her youth. Her face told a story of the life she had lived: the love and the loss, the happiness and the grief, all the emotions that gave the world its colour.

Minou looked again at Antoine le Maistre's letter in its place on the noticeboard, and prayed they would receive confirmation from him soon. Over the years, she and Piet had learnt never to hope – they'd had too many false alarms – but now? This news had the ring of truth about it.

Since discovering what Mariken's package contained – the letter from Piet's mother and the testament of her marriage to Philippe du Plessis – Minou and Piet had put all their spare time and limited resources into trying to find Vidal. Working on the assumption he was still alive – the common gossip about the Duke of Guise's attempts to hunt him down confirmed it – they followed every lead, but the mass displacement of people in the continuing sequence of religious wars, and the looting and destruction of records in French towns and cities, meant they'd had little to go on. Du Plessis' estates outside the town of Redon in Brittany had been sold and his only relative, a nephew, had been the sole beneficiary. No one resembling Vidal had been seen in the area since his uncle's illness and death in March 1572, and there had been no talk of a legitimate son born to a Dutchwoman in Amsterdam many years before.

Because Vidal's survival depended on disappearing from Guise's omnipresent spies, Minou was convinced he would have taken on another identity altogether. So they'd turned their attention to the only other clue they had, tenuous as it was, namely Willem van Raay's dying words that the French cardinal was now a relic hunter.

Cornelia had found nothing in her father's papers to explain his words, nor any indication as to what information Wouter might have had to trade. But, from their previous history with Vidal, Minou had thought it was a route worth pursuing. Since the very beginning of the religious wars in 1562, sacred objects looted from monasteries and convents circulated freely within France, and the trade in relics was particularly lucrative. Many of the most significant Catholic sites were now guarded around the clock and information about attempted thefts was circulated. Aunt Salvadora, still ensconced in her widow's weeds in the house in the rue du Taur in Toulouse, had never forgotten Vidal's cruelty – and what evil he had done to acquire the Shroud of Antioch – so she did everything in her power to try to help them.

But, until le Maistre's letter, nothing had come of anything.

Minou turned to the oak table in the middle of the chamber, which was covered by a huge map of France. It was marked with black crosses, each indicating a place in the past six years where a relic hunter answering Vidal's description had been sighted: Saint-Antonin, Toulouse, Carcassonne, Reims, Vassy, Rouen, Nantes, Amiens. Minou picked up a piece of charcoal and drew a fresh cross against the city of Chartres.

A sudden sound roused Minou from her reflections. She looked up to see her daughter in the doorway to the terrace shuffling from foot to foot.

'Bernarda, you surprised me!'

'*Het spijt me.*'

Now eleven years old, her freckled skin and copper hair clearly marking her as Johannus' sister, she was also of average height and sturdy build. Born and bred in Amsterdam, she was

Dutch through-and-through. She spoke French hesitantly and with a blunt Amsterdammer accent.

Minou waved her hand. 'Don't just stand there, child. Come in.'

The girl took a single step into the room and stood with her hands folded neatly in front of her. 'I didn't want to disturb you.'

'I was only thinking.'

Since Bernarda was a child blessed with a lack of curiosity, she accepted the comment at face value.

Minou sighed. 'What can I do for you, Bernarda?'

'Might I go to see Aunt Alis? She promised me a book and I have run out of things to read to the children.'

'That is kind of you. Of course, you may go. Ask Johannus to accompany you to Warmoesstraat.'

'I don't need a chaperone,' she mumbled.

'I don't want you going on your own. Take your brother as I ask.'

The girl looked at her feet. It made for an easier household, but Minou sometimes wished Bernarda would show a little more spirit. And as so often, even now, she could not help comparing her very Dutch daughter to the French daughter she had lost.

Marta's loss was now a permanent ache, always there but less sharp with each passing year. Twelve winters and summers had passed since she'd last seen her mercurial, spirited daughter, and though she fanned the tiniest flame of hope in her heart that Marta had somehow survived, in truth, Minou no longer believed it.

She tried to keep her memory alive in the life of the household. The tapestry of the Joubert-Reydon family Alis had smuggled away from Puivert hung in the main family living chamber, and Minou had always made a point about talking to Johannus and Bernarda about their older sister, with her blue dress and her mismatched eyes, one blue and one brown. But Minou knew Marta meant nothing to them. She was just the girl in the tapestry.

'I don't want you walking through the streets alone, Bernarda.'

'As you wish, Mother.'

Feeling guilty for finding her obedience so vexing, Minou put her arm around her shoulders and hugged her a little too tightly.

'You are a good girl,' she said. 'Take Agnes with you, if you prefer. Give my best regards to Alis and to Cornelia, and ask them to dine with us this evening. Would you like that?'

Bernarda shrugged. 'I don't mind.'

Minou sighed again. 'Then ask them to come at six o'clock.'

As Bernarda took her leave through the garden, Minou went to her bureau and took out her journal, then settled down to write. Doing something was better than simply waiting for further word to arrive from le Maistre. It could be days, it might be weeks.

In the years between their flight from Paris and Alis's arrival in Amsterdam, her ink and quill had sat untouched in her drawer. It was Alis who had encouraged her to begin again. With Alis's passionate support, Minou began to write every day, driven to make sure that the voices of ordinary women like her were not lost, filling journal after journal with how this one family had survived the wars, describing what it was to have to flee your home and build a new life in a faraway city.

Now writing was as necessary to her as breathing. A necessity, a responsibility. Her journals were no longer a history of her own hopes and fears, but rather the story of what it meant to be a refugee, a person displaced, a witness to the death of an old world and the birth of a new. Minou knew that it was only ever the lives of the kings and generals and popes which were recorded. Their prejudices, actions and ambitions were taken to be the only truth of history.

Minou picked up her quill and dipped it in the ink, but got no further than writing the date when she heard the front door slamming shut.

She looked up. Neither the children nor the servants were permitted to enter that way – they all went through the gate in the garden directly onto Zeedijk – and at this time of day Piet was usually at the van Raay warehouse. He and Cornelia, with Alis's help, had taken over the running of her father's business some years ago.

'Piet? Is that you?'

He strode into the War Room, his handsome face alive with news. Minou leapt to her feet. 'What is it? Has a second letter from le Maistre come?'

'The Prince of Orange is dead. Assassinated three days ago in his headquarters in Delft.'

CHAPTER SEVENTY-FOUR

THE RELIQUARY
CHARTRES

Lord Evreux sat in the middle of the chamber, his thin fingers grasping the carved arms of the cathedra, his bishop's throne.

The wicks on the tall silver candelabra, which stood either side of the altar, were lit, though there was no need. The summer's afternoon shone rich and bright through the glass lantern skylight set in the white plaster ceiling, flooding the heart of the chamber with light. The corners and walls were in shadow, protecting the exquisite frescoes of the Stations of the Cross and the caskets in front of them, from the force of the sun.

Vidal raised his hand to his right temple. The canker was the size of a fist now, his skin stretched white above his right ear. It no longer caused him pain and, though still plagued by blackouts, which stole days from him, Vidal believed God would continue to spare him until his work was done.

Six years.

He had not thought it would take so long to complete his collection. The Shroud of Antioch in 1562, a spine from the Crown of Thorns in 1572, the Sancta Camisia in 1578. Since then, with the benefit of his son's exquisite painting of what he had seen in the Sainte-Chapelle, Vidal had commissioned a Venetian glassmaker to produce an excellent replica of the Crown of Thorns – a twist of rushes held within a crystal circle. If the people believed, and invested their faith and trust in an object, even if it might be a copy, then God's purpose was also fulfilled.

In the casket in front of the second Station of the Cross was a phial of light-brown earth from the Via Dolorosa, where Christ had fallen for the first time and now, in the fifth casket, another vial holding a single spot of Christ's blood, where he had fallen for the second time.

Only one casket still remained empty.

The swirl and rage of the religious wars in France, and the periods of armed peace, had helped keep Vidal out of sight of Guise's spies. But they had also made it harder to acquire information. Vidal understood that until the final relic or copy was brought to Chartres, his ambition to establish a true Catholic Church in France, to rival the false piety of Guise's Catholic League funded by Spain, could not be fulfilled. To do this, he needed his collection to be complete.

Feeling his age and the sickness in his bones, Vidal stood up. He walked with a cane now. The potions and treatments of the apothecaries had taken a harsh toll. His head was covered with a rough white stubble, like a winter field under a fall of snow. His distinctive hair was gone.

The silver ferrule tapped on the tiled floor of the reliquary as Vidal walked to stand before the empty casket.

The time was right.

A month ago in June, after a disastrous military campaign in Flanders, Catherine de' Medici's youngest son had died and the world shifted on its axis. His brother, the King – the Duke of Anjou, as Vidal had always continued to think of him – had no children, which meant that the Huguenot Henri of Navarre was now heir-presumptive to the French throne.

No one believed the Catholic League would accept a Protestant monarch, but would Guise be brave enough to stand against the lawful succession? Navarre was a prince of the royal blood. Guise had no authority to challenge him, but Vidal had no doubt he would try.

France was already descending into chaos. And Vidal sensed that, soon, he would finally be able to come out of the shadows. Harnessing the ineffable power of the relics, his organisation would honour the ancient principles of their Holy and Apostolic Church. His God was the God of the Old Testament, vengeful and tyrannical and omnipotent. It was what France needed to return to her former glory. Only might and force could now bring peace to their divided land. When his power was assured, invincible, Vidal would offer his support to Guise.

But he needed the last relic first.

CHAPTER SEVENTY-FIVE

Minou put her head around the door to the War Room.

'What is it that keeps you from me, *mon coeur*? You said you would accompany me to the market.'

Piet looked up from the table. 'I lost track of the time.'

Minou slipped inside and closed the door, then kissed him. 'You've been cloistered in here since first light.'

'And I am sorry.'

She smiled. 'No need to apologise.' She took out her kerchief and wiped a smudge of charcoal from his face. 'I just worry for you, cooped up in here. We'll hear from Antoine when we do. There's nothing we can do until then but wait.'

Over a week had passed since the Prince of Orange had been assassinated in his headquarters in Delft, shot at close quarters with a pistol by a fanatical French Catholic. The leadership of the Revolt had passed into the hands of his oldest son and most trusted general, but no one knew what might happen next. The atmosphere in Amsterdam was volatile. Tempers were running high.

Yesterday, Minou had met Cornelia and Alis in the Reydon pew at the Oude Kerk to listen to the women exchange morsels of gossip in the cool of the morning before the pastor began to preach. By the evening, there had been huddles of men gathered on the shaded street corners and beside the wharves to pass on the latest news. What would the Prince's murder mean for Holland? What did it mean for Amsterdam?

'Is it something else that occupies your thoughts?' Minou asked.

Still, Piet didn't answer.

'You have worked long enough. Come into the garden and take the air for a while.'

'I cannot.'

Minou rested her hand against his cheek. She knew her husband well in this mood. He was like a terrier with a bone, unable to step away – night or day, however long it took – until he had finished whatever it was that concerned him.

'What is it you're doing?'

Piet did not reply and Minou rubbed absently at a brown spot. The servants had scrubbed, and polished, and scrubbed again the surface of the oak table where Willem van Raay had bled to death, but that one mark would not be shifted. The blood had soaked too deep into the grain of the timber. She slid a piece of paper across the table to cover the stain.

Minou looked at the chaos of papers. 'It might be that another set of eyes might help?'

'It's not that.'

'Then what, my love?'

For a moment, Piet said nothing. Then he picked up the compass and bent over the table, cradling the instrument in his hands.

'It puts me in mind of your father's old box compass,' he said. 'The stories it might have told of its travels.'

Minou smiled. 'You only knew him as an old man, but in the days before the wars began, he journeyed all over France in the 1550s and 1560s – even London once and here to Amsterdam – sourcing stock for our bookshop in the rue du Marché.'

'That was where I first saw you. You sent packing the soldiers come to arrest me!'

'I was young then and foolish!'

'You saw an injustice and did not turn away.' Piet put his hand on her cheek. 'You haven't changed, Minou.'

She leant in to his touch. 'You are gallant to lie so prettily.'

Piet put the compass back on the table. 'Marta loved Bernard's compass. She was always "borrowing" it,' he said. 'Do you remember?'

At the unaccustomed mention of her daughter's name, Minou caught her breath. Piet rarely – if ever – spoke of her. 'Marta was a terrible magpie.' She hesitated: 'I didn't know you thought about her still.'

'How could you doubt it!' Piet cried, looking at her with such anguish that it turned her heart. 'I found speaking about her undid me, so I kept my peace. I know that hurt you, Minou – and I wish I had been a better comfort to you in those early days – but speaking her name caused me such pain. When I tried to talk to you, I only made things worse.'

Minou chose her words with care. 'We saw things differently. It was nobody's fault. You were grieving for a daughter you believed dead. I, for a daughter I believed lost but still alive.'

He bowed his head. 'You blamed me for forcing you to leave Paris without her.'

Minou flushed. 'I did. For many years, I did. It took me a long time to forgive you, but I know you did your best, Piet. We both did.'

He gave a heartfelt sigh. 'Do you think about Marta now?'

She smiled. 'Of course, every day. But I no longer expect to see her – in a crowded street, in church, when I say my prayers at night. Too many years have passed without word of her, Piet. Whether it's the wisdom of age, or simply the passage of time, I have come around to your way of thinking.'

To her surprise, Piet took something from the table, then walked to the wooden settle.

'Minou, sit with me.'

'What is it?' she asked quickly, her heart skipping a beat. She felt suddenly fearful of what Piet might be about to say. There was no life without sorrow, but the home they had made for themselves here was good.

'What is it?' she asked again, sitting nervous and upright beside him, as if posing for an artist's portrait.

'Don't be angry with me, but this morning, I received the letter from le Maistre we have been waiting for.'

'What!' Minou's face flooded with hurt. 'Why didn't you tell me straight away? I've been on tenterhooks. It's unkind.' She tried to stand up, but he took her hand. 'No, Piet! So many times in the past – too many – we have talked about this. Every time, I beg you to confide in me, not to keep things from me. Every time, you give me your word that next time you will and yet . . .'

'I'm sorry.'

'I don't understand.' Minou forced herself to take a couple of deep breaths. 'Well, what does the letter say? Was he right? Is it Vidal?'

Piet didn't answer directly. 'You remember, after the Alteration, Antoine le Maistre joined the Prince of Orange's army and travelled south.'

Minou waved her hand. 'I know this.'

'He was caught up in the massacre in Antwerp and only just escaped. He left Flanders and settled in Chartres, where he has relatives.'

'Why are you telling me things I already know?'

Piet kept talking. 'Which is where he heard the rumours

about a local landowner by the name of Lord Evreux. Evreux is considered something of a recluse.' He tapped the letter he was holding. 'Antoine has further news.'

'Confirmation that Evreux is Vidal?' Minou said quickly.

'Not definite, but three things he has further discovered that seem to support the theory: first that Evreux has a son of some nineteen or twenty years. Which would be the age of the boy I saw in Vidal's company in Paris on the day of the wedding.'

Minou shook her head. '*Mon coeur*, as I said at the time and since, many men have sons of such an age! That's no proof.'

'Second, Antoine also writes that shortly after Lord Evreux first settled outside Chartres – in the autumn of 1572, which also fits with the date Vidal disappeared from view – a novitiate priest was found murdered in the cathedral. The official explanation is that he was trying either to steal – or possibly protect – the Sancta Camisia and was killed in the attempt.'

'Surely the Sancta Camisia is still in Chartres Cathedral, is it not?'

Piet gave a ghost of a smile. 'There is a relic on display.'

Minou understood. 'But the fact of the murder gives weight to the idea that an exchange was made – a false relic for the true one – just as Vidal did with the Shroud of Antioch.'

'Yes.' He nodded. 'And the timings fit between Vidal's disappearance from Paris and Evreux's appearance in Chartres.'

This was strong corroborating information, but Minou still didn't want to rush to a conclusion.

'You said there were three things.'

'In the last week, a captain in the pay of the Duke of Guise – a Pierre Cabanel – is rumoured to have arrived in Chartres asking questions about Lord Evreux.'

'A local man?'

'From Paris. It sounds as if Guise has come to the same

conclusion, that Lord Evreux is indeed his errant confessor.'
Piet turned to face her. 'I know you counsel me against false
hope, Minou, but I have a feeling in my bones. I'm certain it's
him.'

Minou felt it too. She sat back, hearing the creak of the settle,
then put out her hand.

'May I read Antoine's letter for myself?'

For some reason, Minou felt the air in the chamber sharpen.
She glanced at Piet, trying to read the look on his face, but he
said nothing. Slowly, he passed the paper over.

Minou started to read, seeing no reason why Piet would have
withheld news of the letter from her all day. It contained no
more than he had just told her. Until she reached the postscript,
scribbled in a hasty hand at the foot of the page.

She turned cold.

'That's why I have been cloistered in here all day,' Piet said
quietly. 'I didn't know what you would feel. I didn't know
what I felt.'

'Yes, I see,' Minou's voice was barely a whisper. Her thoughts
were roaring in her head. Her heart was thudding.

Piet reached out and took the letter gently from her shaking
hand.

'"Cabanel is said to be accompanied by his daughter",' he
read. '"I have not laid eyes on him, but she is a beautiful creature of some eighteen or nineteen summers. Strange to say,
Reydon, there was something about her that strongly reminded
me of your dear wife: the same long brown hair, the same pale
skin, and an extraordinary coincidence – the girl has one blue
eye and the other one brown."'

Piet took her hand. 'Cabanel comes from Paris. What if it's
her, Minou? What if it is Marta? Our daughter found at last.'

427

CHAPTER SEVENTY-SIX

CHARTRES

A single band of sunlight shone through the gap in the shutters, falling like a golden ribbon across the bed.

Marie Cabanel stood at the window, looking out over the rue du Cheval Blanc towards the north door of the cathedral. She had positioned herself precisely so the sacristan would have the most beguiling view: tall, her long brown hair hung loose over her shoulders and down her back, modest. Marie rested one pale hand on the casement, so that the white skin of her inner arm was tantalisingly visible.

'Have I done something to offend you?' she asked in a whisper, though loud enough to bring the cleric rushing across the room.

Marie could feel him close behind her. She felt the heat emanating from him. She could picture the precise way his hand hovered in the air, desperate to touch her. She let him wait a moment longer then, without turning round, she reached out her hand behind her, so that her sapphire ring glinted fleetingly in the light. The sacristan should be in no doubt that she was a woman of exceptional qualities. A woman much sought-after. The kind of woman over whom, in antiquity, wars might have been fought.

The young cleric grasped it, like a drowning man, and entwined his fingers with hers.

Without seeming to move, Marie let the ribbon of her cloak

come fully undone. It fell from her shoulders to the ground, the pale blue material pooling like water, revealing that she was wearing nothing but a shift beneath. Marie heard him catch his breath and slowly turned, so he could see the contours of her body, the soft curve of her waist.

'You are . . .'

Marie placed one finger on his mouth. 'I should not have come, but I could not help myself.'

She leant in so that the sapphire necklace, the blue a perfect match for the ring, fell forward against his black robes. Her body pressed against his just for a moment. Then she pulled back. Marie needed him to be tortured by the memory of what he might have. Without that, she would not acquire the information she needed from him.

'This cannot happen –' he murmured, though the words caught in his throat. He closed his eyes and she saw his lips move.

Marie knew he was praying and she smiled. Men of God were all the same. Mind over matter was all very well when they were alone in their monastic cells at night. But when she was there, their vows were easily broken.

Her last lover, a sweet young priest serving at the Sainte-Chapelle in Paris, had told her in precise detail what went through his mind when he tried to resist temptation. He imagined himself on his knees before the grand altar, filling his head with images of the vaulted stone ceiling, the bloodied hands and feet of Jesus upon the cross. He tried to replace the beating of his pulse with the melody of the choir, voices soaring through the nave and up to the highest rafters. He forced himself to remember the promise of the resurrection and of the life to come for those who followed Him and obeyed God's laws.

Marie reached out and tenderly forced the sacristan to kneel. His breathing came faster.

'I wish only to give you comfort. You toil so hard for the good of others.'

He rested his head against her belly and she heard him groan as he drank in the scent of her. He tried to wrap his arms around her thighs.

'You remember those days, after we first lay together?' she said, pulling away slightly from his reach. 'My love, I could not sleep or eat or drink. I was sick for the lack of you.'

'You were?' She could hear the desperation in his voice now.

'You were so sweet.' She smiled. 'My little songbird.'

He closed his eyes. 'But I cannot. This is a sin. My vows do not permit it.'

Marie fell to her knees in front of him, so that they were facing one another.

'Will you give me your blessing,' she murmured, taking his hand and pressing it against her heart. 'Or is that also contrary to your vows?'

She could see how desperately he wanted her and how hard he was trying to resist. Then she felt the slightest increase of pressure as his hand cupped her breast.

'Thank you for your kindness.' She slipped her expert hand beneath his robe. 'No one need know.'

'The Lord sees all.'

'And forgives all those who truly repent,' she whispered, tracing a finger up the inside of his thigh. The sacristan rocked back on his knees and Marie knew he was limed.

Suddenly, he swept her up from the floor and carried her to the canopy of the bed, dragging back the curtains so roughly that the rings rattled on the rail.

'In Chartres, they talk of you highly,' Marie said, allowing him to lay her down across the sheets. 'I can teach you to be the man you were born to be.'

He had forgotten his vows, he had forgotten how the chamber overlooked the cathedral.

'That's right,' she encouraged, opening herself to him.

He closed his eyes, aware of nothing now but the movement of his body inside hers, desire blotting out any thought.

'Did you discover what I asked of you?' she murmured into his ear, moaning as if his thrusting was giving her pleasure.

He did not answer. He could not. He had lost any sense of where he was. But Marie knew she needed him to speak now. Some were unguarded after the act was over. Others felt an immediate shame and were anxious to be gone.

She grabbed a twist of his hair and roughly dragged his head back. He cried out, then she silenced him by bringing her mouth to his and biting his lip. He moaned with an exquisite jolt of pain.

'Where is he to be found?'

'Marie –'

She wrapped her legs around his back and, before he realised what she was doing, she rolled him over so she was now sitting astride him.

'Where does Lord Evreux live?' she pressed, letting her hair fall over him like a veil. 'You promised you would discover this for me.'

'I have the information you asked for,' he panted.

'You brought the papers with you as I commanded?'

'Yes,' he cried. 'I kept them hidden in the sacristy in case. In case – I hoped you would come back.'

'You have done well.' Marie encouraged him by kissing him full on the mouth. 'And Evreux's estates are?'

'It is all there,' he stuttered, no longer the master of his words. 'I wrote it down. For you.'

She rocked back, arching her spine. As he came to his end, he called out her name.

Afterwards, Marie lay beside him, soothing him and murmuring to him until he fell asleep. She was good at what she did. She was not one of Catherine de' Medici's *escadron volant* – she was not high enough born for such an honour. But growing up in the heart of Paris, Marie had watched and observed their methods and adapted them for her own.

A sudden sharp flash of memory pierced her. Like a bead rolling away through dusty attic rooms, the sense of something always just out of sight, out of reach: the memory of a white bonnet, of a man overheard in the street, of a baby crying and crying, of questions never answered.

Glimpses of a life before the life she remembered. 'What is a *fille d'escadron*?' Who had said those words? Had she? 'Boys are fools, to give away secrets for trinkets.'

She hated these moments, echoes of some previous time. They were becoming more frequent and there was no one she could ask about them. Other faces, other voices she could not identify, but which seemed to be lodged somewhere deep inside her. From a time before she was Marie Cabanel.

She closed her eyes and focused on the present. She had no need of the past. All that mattered was now and taking care of herself. There was no one else.

Marie waited until the sleeping man became heavy in her arms, then she slipped out from under him. As the great bells of Chartres Cathedral marked the passing of the hour, the sacristan was unaware of her expert fingers rifling through the folds of his cassock, searching the leather satchel until she found the papers. He did not see the look of satisfaction in her eyes as she read the details.

Standing in the rue du Cheval Blanc in the four-o'clock

shadow of the hot afternoon, Marie allowed herself a moment of triumph. Amongst many other things, she had confirmed that, although Lord Evreux possessed a town house in this very street, his main estates lay to the west in the Orléanais countryside; that he lived on the estate with his son, a man of some twenty-one summers; that Evreux was rumoured to be a relic hunter.

It was him, Marie was sure of it.

What she needed to do now was to get a letter to Vidal, offering a trade he could not resist. What would happen after that was in God's hands. She twisted the silver chain of her necklace, letting the gemstone dazzle in the light. Of all the shades of blue, sapphire was her favourite.

She smiled. Her father would have been pleased.

CHAPTER SEVENTY-SEVEN

WARMOESSTRAAT, AMSTERDAM

'What are you going to do?' Alis asked again.

After dining at six o'clock, the children had gone into the garden to enjoy the cooler air of evening while the adults retired to the family chamber. Minou and Piet had told Alis and Cornelia about le Maistre's letter. The air had grown stale with talking.

When it was time for them to return home, Minou had decided to walk with Cornelia and Alis back to their house in Warmoesstraat. Cornelia had excused herself, claiming there were shipping documents she needed to ratify, leaving Alis and Minou alone.

Now it was dusk and the two sisters were sitting in the main chamber of the house. The tall elegant windows were open over the canal. Fireflies fluttered around the candles set on the window sills. The room was infused with the scent of citronella.

Minou was unable to settle. Having lived for twelve years trying to accept her daughter was dead, the idea that she might in fact be alive was almost too much to bear. She felt as if a layer of skin had been removed, every nerve tingling. She felt excited, yes, but at the same time utterly undone.

'You know what Piet wants to do. What about you, Minou, what do you want?'

She looked at her sister. 'I don't know. I want to believe the girl is Marta. But in the next instant I can't bear the thought she might be.'

'Why not?'

Minou took a deep breath. 'Because I gave up on her, Alis. I stopped believing she could be found.'

'That's not true,' Alis said loyally. 'You did everything you could, but you were in Amsterdam. Too many people went missing or died that night; there was no way of finding one seven-year-old girl from so far away. And Paris was – is still – too dangerous for us. You are too harsh on yourself. You should not feel guilty.'

'But I do,' Minou cried.

For a moment, she allowed herself to be soothed by the sounds of the barges on the canal, the dip of oars in the water, the gentle wash against the walls. Minou realised she had never allowed Marta to grow up. Having pictured her daughter's face over so many years – an image that had grown fainter and fainter with time – Marta was still the same girl, clutching her white cap in her hand and dressed in her favourite blue dress, who'd come complaining about being confined to the nursery with her sick brother on that hot August day. The courageous, bold, disobedient child who, impatient with waiting, had gone alone into the streets of Paris and never come back.

'What if it is Marta and she doesn't know me? She'd be nineteen now.'

'Of course she'll remember you,' Alis said firmly.

'Or what if it is her, but I cannot love her?'

Alis smiled. 'You will. It might take a while, and it might be hard, but she will find her way back to your heart eventually and you to hers. You're her mother. She will not have forgotten you.'

'She might. It has been so long.'

Minou felt misery seeping into every pore, her limbs heavy, as if she had woken too early from a deep sleep. She felt disjointed and confused. For twelve years, Minou had prayed for her daughter to be given back to her. Now, at the thought of it, she felt only terror.

Minou twisted her pale white fingers in her lap. 'What if she has suffered – what then?'

'The girl le Maistre describes in the letter does not sound like that,' Alis said, though Minou saw a flash of pity in her sister's eyes. 'But whatever might or might not have happened in Marta's life, for good or for ill, you will be equal to it. It is possible she will tell you things you will not want to hear. That she has lived a life very different from the one you would have given her. It would be foolish to pretend other-wise. It is hard to be a woman in times of war, let alone a girl.'

'If it is her,' Minou said again.

'If it is her.'

She took a deep breath. 'Piet is excited, both at the thought that we might have found Vidal after all these years and that we have found Marta. He has no doubt. But there's no reason to believe Cabanel or his daughter are still in Chartres.'

'There's no reason to think they are not,' Alis countered.

Minou looked at her sister. 'So you think I should go?'

Alis laughed out loud. 'Of course you must go. You cannot sit here in Amsterdam wondering. Or waiting for Piet to come back. The sooner you go, the sooner you will know. One way or another, you will know.'

There was a sound behind them and Cornelia put her head round the door. Alis's face lit up.

'Am I intruding?' she asked.

Alis held out her hand. 'Of course not.'

Cornelia walked in, carrying a pewter tray with three tankards and a jug.

'I thought you might be in need of refreshment.'

Minou marvelled at how little Cornelia had changed in the years since they'd first met. Her brown hair was a little thinner now and her features had not softened over time, yet she had somehow grown into herself. Age suited her.

Minou saw Cornelia drop a hand on Alis's shoulder as she passed, and Minou smiled. Love suited her. It suited them both.

Cornelia had never had to marry. She was financially independent, so had no need of a husband to support her. With Piet's assistance, she had continued to grow her father's business and the van Raay fleet was now one of the most successful in Amsterdam.

From the earliest age, Alis had made clear her disdain for boys, then the institution of marriage. Minou had thought it was something she would grow out of, but as Alis settled into life in Amsterdam and Minou got to know her sister again, she realised she knew her own heart.

'What are you thinking?' Alis asked.

Minou smiled. 'Nothing.'

For a while, the three women sat in silence, sipping their beer. Alis and Cornelia occupied their usual chairs either side of the fireplace. Minou remained at the table, tracing patterns on the polished wood with her finger.

'If we go to Chartres,' she said eventually, 'will you look after Jean-Jacques and Bernarda? And the *hofje*?'

Minou saw Cornelia and Alis exchange a look and realised they had already talked about it.

'Of course,' Cornelia said.

Alis grinned. 'Bernarda and Johannus will be more than happy in our care. I will move back to Zeedijk and keep everything going until you return.'

Minou smiled. 'You realise we might be gone for a month. Longer, possibly, depending on what we find?'

Cornelia and Alis exchanged another look.

'I wondered if we might invite Salvadora to come and stay,' Alis said tentatively. 'To help look after the children. Johannus is very fond of her.'

'You don't even like Salvadora!' Minou exclaimed. 'I seem to remember when she nursed you at Puivert after . . . you said if we didn't take her with us to Paris you would throw yourself out of the window.'

'You did not!' Cornelia laughed.

Alis put her hands up. 'I will admit I found her tiresome. But I was younger then. And she always liked Aimeric more.' Her face grew serious. 'I think she would be grateful to be here when you return. If it is Marta. Salvadora hasn't forgotten those days or your flight from Paris. It lies heavy on her heart, too.'

'She was always so abrupt with Marta.'

'That was just her manner. In her letters, she never fails to ask.'

'You correspond with Salvadora?' Minou asked, genuinely surprised.

'She likes to reminisce about Aimeric.' Alis sighed. 'And so do I.'

'You could have talked to me,' Minou said, trying not to feel snubbed.

'You had Marta to think about,' Alis said simply. 'Besides, Aunt Salvadora misses the children. She asks often after them.'

Minou frowned. 'I begged her to stay with us here, but she was set on returning to Toulouse.'

Alis grinned. 'Forgive me, Cornelia, but Salvadora disliked Dutch society and hated Amsterdam. A "nasty, damp place" was how she described it in one of her letters.'

Cornelia laughed. 'My father said she often complained.

Whenever he escorted her to Mass at the Nieuwe Kerk, he said she always found fault with something.'

Minou watched them smile at one another, still wondering at the relationship between her aunt and her sister she'd had no idea existed.

'Do you think Salvadora would come?' she said. 'With the situation in France after the death of the King's brother – and now the instability here after the assassination of the Prince of Orange – these are dangerous times to travel.'

'Cornelia had an idea,' Alis said. 'She suggested that – if you decided to go to Chartres – it would be safest to do as much of the journey as possible by sea. The same vessel that takes you and Piet into France could then sail down the western coast of France to Bordeaux and collect her there. If Aunt Salvadora could arrange safe travel from Toulouse.'

Minou nodded. 'It would be reassuring to have Salvadora here again.' She turned to Cornelia. 'Do you think you could find room for us on one of your ships?'

'I will need to look at the chart, but I believe we have a ship sailing the day after tomorrow. You could sail to Rouen, then ride west to Chartres from there. It's dangerous to travel through the southern provinces – the fighting there is worse than ever. Such devastation, such a lack of food, so the reports say. You'll be safer on the water.'

'And bring Salvadora back on the return journey?'

'Of course.'

Finally, Minou smiled. 'The same journey we did together all those years ago, but in reverse. You are saving us again, Cornelia.'

To her surprise, the Dutchwoman blushed. 'No need for thanks,' she said gruffly. 'You have done me at least as many kindnesses in return.'

Alis clapped her hands. 'So that is settled, then.'

Minou felt a sudden lightening of her spirits. 'If Piet agrees – and you are both certain it is not an imposition for you to run the *hofje* until we return – then yes, it is settled. We will sail for Chartres on Sunday.'

CHAPTER SEVENTY-EIGHT

EVREUX ESTATE, CHARTRES

'You believe the letter is genuine, Father?'

Since word had arrived via a sacristan in the cathedral that there was a woman claiming to be in the possession of the Sudarium, the Veil of Veronica, Louis had been anxious.

'The letter or the relic?' Vidal asked sharply.

'Both.'

'I would like to think so.'

Louis hesitated. His father's moods were so changeable these days and he did not want to provoke him. Vidal had been bled again this morning and while Louis knew his father was in pain, he believed the visits from the apothecary did more harm than good. Such was his concern, he had made the mistake of trying to talk to Xavier about it. Later that day, when he had gone out to ride, Louis found the girth on his saddle cut. It was only luck that stopped him from being seriously hurt. It had always been thus between them, but recently Xavier's hatred of him seemed to burn even more fiercely.

He chose his words with care. 'Even so, is there any need to invite her to come here, my lord?'

'Are you questioning my judgement?'

'Of course not, it just seems an unnecessary risk. You have protected your privacy so well. Surely it would be better to rendezvous in Chartres? I could meet with this sacristan on your behalf and learn more about this woman.'

'No.'

Louis bit back his disappointment. 'Or accompany you, at least.'

Vidal shook his head 'There are spies everywhere.'

They were sitting in the library of their manor house. His father was tapping his fingers on the arm of his chair, a steady drumming. Louis had lived in his company long enough to know he only did this when troubled.

'Has something particular happened to make you want to avoid Chartres?' he asked cautiously.

Louis saw the indecision in his father's eyes and guessed Xavier had been dripping poison into his ear again. He was sly and he was clever. Xavier never said anything explicit that Lord Evreux could take exception to, but even the tiniest barbed comment about Louis's loyalty could do him a great deal of damage. And with his father so sick now, his judgement was impaired.

'It has been brought to my attention that someone has been asking questions,' Vidal said eventually.

'Did Xavier tell you this?'

He saw annoyance flicker in his father's eyes. 'It doesn't matter who told me, I believe it to be true.'

'There's always someone asking questions, Father.'

'Not so close at hand.'

Louis stood up. 'In Chartres itself, do you mean? Do you know who?'

Vidal put his hand to his temple. 'The threat is credible, that's all you need to know.'

'If that is the case, Father, then forgive me, the decision to allow this woman – this stranger – to come here seems even more unwise. I am surprised Xavier counselled you this way.'

'Xavier has everything in hand.'

Louis did not like the sound of this at all. 'Father, I don't wish to speak out of turn, but do you think it possible this so-called credible threat, and the letter offering you the Sudarium, are connected?'

For the first time, Vidal looked at him. 'The timing gives me pause for thought, yes.'

'In which case – '

'Enough!' His father's fingers drummed faster. 'If the Veil is genuine, it is a risk worth taking. I will not know unless I see it for myself.'

'And if it is a forgery?'

He gave a hollow laugh. 'I cannot see Guise sending a mere woman to kill me, it would insult his sense of justice! Besides, soon he will be coming to me on bended knee.'

Louis looked at his father with unease. Vidal was usually so careful, so measured, despite his illness. Yet today there was some wildness to his thinking. One moment he was hiding from Guise, the next he seemed to be courting attention.

'I am yours to command, Father.'

'I shall write a letter to the sacristan informing him that this creature will be invited to present herself once she has the object in her possession. Xavier will deliver it.'

'I can do this service for you, my lord,' Louis offered quickly, thinking it would at least give him the chance to investigate the woman on his own.

'I want you here.'

Vidal's mood suddenly changed again. His features seemed to relax and the light came back into his eyes.

'There is no one who has attempted to do what I am doing. I am so close now. No one, since Saint Louis built the Sainte-Chapelle to house the holiest relics of the Passion, has ever had such ambition.'

Louis stood listening, his hands clasped respectfully.

'You have the impatience of youth. I have been patient, but now at last things are within my grasp. The time is right. The King cannot decide whether to crush the Huguenot threat or embrace it. Navarre is now the heir apparent and Guise will not stand for that. France will fall. And when that happens, I will be ready – the Priest-Confessor of a new Church rising from the ashes to challenge the power of Spain and Rome.' He poured himself a goblet of wine and held it up in a toast. 'And if I die, you will finish my work. To make sure my legacy lives after me. That is your purpose as my son, do you understand? That is why I brought you here.'

Vidal put his goblet back on the tray.

'Bring me paper and ink, I will write the letter now.'

Louis didn't trust himself to answer. He feared his father had lost his wits.

CHAPTER SEVENTY-NINE

Damrak, Amsterdam

Two days later, when the sun was high in the sky and Amsterdam looked at her best, Minou and Piet walked to the end of the can Raay wharf on Op 't water.

Minou embraced Bernarda and Johannus in turn, promising they would return before the autumn was far advanced and pleading with them to be good for Aunt Salvadora when she arrived. Piet told Johannus to be the man of the house in his absence.

'Though Aunt Alis is really in charge,' Minou said, smiling.

While Cornelia's servant lowered their travelling chest into the barge, Piet checked his leather satchel. Minou turned to take her leave of Alis.

'Remind me once more that this is the right thing to do,' she said, looking at the Amsterdam skyline. 'To leave all this. To leave you all.'

Alis took her hands. 'Dearest Sister, you have no choice. You are doing the right thing.'

'So long as one of us is certain.'

Minou turned to the row of high houses on the other side of the water, feeling oddly nostalgic.

'But what if we – ' she began to say.

'You will be back before the leaves are turning gold, and before the last of the late crops of apples have fallen in the orchard you will be home.'

'Home . . .' Minou murmured.

She suddenly remembered standing on Plaats with Alis, Jean-Jacques and Bernarda in March 1580 to witness the arrival of Willem of Orange. On the foredeck of a galley draped with his noble colours of orange, white and blue, he had sailed along Damrak at the head of a flotilla. As the Prince had stepped off the ship, Minou had seen his thick white ruff above his fur collar, an embroidered velvet doublet with gold clasps. He had looked every inch the man who would free them from Spanish rule.

'Are you ready?' Piet said, reaching up and offering his hand.

Minou looked at his familiar face, at the purpose in his eyes and the set of his shoulders, and was reassured. She was ready. Alis was right. They had to go. For although it was so small a piece of information on which to stake their hopes – the coincidence of a pair of mismatched eyes – they were right to have faith.

Minou's hand stole to her pocket. Earlier this morning, she had put Marta's old bonnet there. A talisman for good luck, or something to prompt her daughter's memory, she wasn't certain.

If they found her.

At the last moment, Minou had added her journal to the chest, too. 'Yes, I'm ready,' she replied and stepped down into the barge.

'We will take good care of things while you're gone,' Alis said. 'You don't have to worry about anything. Au revoir!'

'*Tot ziens!*' Minou called in reply. As Bernarda and Johannus started to wave, she felt a pang of guilt at leaving them. 'I will miss you, my little ones. I love you.'

Cornelia gave the instruction to the boatman. He pushed the craft away from the wharf, jumped in and steered them into the middle of the water to join the steady line of little craft heading for the lock, then through to the harbour and the open sea beyond.

CHAPTER EIGHTY

Four Weeks Later

RUE DE LA POISSONNERIE, CHARTRES
Tuesday, 21 August

Minou and Piet arrived in Chartres at dusk.

The voyage from Amsterdam had taken some four weeks. With a fair wind behind them, they had sailed from Amsterdam to Rouen – north through the IJ, then south-west along the Flanders coast, then east down the river Seine. In Rouen, they had rested for a few days. Piet had been relieved to find a message from Antoine le Maistre informing him that Cabanel and his daughter were still in Chartres. He had sent a letter in return advising him of when they hoped to arrive.

Bright July sunshine gave way to slate-grey skies and relentless rain in August as they began the next stage of their journey.

They travelled due south through Normandy and into the Orléanais, passing through Evreux, Nonancourt, Dreux and on towards Chartres itself. Crops were rotting in the fields. The land was sodden underfoot. Several rivers had flooded.

The monotonous thudding of the horses' hooves on the damp ground, the relentless drizzle, the rumbling of the carriage wheels until Minou thought her teeth would be shaken out of her head – had all taken their toll. Many times she wished herself home in Amsterdam, rather than on what she now feared was going to turn out to be a fool's errand.

'You are sure he expects us today?' Minou asked again, as the carriage rattled through the narrow, cobbled streets to the address le Maistre had given them.

'Yes,' Piet snapped, his impatience a sure sign he was also concerned that his latest letter to le Maistre might not have been received. 'I hope so.'

But when they stopped at the half-timbered house in the rue de la Poissonnerie, the servant who opened the door was waiting, Antoine standing in the entrance hall to greet them in person. Minou and Piet were shown to a comfortable chamber, where they could wash the dust of the road from their faces, and within an hour of their arrival, they were sitting with their host in a sheltered courtyard at the rear of the house drinking sweet white wine and eating *cochelins*, a local sweet pastry.

'I apologise for the weather.' Antoine smiled in apology. 'Chartres is not at her best in the rain. It has been an unseasonably wet August.'

'We are used to living in a world of water,' Piet laughed.

Exhausted by the journey and with her senses pleasantly numbed by the wine, Minou was happy to listen to the two men talk.

'You were never tempted to come back to Amsterdam?' Piet asked.

Le Maistre shook his head. 'I always felt an outsider. I couldn't learn the language and after Antwerp – and the loss of so many of the men I was fighting alongside – I wanted to come home to France. Not to Limoges. I would have taken no pleasure to be reminded every day of the loss of my wife and children. Here, at least, there are no memories to be disturbed.'

Piet nodded. 'You have friends here?'

'There are but few of us of the Reformed faith in Chartres.

This is a very Catholic city and some sections of the northern city walls still bear the scars of the Huguenot siege during the second war, so there is no love lost. But we meet in secret to worship and things are, for the present at least, as peaceful as anywhere.' Antoine smiled. 'And there is a widow, a woman of gentle bearing and middle years. She will never take the place of my dear wife, but we enjoy one another's company. These days, to be safe and contented is enough. The fire of my youth has gone.'

Piet raised his glass. 'I am glad for you, my friend.'

In the branches above their heads, a blackbird began its lament for the fading day.

'And the matter that brings us here?' Minou asked.

Le Maistre glanced up the ivy-covered wall, then stood up. The mood of the evening changed.

'Shall we repair inside?' he said. 'I would not be overheard.'

RUE DE LA PORTE CENDREUSE

Marie Cabanel pulled her blue silk hood over her head, told the carriage to wait, then set off on foot through the darkening streets.

She hurried through tiny squares and past half-timbered houses standing morosely in the driving rain. At her heels, the river Eure threatened to burst its banks.

At the appointed hour, Marie was back at the artist's studio in the shadow of the Priory of St Vincent. She glanced around. She did not believe anyone had followed her – she had taken a circuitous route and, besides, it was dark – but it was as wise to be sure.

The rain was seeping through her hood and dripping down

between her gown and her ruff. All the same, it was a relief to be out of the confinement of the boarding house. Since commissioning the forgery three weeks ago, Marie had remained out of sight in the rooms she had taken in her father's name. A local man was being paid handsomely for masquerading as her father, eating and drinking himself into a stupor every night, but it was a necessary precaution. If people knew she was a woman unaccompanied, she would not be safe.

She hated it. The quiet, the lack of society and entertainment. But, God willing, it would not be for much longer. If everything went according to plan, in a matter of days she would finally be on her way home.

Just for a moment, Marie allowed her thoughts to take her there. She remembered almost nothing of her younger life, just occasional glimpses, but her memories always led her back to the city she loved. Paris. She remembered standing in the doorway of a beautiful blue chamber and seeing other rooms opening out and out into the distance and beyond. A feeling that if only she could get to the final room, there was something there that she needed to see. After that, the memories darkened: the ghost of a memory of a man with black curls lying dead on the floor. So much blood.

And, nothing.

One of the few things her father had told her about her childhood was that she'd suffered a serious fall when she was seven and had hit her head.

Marie's fingers stole to the rosary at her waist, as they always did when her thoughts turned in upon themselves. Once, she had asked her father if it was possible she might have witnessed a murder. He had not answered and now he was dead, too, leaving her alone to carry out the mission that had obsessed him.

Marie was jolted back to the present by the door to the atelier opening.

'Mademoiselle, you are welcome. Will you step inside?'

She looked at the old man, a gifted tailor and forger. He had a spider's web of lines around his eyes, and magnifying spectacles perched on the tip of his nose as if she had interrupted him in the middle of a delicate piece of sewing. Needles of different sizes were pinned into his felt jerkin, making a silver ladder like the bands on a soldier's coat.

'Is it finished?'

'It is.'

Marie followed him through a warren of tiny rooms, until they reached a large workshop at the back of the building. A row of lighted lamps hung above a long wooden counter, and the surface was covered with swatches of fabric, scissors and paints. Marie was relieved to see he had obeyed her instructions and sent away his apprentices.

'Where is it?' she demanded, anticipation sharpening her voice.

The old tailor smiled. 'I do not think you will be disappointed, mademoiselle.'

Marie hoped it hadn't all been for nothing. The expense, the waiting, the inducements to ensure the work was done on time. Though little was known about Evreux, he was reputed to have a fine eye and an uncommon depth of knowledge of antiquities. Marie had forged letters of recommendation from the port of Alicante in Valencia, the most promising of the sites claiming to have possession of the Sudarium, the Veil of Veronica, one of the most elusive of the relics of the Passion.

Evreux was said to be keen to acquire it.

'Show me,' Marie said.

The old man opened a carton. He slid out a roll of cloth and laid it flat on the table. Marie knew better than to touch it, but instantly she admired the way he had skilfully captured the scent and the shimmer of the Holy Land. The cloth seemed to smell of olive groves and sandalwood and cedar. The image on the cloth showed a gentle man with sorrowful eyes filled with the suffering of the world.

'Will it suffice?' the tailor asked nervously.

Marie gave a long exhalation of breath. 'It will.'

RUE DE LA POISSONNERIE

Minou and Piet were sheltered in Antoine le Maistre's study poring over the map of the local region.

'Evreux's estates are here.' Le Maistre pointed to a large expanse of land some five leagues to the west of Chartres. 'I have never seen the man, but common gossip has it that Pierre Cabanel, a captain in the employ of the Duke of Guise, has been keeping an eye on Evreux's townhouse in the rue du Cheval Blanc, not far from here, and also has men watching the manor house on Evreux's estate itself.'

'You are certain this Cabanel has been sent to kill Evreux?'

'If Evreux is indeed Guise's former confessor, then yes, I am. It is common gossip that the duke put a price on the cardinal's head.'

'Why has Cabanel not acted before now?'

Le Maistre shrugged. 'Evreux rarely leaves his estate. It is well guarded: he employs mercenaries from the wars. And even in these lawless times, I imagine Guise – whose leadership of the Catholic League is based on his moral authority and his pious character – wouldn't want to be held responsible for the murder of a priest.'

'That makes no sense!'

Le Maistre laughed bitterly. 'None of this makes any sense, Reydon. Hundreds of thousands of people slaughtered in God's name, women and children, not only soldiers on the battlefield, for the right to worship as we please, for the right to worship in our own language. We have destroyed our country with this madness. None of it makes sense.'

Piet put his hand on his friend's shoulder. 'I know.'

Le Maistre sighed. 'Forgive me, I am so weary of it all.'

'Where is Cabanel now?'

'I have managed to find out he's been lodging in a coaching house on the road that runs north of Evreux's estates. Presumably waiting for further orders.'

'Is his daughter still with him?' Minou asked anxiously.

'I confess I don't know.' Le Maistre sighed. 'Madame Reydon, perhaps I should not have said anything. After I had sent the letter to Amsterdam, I realised I might have raised your hopes for no reason. It was just the resemblance was so marked, and I have such a strong memory of your daughter. I couldn't help but wonder.'

Minou nodded. 'Will you describe her to me?'

'She is of your stature, Madame Reydon, in both her bearing and her manner. There was something about her. An elegance and a confidence, a boldness in the way she carried herself.'

'What colour was her hair?'

'It was covered beneath her hood, but I could see glimpses of brown.'

'The colour of autumn leaves,' Piet said, smiling.

Le Maistre nodded. 'Her features put me immediately in mind of you, Madame Reydon, it took me aback. The turn of her nose, her pale complexion, the set of her mouth. But, most of all, it was her eyes. We passed on the street. She was walking along the rue du Cheval Blanc and I was going in the opposite direction.'

'You saw her eyes clearly?'

'One brown eye and one blue, I remembered my dear wife remarking upon it when you stayed with us in Limoges. You and your daughter both.'

Minou smiled. 'I have the enamel box Madame le Maistre gave me, I treasure it still.'

Le Maistre smiled too, for a moment lost in happier times. In the courtyard, the blackbird still sang in the plane tree.

'What do you propose we do?' Piet asked.

Le Maistre raised his hands. 'It is up to you, my friend. I can take you to Evreux's estate, though how you get access to the manor house itself once we are there, I know not. Or I can take you first to where Cabanel and his daughter are lodging. I will give you what assistance you need. The choice is yours.'

Piet hesitated, then turned to Minou. 'What would you do?'

She looked at him. The lines of concern on his face seemed deeper in the flickering light of the candles.

'Do you realise what the date is tomorrow, *mon coeur*?'

'The twenty-second day of August –' He stopped. 'Oh.'

Minou's fingers stole to Marta's old linen bonnet in her pocket.

'Tomorrow it will be exactly twelve years ago to the day that we last saw her. I remember every moment of that day as if it was yesterday: the oppressive heat, the smell from the street, the sounds in the rue des Barres. It was a hot and humid day. Aimeric came – it was the last time I saw him also; Jean-Jacques had colic and had been up all night crying; Marta came bursting into our chamber demanding to be taken out into the city. She was only seven.'

'Minou,' he murmured. 'My love.'

'I must see this girl,' she said, her words coming in a rush. 'Tonight, tomorrow, as soon as possible. I cannot bear another day not knowing.'

CHAPTER EIGHTY-ONE

CHARTRES COUNTRYSIDE, ORLÉANAIS

In the dark heart of the Chartres countryside, Marie Cabanel sat in the chamber and listened to the rain lash against the window pane. God willing, this would be her last night in this noisy, foul-smelling place.

After Marie had left the artist's studio in Chartres, she had sent a letter to Lord Evreux requesting an audience, this time in her own name rather than from the sweet sacristan. She had then returned here to the coaching house that had been her base for these past seven weeks, to wait and to rest, but Marie could not settle. Every tiny thing that might cause her plan to fail was pricking at her mind, chief among them that Evreux might not take the bait at all. Had she put enough in the letter to convince him to receive her? What if he did not even reply?

Marie stood up and began to pace the room. Her plot was excellent. She had to have faith that it would all fall into place.

'It must work.' The sound of her own voice gave her courage. 'It will.'

She had suggested she could go to his house in the Rue du Cheval Blanc. That would be safer. Pierre, the ale-soaked labourer she'd recruited to masquerade as her father – now snoring his guts out in the box room next door – would keep watch at a suitable distance. Though everything depended on Marie convincing Evreux to trust her, she was not foolish enough to go alone.

She took a deep breath. Her nerves were strung tight tonight. Anxiety fluttered in her stomach. All she had to do was confirm that Evreux was Vidal – she knew his every distinguishing mark from her father – and take her leave before he had any idea the relic was a fake.

The forger had done an excellent job. But was it good enough to deceive so practised an eye as Evreux's? She would only know when she laid the false Veil before him.

Her heart skipped a beat. She had to believe the stars would align.

All being well, she would quit Chartres immediately after-wards and make her way home to Paris. With luck, she would be there by Michaelmas and back in their modest lodgings on the rue Saint-Antoine. They had been gone for over a year.

There was no one waiting for her now. She'd no brothers and sisters, she barely remembered her mother – a drab streak of a woman, who had died in the epidemic that swept Paris after the St Bartholomew's Day massacre – and her father had died last winter. A stupid brawl in a boarding house in Rouen.

Cabanel had been a rough and taciturn man, not one to show affection, but he'd never raised a hand to her. In his own way, she thought he had been fond of her. She had no illusions about his character – he was a paid assassin, a murderer and a schemer – but he had treated her like a son and educated her in the way of life lived in the shadows.

The next stage of her plan would be to seek an audience with the Duke of Guise. She would wear her finest blue dress and would be demure and charming, without guile. She would beg his forgiveness as she told him how she, a girl of nineteen, had fulfilled the mission he had set her father, Pierre Cabanel. Marie had been in the duke's presence with him once before – she must have been thirteen or fourteen. The duke had honoured her with his attention, commenting favourably on her boldness and the unusual colour of her eyes, one brown and one blue. She thought he would remember her.

And then?

Marie allowed herself to dream.

What she hoped for – with a recommendation from Guise – was that she might come to the attention of Charlotte de Sauve, the leader of Catherine de' Medici's *escadron volant*. A former mistress of both Navarre and the King's younger brother, 'Monsieur', it was known in Paris that the duke's eye had been caught by Charlotte. Surely, if Guise was satisfied with what Marie had achieved in Chartres, then might he not effect an introduction? And she would change her name. Cabanel was too ordinary, she had never felt it suited her. With a new identity, she would start afresh as the woman she was meant to be.

Then, suddenly, she experienced an unaccountable feeling of loss. And shame. Marie's fingers curled into a fist. She pushed the emotion away. She did not have to justify herself to anyone. There was no one who would even care. She had not chosen the life she lived, and she had no choice but to survive on her wits and her looks. There would be time enough to repent and live a better life when she had money of her own, when she was finally safe.

A shout below drew her back from the precipice of her treacherous thoughts.

Marie rushed back to the window in time to see the youngest stable hand, a sweet boy with a claret birthmark on his face, rush out and grasp the reins of a carriage-and-pair cantering too fast into the courtyard.

'Steady,' he cried. 'Steady now.'

Marie's spirits fell. It was not the messenger returning from Evreux, but rather guests arriving for the night.

For a while longer, she stood in the window looking out over the empty countryside, still listening for the sound of a horse's hooves. It had stopped raining, but the evening was humid and there was now a white night mist lying over the dark flat land. Without warning, a phrase came into her mind.

'My lady of the mists.'

Now she was assailed by a faint half-memory: of a winter's night and cobbled streets, of a girl and a boy meeting in the shadow of the misty cathedral. A girl who looked like her.

Shaken, Marie pushed the glass open as far as she could to drink in the night air. The tavern below had fallen silent. Nothing was stirring. Only the sour scent of straw after rain and horse piss and manure drifted up to where she stood watching.

Marie sat down on the chest by the window and picked up her father's dagger. He'd valued it more than anything, never letting it out of his sight. His lucky charm, he'd told her, a symbol of the night his fortunes had changed. He had been holding it when he died, his life bleeding away for the sake of a quart of ale in a harbour tavern. Suddenly, Marie remembered the last words he'd uttered.

'I didn't mean to keep you,' he'd whispered.

Marie relived the moment in her mind's eye: the ice on the ground; the sailor swaying, horrified at what he'd done; the sound of the tavern door and the smell of sweat and ale as men came to carry her father inside. The crying of the gulls over the water. She hadn't cried. There'd been no point.

'I didn't mean to keep you . . .'

CHAPTER EIGHTY-TWO

Evreux Estate

Louis stood outside the library door, holding his father's letter in his hand. The message from the woman claiming to be in possession of the Sudarium had arrived nigh on midnight. It was now two o'clock in the morning and the messenger was still waiting for a response.

It was dark, but still he hesitated. Listened. Not a mouse was stirring, the servants were in their quarters, his father had retired to his bedchamber. Satisfied he was unobserved, Louis slipped the tip of his dagger under the Evreux seal and cracked the wax. He told himself his actions were justified to protect his father's interests.

Louis tilted the paper towards his candle and read the few words set down – nothing more than he already knew, that Marie Cabanel was to come to the estate tomorrow at sunset. The name Cabanel meant nothing to him.

He passed the red seal across the flame, just long enough to soften it, and resealed the missive. Then, full of misgiving, he went out into the courtyard and round to the kitchen garden where the messenger had been sent to wait.

The boy was dozing on a bench.

Louis stood over him. 'How now?'

The boy scrambled to his feet. 'Sire!'

'With Lord Evreux's compliments,' Louis said, pinching the letter between his thumb and forefinger: 'Where are you to deliver this?'

'I cannot say, sire.'

Louis stared at him. 'Cannot, or will not?'

'The lady asked me not to – her reputation.'

'Do you imagine my father is in the habit of –' Louis slapped the boy on the shoulder. 'In which case, I hope for your sake that you do not have too long a ride ahead of you.'

'No, sire.'

'I warrant Mademoiselle Cabanel is staying close enough at hand, but far enough to be discreet.' Louis handed over a coin. 'Lord Evreux will be grateful for your tact in this matter. You know how people talk.'

'Thank you, sire.' The messenger sighed with relief. 'The lodging is but a league away, then I will ride back to Chartres.'

RUE DE LA POISSONNERIE

Minou sat in the dark in their bedchamber. Her restless mind would not let her sleep.

She felt as if she was going into battle. Resolved, full of anticipation yet also terrified at what might lie ahead. Her head was filled with thoughts of her beautiful daughter and what she might be like. What would she say when they stood face to face after all these years? How would she feel?

Minou tried to remember all the versions of Marta she had conjured into life over the past twelve years of grieving: her daughter at ten years old, a little taller but the same; at twelve, with her hair braided and dressed; at fifteen, on the verge of womanhood. Now, if Antoine was to be believed, as alike to her as a reflection in a looking glass. The same manner and bearing, he had said. The same unusual eyes, blue and brown, so rarely found together. Minou would be looking at a young version of herself, and that thought both pleased and terrified her. But, in truth, only the child who had gone missing on this same day in 1572 was clear in her mind. The girl in the tapestry.

Minou felt a sharp pain in her chest and she pressed her hands against her ribs to stop herself crying out. After so many years of being careful, she had let down her guard and allowed herself to hope. If she was disappointed again, Minou was not sure her heart could bear it.

EVREUX ESTATE

Louis rushed to the stables.

There was only one lodging house within striking distance of the estate. If his suspicions were right, and Marie Cabanel was there, then he could observe her as she received his father's invitation and assess the situation. If she seemed genuine, then so be it. But if something seemed awry, then at least he was forewarned.

'Where the hell do you think you're going?'

Louis felt himself punched between his shoulder blades. He spun round.

'Don't you dare touch me!'

Xavier shoved him again, pushing him back against the rail. Louis heard the stamp of the horse's hooves on the straw.

'I'm warning you, do not try my patience.'

The steward laughed. 'Or what? You'll go crying to Papa? How do you think our noble lord would react if he knew you were opening his private correspondence? Or if he learnt you were absconding in the middle of the night?'

Louis stood his ground. 'It is none of your business. Get out of my way.'

'I asked you a question, boy. Where are you going?'

To his horror, he saw a flash of silver in the steward's hand.

'Don't be a fool,' he said, glancing desperately around for something with which to defend himself. 'Neither of us wants trouble.'

Xavier jabbed the knife towards him. 'From the moment we went to Saint-Antonin you have been nothing but trouble. I told his Eminence then, and I remind him now, you are no good. You have no loyalty, no affection. You're vermin. He cannot trust you, especially now he is sickening.' Xavier gave a crooked smile. 'So terribly sick. Not long for this world, I'd say.'

Louis turned cold. 'What do you mean?'

Xavier's answer came with another jagged thrust of the knife, slashing Louis's forearm.

'Just because you have his blood in your veins, because you have his countenance, did you think I would let you displace me when I've served him for so long?'

Out of the corner of his eye, Louis saw a rake leaning against the wooden strut at the end of the horse's stall. He flung out his arm, grasped the rake and sent the handle slamming down on Xavier's shoulder.

The man howled, but didn't drop the knife.

'Don't do this, Xavier,' Louis shouted and swung the rake again.

There was a stomach-turning crunch as the wood connected with the side of the steward's head, and he went down. In the stalls behind him, the horses started to whinny and stamp.

For a moment, Louis just stared in horror. Was he dead?

He knelt down. 'Xavier?'

Louis pressed his fingers to the man's neck, but could feel no pulse. He didn't seem to be breathing. Had he killed him?

A wave of pure horror swept through him, and he felt like the same powerless child incarcerated in the monastery in Saint-Antonin all those years ago.

Then Louis stood up. He was no longer a weak boy waiting in the dark for the punishment that would surely come. He was the son of Lord Evreux, his father's legitimate heir. He had acted in self-defence. He had been protecting his father's interests.

But would Vidal believe him?

Louis looked out through the open stable door and saw the first glimmers of dawn in the east. One thing was certain. He could not leave Xavier here. His best hope was if Xavier's absence went undiscovered for as long as possible. His father's attention would be focused on the arrival of Marie Cabanel at dusk. Vidal's obsession was to complete his collection. Surely he would have no thought for anything else this day?

Hoping he was right, Louis hid the blood-stained rake, then, praying none of the estate workers were yet awake, he grabbed Xavier by the legs. Carefully, slowly, in the gathering day, he dragged the body away from the stables all the way down to the lake. It was hard going and the grass was damp with early morning dew, but he made it.

Panting, Louis took a moment to catch his breath, then rolled the corpse over into the water and watched Xavier sink beneath the dark surface. Then, shocked by what he had done, he ran back to the manor house before anyone could notice he was not in his bed.

CHAPTER EIGHTY-THREE

As the day was dawning, Marie Cabanel and her two companions made their way through the woodland that marked the northern boundary of Evreux's lands. They had assured her that no soldiers would be on duty in this part of the estate so early in the day. If they were unlucky, a gamekeeper might see them, but so long as there were no dogs, they should be safe enough.

Marie had received word from Evreux in the middle of the night. He had agreed to receive her, but the rendezvous was not to be at Evreux's town house in Chartres, as Marie had hoped, but rather his countryside estate. At that point, her resolve had wavered. No doubt it made the operation more dangerous and her position more perilous.

But as a pink sunrise crept over the window sill, she had strengthened her resolve. She'd come too far to give up now. Success was within her grasp, she just had to hold her nerve.

At six o'clock, Marie had vacated her chamber, settled her debts with the landlord, then loaded the carriage with her belongings. It seemed wise to familiarise herself with the estate before she returned there at nightfall. Though the expenditure would further dent her dwindling resources, she had elected to take with her for protection not only Pierre, who was pretending to be her father, but Pierre's brother also. With the coachman,

465

that made three. All were local men, they knew the lie of the land. Besides, if all went according to plan, the money Evreux would give her for the forged Sudarium would easily cover these additional costs.

If he was deceived by the forgery.

Marie moved forward to the edge of the line of trees, then stopped. In the far distance she could see the manor house standing alone in the middle of a wide and open space at the top of the hill.

'I will approach the house by carriage along the main drive.'

Pierre cleared his throat. 'It's not the house you need. It's here you will find him.'

Marie followed the direction he was pointing in and saw a shimmer of water. She narrowed her gaze. In a dip in the green expanse she saw an ornamental lake. In its centre was an island and, on it, a white building.

'A church! I'm not intending to pray, messieurs!'

Jean gave her a sly look. 'Lord Evreux is accustomed to go across to the island each evening at sunset.'

Marie frowned, feeling nerves flutter in her chest. This complicated matters further. To walk into Evreux's house alone was risky enough, but this?

'And he is usually unaccompanied?' she asked.

'Except for the boatman who takes him across, yes.'

'His son does not go with him?'

Pierre shrugged. 'From time to time.'

'On whose authority do you know this?'

Pierre and Jean exchanged a look. 'We have a man on the inside,' the older brother said. 'Lord Evreux's steward.'

'He is to be trusted?'

'Xavier has served Evreux for some twenty years.'

Marie stared at the building. As the light grew stronger, the white tower stood even more starkly against the blue sky. Was it a private chapel? A mausoleum? Then, she realised. If everything she knew about Evreux was true, wasn't it likely to be a reliquary?

Marie felt her confidence soar again. This raised the stakes. Her thoughts started to run ahead, now imagining how grateful the Duke of Guise would be if she brought him not only news of Vidal's whereabouts but also information about his cache of relics. They would be of inestimable value to the Catholic League.

'There is a boat?'

Pierre coughed. 'There is a chain on the far side, linking a jetty below the manor house to the island.'

'Though there is no need for it,' Jean said. 'Unless there's too much rain, or the river bursts its banks, the water is no deeper than this.' He made a mark at his shoulders.

'So, if we are to be in the reliquary,' Marie said, thinking aloud, 'you would be able to be there, too.'

Pierre nodded. 'Exactly so.'

Marie frowned. 'How will you know? I doubt if I will be able to get any message to you.'

'We will watch the house, mademoiselle. If we see you come out and down to the lake, then we will get across to the island, too.'

Marie's hand went to her father's dagger at her waist. Many times sharpened on the whetstone, it had served him well until the day of his death. Perhaps it would protect her now, too.

She knew she was taking a huge risk. Even if he was deceived by the relic, what guarantee did she have that Lord Evreux would let her go? All the same, the stakes were high. If she succeeded, then she would be able to start fashioning for herself the life she deserved. She would, at last, be safe.

Marie took a final look at the manor house at the top of the hill and the white tower in the middle of the island, then turned back to the woods. As a Parisian girl born and bred, she had always thought it strange how she felt so at home in woodland. It spoke to her of long and happy summer days, of picnics in the open air and freedom. For a moment, she had an image of a child sitting beside an old man: a table covered with paper and coloured chalk, a map drawn by hand. Feeling loved and cherished.

'*Les fantômes d'été*,' she murmured.

'Mademoiselle Cabanel?'

Marie blinked and was surprised to find herself standing in the Chartres countryside. The ghosts of summers past slipped away.

'We will return at dusk,' she replied briskly, then turned and walked back to the carriage.

CHAPTER EIGHTY-FOUR

RUE DE LA POISSONNERIE, CHARTRES

As the bells of the cathedral were ringing for noontide prayers, Minou, Piet and Antoine le Maistre rode out through the western gates of the city.

It was the twenty-second day of August. The anniversary of the day Marta had gone missing. The sun was high and the sky was an endless blue, though wisps of flat white cloud on the horizon threatened the weather might turn.

The three old friends rode in silence, each locked in their own thoughts. To the outside eye, Minou seemed poised and calm. She was wearing her faithful green travelling cloak, in case the sight of it jogged Marta's memory, and had dressed her hair as she had back in their Parisian days rather than in the contemporary Dutch manner. She had packed her last journal from Puivert and Marta's old bonnet in her saddlebags. But beneath the surface, her heart was beating like waves crashing over and over on the shore.

At a junction in the flat green countryside some three leagues out of Chartres, le Maistre pulled up his horse. One road carried on due west, the other small track turned to the left.

'That leads to Evreux's estates.'

'How far is it?' Piet asked.

'Some two leagues south,' le Maistre replied. 'The lodgings where Cabanel and his daughter are supposed to be staying are on this road itself, some half-hour's ride further.'

'You're not certain?' Piet asked sharply.

'As certain as I can be,' le Maistre answered, 'but you know how it is. A message is passed, then passed on, then passed on again. By the time it reaches the ear for which it was intended, the truth has worn thin.' He pulled a face. 'Until we arrive and speak to the landlord in person, I cannot be certain. You understand?'

'Piet understands,' Minou said quickly. 'We both do.'

EVREUX ESTATE

'And from His presence earth and sky fled away, and no place was found for them.'

Vidal was not sure if he spoke the words out loud. He seemed now to exist in a liminal state between waking and sleeping, caught by the pain and the sickness in his head. He felt the weight of the Bible on his lap. It was open at the Book of Revelation, though he had no need of its reassurance. The words were scored on his heart.

'And I saw the dead, great and small, standing before the throne, and books were opened. Then another book was opened, which is the book of life. And the dead were judged by what was written in the books, according to what they had done.'

Such dreams. Such terrible, dark dreams. The day of judgement as foretold. Would he be spared long enough to tip the scales back in his favour? To see the white light of Heaven and stand in the company of angels and archangels? If the Cabanel woman brought what she promised, then maybe he would. Except, said the Devil at his shoulder, God will see the false from the true. What Grace could be there?

'Father?'

Vidal jolted, sending the Bible flying from his knees to the ground.

'Xavier, is that you?'

'It's me, Father. Louis.'

It took a moment for his eyes to adjust. The tall windows looking out over the gardens, the glass-fronted shelves. He was in the library, waiting for the sun to set. He remembered now.

Vidal fixed his eyes on his son. For an instant, he thought he was seeing a reflection of himself in a looking glass. The same dark direct gaze, the tell-tale white strip of hair. Was the boy equal to the task required of him? He wanted to be sure, but Louis kept his thoughts to himself. Vidal never knew what his son was really thinking. For that reason, Xavier didn't trust him, he never had. Vidal rubbed his hand over the stubble of his shaved head.

'Where is he? I would be ready for our visitor this evening.'

'I'm sorry, Father. I've looked everywhere – all through the house, his personal quarters, the stables, the kitchens. I even rode up to the village. No one's seen him.'

Vidal let his hand drop back into his lap. This lassitude was no good.

'Bring me some wine and my tonic.'

He watched while Louis poured a generous measure, then tipped a paper twist of powder into the wine and stirred.

'Here you are, Father.'

Vidal drank deeply, draining the goblet in three mouthfuls. Instantly, his blood started to revive. He held out his cup to be refilled.

'I could do it,' Louis said, returning with the decanter.

'Do what?'

'Given Xavier is not here – and you would make your usual preparations – I could serve as barber in his stead? I have watched him often enough with the razor and cloth.'

Vidal rubbed his hand over his head again, then nodded.

'Take care your hand does not slip.'

By the time Minou, Piet and le Maistre arrived at the coaching house, the sky was grey and the air had cooled. Black clouds now scudded across the horizon as another storm gathered its strength. Minou pulled her cloak tight around her shoulders and wished she had worn warmer riding gloves.

'Leave it to me,' le Maistre said, jumping down from his horse and vanishing inside.

Minou and Piet dismounted. Through the open door, she could see the coach house was crowded. Long wooden tables and benches, occupied mostly by men. A full-figured matron was setting platters of bread and dried ham along the centre of the board, with plates of sweet *cochelin* biscuits and sliced plums. A servant ran up and down the rows filling wooden tankards with ale from a jug. It was exactly the sort of place where people might come and go without comment or notice. A place in which to wait out of the sight of prying eyes.

Shortly, le Maistre returned. 'This is what I know. The landlord confirms he rented two rooms on the second floor in June to a Pierre Cabanel and his daughter. She came first, to check the chambers were suitable on account of her father being an invalid from the wars.'

'An invalid!' Piet exclaimed.

'I imagine that was merely an excuse to keep him hidden. The landlord admits he rarely saw him. All his meals were taken up to him. The rent was paid on time. The pair of them were quiet and caused no trouble.'

'What about the girl?' Minou said anxiously.

Le Maistre raised his eyebrows. 'The good landlord was most struck with Mademoiselle Cabanel. Charming, polite. Fine clothes. He described her in great detail and, though the man's a drunk, I have no doubt it is the same young woman I saw in Chartres. He could not stop talking about the beauty of her eyes. She led him to believe they had relatives in Chartres itself. Unlike her father, she did sometimes ride out.'

Minou looked up at the windows overlooking the courtyard. Her legs felt suddenly weak. 'Are they here now?'

Le Maistre's expression changed. 'I regret to say, as of this morning, they are not. Mademoiselle Cabanel settled their outstanding bill early, and with great haste, then they left before the sun had risen.'

Minou felt a crushing disappointment. To be so close, and yet be frustrated again, she couldn't endure it.

'Why so suddenly?' Piet asked. 'Did the landlord say?'

Le Maistre shook his head. 'No, nor where they were going. He did mention, however, that a messenger arrived for Mademoiselle Cabanel before dawn. Fair woke the whole house with his banging.'

Piet looked at Minou. 'What if Cabanel discovered that Evreux is not Vidal?'

Minou gathered her thoughts. 'No, I think it's more likely he received confirmation that he is. I think Cabanel has gone to kill him.'

She felt Piet's eyes upon her. 'You are saying we should follow?'

'I don't see what else we can do. If I'm wrong, there's no way of finding them now. They could be anywhere. Our best chance is to go to Evreux's estate and hope to find Cabanel and his –' Minou checked herself. She was now so convinced that it was Marta they were tracking down, that she could no longer bear to refer to her as Marie Cabanel. 'Our daughter is in grave danger.'

'If it's her,' Piet said softly.

Minou turned away.

CHAPTER EIGHTY-FIVE

EVREUX ESTATE

Marie shot out her hand to steady herself, as the carriage turned sharply off the road onto the long drive leading to Evreux's manor house.

At last it was dusk. Pierre and his brother Jean should already be in position in the woods beside the lake. She closed her mind to what would happen if Evreux broke his usual habit and remained in the manor house itself. It would leave her with only the groom to protect her, should there be trouble.

Marie was more nervous than she could remember. Her hand went to her father's knife at her waist, hidden beneath the folds of her cloak. She could look after herself. Had she not survived alone these past seven months?

She had dressed with care – elegant, but not too much so. Her hair was rolled beneath a coif and blue hat, so the shimmering tones of her brown hair were visible. Rather than a gown, she wore a doublet shaping to a point at her waist. A wide skirt over a French farthingale, also blue, completed her outfit with a white ruff of cutwork lace.

The carriage continued on in a straight line to the manor house. Marie took another deep breath. Then she placed her hands firmly in her lap, pressing down on the carton containing the Sudarium, to stop them from shaking.

As she stepped down from the carriage, it began to rain.

'Wait here,' she ordered the groom.

It was oddly quiet. There was no one in sight, no servants or gardeners, no guards on duty, no signs of life at all. As Marie walked along the path through a formal garden of box and privet towards the front door, she was conscious of the tread of her feet on the damp ground and the rustling of her skirts. She glanced up, sensing someone watching, but the mullioned windows were dark and she could see no one.

Marie reached up to the heavy black iron ring. She knocked and the sound echoed inside the house. Then, the sound of feet and a bolt being shot.

A servant in black livery stood on the threshold. 'Mademoiselle.'

'Lord Evreux is expecting me,' she said, finding a confident smile.

He inclined his head. 'If you will follow me.'

As Marie stepped into the tiled entrance hall, she heard the heavy front door close behind her and she shivered.

From the first-floor gallery at the far end of the hall, Louis was watching.

She was younger than he had expected. She was well dressed and assured, but he was still surprised she had come unchaperoned. It was possible she had a maid or a bodyguard in the carriage, but it seemed exceedingly stupid that she should have entered the house alone.

He watched as the servant led her across the hallway and into the library, as agreed. His father's orders were to leave her for some few minutes, then to present himself and explain that Lord Evreux would receive her in the reliquary itself.

Louis still thought this a mistake. But as the hands of the clock had turned, his father had seemed more his usual self. His wits were sharp, he'd shaken off his lethargy and taken pleasure in the arrangements. If his eyes shone just a little too brightly, and his moments seemed charged with an energy lacking in previous months, Louis decided to see this as a sign of improvement. And, finally, he had let Louis help him dress. He had not asked after Xavier since.

Louis waited for the servant to withdraw, then walked down the stairs and towards the library, ready to play his part.

As soon as the servant left her alone, Marie opened the window and poured the wine into the flower bed below, then put the empty goblet back on the pewter tray.

She was not so green as to accept sustenance in a stranger's house. Though she had never been into the Louvre Palace, it was common knowledge the court was plagued by the fear of poisoning. The King had his own taster sample every dish, even kissing the plates and napkins before the royal hand would touch them. The Queen Mother, too. So many spices from the Indus could be used to mask the presence of henbane or belladonna and a strongly flavoured wine could be drugged.

A clock chimed the quarter-hour.

Marie took down a book, admiring the quality of the binding, then replaced it. She walked a little further, her fingers running along the spines of the books until she had reached the end of the shelf. Then, bored with the library, she went to the double doors and opened them into the room beyond.

This next chamber was more to her taste. Well appointed and light, it was filled with rosewood furniture. A walnut tallboy that shone golden in the reflected rays of the setting sun, embroidered silk cushions and silver-white upholstery the colour of apple blossom. There was much to admire.

Her attention was caught by a beautiful enamel box. Fashioned in the *champlevé* style so popular in Limoges, golden figures danced and revelled on a blue background – satyrs and nymphs –

a banquet in the woods. Marie turned it over in her hand, sure she had seen one just like it somewhere before. A memory started to whisper in her mind, speaking of a warm summer's afternoon in the company of children, the gift of a box as alike to this as to be its twin. A blue dress and a white cap with—

'Would you care to tell me what you are doing in here?'

Caught unawares, Marie nearly dropped the trinket. Composing herself, she placed it carefully back on the table while she gathered her wits.

'You startled me,' she said, turning towards the voice.

The tall young man held his stance in the doorway on the far side of the room. Marie approved of what she saw. Tall and broad, his dark beard was well-trimmed to a point and his long black hair was combed back from his forehead beneath a grey velvet hat. He wore pale hose, a doublet with jewelled buttons fastened at the side in the modern fashion, a cutwork linen collar rather than a ruff.

'Who are you?'

He laughed. 'More to the point, who are you?'

'I am waiting for Lord Evreux. He is expecting me.'

'Is he now?'

'Yes, though I doubt it is any business of yours.'

He continued to stare at her from the doorway.

'Except that these happen to be my father's private chambers and you were shown to the library. Try again, Mademoiselle Cabanel.'

Marie felt her face flush, but she decided to brazen it out. 'The door was ajar.'

He folded his arms. Something about the gesture sent another recollection scuttling through her mind. She racked her brain, but the memory wouldn't come.

'Forgive me, but might we have met previously?'

'Have you been to Chartres before?'

'No.'

'Then, I cannot think so.'

Marie stared at him, bewildered by his odd conversation. She waited for him to say something more, but he continued to stand in silence.

'Your father is expecting me,' she said eventually. 'I have something of great value to show him.'

Marie stepped forward, into the light, holding the carton out before her. To her astonishment, he turned white.

'Whatever is the matter?' she asked, growing impatient with his behaviour. 'Where is Lord Evreux? Our appointment was at this hour. Why is he not here to greet me? Is he so discourteous?'

'Forgive me, Mademoiselle Cabanel,' the young man said, suddenly charming again. 'I am charged to take you to my father. He will receive you in the reliquary. He thought it was more appropriate given the nature of your visit.'

Though this was what Marie had planned for, she felt suddenly afraid. Then Evreux's son reached out his hand towards her, and something about that gesture, too, was familiar. A shiver went down her spine.

CHAPTER EIGHTY-SIX

Minou, Piet and Antoine le Maistre dismounted and led their horses through the woods, the sound of their hooves muffled on the damp ground.

They saw no one, heard no one.

Dusk was giving way to night, bringing with it a chill, damp breeze. Beyond the shelter of the trees, the drizzle had turned to rain.

They got as close as they could without being seen. The carriage they had glimpsed turning into the estate from the road was now standing in front of the manor house, but there were no lights burning in the windows. Even the servants' quarters and stables appeared to be deserted.

'Where is everyone?' Piet whispered. 'Could Vidal – Evreux – have left?'

Le Maistre shook his head. 'We would have seen. We've been watching all afternoon.'

'Could he have gone by another route? Through the woods, perhaps?'

'It's possible, but not if the household had gone with him. This is the only passable way in and out.'

'Let me check the house first,' Piet said. 'It may be that all the living quarters are at the rear of the building.'

'I'll come with you,' le Maistre replied.

'Be careful,' Minou whispered, squeezing Piet's arm.

She watched the two men slip from the cover of the woods,

using the box hedge of the formal gardens for cover, then approach the house and disappear from view.

The boatman started to slow as they drew close, setting his hands at shorter intervals on the chain as he pulled them to the island.

'Are you all right, Mademoiselle Cabanel?' Louis asked.

She was sitting bolt upright, clutching the package in front of her like a shield.

'Quite all right, thank you,' she replied, in a tone that gave the lie to her words.

Nearly an hour had passed since Marie Cabanel had arrived and Louis's thoughts were still in turmoil. It didn't seem possible that the woman come to trade with his father – to deceive his father – was the girl he had abandoned in the blue chamber in the rue d'Orléans twelve years previously, but yet there was no doubt. The instant she'd stepped out of the shadow in his father's study, he'd known. Those eyes were unmistakable.

Marie Cabanel was Marta Reydon-Joubert.

It changed everything. Was it possible that the threat to his father's life – for Louis was sure that the relic was a forgery and being used as a pretext to gain access to the estate – came not from an assassin in the pay of the Duke of Guise but Vidal's old enemy? Louis knew Piet Reydon haunted his father's waking hours, especially now his mind was failing. It bordered on an obsession. The mountain of documents and papers he kept in his desk, legal judgements and testimonies, his late uncle's will, all attested to it.

What Louis couldn't work out was whether or not Marta had recognised him, too. She thought she knew him, she had admitted as much, but he didn't think she was sure. The moment they were inside, Louis had to tell his father who she was. Then it was in his hands.

In the fading light, Louis glanced down into the water. For an instant, he thought he saw Xavier's face staring up at him from the shimmering green void beneath the boat. Dead eyes wide open. Startled, Louis pulled back, causing the boat to rock.

'Be careful, else you'll tip us out. I'm wet enough as it is.' Marie Cabanel turned to look at him. 'What's wrong? You look strange.'

Her words took him back to his nine-year-old self being challenged by a precocious girl to explain why he had a strange strip of white hair. Self-conscious, Louis pulled his grey cap lower on his forehead.

'We're here,' he said unnecessarily, as the boat bumped the shore. 'Let me help you, mademoiselle.'

Louis held out his hand. After a moment, Marie took it.

'Could you see anything?' Minou asked quickly, when Piet and le Maistre reappeared. 'Are they there?'

Piet shook his head. 'I can't be sure without going inside, but the house seems completely deserted.'

'Yet the horses are in the stables,' le Maistre mused. 'There was a solitary groom, fast asleep. It's odd.'

'What about there?' Minou said, pointing down to the lake below the house. In the dying light of the day, a white tower was just visible in the dusk. 'There are lights burning.'

Piet peered. 'So there are. What do you think, le Maistre? Should we attempt to get into the house or—'

'Of course!' le Maistre interrupted. 'It's common gossip Evreux constructed his own reliquary here. I'd always assumed it was within the house itself, but that could well be it.'

They all turned towards the lake.

'Listen.' Minou put her hand on Piet's arm. 'Did you hear something?'

'No.'

'It was like the drag of a chain. You know, like at Lastage when the boats are winched out of the water for winter repairs.'

They all listened, but the evening air was silent now.

'Shall we go down and see, or try to get into the house?' le Maistre asked. 'It's up to you.'

'Minou?' Piet looked at her.

She thought for a moment. 'You both sense the house is empty, but the carriage is here, so they have to be somewhere. I think we should go down to the lake and see.'

Piet nodded. 'Let's head for that copse of trees close to the water. We'll go separately, just in case there's anyone watching. I'll go first, then you, Minou. Le Maistre, you go around the far side and see if there's any sign of life, then join us.'

Piet made his way quickly down the grassy slopes between the house and the lake, running into the rain. Minou waited until he was out of sight, then followed, holding her cloak tight around her neck.

'What can you see?' she whispered, when she reached him.

'There's a boat moored at the jetty there.' Piet pointed towards the water. 'And can you see the struts? There's a chain stretched across the water from here to the island for the pilot to pull the barge across. That must have been the sound you heard.'

'Is there anyone on the boat?'

'Not so far as I can see.'

'So I must have heard it coming back from the island before,' Minou said. 'But what about a boatman, is he there?'

'Not that I can see.'

As they waited for Antoine to join them, the last of the light faded from the sky and a brisk wind started to blow. A mist rose lightly up from the surface of the shallow lake, shrouding everything in a strange grey light. The evening lament of nightjars and nightingales began to fill the air.

'What news?' Piet asked when le Maistre reappeared.

'There are two men watching the reliquary from the far side of the lake.'

'Cabanel?'

'I have never seen the man, but it stands to reason.'

'And the other?'

Le Maistre shrugged. 'I don't know.'

'Did you see her?' Minou said, her words coming out in a rush. She hadn't realised she'd been holding her breath.

'I'm afraid not, Madame Reydon.'

Piet squeezed her arm. 'At the very least, it suggests Cabanel thinks Vidal is on the island. If he's there, then surely his daughter will be with him.'

Minou was aware they were making too many assumptions to suit the story they wanted to be told. She didn't know what they should do next. Wait, watch, try to intervene? All possibilities carried some measure of risk. They couldn't do nothing, but what if their actions put Marta in danger?

'You're quite sure she wasn't there?'

'She might have been concealed in the trees,' le Maistre said doubtfully. He turned to Piet. 'What do you want to do now?'

He thought for a moment. 'I will cross to the reliquary and—'

'I'm coming too,' Minou said.

Piet sighed. 'Very well. Le Maistre, you keep watch on Cabanel and his accomplice. If they cross to the reliquary, follow them.'

'I've seen two guards patrolling the island,' he said. 'There could be more. A circuit lasts some quarter of an hour.'

'In which case, I shall time it so they do not see me. Shall we rendezvous back here in an hour to report what we have discovered?'

Le Maistre nodded. 'Good hunting, my friend.'

CHAPTER EIGHTY-SEVEN

The Reliquary

As they walked into the white tower, Marie's senses were assailed by the smell of incense and wax in the confined air.

They were in a long and narrow corridor lit by candles set in wrought-iron double sconces along the wall. The dancing flames cast light on the wall opposite, illuminating a sequence of religious paintings in the alcoves: Christ on the Cross at Golgotha, the Crown of Thorns being carried to the Sainte-Chapelle, all images of the Passion.

'It is not much further,' Louis said.

As they drew level with a painting of St Veronica, Marie stopped. The replica of the Veil she carried was excellent, but was it good enough to convince a relic hunter such as Lord Evreux, Guise's cardinal, as her father had believed him to be? She didn't know.

She realised Evreux's son was staring at her again. She spun round, so they were standing face to face.

'Have I done something to offend you that you should so fix your attention upon me?'

'Why, does my attention distress you?'

'It is impertinent.'

He gave a mock bow. 'In which case, my apologies.'

Marie felt her temper rise. 'And uncivil. You didn't even pay me the courtesy of telling me your name.'

A smile flickered in his eyes. 'What need you with my name,

Marie Cabanel? It is my father you have come to see. I am Lord Evreux's son, is that not enough?'

Marie frowned. 'Why do you keep saying my name as if there is some mystery to it?'

'Don't you know?' he said, sounding genuinely interested.

Again, she felt the full force of his gaze. 'Know what?'

He whistled. 'My God, you really don't know . . .'

'What is your name?' she asked curtly, impatience making her short tempered.

'If that is all that concerns you, that is easy enough to remedy. It's Louis.' He gave a deep bow. 'At your service.'

Antoine le Maistre retraced his steps around the edge of the lake.

He watched Cabanel and his associate climb up onto the island, before stepping out of the cover of the trees to follow. He had thought himself unobserved and safe. But suddenly he'd felt the air move behind him, and now the point of a knife was pressing at his back.

'You're making a mistake, friend.'

'No mistake.' The man laughed, then plunged the knife between his ribs.

Le Maistre gasped as the blade went in, cleanly and expertly. For a moment, he felt no sensation at all. Then he felt the first blossoming of blood beneath his chemise, and a terrible cold like a winter's frost reaching right to the tips of his fingers. He fell down to his knees and tasted blood in his throat.

Why couldn't he breathe?

He didn't understand. The man spoke with a local accent, but Cabanel was supposedly a Parisian? The knife wound began to ache, intensifying until there was no part of his body that wasn't afflicted.

Everything seemed suddenly bright. Now the pain was melting away. He could see the face of his dear wife. She was smiling and holding out her hands to him. Their children were there, too, just as he remembered them before the soldiers came.

He almost laughed. He had survived seven wars, had fought nobly and with courage at the sides of the great Huguenot commanders of the age. But in the end he would die at the hands of a hired assassin. He wanted to shout out a warning to Piet and to Minou, but his words were trapped in his throat.

Le Maistre was aware of the man grasping his doublet and rolling him over in the water. Then, the pressure of a boot on his neck, holding him under. As oblivion rushed into his lungs, he saw his wife and children again.

They were waiting for him.

Marie frowned, another memory slipping quicksilver fast through her mind. Why did his words sound familiar, why did his name?

Louis pulled back a heavy red curtain. 'We're here.'

She managed to gather her wits. 'Is Lord Evreux within?'

In reply, she felt the press of his hand in the small of her back propelling her through the door. Marie found herself standing in a cavernous chamber of light and shadow. There was an altar in the middle of the room with two ecclesiastical chairs in front. Tall candelabra stood like sentinels either side of them, their flickering light sending shadows dancing into the corners of the chamber. A full moon shone down through the vast lantern skylight in the ceiling, bathing everything in a strange, white light. At the far end of the room, she could just make out another, smaller, door.

As Marie's eyes became accustomed to the gloom, she realised there were frescoes on the walls in here, too. Seven paintings, each with a casket in front, a single flame burning before each one. And despite her fear of what might happen, Marie's eyes sparkled with wonder.

'I felt the same when I came here for the first time,' Louis said quietly at her shoulder. 'It is magnificent.'

'It is. Relics for each of the seven Stations of the Cross.'

'Yes, only the sixth of our caskets is empty.'

Marie was abruptly brought back to the matter in hand. 'Though not for much longer,' she said, with a confidence she did not feel.

Louis laughed. 'If what you have brought us is genuine.'

'I have it on good authority, though I am no expert.'

'Yet you are bold enough to come here to offer this relic to me.'

Marie jumped at the voice coming out of the darkness. She had thought they were alone. Louis's hand lightly touched hers as he took the carton from her, then walked towards the voice.

'Thank you, Louis. This is the Sudarium?'

Marie turned in the direction of the voice. A man in liturgical vestments was now sitting in one of the cathedra chairs. He was wearing a white chasuble, with a red pallium and stole, the silk shimmering in the candlelight. Marie was uncertain. Her father had told her Vidal had relinquished his office of cardinal and taken a new identity to avoid being captured, yet here he sat now attired like a bishop.

'Mademoiselle Cabanel says it is.'

Marie waited for Evreux to rise and greet her. He did not. She waited for him to introduce himself. He did not. Nerves fluttered against her ribs as she watched Louis hand over the relic, then lean forward and whisper in his father's ear.

Both men turned to look at her. The family resemblance was so strong, there could be no doubt they were father and son. Why were they staring?

A wave of panic rushed through her. How stupid to have let herself be brought to the island. If something went awry, Pierre and his brother were too far away to help her, and her groom had remained at the house with the carriage. She took a deep breath. Her only chance was to stand firm. She could not allow fear or guilt to give her away.

Marie stepped forward. 'Lord Evreux, it is a pleasure to make your acquaintance.'

'Who sent you?'

Evreux's voice was cold.

'No one sent me, my lord.' Her courage faltered. 'I have brought you the most extraordinary and beautiful object, one which will – from what your son has shown me – complete your collection.'

She drew closer. Now she could see he was wearing a red velvet camauro, the cap only the Pope himself was authorised to wear. Her confusion grew.

'Are you an honest woman?'

She met his gaze. 'I am, my lord.'

Vidal looked up at his son, then back to Marie. 'All the same, it would be best to be certain. Bind her.'

CHAPTER EIGHTY-EIGHT

Minou and Piet waited until the guards had begun another circuit, then climbed out of the boat onto the shore. Quickly, they shook the rain from their clothes, then ran through the puddles towards the white tower.

'What if they notice the boat has been brought back?' Minou whispered.

'There's nothing we can do about that.' He caught his breath. 'Perhaps we should wait for le Maistre to—'

'We're not turning back now. I have to know.'

Stooping beneath the height of the balustrade, Minou darted up the steps. She felt fearless, full of valour and adventure. Minou remembered how, before they were husband and wife, she'd run hand in hand with Piet through the streets of Toulouse: evading soldiers, helping innocent women and children to safety, then riding through the night to Puivert to rescue Alis and their beloved father, held captive in the castle. She had been courageous then.

In the space between one beat of her heart and the next, Minou allowed herself to stand momentarily in the company of the ghosts of the past, with those she had loved and lost, the missing and the dead. Then she took a deep breath.

But not Marta. Marta was not dead.

Minou beckoned at Piet to join her, then pushed at the heavy door. To her amazement, it swung open.

'Minou, wait,' Piet said, slipping in front. He peered inside, then nodded. 'It's clear.'

Now it was Minou who hesitated. 'What if we're wrong? What if they are in the house after all?'

'Someone's been here recently,' Piet whispered. 'Look, the candles are newly lit. Pull the door to, so the guards don't notice.'

Expecting to be challenged at any moment, Minou moved silently along the corridor with Piet behind her. She was aware of the paintings on the walls but she took nothing in. Her entire focus was the door at the far end of the passageway and what lay behind it. A heavy red curtain had been pulled to one side and a narrow band of light was just visible between the edges of the door and the frame.

Then, behind them in the corridor, she heard the sound of feet.

'Hold the lamp higher,' Vidal instructed.

Louis did so, sending light flooding across the fragment of cloth lying on the altar.

Tied to the chair, Marie struggled desperately to loosen the cords around her wrists without drawing their attention. She'd tried to run the instant she realised Vidal meant to take her hostage, but Louis had blocked her exit. He'd found her father's knife at her belt and taken it, then bound her wrists and slipped a loop through the rail at the back of the chair to secure her in place. But the bindings were not tight. If she could slip her hands free, there was a chance she could get away while their attention was focused on the relic. Louis hadn't locked the door when they'd entered the chamber and there appeared to be no servants or guards on duty.

'Do you see, Louis? This is supposed to be the imprint of Christ's face.'

Hearing the doubt in Evreux's voice, Marie desperately tugged at the cords binding her wrists.

'Several times before, I have been offered an artefact purporting to be the veil with which St Veronica wiped Christ's face on the Via Dolorosa. Some say it never left Rome, others claim it was taken to Vienna or San Jaén, or Alicante, where Mademoiselle Cabanel claims to have found this.' Vidal looked down at the cloth. 'And this is very good. Excellent work, in fact. Almost to your standard, Louis.'

'My lord?'

'Your Crown of Thorns. One day we will return to the Sainte-Chapelle and compare it to the original.'

Marie became still – the Crown of Thorns, the Sainte-Chapelle. Was it possible she had seen Louis before in Paris? The timing made no sense. If Louis was indeed Vidal's son – and Vidal had not been seen in Paris since the night of the St Bartholomew's Day massacre – she would have been no more than seven or eight years old. And Louis not much older.

A shiver went down her spine at the vision of a boy with a white stripe in his hair reaching out his hand to a little girl . . .

'Come, it's not far,' he'd said, and she had followed.

The memories became even sharper: a blue chamber of mirror and gilt, the polished virginals, being left alone for hours in the dark, the shouting and ale on a soldier's breath; a dying man clutching a knife in his hand, the weapon that became her father's talisman.

'But, there's the rub,' Evreux was saying. 'This here, you see, is just a little too good. Can you see the brushstrokes?'

'I can.'

'They are hardly there, but if this truly was an imprint of Christ's face there would be no man-made marks.'

Marie quietened her racing thoughts and forced herself to concentrate on the present. Now, more than ever, she had to get away. What if Louis recognised her, too?

'As for the material,' Vidal continued, 'that, too, is an excellent match. Possibly this weave does come from the Holy Land. It may have been brought back by a Crusader, centuries ago. Who's to say?'

Marie gave a final sharp tug and, at last, got her right hand free. With blind fingers, she started to untie the cord from the chair.

But she was too late. Vidal suddenly pushed his chair back and stood up. He removed his skull cap, ran his fingers over his bald head, then began to walk slowly towards her. As he drew closer, Marie saw his pallium was decorated with six small crosses, white rather than the customary black.

She sat very still, keeping her hands behind her.

'Expensive and skilled as this Sudarium is – it would fool any untrained eye – I regret it is a forgery, mademoiselle. What did the person responsible for this hope to achieve by this charade? And why did he send you rather than come in person?'

Marie forced herself to hold her voice steady. 'I don't know what you mean. No one sent me.'

As he stood towering over her, she could see he was sick. There was a canker on his temple, a grey pallor to his skin and his eyes were sunk in their sockets. All the same, Marie could feel the power of the man.

'Your father,' Vidal said. 'Why did he send you?'

'My father is dead this past winter, my lord.'

He put his arms on either side of her chair. 'I do not believe you.'

Marie shrank back. 'The Sudarium was sold to me as genuine,' she said, trying to inject a confidence into her voice she did not feel. 'The priest from whom I acquired it carried it himself over the border from Spain.'

'Is that what he told you to say?'

'It is the truth, my lord.'

He gave a hollow laugh. 'Is it? In that case, how did you pay for it? In the usual way women use to get what they want from men?'

Marie flinched as Vidal put his hand on her breast.

'Father!'

She saw Vidal's other hand come up and tried to twist away, but she was too slow. The blow caught her hard on the cheek.

'Father, please!' Louis protested.

Vidal ignored him. 'Where is he?'

Marie tried to shake free, but he held her shoulder tightly.

'Do you think you can gull me? My son has told me how he found you wandering around Paris years ago. He recognised you. What father would send his daughter to do his traitorous work for him?'

'I swear, I don't know—'

Vidal raised his hand again, but this time Louis stepped between them and took the force of the blow. He stumbled back, sending his hat flying to the ground, giving her the final confirmation that Evreux was Vidal. Louis had the same stripe of white hair his father once had.

'She came alone, Father,' he was saying. 'I watched her arrive. And the groom remains up at the house.'

Vidal threw him a contemptuous look. 'If you believe that, you're a fool.' He turned back to Marie. 'Where is your father, Mademoiselle Reydon? I won't ask you again.'

'Reydon?' Marie stared at him in confusion. If this was a trick, she had no idea of the purpose of it. 'I am Marie Cabanel. My father was Pierre Cabanel, captain at arms. He died last January in Rouen, I swear it.'

'Cabanel!' Vidal laughed. 'I wouldn't expect you to come here under your own name, Mademoiselle Reydon. Even for a woman, that would be the height of stupidity. I will ask you one last time. Where is Reydon?'

Marie braced herself for another slap, when the doors behind them were flung open.

Marie didn't understand. Pierre and his brother Jean were standing in the doorway, soaking wet, holding a tall woman in a green cloak captive between them. She had paid them well for their service, but were they now in the pay of Lord Evreux instead?

Minou felt as if she was looking down on herself from a great height. Like the gargoyles of Saint-Nazaire in la Cité that had so scared her when she was little. Everything in the chamber seemed distorted by the flickering candlelight sending long shadows dancing up the wall covered with images of death and dying. Seven gold-edged caskets in a row, like gifts for a king.

She took in the scene before her in a single blink of her eye. A tall man, dressed in liturgical vestments, a fuzz of white stubble on his head. Beside him, next to an overturned chair, a girl. Pale skin, long brown hair, dressed all in blue, she was being held by a boy the spitting image of Vidal. Almost as if they were dancing.

Minou caught her breath, feeling as if she was seeing herself in a looking glass. All doubt was gone. She felt dizzy and grateful and wild with relief.

'Marta . . .' she said, hardly daring to speak her name.

The girl didn't seem to hear her. And though she had prepared herself, Minou felt her heart crack like a piece of ice.

Then there was a roar in the passageway outside. Seconds later, Piet came charging into the room, knife drawn, defending himself against two armed guards.

For a moment, Minou watched Vidal sway, as if he'd been struck.

'Seize him!' he screamed, then turned on the boy. 'Take the girl away! You know what to do.'

Louis hesitated, then started to drag Marta, kicking and screaming, towards a door at the rear of the chamber.

'Marta!' Minou couldn't let her daughter be taken away.

Taking her captors by surprise, she broke loose and ran. But almost instantly, they were on her. Minou felt a rough arm go round her neck and pull her backwards off her feet. Dirty fingers were spread across her mouth, disgusting and intimate. For a moment, Minou thought she could hear Piet's voice, shouting from the other end of the room. But then she heard a grunt as a fist slammed into his stomach, and she knew he was down.

When she turned back, her daughter was gone.

CHAPTER EIGHTY-NINE

Piet tried to raise his head. The pain in his shoulders was so sharp that he groaned.

'Minou . . .'

Piet breathed out, then tried again to sit up, more slowly this time.

Everything hurt. He pulled at his hands, realising that they were tied behind him. He forced himself to open his eyes. He focused on his boots, still wet, then on the stone floor, then on the wooden legs of a chair. Only when the room had stopped spinning did he manage to lift his head and look at the face of the man sitting opposite him.

'Vidal,' he breathed through swollen lips. He could feel a loose tooth and the metallic taste of blood on his tongue.

'As you see.'

'Where's my wife?'

Vidal didn't answer.

'Where is she?'

Piet met Vidal's gaze. Instantly, he could see he was sick. His pallor and over-bright eyes spoke of a fever and there was a large growth on his temple. It was extraordinary that a man could be so altered by the passing of years but yet be fundamentally unchanged.

'What have you done with my wife?'

'You'll be reunited with her soon enough.' Vidal pressed the tips of his fingers together. 'Why did you come, Reydon?'

'You know why I'm here.'

Piet saw something flash across his old enemy's face. Anger perhaps? Then he realised, confirmation of what Vidal had dreaded.

'Ah, so the papers came to light in Amsterdam after all. I feared they might. I did everything I could to stop that.'

'I would never have known there was something to find. It was your meddling that brought it all to light.'

Vidal gave the same odd smile. 'That, I fear, is the way of things.'

Piet took stock of his situation. The chamber was empty apart from the two of them, though he had no doubt the guards were outside the door. He didn't know where Minou had been taken. The odds were against him. The best he could do was to keep Vidal talking for as long as possible and pray that le Maistre found a way to help them.

'Did you kill her?' he asked.

'Your whore of a mother? You overestimate my power, Reydon. I was no more than a babe-in-arms when she died.'

'Mariken Hassels from the Begijnhof community knew the truth.' Piet kept his voice steady. 'And my mother and father – your uncle – were legitimately married, as you know.'

'There is no proof of it.'

Piet met his gaze. 'There is a document attesting to it.'

'Which you now have?'

'Yes.'

'Ah.'

Piet caught his breath. 'How long have you known we are cousins?'

Vidal drummed his fingers on the arm of his chair, a gesture Piet remembered well.

'Answer me.'

'My uncle confessed to the liaison on his death bed.'

'Their marriage,' Piet said again, then even though he knew it was a mistake, he asked: 'Did du Plessis talk of her?'

'Your mother?' Vidal said with contempt. 'No. She meant nothing to him. An indiscretion from his youth.'

Piet forced himself to keep calm. He could not let Vidal provoke him.

'Did he know he had a son?'

'Would it matter if he had?'

'It matters a great deal,' Piet said, struggling to keep the anger from his voice. 'Isn't that what all this is about? And you evidently have a son of your own. Do you acknowledge him as such?'

Vidal glanced to the door at the rear of the room. 'The boy is useful. If he ceases to be of use, I will send him back to where he came from.'

'You have no love for him?'

He laughed. 'I have no use for such mewling emotions, Reydon.'

'Did you order the attack on my wife in Puivert?'

Vidal pretended to think. 'I don't —'

Finally, his temper snapped. 'Answer me!'

Vidal gave the same, slow smile Piet remembered from their student days in Toulouse.

'Very well. Did I attempt to rid Puivert of the false châtelaine? Yes. It turned out the man chosen to carry out the task was not equal to it. He shot the wrong Huguenot whore.'

Piet shook his head. 'Alis was wearing a green dress that day.'

'Ah, so that's what happened. Alis, yes. I remember her.' Vidal paused. 'In truth, I simply intended to detain you in Languedoc while I ascertained where my uncle's confession of his childhood mistake might be.'

Piet stared at him in horror. 'That was your reason? You would kill so casually?'

Vidal swept his arm around the chamber. 'All this comes at a cost, Reydon, you should know that. In any case, the assassin failed. You and your family came to Paris all the same. And I gather Puivert has now returned to the true Church without my further intervention. I live only to serve God.'

'So I see.' Piet looked at him. 'Though you appear much elevated in rank since last I saw you. I was under the impression that only a Pope was permitted to wear a pallium.'

Vidal gave a wry smile. 'I see you have not forgotten everything we were taught in our seminary days.' He fingered the silk. 'Though you will see I have made a modification of my own. White crosses instead of black, as a reminder of the joyous rebellion of St Bartholomew's Day where God's true Church started to take back control from the false Christians.'

Piet could see zeal shining in Vidal's eyes. 'Is Guise aware of this?'

'I do not have to account to anyone.'

'You have been hiding from him for years.'

'Guise will not live for ever.'

'Maybe not. But you will be judged for your sins, Vidal. In the final reckoning, you will be called to account. You are a murderer and a thief.'

'And you are a heretic,' Vidal shouted. 'You will be judged more harshly than I.' He sat back in the chair, his expression exultant. 'Look what I have done. This is the beginning of a new era, a new Church, with me at its head. Sacred relics gathered for the glory of God. My place in Heaven is secure.'

Piet laughed. 'You forget that I know you. You don't believe that these relics matter, whether their provenance is authentic or not.'

'You have no idea what I believe,' Vidal mocked. 'But to send your daughter to do – well, to do what, Reydon? Did you really think I would be so easily deceived? I learnt the tricks of that trade from you, remember.'

Piet's breath caught in his throat. 'My daughter?'

Vidal waved his hand dismissively. 'There is no one else here, Reydon. There is no need for these charades.'

Piet couldn't speak. He had never allowed himself to believe that Cabanel's daughter could possibly be Marta – though he had realised they had to see for themselves – but what if it was true? What if their daughter was alive? What if she was here?

A myriad memories rushed into Piet's mind. All the moments of joy and sweetness he had suppressed for twelve years, knowing they would be too much to bear, now came flooding back to him: carrying Marta on his shoulders through the *basse cour* in Puivert, teaching her to play Queen's Chess, lifting her onto a horse for the first time.

Then, scouring the streets of Paris in desperation, the white crosses painted on the doors and white armbands. The massacre. Leaving without her. There were no words that would ever expiate his guilt.

'Where is she?' he said in a hollow whisper.

Vidal gestured to the door at the rear of the chamber, as if the question was of no matter.

'How did you know it was her?' Piet managed to ask.

Vidal waved his arm. 'Extraordinary, really. It seems my son found her wandering in the rue du Béthisy two days before the St Bartholomew's Day rebellion and took her away from the fray. He only told me of this tonight. He saved her life, of that I have no doubt. When she arrived here calling herself Marie Cabanel, he recognised her and I realised you'd sent her.'

Piet's thoughts were spinning. Could it be true Vidal had no idea that Marta had been lost to them?

'So, I will ask again,' Vidal said abruptly. 'Why are you here,

Reydon? You can't imagine that I will relinquish my inheritance?'

'I am my father's heir.'

'My uncle didn't even know you existed.' For a moment, Vidal's eyes drifted, then another change seemed to come over him. 'You should not have come,' he said in a cold voice. 'None of you. Look around you. Only one casket remains to be filled. You have taught your daughter well. The copy she brought to me tonight was excellent. Not quite good enough, but excellent all the same.' Vidal's right hand briefly touched the replica Sudarium. 'I will place this excellent copy in the sixth casket. It might prove useful until the true relic comes to light.'

Then he reached out and took a knife from the altar. 'All this is for God's glory, Reydon. He will understand. He will forgive me for what I do in his name.'

Piet stared at the blade. It had been twelve years, but he would recognise his knife anywhere. The one he'd given to Aimeric when he rode out from Puivert for the last time.

'Where did you get that?'

Vidal raised his eyebrows. 'It's your daughter's weapon, surely you know that?' He turned the point towards Piet. 'We're wasting time. You and I have stood on opposite sides for too long. I will not let you take from me what it rightfully mine. That you should be foolish enough to come here surprises me. I confess, I shall sleep easier at night without you haunting my dreams.'

'The inheritance will come to me,' Piet said, trying to keep him talking.

'You will be dead, Reydon. Guards!'

'Have you no courage to do the deed yourself?'

Vidal held the point close to Piet's throat, then withdrew. 'I would not sully my hands with your blood.'

The two soldiers stepped back into the chamber.

Piet tried to resist as he was dragged to his feet, but there was nothing he could do. His hands were tied and they were armed, Vidal too. Thinking furiously, he realised his only chance was to attempt to get away from the guards once they were outside. Then, he had to find Minou and . . . and his daughter.

'Guards!' Vidal called after them. 'Where is my son?'

'He is waiting at the quayside,' one replied.

'Send him here to me.'

'Very good, my lord.'

Piet felt the guard's hand on the back of his neck, forcing him forward and into the passageway. Out of the corner of his eye, he glimpsed Vidal's son stepping back into an alcove. Piet wondered how long he'd been there. And if he'd heard his father disavow him.

CHAPTER NINETY

When Minou came round, it was to the sound of water and the smell of damp underground tunnels. In the distance, muffled by the thick stone, she could hear the steady rhythm of heavy rain on the lake.

She had no idea where she was. For a moment, Minou thought herself back in Amsterdam, a city built on water. Then everything came rushing back.

Minou shivered in her damp clothes, the fabric heavy on her legs. She tried to sit up, but the effort sent her head spinning and she had to close her eyes. Her feet were like ice. When she moved them, she realised water was lapping round her ankles.

Minou waited until her eyes had adjusted to the dark, then took her bearings. She was in some kind of covered channel, or storm drain, but there was fresh air. White moonlight shone in under the stone arch that divided the channel from the open water, causing the colours to shift from green to purple to silver. And beyond, just visible, was the line of poplar trees at the edge of the lake. But the shadow cast by the bars of the iron grille made the chamber seem like a prison cell. She could just see the sluice gate beneath the level of the water.

'You're awake.'

Minou's heart leapt.

It had been twelve years, but she knew Marta's voice. Grown up now, but unmistakably her voice. For a moment, every single minute lost since Marta went missing came flooding back. All Minou wanted to do was throw her arms round her daughter and hold her. To kiss her and promise she would never leave her side again. Then Minou checked herself. She had called out her daughter's name in the chamber, but Marta hadn't responded. She hadn't recognised her voice.

'Are you all right, madame?'

Minou composed herself. 'My throat's a little sore, but yes.'

'Have they left us here to drown?'

Minou narrowed her gaze. Through the gloom, on the opposite side of the chamber, she could just make out Marta sitting on another stone ledge close to the grille. It was too dark to see her face – she saw her only in outline – but she felt a jolt of recognition in her guts. For so long Minou had imagined this moment. She had dreamed of what she might say. Now it was here, she had no idea how to begin.

'My name is Marie Cabanel,' Marta said.

Minou's heart cracked a little. She chose her words with care, realising she could not hurry things.

'I am Marguerite Reydon, though everyone calls me Minou.' For a moment, the words seem to hang between them in the air. Was it Minou's imagination that Marta caught her breath?

'I am pleased to meet you, Madame Reydon,' she said in a courteous, formal voice. 'I am glad not to be alone.'

Minou's heart cracked a little more. 'You're not alone. I won't leave you.'

Though every nerve in her body cried out for her to speak, her words seemed to turn to ash in her mouth. She had to tread gently. Minou had to persuade Marta to trust her before she told her the truth.

'While I was waiting for you to wake,' Marta said, 'I looked for a way out. This grille here divides us from the lake and a sluice. I tried to turn the handle, but it's stuck and I couldn't move it. The grille is set fast into the wall.' She rattled the bars.

'The water keeps getting higher.' Her voice broke and she sounded suddenly very young. 'This wasn't what was supposed to happen. I thought I would be safe. I planned it all so carefully,' Marta continued, then burst into tears.

The sound of her daughter weeping was too much to bear. Now the only thing in Minou's mind was how to comfort her. The rest could follow. There would be time enough.

'Come sit with me,' Minou said into the darkness. 'Tell me something of your life. It will pass the time while we wait for someone to come.'

'Will someone come?' Marta asked in a small voice.

'Piet will come,' Minou replied. 'My husband will come. He won't abandon us.'

There was a silence, then Minou heard the sound of the water splashing as Marta waded through the stone chamber towards her and settled herself at the far end of the bench.

For a moment, neither woman spoke. The only sounds were the relentless pounding of Minou's blood in her head and the ceaseless rain on the rough surface of the lake.

'I grew up in Paris,' Marta said.

CHAPTER NINETY-ONE

Louis stepped back into the chamber and closed the door.

With his father's words ringing in his ears, he walked round the periphery of the room into Vidal's line of vision. He was bent over the altar in the middle of the room, examining the Sudarium.

'I never knew what it was to be cared for,' he whispered.

Vidal paid him no heed.

'You made me believe I was worthy enough to be loved. But it wasn't true. I mistook my usefulness to you for affection. I'm your son.'

Vidal picked up the magnifying glass and leant over the cloth, focusing on the imprinted face. 'This really is an excellent copy. In fact, I would be glad to know who made it . . . I will send Xavier to find him.' He frowned, only now remembering his steward had disappeared.

Louis shuddered. Many times, in the orphanage, he had imagined what it would feel like to kill a man. In those perilous hours between dusk and dawn when the monks came, he had removed himself from what was happening to him by picturing a knife in his palm or putting his small hands around his torment-or's throat. He had imagined then that he'd feel powerful and free. But all he could see was Xavier's dead eyes staring up at him from the depths of the lake. He felt nothing but revulsion at what he'd done.

Vidal suddenly looked up. 'Louis. Since you're here, you can make yourself useful. Ask the girl who made this.'

Louis forced himself to speak. 'Father, the rain is getting

heavier. Can't you hear it on the roof? The water is getting dangerously high.'

'And?'

He faltered. 'The men have already left the island for fear of being trapped.'

'Which men?' he snapped.

'I don't know who they are. Who came with Mademoiselle Cabanel, though I assume are working for you since they—'

Vidal sighed impatiently. 'What is your point, Louis?'

'The waters are rising quickly. Should I not move the girl somewhere safer? And Madame Reydon too.'

To his horror, his father began to laugh. Louis could see a sheen of sweat on his brow.

'Father, are you ill?'

'Are you that much of a fool as to think I intend to let them walk out of here? Reydon, his heretic wife and daughter?'

His father straightened up and stared at him with such loathing that Louis took a step back.

'If the guards have done their job, the water already has him. As for the girl, in whom you appear to be so interested, if the lake rises beyond usual levels, she will soon join him. Her mother too. If not, they can rot there until the Devil takes them.'

'You cannot mean that.'

His father looked at him with maddened eyes. 'Think of the words of the Book of Exodus, of Leviticus. It is quite clear.' Vidal waved his arm around the chamber. '"There shall be sacrifice in God's name. The righteous shall rise on the bones of our enemies, any who would seek to frustrate the ways of the Lord."'

Louis had no illusions about his father – in the past twelve years in Vidal's company he had seen evidence enough of his cruelty, the vile deeds done by men of faith in God's name – but Marta had done nothing wrong. There could be no justification for this.

'You're going to leave her to drown?' Louis asked desperately. 'But Marta doesn't know who she is, couldn't you see that? The name meant nothing to her. For whatever reason Reydon is here, it's nothing to do with her. She is not your enemy.'

Vidal took a step towards him. 'Are you questioning my judgement?'

Louis faltered. 'No, my lord, only—'

'You are disobeying my orders?'

'She doesn't deserve to die.'

His last words were taken from him as Vidal struck him hard in the face. Shocked, Louis put his hands up to defend himself, but his father hit him again. Louis kept telling himself his father was sick. Often these days, he vanished inside his tangled mind, unaware of where he was or who he was. Louis didn't want to fight back, but he might have no choice.

'Father! It's me.'

The next blow caught him on the jaw. Louis stumbled back into the chair, knocking over the candelabra. Wax spilling across the stone floor, the flames quickly extinguished, plunging the chamber into blackness. Now the only light came from the white moon shining down through the lantern and the tiny flames burning before each reliquary casket.

'I beg you, stop!'

Vidal didn't seem to hear. A red mist had descended. Louis could see his knuckles were cracked and bleeding. His silk pallium was splattered with blood, his or his father's Louis couldn't tell. Why did nobody come to help? Where were the guards? Louis blocked the next punch, but the one after sent him flying to the ground.

Blood streaming down his face, in the darkness his hand found something cold and hard. Scrambling to his feet, he held the dagger full out in front of him.

'I don't want to hurt you! Stay back.'

Vidal charged at him and, in the fraction of a moment before Louis realised what was happening, he felt the knife slip in between his father's ribs.

Vidal's eyes opened wide with surprise, his wits suddenly clear again, and stared at him.

'I didn't mean to . . .' Louis whispered in horror.

'A new kingdom on earth –' Vidal swayed on his feet. 'To God's glory – it is you who must continue . . .'

'Father!' Louis shouted, falling to his knees. 'Father!'

CHAPTER NINETY-TWO

Minou watched another surge of water flood the chamber. She was powerless to stop it. She had learnt to live surrounded by water in Amsterdam, her city of tears. She had learnt to respect and fear and love its power. She had not thought to suffer such a fate in the flat Chartres countryside.

But there was no respite from the rain. They had moved away from the grille to the highest point, perching themselves at the top of the stone steps directly beneath the wooden hatch through which they'd been dropped, but even so the lake water was already up to their knees. If no one came soon, they would drown.

Minou looked down at Marta, leaning against her just like when she was a little girl, and smiled. Whatever happened, whether Piet found them or if they were to die here, Minou knew without a shadow of a doubt she wouldn't have exchanged this time with her daughter for anything.

Marta had been reserved at first, the independence of a girl used to looking after herself. But as she'd become accustomed to the swell of the water, she had begun to trust her. Minou had listened with a mixture of melancholy and wonder and relief. All the terrible imaginings that had haunted her these past twelve years faded – her daughter was a confident, self-possessed woman – leaving Minou with a suffocating sadness that she had not been there to see her grow up.

Minou continued to listen, still waiting for the right moment. But the more Marta had talked, the clearer certain things became:

first, that the life she had lived with the man she thought of as her father, Pierre Cabanel, was a complicated one. From what little Marta let slip, he was a captain at arms and, Minou suspected, a mercenary. Of what she was doing in Chartres, she said nothing and, not wanting to damage the fragile trust between them, Minou had not pressed her.

Marta genuinely appeared to have no idea that she had been born into a different life. She was Marie Cabanel. It was as if the first seven years of her life had been wiped clean. She talked of her love of Paris and how she had never lived anywhere else. She talked with disdain about Henri of Navarre and his Huguenot supporters, clearly holding him responsible for the wars that never ended. She talked with admiration about the Duke of Guise and the Valois court.

While she tried to decide what to do, Minou took pleasure in glimpses of the girl Marta had been in the woman she was now: her love of jewels, her quick wit, her contempt for men who gave their secrets away in the bedchamber, her confidence.

Marta had moved closer, until finally she had rested her head on Minou's shoulder and fallen asleep. She'd wrapped her own green cloak around her for extra warmth, but she could still feel her shivering beneath the layers.

While her daughter slept, Minou had murmured stories of their lost past, hoping to replant memories in her mind. She had whispered of the mountains and the vineyards of Languedoc, of their home at Puivert and her family's life there. Then, not wanting to wake her, she kissed her fingers and placed them softly on Marta's forehead.

'*Ma petite*,' she whispered, an endearment she had thought lost to her for ever.

CHAPTER NINETY-THREE

Holding him fast between them, the guards forced Piet down the steps in the driving rain. The wind cracked and slammed into them, driving their cloaks up into Piet's face. A torrent of water was pouring down the curving steps from the main entrance and flooding the ground.

It was not until they were almost at the quayside, and one of the guards slipped, that Piet could take his chance. Drawing back his leg, he sent a kick pummelling into the man's side and he went plummeting down, cracking his head on the stone balustrade. The other guard drew his sword, but he was too slow. Piet drove his bound hands upwards into the man's nose, shattering the bone with a sickening crunch.

Piet cast desperately around for a rock or a stone, anything sharp to rub the rope against. The guards were unconscious for now, but they might recover at any time. If he could find something to cut through the cords binding his wrists, there was a chance he might hold them off. There was nothing.

The lake water had risen quickly, and was rising still. The moored barge was now almost at the level of the landing. Piet couldn't delay. He had to find his wife and daughter.

Turning, he ran through the deep puddles, two-by-two up the steps and back into the reliquary. Already, water seemed to be seeping inside. Small cracks were appearing in the plaster. There was no time to lose. He had to find Minou and Marta. Her name caught in his throat. He prayed to God that they were together. That Minou knew her faith had been justified in believing her daughter was alive.

Piet hurtled along the passageway, past the frescoes and images and into the chamber. Then he stopped dead.

Louis was standing in front of one of the chairs. The other was lying on its side in a chaos of broken candles, the altar cloth and plate. In the darkness, Piet could see the blade of a knife glinting in the moonlight from above.

'This was my fault,' the boy said in a hollow voice. He looked back to Vidal's body, slumped in the cathedra. 'It didn't seem right to leave him on the ground. He would have hated that.'

Cautiously, Piet moved closer.

Though his eyes were open, Vidal was no longer there. Piet could see the gash in his stomach where the knife had gone in. His papal robe was saturated with blood, the white crosses soaked to red. On the floor, the cloth with the image of Christ's face lay trampled and bloody beneath Vidal's feet.

Piet took a step closer.

'He never wanted a son. I thought he did. I was mistaken.' Louis looked at Piet with anguish in his eyes.

'You overheard what he said,' Piet said, slowly understanding the scene before him.

'He didn't even notice I was here. I was of less importance to him than a forged piece of cloth.'

'So you killed him.'

'No.' Louis sounded shocked. 'I didn't mean to.' He tapped his head. 'The sickness made him do things. He was beating me. I didn't want to fight back – but then he came at me. The blade went in.'

Louis picked up the dagger and turned to Piet.

Piet stepped back out of reach. 'I'm no threat to you,' he said, holding up his tied arms.

To his surprise, Louis took his wrists and cut the rope. There was no doubt this was his old weapon.

'Where did you get that knife?'

Louis frowned. 'My father asked me the same thing. Your daughter had it.' Louis looked at him with blank eyes. 'Marta is your daughter.'

Piet caught his breath. 'She is.'

Louis gave an odd smile. 'I don't think she knows that.'

'What do you mean?'

'She doesn't remember. My father thought you had sent her. He called her Mademoiselle Reydon, but she didn't understand. She believes she is Marie Cabanel, the daughter of a man hired to kill my father.' He paused. 'At least, I think that is how it goes.'

Piet's heart was thudding. 'Vidal said you found Marta in Paris.'

For a moment, Louis's face lightened. 'It was the day Admiral de Coligny was assassinated. My father knew what was planned, so we left suddenly that night before the killing started. I couldn't do anything. I left Marta in our house in the rue d'Orléans. I always wondered what had happened to her.'

'You saved her life.' Piet put his hand on the boy's shoulder. Louis flinched and pulled away. 'Will you help save her again? Where is she?'

Louis answered as if he was in a daze. 'Below the reliquary, there's a chamber. There's a hatch giving into a tunnel with a sluice. My father explained it to me once. It floods when the water gets too high.'

'And my wife? Where is she?'

'With Marta.'

Piet put his hand on the boy's arm. 'Show me. The whole building could collapse at any moment, we have to get them out.'

'If the sluice gate isn't closed, once the chamber fills up the island will flood from within. That was my father's safeguard. If Guise came before his preparations were complete, he intended to destroy the relics rather than relinquish them.' Louis looked around the chamber. 'A flood. Everything to be swept away. The Book of Genesis, chapters six to nine.'

'What if we close the sluice?'

'It's too late. That's why the guards have gone. They knew to flee.' Louis stared at his father. 'Everyone is deserting him. I am the last.'

Piet looked down into the face of the man who had haunted his dreams for a lifetime, and felt nothing but pity. He leant across and gently closed Vidal's eyes.

'May God have mercy on your soul.'

Then he grabbed Louis's arm. 'Take me to where they are. Quick, now.'

CHAPTER NINETY-FOUR

No one was coming.

Minou was holding the old embroidered cap in her lap though she couldn't feel her fingers.

'What's that you're holding?' Marta asked, stirring beside her.

'Nothing,' Minou said quickly. 'Are you cold?'

'No more than before. Please may I see it?'

Minou hesitated, then passed the cap to Marta. She watched her turn it gently over in her hands.

'I –' Marta began, then stopped.

Minou held her breath. Perhaps there were some memories of the girl she had once been buried deep inside.

'It belonged to my daughter,' she said.

Marta traced her fingers over the embroidered letters. 'It's strange. I think I had a cap rather like this when I was little. The letters were red.'

'As are these: M R J.'

Minou sensed Marta's confusion as she moved away and pushed her hands into her pocket, clearly looking for something.

'I have a kerchief, if you need one.'

'It's not that.' Marta opened her hand to show her a plain wooden rosary, nestling in her palm. 'It was my mother's, I think. She died in the plague in Paris when I was little. I don't remember her.'

Even in the semi-light of the chamber, Minou recognised her old chaplet. It had been lost for twelve years, she had thought for ever, but her quick-fingered daughter had had it all along.

'You always were a magpie,' she whispered.

The water was still rising, they were both blue with cold, and no help had come. These might be their last moments on God's earth.

Feeling oddly calm now the time had come, Minou took her daughter's hand.

'There is something I must tell you,' she began to say. 'You are not who you think you are.'

Suddenly, someone was banging on the wooden trapdoor above their heads and the moment was lost.

'Minou? Minou, are you there?'

Her heart leapt at the sound of his voice.

'Piet!' she shouted, jumping to her feet. 'I'm here. We're both here. We are all right.'

Minou heard the bolts being undone then the trapdoor was thrown back and Piet's face appeared in the opening.

'I feared you wouldn't find us.'

'We need to get you out of there.'

'Take Marie up first.' There was no time to say anything more.

Piet lay down flat on the floor above and stretched his arms down. 'All set.'

'Can you manage alone?' Minou called up.

'Vidal's son is with me,' he said, giving a signal with a brief shake of his head not to ask more.

Minou nodded, then turned back to Marie.

'What were you going to say? Madame? Tell me.'

'As soon as we are free, I will,' Minou replied, keeping her voice light. 'Now we need to put all our efforts into getting out.' She laced her fingers together. 'You climb on my hands, then once you have your balance, reach up. My husband will pull you out.'

'What about you?'

'Don't worry about me.'

Marta did as she was told. She wobbled a bit, then steadied herself and clamped both her hands around Piet's wrist.

'Ready?'

'Yes, monsieur.'

'Here we go.'

He grunted, and then started to pull Marta up. Her legs flailed in the air, but she held on tightly and, within moments, she was safely out.

Piet's face, red from exertion, reappeared in the opening.

'How are you going to manage, Minou? Is there anything to stand on?'

'If I can brace myself into the angle of the wall, I should be able to raise myself high enough to reach you.'

He leant further down and whispered. 'It is her, isn't it?'

Briefly, Minou smiled. 'It is, but she doesn't remember.' Then she raised her voice for the benefit of the listeners. 'Here I go.'

At the first attempt, Minou slipped. Her wet clothes were dragging her down and she couldn't seem to get purchase on the slippery walls. The second attempt was little better. The third time, she managed to stretch her fingers just a little further, and Piet reached down just a little bit lower and, though it was a struggle and took the last of her strength, suddenly she was free.

'My lady of the mists,' Piet murmured, wrapping her tight in his arms.

She drank in his familiar scent of sandalwood and hair oil, then looked up, becoming aware of the two young people next to him. The boy looked dazed, but Marta was now staring hard at her. The first of the morning light was creeping through a small high window in the antechamber, so for the first time, Minou saw her daughter's face clearly. As Antoine le Maistre had said, she was a mirror image.

She smiled. But Marta frowned, and turned away.

'Minou, this is Louis,' Piet said.

Keeping her eyes on her daughter, Minou nodded. She didn't understand why the boy seemed now to be allied with them rather than with his father, nor why Marta seemed to have withdrawn from her. She'd thought they had established a rapport.

'Where is Vidal?' she asked.

'He won't disturb us,' Louis said in an odd, detached voice. Minou saw Piet glance at him. 'The guards are our main concern. I managed to hold them off, but they could be anywhere now. I'm surprised they haven't already found us. The building is not stable. We need to get to the boat and get clear.' He shot another glance at Louis. 'We have no choice but to go back through the reliquary.'

Piet then drew Minou to one side. 'Go quickly through the chamber to the other side,' he whispered. 'Keep her at your side and don't let her stop.'

Minou's eyes widened. 'Why, what's happened?'

'Just keep walking. Don't look round.'

CHAPTER NINETY-FIVE

Minou put her arm around her daughter's shoulders and Marta didn't pull away. She was shaking, from cold or relief or fear, Minou wasn't sure. Marta had not said a word since they'd been pulled out of the chamber.

The dismal grey dawn was filtering down through the lantern as they rushed into the reliquary. Louis had already gone ahead into the chamber, with Piet following closely behind.

Minou stopped. Vidal himself was sitting in a chair in the middle of room.

'Piet!' she hissed. 'He'll see us. There must be some other way.'

'He can't hurt us now, Minou, keep going.'

'What do you mean?'

There was another sharp sound, louder this time like a mountain animal waking from its winter sleep. A crack appeared in the wall, snaking across the chamber like a fork of lightning, widening as it went.

'The building could collapse at any moment, keep going, Minou.'

Piet ran further into the chamber. After a moment's hesitation, Minou followed. Still Vidal did not move.

As they drew level with the altar, Marta suddenly broke away and ran to the chair. In the strengthening of the light, Minou took in the stains on the ground, the trampled Sudarium and Vidal himself, slumped in bloodied robes.

'Don't look,' Minou said, trying to draw Marta away. She shook her off.

'My father spent his entire life looking for this man. Everything we had was spent trying to find him and now –' She turned on Piet. 'Did you do this?'

'Not I.'

'Then who?'

Louis was standing by the far wall.

'It was an accident,' he said calmly, as if it was a matter of no great importance.

There was a shuddering beneath their feet. The ground was giving way.

'The relics don't matter,' Piet shouted. 'Leave them.'

Louis lifted the lid of the third casket. 'This is the Sancta Camisia. It is genuine. It should be saved. And the Shroud of Antioch, too, but then of course you know that, Monsieur Reydon.'

'There isn't time!'

Minou grabbed Marta's arm as fissures opened in the walls, each giving life to another and renting the chamber in two.

'Run!' shouted Piet.

They cleared the chamber and charged along the passageway, feeling another mighty lurch beneath them. The frescoes on the walls began to crack, brickwork falling from the alcoves. A huge piece of blue plaster fell, sending a fragment of Charlemagne's painted cross smashing down to the floor near Minou's feet.

Piet threw open the outer door. The stone staircase was already coming away from the wall. They took the steps two at a time, the wind snapping at their heels, and managed to jump clear of the building and down to the water.

'The boat's not here, Piet,' Minou cried. 'The guards must have taken it. What are we going to do?'

Shielding his face against the driving rain, Piet pointed into the lake.

'It's there. It's come away from its moorings.'

'Can you get it?' Minou yelled, struggling to make her voice heard over the storm.

'I can try.'

Her heart in her mouth, Minou watched Piet launch himself into the torrent. A huge wave washed over him. Minou screamed as he disappeared beneath the surface of the water, but then she saw his head a little further out. Fighting the current, Minou saw he was gaining ground. Several times more, he disappeared from view, until finally he managed to get hold of the rope. He didn't give up, just started to drag the boat back towards the island bucking on the tide like an unbroken horse.

'You're nearly here,' Minou screamed into the storm.

'You're going to have to jump,' he yelled, trying to hold the rocking craft steady. 'I can't get any closer for fear the hull will smash.'

'Wait,' Marta suddenly shouted, speaking for the first time since running from the reliquary. 'We have to wait for Louis.'

'He knows the island,' Minou said quickly. 'He will know where to take shelter until the storm passes.'

To her relief, Marta didn't argue. With a last look over her shoulder at the white tower, she lifted her skirts and jumped.

'Brave girl,' Minou heard herself say. Then she took a deep breath, and did the same.

As soon as they were set, Piet hauled himself in, too, setting the flat-bottomed boat plunging sideways. Water broke over the stern. Then he braced his knees and tried to stand up so he could reach the chain.

'It's too dangerous,' Minou cried. 'You'll be thrown out.'

'There's no choice.'

With Minou grasping his legs to hold him steady, Piet set his face to the wind and, hand over hand on the iron links, started to haul them away from the island. Years of living in Amsterdam had taught her what happened when huge bodies of water were violently displaced. If the building collapsed – when it collapsed – it would cause a massive surge. Their fragile boat would be dragged under.

Tossed and thrown in the plunging waters of the lake, Piet nearly fell several times, but they kept going.

They were nearly there when the wooden pole supporting the chain on the island gave way and tipped forward into the lake, like a felled tree, sending a reverberation all along the chain. It cracked like a whip, smashing into the water and capsizing the boat.

Minou threw out her hand and grabbed Marta. Together, they managed to swim the last few yards to shore, bruised and soaking wet, but alive.

Behind them, there was an enormous eruption, as if the earth was being split in two. Minou, Piet and Marta turned. The sound seemed to echo around the hollow of land, reverberating like thunder in the mountains.

'Louis!' Marta shouted.

For a moment, Vidal's son was briefly visible standing at the doorway to the white tower. Then he disappeared. Moments later, an enormous surge of water swept up from the lake onto the island. The reliquary seemed to sway on its foundations, then disappeared into the underground vaults Vidal had built. White clouds of debris flew up into the grey dawn air.

Water had reclaimed the land.

CHAPTER NINETY-SIX

Two Days Later

It was the blue hour, that magical time in an August afternoon when the sky turns from blue to orange to white. All around, so far as the eye could see, stretched green fields and golden wheat and shy red poppies.

At this time of the day, with a light breeze, long shadows seemed to dance along the pathways as if they were late for some charming rendezvous. Butterflies fluttered, dipped, settled and spread their wings, before spiralling up into the sky again. The air was alive with the conversation of songbirds and the humming of bees. A wood thrush called to its mate. Sparrows shimmered in and out of the formal hedges of box, rosemary and privet that led to the front door.

The façade of the manor itself was bathed in late afternoon sunlight. It was a house that was most itself in late summer when the honeysuckle transformed the walls from grey to green, yellow and white.

The estate was elegant and serene and beautiful. It seemed impossible that only two days previously, a flood could have caused so much devastation. The storm had blown through as quickly as it had come. Today, the lake was as still and tranquil as a millpond. The island was visible again above the surface of the water, but the white tower had vanished.

Chartres had never known a natural disaster like it: as the waters receded, the corpses of two local brothers and two estate guards were discovered; a nobleman from Chartres, Lord Evreux himself and his steward, Xavier. Although their injuries were not consistent with drowning, there was no one prepared to ask questions. Piet grieved for the loss of his friend, Antoine le Maistre, though Minou imagined him reunited with his beloved wife and children again, and thought he was at last at peace.

Only the body of Evreux's son, Louis, had yet to be found.

Minou and Piet were sitting in the library waiting for their carriage to be brought to the door. Yesterday, they had repaired to the house and found that the servants had returned. Each told the same story: that Lord Evreux had dismissed them on the eve of the twenty-first day of August, giving them a night and a day with their families, asking them to return at dawn on the following day. Marta's coachman, who had stayed at his post through the storm, confirmed it. And although some admitted their master had been capricious of late, his moods changeable, Piet had noticed they were all saddened by his death. That Louis's body had not yet been found gave them hope that the future of the estate would still be secure.

'I should not have told her,' Minou said again. 'It is too much. After everything that happened, I should have given her time to—'

Piet put his hand over hers. 'My love, stop this. Marta deserved to hear the truth. Even if she didn't want to hear it, even if she has no memory of her life before Paris, she cannot fail to see herself in your features, and that confuses her. Give her time. She will come back to us when she is ready.'

'But if she does not?'

Piet looked out across the green countryside. 'We must give her time.'

Minou had less hope. After they'd staggered, half drowned, to the manor house yesterday, Marta had barely spoken. Her colour was high and her temperature spoke of a chill. Taking up residence in Vidal's private quarters, Minou had sat with her daughter all afternoon, cooling her brow and cindering herbs to purify the room. It eased some of the loss of the past twelve years. Just a little.

As the fever burned, Minou had told Marta who she really was and how she had been lost, trying to bring her back to her memories: of Puivert and Carcassonne, of the tapestry of the Reydon-Joubert family that now hung over the fireplace in Amsterdam; of her brother and sister and aunt; of how loved and cherished she had been.

'You were always in my heart,' she'd whispered as Marta slept. 'Not a day went by when I didn't think of you.'

At sunset, Marta's fever had broken and Minou had rejoiced. But when her daughter came back to herself, she had turned her face away. Minou tried to recapture the intimacy she'd shared in their stone prison, but Marta had been formal and courteous. She did not want to listen.

In the end, feeling as if her heart was breaking, Minou had left her journals on the table beside the chaise longue and withdrawn. She didn't want to cause her any more pain – she could not.

'I am not sure we should leave,' Minou said again. 'What if she will not come with us? What if Louis survived? We should stay.'

'We are her blood family, Minou,' Piet said gently, 'but she is a grown woman. And even if Louis is not dead, she cannot stay here. She wouldn't tell you why she came here, would she? We know she brought with her a forgery of a relic. We know too that the man she thinks of as her father, Pierre Cabanel, was the man hired to kill Vidal.'

'What are you saying?' Minou asked, her own fears making her snap.

Piet sighed. 'She came here with some purpose, Minou.'

Minou fell silent. Whatever her daughter had done, whatever the life she had lived, she would accept it. Forgive it. Who were they to judge, they who had abandoned their child when she'd needed them most?

But now, at the idea that they might have found her only for Marta to turn away – Minou knew she would never recover from this second loss.

'I don't care about any of that, Piet. She's our daughter.'

Piet raised his hands. 'I don't want to quarrel. But twelve years is a long time, my love.'

Biting back her tears, Marta stepped away from the door.

She had pretended to sleep. She had heard Minou whispering to her in the cellar when they thought they would drown, and yesterday as the fever burned. She feared what she might have said in her delirium. Memories she had not known were there, clouded but glimpsed, had flooded back, melding with the fragments of her life she had never been able to account for: being carried through a courtyard in a mountain castle; playing with the pointer on a compass in a box and being gently scolded by an old man with a sweet voice; picking a black feather plucked from a fan; stealing a wooden rosary from a casket; remembering an embroidered cap covered in blood.

The boy who'd left her in the blue room. Louis.

Marta's fingers tightened round the chaplet, feeling shame

curdle in her stomach. They were good people. They loved one another, she could see it. If they knew the truth about her, they would despise her. The life she had lived was not one of honour, she knew that, but it was the only life she had.

'My lady of the mists . . .'

She shook her head. If they knew what she was, what she had done, they would reject her. They were decent people, how could they possibly accept her as their daughter again? It was no good. She would go to Paris, as she'd always intended. She would tell the Duke of Guise what she knew and throw herself on his mercy. All would yet be well. All would yet be as she'd intended it to be.

As she looked around the room one last time, her eyes alighted on the journal Minou had left. Tears caught in her throat, recalling the last conversation they'd had yesterday evening.

'I have something for you,' her mother had said, oddly nervous.

'Before you do, Madame Reydon, may I say something?'

'Of course.'

'I understand you believe there is some connection between us. The resemblance is marked, everyone can see. Our demeanour, our eyes, it is extraordinary. But there is no need for you to feel responsible for me. My father left me well provided for.'

Marta blinked away the memory, the look of devastation in Madame Reydon's eyes, though she had done her best to hide it. It was then Minou had reached into her pocket and taken out her journal. 'Take this. Read it if you will.'

'What is it?'

Minou had forced herself to smile. 'It's the story of a girl.'

In the blue light of the afternoon, Marta opened the book and read the first date out loud: 'Chateau de Puivert. Friday the sixth day of June. Fifteen seventy-two.'

Marta took a final look around the chamber, then slipped the journal into her purse and stole to the stables, where her coach was waiting.

'I should talk to her again,' Minou said. 'She must return with us to Amsterdam, everyone is waiting.

'You have done everything you could.'

Minou waved her hand. 'What of this, *mon coeur*?' she said in a falsely bright voice. 'Even if Louis survived, this is rightfully yours. This is all built on the du Plessis fortune.'

Piet dropped his head between his hands. 'I cannot believe he's gone.'

'Vidal?' Minou pulled at a thread on the arm of her chair. 'Vidal believed himself invincible. He never thought that death would come to him – at least, not before he was ready.' She paused. 'Do you believe that his death was an accident?'

Piet ran his fingers through his grey hair. 'It's hard to say. The boy was shocked at what he'd done, I believe that. In the brief time I spent with Vidal there was a wildness, a zealotry, an obsession with what he thought he would do here.'

'What did he want?'

Piet sighed. 'He saw himself as the Priest-Confessor of a new Church, to rival the Catholic League. To rival Rome. The acquisition of relics was the way in which he thought to achieve it.'

'Power, then.'

Piet thought for a moment. 'No. He feared the dying of the light. He feared what was to come. Hell, not Heaven. He died afraid, Minou, and unshriven.'

Minou covered his hand with hers. 'It's over now. There is nothing more you can do.'

There was a knock at the door.

'Come,' Piet called.

'Monsieur, your carriage is waiting.'

'Very well.'

Minou stood up. 'I'll go to her now,' she said quickly. 'See if she is ready.'

The servant cleared his throat. 'Mademoiselle Cabanel asked me to give you this, Madame Reydon.'

Minou felt the ground shift from under her. She felt as if she was watching another's hand reach out and unfold the paper, though she already knew what it would say.

'Minou, what is it?'

Piet's voice seemed to be coming from a long way away.

'Minou?'

Unable to speak, she handed the note to him. There were only two words, but enough to break her heart in pieces.

Forgive me.

CHAPTER NINETY-SEVEN

The bells of the Oude Kerk were ringing out over the canals and waterways of Amsterdam. In Plaats, buyers and sellers haggled over the price of herring and peat as they always did. Women and men breathed warm air into their cold hands beneath the colonnades of the old medieval Stadhuis, a predominantly Calvinist council now.

After a gentle September, when the leaves on the trees were claret and golden and copper, painting Amsterdam bright with their colours, the weather was beginning to turn. There were few masts left in the IJ. The last of the ocean-going ships had all sailed on the October tides. The birds were making their final preparations for the journey south to find the sun. To the Islas Canarias, to Lisbon and Seville, to the Cape of Good Hope.

Minou had finished the last quarter's accounts. As the air became cooler in the room, she rolled down her sleeves and considered calling Agnes to bring kindling for the fire. She looked at the cold grate. The drawing in of the evenings always saddened her, though she liked the winter in Amsterdam, too, when the canals froze and the children could skate on Singel, tearing up the ice on wooden skates, creating such beautiful white pictures.

She turned back to her papers. They were all expected at

Cornelia's and Alis's house to honour her feast day. Salvadora was already there, preferring the comfort of Warmoesstraat to the busy working environment of the *hofje*. Today, Minou was forty-two years of age. She had lived to make old bones. She and Piet, Johannus and Bernarda were all going, together with Frans and Agnes, the two longest-serving residents of their orphanage.

There was only one person missing.

Minou blotted the row of figures. She was glad of the diversion. The Eve of All Hallows was little observed in the Calvinist Church but, on days such as today, she remembered the observations of her Catholic childhood – the rose-water biscuits, the sip of hot wine, the flowers laid on the graves of the dead. She and Aimeric and Alis, standing with their father in the shadow of the Basilica of Saint-Nazaire in Carcassonne, listening to her father speak a prayer at the grave of their mother, before hurrying back inside to the fire.

She opened a brown cardboard file and turned her attention to the latest proposals being advanced by the governors of the new city orphanage, on the site of Saint-Lucie's Convent, on Kalverstraat. Their success in Zeedijk meant that she and Piet were much in demand to advise. Aunt Salvadora, in residence since August, had proved herself an excellent counsellor, too. She had proved a staunch ally and support in the dark days after her and Piet's return from Chartres alone.

She pulled the candle towards her and started to read.

'Moeder.'

Minou looked up. 'Bernarda, you are ahead of the clock. It's not yet time to go. Can you amuse yourself for a while longer?'

'There is someone at the door asking for you. A lady.'

Minou leant back in the chair. 'Did she give her name? Or what business she had with me?'

The girl frowned. 'I am not sure. She spoke in French, and so fast. I fear I misunderstood.'

Minou smiled. 'I'm sure you understood more than you thought. What do you think she said?'

Bernarda looked at her feet. 'I don't know. She is very beautiful.'

Minou felt a wave of pity for her awkward daughter, who stumbled and blushed and always felt in the wrong.

'It doesn't matter. I am sure you did very well.' She stood up. 'Show her in. You go and bid your brother and father get ready. I'm sure it won't take long. Then, at six o'clock, we shall go to Warmoesstraat and eat pancakes.'

Bernarda's face brightened. 'And drink beer?'

'Since it is my feast day, you may have a little beer, yes. But only a little, mind. Off you go.'

Minou tidied the papers on the desk. She put the lid on her inkwell and wrapped the tip of her quill so it was ready for the morning.

She heard footsteps and turned to greet the visitor, hoping the matter would not take too long.

The woman came into the chamber in a haze of blue velvet and silk. Minou watched as her eyes went to the tapestry on the wall, then returned to settle on Minou herself. Such extraordinary eyes, one blue and one brown.

'I am Marta,' she said.

Minou nodded. There was no need to say more.

EPILOGUE

CHARTRES

February 1594

Ten Years Later

CHARTRES CATHEDRAL
Sunday, 27 February 1594

In the cold sunshine of a February afternoon, Minou and her family stood with the other honoured guests in the soaring nave. Wearing velvet and fur and jewels, diadems and crowns, all had come to witness the first ever crowning of a French king in the mighty cathedral of Chartres.

Nominally monarch for five years, neither the Catholic League nor Catherine de' Medici had been prepared to accept a Huguenot on the throne of France, so the wars had dragged on. Now, at last, Guise was dead and, pragmatic to the last, in order to win Paris over, Navarre had converted to Catholicism in July 1593. Though his decision had not pleased many, Minou believed it was the best chance of a lasting peace for a generation. Salvadora, having despised Navarre for years, was now his greatest advocate. A prince of the royal blood, indeed.

Minou turned to smile at Piet, his eyes shining bright with the occasion. All the Huguenot nobility were here, standing shoulder to shoulder with their Catholic brothers and sisters. Alis and Cornelia had remained in Amsterdam with Salvadora, who was too frail to travel, but everyone else had come with them: Johannus, Bernarda and Marta.

Henri of Navarre stepped up to the altar where the Bishop

of Chartres stood waiting. Dressed in a crimson satin shirt, he kissed the sword of Charlemagne, then prostrated himself before the altar.

'Why is his Queen Marguerite not with him?'

Minou smiled at her eight-year-old granddaughter. 'They are estranged.'

'What does estranged mean? And why is he lying down?'

Minou put her finger to her lips. 'It's a tradition.'

The Bishop of Chartres prayed over the King, anointing him on the head, on his chest, between the shoulders and on the elbows, each time saying the same words.

'*Ugno te in Regem.*'

'Why does he keep saying the same thing always?'

'Hush,' Marta whispered. 'You must not talk.'

Minou and Piet grinned at one another, remembering every occasion in Marta's childhood when they'd had to beg Marta to hold her tongue. They knew nothing about the father of Marta's child – she had refused to speak of what had happened or where she had been in the two months since leaving Chartres in August 1584 and arriving in Amsterdam on the eve of All Saints nearly ten weeks later – but, in her temperament and character, the little girl was the mirror image of her mother: quicksilver smart, impatient, bold beyond her years.

Navarre stood to be vested in a blue tunic sewn with gold lilies and a chasuble damascened with pomegranates, then he knelt again to be anointed in the palms of his hands.

'Why is it taking so long?'

This time, Bernarda put her arm around her little niece's shoulder.

Gloves, velvet boots, the ring and the sceptre were then presented to the King by the lords of the realm, then finally the bishop took the crown from the altar and placed it upon his head.

'*Vive le Roi!* Long live the King. *Vive le Roi!*'

The cry echoed around the cathedral, spreading out into the streets where the crowds had gathered. Then the hautboys, bugles, trumpets, fifes and drums sounded, the cannons roared out the salute, the musketeers fired volley after volley and the Te Deum was sung. Minou put her hand upon Piet's cheek. His hair was white now, but his spirit was undimmed.

'This is a great day.'

'France is finally united once more. A new era begins.'

Smiling, Minou turned to Marta and was astonished at the change that had come over her daughter. Her eyes were wide with shock and the colour had drained from her face.

'Whatever is it? What's the matter?'

Shaking her head, Marta clamped her hand over her mouth.

Minou followed the line of her gaze. Up towards the altar, where the noblemen of Chartres were providing a guard of honour around the new king. In the middle of the row stood a tall, dark-haired man with a stripe of white in his hair.

She turned cold. Minou looked back to her daughter, then at her granddaughter, who was tracing patterns in the dust with the toe of her shoe. And she realised.

'It was him?' she said in a horrified whisper. 'He's Louise's father?'

Marta met her mother's eye, then she nodded.

Outside, heralds threw gold and silver coins into the crowd.

ACKNOWLEDGEMENTS

There are so many generous people who've given practical, professional and enthusiastic support during the writing of *The City of Tears*:

My dear friend and publisher at Mantle, Maria Rejt, and the entire London Pan Mac gang, especially Anthony Forbes Watson, Josie Humber, Kate Green, Sarah Arratoon, Lara Borlenghi, Jeremy Trevathan, Sara Lloyd, Kate Tolley, James Annal, Stuart Dwyer, Brid Enright, Anna Bond, Charlotte Williams, Jonathan Atkins, Laura Ricchetti, Cormac Kinsella; and everyone at Pan Mac Australia, New Zealand and India, and Terry Morris and Veronica Napier at Pan Mac South Africa.

My fabulous agent, Mark Lucas, and everyone in my corner at The Soho Agency and ILA, including Niamh O'Grady, Alice Saunders, Nicki Kennedy, Sam Edenborough, Jenny Robson, Katherine West, Alice Natali and George Lucas at Inkwell Management in New York.

I'm lucky to have so many exceptional foreign publishers and translators, in particular: Maaike le Noble, Frederika van Traa and Jorien de Vries at Meulenhoff-Boekerij, and Rienk Tychon for his superb help with sixteenth-century Dutch history (and spellings!); my editor Catherine Richards at Minotaur Books, and the whole St Martin's team in New York, including Hector DeJean, Danielle Prielipp and Nettie Finn; everyone at Planeta de Libros, especially Míriam Vall Rosinach; at Sonatine Éditions Marie Misandeau, Carine Fannius, Auxanne Bourreille and Muriel Arles; Lena Schaefer, Stefanie Zeller and Barbara Fischer at Bastei Lübbe; everyone at Newton Crompton Editori.

Many thanks for superb advice from Dr Emily Guerry (Senior Lecturer in Medieval History at the University of Kent and Director of the Centre for Medieval and Early Modern Studies) about the

Acknowledgements

Sainte-Chapelle and sixteenth-century Paris (any mistakes are mine!); Dr Diana Winch, Director of the Huguenot Museum, and her team; Dr Tessa Murdoch FSA, for so many helpful introductions to Huguenot organisations in New Paltz, New York and South Carolina; the staff of the Huguenot Museum in Franschhoek, South Africa. Huge thanks to Alain Pignon, Manager du centre-ville de Carcassonne (who knows everything there is to know about Carcassonnais history) and to Christine and Adélaïde Pujol for their hospitality at the Hôtel de la Cité over many years.

I was so grateful to be invited by Nederlands Letterenfonds/Dutch Foundation for Literature to be Writer in Residence in Amsterdam in April 2019 while researching this novel. My special thanks to Maaike Pereboom.

All writers know how family, friends and neighbours help keep daily life going during the writing of a book, bringing coffee, wine and good cheer from the outside world, so special thanks to: Jon Evans, Clare Parsons, Tony Langham, Jill Green, Anthony Horowitz, Saira Keevil, Stefan van Raay (who also allowed me to 'borrow' his name), Linda and Roger Heald, Dale Rooks, Syl Saller, Tessa Ross, Margaret Dascalopoulos, Sylvia Horton, my cousins Anne Renshaw and Phillipa and Kerry Towlson-Mulbregt, Pierre Sanchez and Chantal Bilautou.

All love and thanks to my family, especially my legendary mother-in-law Rosie Turner; my brothers-in-law Mark Huxley and photographer Benjamin Graham, who's so generous with his time and always on hand to step in; my lovely sister Caroline Matthews; my brilliant sister Beth Huxley (and Thea and Ellen) for her endless support (not limited to dog-walking, balloon-buying and tea-making!); to Ollie Halladay for puzzle-doing and cheese; and to the memory of my parents, Richard and Barbara Mosse, much loved and much missed.

Finally, as always, I could do none of this without my beloved husband Greg Mosse – my first love and first reader – and our brilliant, amazing (grown-up!) children Martha Mosse and Felix Mosse. Were it not for you three, there'd be little point to any of it. I'm so proud of you.